CW00550524

ILLICIT CAPTOR

MAFIA WARS IRELAND
BOOK TWO

MAGGIE COLE

PULSE PRESS INC

This book is fiction. Any references to historical events, real people, or real places are used fictitiously. All names, characters, plots, and events are products of the author's imagination. Any resemblance to actual events or places or persons, living or dead, is entirely coincidental.

Copyright © 2023 by Maggie Cole

All rights reserved.

No part of this book may be reproduced in any form or by any electronic or mechanical means, including information storage and retrieval systems, without written permission from the author, except for the use of brief quotations in a book review.

WARNING

This is a dark mafia romance. The heroine has experienced sexual abuse, kidnapping, and other horrific things. While it's not depicted in detail, it may trigger survivors. Mature audiences only.

IRISH TERMS

Below is a list of some terms used in Ireland and England that ya may or may not be familiar with that ya will find in this series.

A stór - my treasure

Arse - ass, butt, OR a stupid, irritating person

Aye - yes

Bloke is a slang term for a common man

Burd - girl, girlfriend

Garda - police in Dublin

Plonker - idiot, moron

Runners - workout shoes

Da - Dad, father

Mum, mammy - Mom, mother

Ya – you

Yea - Yes

PROLOGUE

Aidan O'Connor

Cold wind blows harder through the field, whipping through the air, mimicking a razor slicing my cheeks.

I welcome it.

It's a perfect accessory to my hatred, ramping up the pulse throbbing in my neck.

Revenge can finally start. Tommy Ahern's on my list, and he's been there longer than I normally have any man. Now, I'm drawing out his time on it. He'll pay for his sins, but before I end his life, I'm stealing his most prized possession.

His wife.

I pull out my phone and stare at the photo that's mesmerized me for over a year. I never saw her until one of my guys inside the O'Leary clan sent it to me.

Scarlet Ahern, daughter of our biggest enemy, Jack O'Leary, makes my skin prickle with heat. Her hair's the color of her name, a handful of freckles dot her porcelain cheeks, and eyes, bright as a wild animal at night, glow brightly.

Life fills her. There's mischief, confidence, and a bit of defiance in her expression. Everything about those things makes me feel uncomfortable. All I can think about is taming that defiance, seeing what she really has up her sleeve if I were the object of her affection, or watching her strut toward me in a crowded room with all eyes on her, knowing she's mine.

I hate myself for those thoughts.

She's an O'Leary. My brother, Brody, may have overlooked it with his wife Alaina—Scarlet's sister—but I'm not looking to get wrapped up with my enemy. My brother fell hard and I'll be damned if I do the same. So I click the phone and the screen turns black.

Focus, I remind myself, sliding my cell into my pocket and wrapping my fingers around my pocket knife. I glide my thumb over the raised metal, assessing Tommy's guard positioned at the front door of the farmhouse.

He pulls his flask out of his jacket pocket, takes a mouthful of what I assume is whiskey, then wipes his mouth and puts it away. He removes a cigarette from his metal case, then flicks his lighter. Smoke circles his head, and the red butt burns hotter with every inhale.

Every night, it's the same situation. Tommy leaves, and his thug stands guard, drinking from his flask and smoking his cigarettes until the darkness fades into the morning and his boss returns.

There's never any other men. Sometimes, days pass before Tommy returns. When he finally does, his thug crosses the small farm and settles into the shed Tommy's assigned for his shelter.

Each moment that passes that Scarlet's inside with the husband she was forced to marry, my skin crawls. Every ounce of patience I have, I've tapped into, so I don't destroy my chance of revenge.

Tonight, there's no more waiting. I stay in the shadows, moving toward the house, and finally step out of them when I can't hide anymore.

The guard squints, releasing a cloud of tobacco, and belts out in a rough smoker's voice, "Ya better be lost."

I hold my hands in the air, declaring, "Easy, mate. Tommy sent me."

"Mate? I don't know ya," he seethes, stepping closer. He pulls his knife out of his pocket and keeps his cigarette in the other.

"Anthony, I'm Tommy's nephew Jackie from Belfast," I lie.

He remains frozen, assessing me.

I add, "Tommy needed me to come here and give ya a message."

Anthony stays cautious, but his body relaxes a bit. "Aye? What's that?"

I step closer and glance behind me, even though no one is around for miles. Tommy wanted it this way—Scarlet hidden from everyone, with no chance of her having any life outside his prison.

I turn back and lower my voice. "I don't know the details. He gave me a note to give ya."

"A note?"

"Aye, mate."

I wait for him to hold out his hand. He finally does and orders, "Well, then, don't waste my time."

Adrenaline shoots through me. I reach inside my pocket, open my knife, and whip it out as fast as possible, so he doesn't have time to react. I slice his throat, then stab his heart several times.

Blood sprays everywhere, and his knife and cigarette fall to the ground. Wind whistles through the air and Anthony falls toward me, his eyes wide, the life already leaving them.

I step back, and he thuds to the ground. For several moments, I stare at him while breathing hard. Then I take a handkerchief out of my pocket, along with sanitizer, and wipe my face, hands, and any part of my jacket where I see blood.

The scent of tobacco, whiskey, and his blood doesn't leave me. I step under the light, pull up the camera on my phone, and check my reflection. I wipe two missed spots and put my cell back in my pocket.

I reach for the doorknob and turn it.

"Fuck," I mutter. It's locked. I shouldn't be surprised Tommy doesn't trust his guard with his wife. It only makes my vengeance more powerful.

I debate what route to take, assessing the quality of the wood door, the lock, then the windows.

It's not what I wanted. My goal isn't to shake up Scarlet more than necessary, but there are no other options.

I grab a log from the stack next to the side of the house, then slam it into the glass as hard as possible.

It shatters, echoing in the air, and I put on my gloves before I punch out the remaining shards until there's nothing but a hole, then I carefully maneuver my body through the darkness.

It only takes a moment to locate the room where Scarlet is. The door is locked, but there's nothing special about it. I kick it until it splinters.

A muffled whimper fills the air, which I expected. I reach through the door and unbolt it, then open the remaining barricade.

The pitch-black room is due to the wood covering the windows. It's so cold it makes the outside feel warm. I flip the light switch, but nothing turns on, so I use my phone's flashlight, then scan the tiny, empty space.

I freeze, except for the hairs on my neck rising.

A shell of a naked woman, all skin and bones, sits in the corner, hugging her shins and hiding her face. Her scarlet hair falls over her shoulders and legs, a drastic contrast to her purple skin. She shivers, and I assume it's a combination of the cold and fear of me.

Jesus. What has he done to her?

She peeks up, the green glowing from her eyes, then hides them again.

"I'm not going to hurt ya," I say, trying to keep my voice calm, stepping closer.

She shakes harder, cowering closer to the wall. Her hitched breaths grow louder.

I stare at her, wanting to kill Tommy even more, cursing myself for not doing this sooner.

I crouch down and reiterate, "I promise I won't hurt ya. I'm here to get ya out of here. But it's cold outside. I'm going to get a blanket."

She doesn't look up, only trembles harder, gasping for air between her arms.

I race into the bedroom next to her prison cell and grab the quilt off the bed. I return to the room, but she's still in the same spot.

I kneel beside her and assert, "We need to go." I move the blanket toward her.

"Don't touch me! Please!" she shrieks, looking up with tears falling down her cheeks.

My mouth turns dry. I stay still, stating, "There's only so much time to get away from here. We have to go."

"Leave me alone! Please!" she cries out again, shaking harder and burying her head back into her arms.

"Scarlet, your sister sent me," I announce.

It's a half truth. Alaina wanted to come herself, but I wouldn't tell her anything other than I knew Tommy lied and Scarlet was alive.

Scarlet slowly looks up, blinking hard.

"Alaina. She sent me to rescue ya," I repeat.

Scarlet's lip quivers, and she shakes her head hard. "No."

Surprise fills me. I thought my statement would comfort her. "No?" I question.

Another level of fear fills Scarlet's expression. She whispers, "He'll kill me if I go near her."

I attempt to control my reaction, but it's hard. In a stern voice, I try to assure her. "He won't kill ya. I'll make sure of it."

Her intake of breath turns so sharp I'm afraid she's having a panic attack.

I cringe, but there's no other option. When the sun rises, we need to be away from here. So I inform her, "I need to make a choice for your safety, and it's better if ya decide."

She stares at me, confused, her breathing turning even more shallow.

I loathe myself before I say it, but I assert, "We need to go now. I can carry ya out of here while you're conscious, or I can drug ya so ya go to sleep. What do ya prefer?"

Her eyes widen with a new horror in them mixed with hatred.

Sharp pain sears through my heart, but I'm out of options. I demand, "Choose now, or I will."

She shakes her head.

I assume she doesn't want to be drugged. I reach for her.

She screams, her hands jab at me, but she's so weak I barely feel it.

I grab her wrists with one hand and state, "I'm sorry, lass, but ya leave me no choice."

"Go away," she whimpers, tears falling faster.

Guilt fills me, but I grab the syringe out of my pocket, flip the cap off it, and stab her in the arm.

She yelps and then her eyes flutter.

I cradle her body against me, pull the blanket over her, stroke her hair, and murmur, "Shh. Everything is okay. Go to sleep, petal."

When I'm convinced she's fully asleep, I tighten the comforter around her and tuck it between her forehead and my chest to shield her from the wind. I rise with her in my arms and leave through the front door, stepping over Anthony's corpse.

I trek a mile down the road, barely feeling the razor-sharp gusts, my mind racing with a million different thoughts. When I finally get to my car, I put her in the front seat, lean it as far back as possible, and secure her seat belt around her.

For two hours, I drive, sweating from the heat that creates a furnace inside the vehicle. It's well into an hour before a hint of color comes into Scarlet's cheeks.

I don't stop until I pull up to the small cottage, which is just as remote as the place Tommy held her prisoner. I park next to my brother Devon's car and get out. I go around to the passenger seat, unbuckle Scarlet, then pick her up.

She doesn't stir, which doesn't surprise me. I get to the door, and my brother opens it.

He glances at her and steps aside.

I enter and order, "Go into town and buy some clothes for her."

He asks, "What size?"

My anger resurfaces. "Small. Extra small. Whatever ya can find. He starved her."

Disgust lights in Devin's expression. He says nothing and leaves.

I carry Scarlet to the bedroom and pull back the covers. I unwrap her from Tommy's quilt and tuck her in. I carry the comforter outside to the burn pit and douse it with kerosene. I strike a match, study it until my fingers feel the heat, and toss it.

The flames explode, covering the material in seconds. I stay there, lighting more matches, trying to return to a calm state so I don't scare Scarlet further when she wakes.

It's harder than normal. The fire doesn't help the way it usually does. All I can think about is the horror that bastard put her through.

When there's nothing left to burn, I grab a few more logs and return inside. I lock the door, go into the bedroom, and add more wood to the fireplace. Then I sit on the edge of the bed, studying her until my brother returns, tearing me out of my thoughts.

"What else do ya need?" he asks, setting two large bags on the dresser.

I rise and cross my arms. "Nothing. Go back to Belfast."

He peers at Scarlet, then me, asking, "Ya sure about that?"

"Aye. Make sure ya don't speak to anyone about this."

"Ya mean don't tell Brody or Alaina?"

"No one. Not even Tynan," I order.

His face hardens. "What are ya going to do now that ya have her? Ya can't keep her here forever."

Rage builds so fast that I clench my fists at my sides. "I'm going to make Tommy pay for his sins," I vow.

1

Scarlet O'Leary Ahern

*W*armth fills me, giving me the illusion I'm dreaming. For too long, coldness dug into my bones. The scent of cedarwood mixes with a light musk. I turn on my side, snuggle into the comfort of the mattress, hug the pillow tighter, then freeze.

Why am I in a warm bed?

Why is there a pillow?

Tommy only lets me in bed when he has his way with me and then he locks me back in the dark room.

My pulse skyrockets. I try to open my eyes, but my lids feel heavy.

"Easy," a deep voice murmurs, and what feels like a hand strokes my cheek.

My heart races faster. I force my eyes to open, but my blurred vision panics me further. My lungs constrict to the point I can barely take in any oxygen. I blink harder, and tears fill my eyes.

Am I blind? Did Tommy do something to my eyes like he's always threatening?

Fingers swipe at my tears, declaring, "It'll take a few minutes for the fuzziness to go away. Everything will be all right. I promise."

He promises?

I'm unsure if I should believe him or not. I try to sit up, but he holds me down.

He warns, "Don't move too fast. If ya do, your head will pound so hard you'll get nauseous. It's a side effect of the drug."

Drug?

More anxiety expands in my chest. The fuzziness in my vision clears slightly, but all I can make out of the man in front of me is his white T-shirt, chestnut hair, and large frame.

"Wh—" I barely manage a whisper, and a pain shoots through my throat.

A glass comes to my lips. The man says, "Have a few sips of water. But go slow."

I don't question it. My dry mouth could compete with a desert. I swallow a few sips and want more, but he limits my intake. He pulls the glass away and states, "Ya can have more in an hour. I don't want ya vomiting."

I blink again, and his sharp features come into focus. My confusion continues, and nervous butterflies fill my stomach.

Why is he being nice to me?

He drugged me.

Why does he look familiar?

He's one of Tommy's men.

I grip the blankets tighter, as if they could somehow protect me.

When will he put me back in the cold room?

He puts his hand back on my cheek.

I jerk my head backward, but it can't move very far. My insides quiver.

"It's okay. I won't hurt ya," he repeats. He slides his thumb over my jaw. It's gentle and warm, something I haven't experienced since before my da forced me to marry Tommy, yet I don't trust this stranger.

A flashback of my wedding day hits me. I close my eyes, trying to stop the barrage of emotions hammering me, but I can't.

Tommy's leering at me, waiting for me to say, I do. I can't form the words. No matter what my father ordered me to do, I can't make that vow.

Too much time passes. Tommy orders through gritted teeth, "Say it."

I shake my head. "I-I can't. I-I won't!"

Da jumps out of his seat. He's the only other person besides the priest in the room. He steps in front of us and declares, "She does. Move along."

I argue, "What? No! I don't!"

Da seethes, "Who's head of the clan?"

I swallow hard. My lip quivers and I struggle not to cry. One thing Da hates is tears.

"Who?" he barks.

"Ya," I answer, my stomach diving.

He points to the priest, snarling, "As I stated. Move forward."

The priest nods, asking Tommy the same questions. Tommy agrees, and the next thing I know, it's over, and he's dragging me out of Da's house.

"Don't cry. I promise you're safe. Your sister sent me to rescue ya," the stranger states again, tearing me out of my trip down memory lane. I want to block that time out forever.

I sniffle, then force myself to look at him.

My vision clears. He comes into full view, and my butterflies intensify, but I'm no longer sure they're based on fear.

Maybe I've had to look at Tommy for so long that anyone who doesn't reek of tobacco, have an age-spotted, half-bald head, isn't thirty-plus years older than me, or look like a monster, seems appealing. But the butterflies intensify, and a feeling between my legs I haven't ever felt before ignites.

I squeeze my thighs together, happy the blanket covers me, as I stare at the stranger. My pulse beats harder as I study him.

His nose is slightly crooked, and I wonder how many times he's broken it. His thick, wavy chestnut hair looks disheveled. His matching goatee needs a trim, but it isn't too long. Deep brown eyes scream danger, yet there's also another thing I haven't seen since before my wedding day.

He seems concerned about me. Still, I'm not letting my guard down. I don't know this man. And from my experience, men shouldn't be trusted.

My gaze drifts to his thick, chapped lips, and my heart pitter-patters harder.

He shifts his large frame on the bed, pulling me out of my trance over his features.

How tall is he?

Way taller than Tommy.

He can crush me with one move.

I tighten my grip on the covers, not liking the mixed signals my body gives me over my rationale.

Why does he say he knows Alaina?

He must be one of my father's men if he knows her!

More fear attacks me. I blurt out, "Who are ya?"

"My name's Aidan." His gruff voice sends tingles down my spine.

I try to sit up again. A rush of blood hits my brain, fogging up my vision.

He places his palm on my chest again, making my tingles throb faster. He orders, "Ya need to lie flat for a bit longer. The drug needs time to wear off."

"Drug!" I exclaim and try to rise again.

He arches his eyebrows, holding me firm to the mattress. Something passes in his dark expression. I think it's guilt, but surely I'm wrong? He declares, "I gave ya a choice. We had to leave. Ya were too distraught."

Think!

I struggle but finally remember cowering in the corner of my room and him holding a blanket toward me.

Tommy's going to kill me.

I swallow hard, barely getting out, "Take me back."

He jerks his head backward. It's slight, but I don't miss it. "Take ya back?"

My mouth turns drier. Tommy's vile eyes light up in my mind. I find my voice, demanding, "Take me back before my husband finds out."

Aidan's eyes turn to slits. "Ya don't have to worry about him ever again."

"M-my husband will kill ya. He'll... He'll kill me! Take me back," I shriek, trying to sit again, but Aidan's palm holds me firm.

He seethes, "He's not killing either of us."

"He will!" I insist.

Aidan inhales deeply and snarls, "Scarlet, I can assure ya that the only one dying will be Tommy. Now stop trying to sit up."

I freeze, trying to comprehend this situation, but I can't. No one is more powerful than Tommy, except my da.

More anxiety riddles me. I assert, "You've gone against my da and husband. They'll be hunting ya down. Wh-why would ya do such a thing?"

He snorts as if my da and Tommy are no one to scare him. I don't understand it. Everyone I know fears them. He claims, "They don't know I took ya. At least, not yet."

I inhale sharply.

Aidan assesses me, and my cheeks heat while my confusion grows. I want him to look away, but I also want to stare at him forever, unraveling the mystery of whoever this man is who had the guts to defy my father and husband.

I blurt out, "Ya know what happens when an O'Leary defies my da."

A deep hatred fills his expression. He scowls, announcing, "I'm not an O'Leary," as if trying to control his delivery.

Not... I try to sit up again, making my head pound harder.

"Ya aren't listening. Stop moving so abruptly," he states, putting both hands on my shoulders, his face six inches from mine.

Cedarwood and a light musk flare in my nostrils, oddly calming and stirring the sensations between my thighs.

His chest rises and falls faster. He licks his lips, staring at mine for a moment so brief I wonder if I imagined it.

"Who are ya if ya aren't an O'Leary?" I ask.

He hesitates, then answers, "I'm Alaina's friend."

I shake my head, wince from the hammers pounding into my skull, and claim, "She doesn't have friends."

His lips curl tightly. He glances at my mouth again, and I know I didn't imagine it. Then he says, "She has one. It's me."

I furrow my brows. "She would only be friends with an O'Leary."

His face falls. In a firm tone, he repeats, "I'm not an O'Leary. And there's nothing for ya to fear. As I said, I won't hurt ya, and neither will your da or Tommy. I won't let them."

Minutes pass. Both of us stare at the other, and I'm unsure what to think. Part of me isn't scared, but the other knows that's foolish.

No one can defy Da or Tommy.

"Ya have to take me back," I whisper, yet the thought of that cold room or Tommy dragging me into his bedroom...

I close my eyes, fighting the tears welling up, but there's no point. They leak down my cheeks.

Aidan swipes his fingers over them. "Shh. It's okay. But ya aren't returning to Tommy, and I'll only say this one more time. Your da and Tommy won't ever hurt ya again."

I shake my head. "They will. No one can protect me."

"They won't," he declares with so much assurance I almost believe him.

Almost.

He stays planted another moment, then retreats. "It's going to be a few more hours until the drug is fully out of your system. It's best if ya don't make any sudden movements and stay in bed. I'll come back in an hour and give ya more water. Later, ya can have some soup."

He drugged me.

Anger resurfaces. Not only has he put my life in danger, but he also stabbed me with a needle full of who knows what.

Amusement passes on his expression. He mumbles, "There's that defiance."

"What?" I snap.

He blinks as if he didn't realize he spoke out loud. He sniffs hard, then rises. "Can I trust ya to rest, or do I need to tie ya to the bed for your own good?"

Horror fills me. Flashbacks of Tommy restraining me so I couldn't fight him assault me.

Aidan must take my expression as cooperation. "Good choice. Stay in bed so ya don't hurt yourself." His gaze lingers, then he spins and walks out of the room, shutting the door.

I stare at the brown wood and shudder. It's identical to the one in the cold room where Tommy kept me captive.

How many hours did I study that door?

I wait for the sound of a lock to click, yet nothing ever comes. A while passes before I find the courage to glance around the bedroom.

Faded green and cream paper covers the walls. A shopping bag sits on a wooden dresser. Next to it is a matching desk and chair. A gold mirror hangs on the wall above it. There's one window with a shade pulled over it. A hint of sunlight shines through the edges.

How long has it been since I've seen the sun?

I sit up and wince from the pain shooting through my brain. After it turns to a dull throb, I slowly inch my legs off the mattress until my feet hit the wooden floor.

I stare at my thighs, wondering how they got so thin. I remove the quilt and study the rest of my body.

This isn't me.

It is.

It can't be.

I force myself to rise and grip the headboard until the dizziness subsides. Taking a deep breath, I walk to the desk, then reach for the back of the chair to steady myself, swallowing down nausea.

When it passes, I lift my head and stare at myself with horror. Black half-moons underline my emerald eyes. My gaunt face barely resembles who I remember. All my bones are visible, and my muscles seem to have disappeared, along with my breasts.

New tears fall. I shouldn't cry. It's vain of me to do so, and Da always ordered us to hold them in. Yet I can't stop the waterworks.

A long time passes before I pull myself together. I swipe my arm across my eyes. I find my balance, step toward the window, then hold the windowsill with one hand.

I lift the shade, squeezing my eyes closed at the glare of the light, then force myself to open them. Eventually, everything comes into view.

There's a barn and chicken coop. A fire burns in a pit, and I stare at the back of Aidan's large frame. He crosses his arms, and the fabric of his shirt strains against his back.

Sweet Jesus.

The uncomfortable sensation lights up in my core again, and I curse myself.

I'm a married woman.

Tommy will kill me for thinking about any other man.

Aidan drugged me. He's not any better than Tommy.

Isn't he? He brought me to safety.

I'm not safe. Tommy and Da will hunt us down.

If he's not an O'Leary, then who is he?

Aidan spins and catches me staring at him. He frowns, then shakes his head and lunges toward the house.

I panic, but I'm unable to move.

Within seconds the door flies open. He steps inside and freezes. He drags his gaze over my body and then locks his eyes on mine.

I cover my chest with my hands and bend my knees, realizing I'm naked and look like a skeleton. A rush of blood pounds in my head from the quick movement, and I lose my balance.

Before I hit the ground, Aidan grabs my armpits, tugging me into him. "Whoa. Steady, lass."

Horrified, I keep my eyes shut, breathing in his scent and melting into the sensation of his warm arms around me.

His lips graze the top of my head. "I told ya to stay in bed."

Alarmed, I look up, begging, "Please don't restrain me!"

His face hardens.

"Please!" I whisper, blinking hard and admitting, "I-I haven't seen sunlight in a long time."

He takes several controlled breaths, glances at my lips, and adrenaline bursts inside me. Something about his gaze gives me the impression he's thinking lewd thoughts. "I can't have ya hurting yourself. You're too weak from Tommy starving ya. You'll break a bone, or several, if ya fall right now."

I process his statement, wondering if it's true that Tommy starved me.

"I'll keep the shades open if ya give me your word and stick to it that you'll stay in bed until the drug wears off," he adds.

Too many thoughts plague me. I stay silent, taking in his sharp features, then blurt out, "How many times have ya broken your nose?"

His lips twitch. "Who said I've broken it?"

I tilt my head, sure of it, questioning, "Haven't ya?"

"Do ya always ask men about their noses?"

I try to stop my smile, unsure why I'm asking him about his nose or even finding humor in this.

When did I smile last?

"Well? Do ya?" he pushes.

"No." I swear a hint of satisfaction appears in his expression. But maybe I'm crazy and just want it to be? I clear my throat and ask, "So...how many times?"

His head bobs side to side as if he's counting. Then he answers, "Six."

"I knew it."

His grin grows. "Are ya a nose-breaking expert?"

I laugh, but it sounds strange to me. Or perhaps it's just because it's been so long. I stop myself and stare at him.

His face falls. "I haven't heard ya promise me you'll stay in bed."

I start to nod but wince.

"Easy. Jesus, you're not helping yourself, petal."

Petal?

I bite my lip and arch my eyebrows.

"What's it going to be?" he repeats.

I cave. "I'll stay in bed."

He squints. "And I can trust your word this time?"

"Yea."

He repositions himself to the side of me and instructs, "Move slow."

More embarrassment that I'm naked hits me, and it seems to take forever to get under the covers. I sit against the headboard and pull the quilt under my armpits.

He asks, "Do ya want the shade up?"

"Please."

He goes to the window and opens it. Then he returns and says, "I'm trusting ya to keep your word."

"I will," I state.

He crosses his arms, assessing me.

"Do ya have a T-shirt or something I can put on?"

He steps in front of the dresser, rifles through the shopping bags, and tosses a pair of sweatpants, a T-shirt, and a sweatshirt on the bed. He states, "My brother didn't get any undergarments. Sorry."

"Your brother?"

He nods.

Anxiety reappears. "He's here?"

"No. I sent him away. And don't worry. He's sworn to secrecy," Aidan states.

I relax a bit. Something about being here only with Aidan comforts me.

He glances at his watch. "Ya can have some more water in about a half hour. Is there anything else ya need right now?"

"No. Ummm..."

He waits.

"Thank ya," I offer.

"If ya need something, yell. Don't get up. I can't have ya breaking bones," he warns.

"Okay."

He hesitates and then steps toward the door. He reaches for the doorknob.

I blurt out, "Wait!"

He turns.

"Can ya keep the door open?"

He nods. "Aye."

I exhale. "Thank ya."

He says nothing and leaves.

The front door slamming shut echoes down the hall. I glance out the window, and Aidan reappears in front of the bonfire pit. I stare at him, unable to take my eyes off his backside, unsure why my butterflies won't go away.

I'm married.

He's a stranger and can't be trusted.

He took me away from Tommy.

Da and Tommy will kill both of us.

Who is he? Does he really know Alaina?

My sister doesn't have friends and doesn't associate with people outside our clan. If Aidan isn't an O'Leary, then it can't be true.

He's lying to me.

If he isn't an O'Leary, who is he?

Our clan has a lot of enemies. He could be anyone.

What is his motive for kidnapping me?

Oh my God. I'm his captive.

Aidan turns, and his eyes meet mine. Neither of us looks away until he moves toward the house and disappears. The sound of the door opening fills my ears, and I slide down into the bed, closing my eyes.

There are too many unanswered questions that scare and confuse me. I don't know who this man is, nor do I trust the way he looks at me or the sensations he ignites inside me.

Maybe it's better if I pretend to sleep?

The floorboards creak, and the weight of his body sinks the mattress. His warm palm covers my cheek, and electricity sparks on my skin. "Time for some more water, petal."

There it is again. Petal.

Why do I like it when he calls me that?

I open my eyes and take the water. He sets the glass on the table and rises.

When he gets to the door, I ask, "Who are ya? I can't figure it out."

He freezes, then turns, stating, "I told ya. My name is Aidan, and I'm Alaina's friend."

"That doesn't make sense."

"It will soon. Stay in bed for a bit longer. We'll have dinner in an hour," he adds, then disappears, leaving me full of questions and no answers.

2

Aidan

*P*otato soup boils in the pot. I stir it, turn the heat down to simmer, then put the lid on top. I grab the plates and bowls from the cupboard and set them on the counter.

My ringer goes off. The hairs on my neck rise, and I pull my cell out of my pocket. There's a message from my brother.

> Brody: Where are ya?

I double-check that the tracker's off on my phone. I send him one message.

> Me: Tell your wife I have her and she's safe.

I turn off my phone. There's no point in having it on. He'll bombard me with messages, and I don't need to deal with them.

I grab the spoons and a butter knife out of the drawer. A movement catches my eye.

Scarlet's standing in the doorway. The sweatpants and sweatshirt hang on her frame as if they're going to fall off.

Jesus, what size is she?

She shouldn't be standing, let alone walking around.

She's weak. If she falls, I can't take her to the hospital. Tommy would surely find out. So in all reality, I don't know what I would do if she got injured.

My voice comes out as a bark. "What are ya doing out here?"

She jumps, startled.

"Sorry, I didn't mean for that to come out harshly," I confess.

Her eyes widen. She asks, "Can a girl wee?"

I wipe my hands on the towel and then walk over to her. I put my arm around her waist and steer her toward the bathroom.

"I can walk. I'm not an invalid."

"I don't need ya breaking any bones. I thought I was clear about this." I move her into the bathroom. It's small. The two of us barely fit in it.

She looks up. "I'm not going to break any bones. I'm fine. I'm going to go to the bathroom and then I'd like to take a shower in peace...if...if I'm allowed?"

"That's not a great idea," I state.

She looks at me appalled. "No? I have to stay stinky? You're not going to let me shower either?"

Another wave of anger rolls through me. The ways Tommy neglected her piss me off. I keep my voice calm and answer, "Ya can shower, but not by yourself. I'll get in there with ya. You're too weak."

Outrage fills her expression. She declares, "I'm not letting ya take a shower with me."

"I'll keep my clothes on if ya want."

"If I want?" She arches her eyebrows.

I arrogantly claim, "Most women prefer me naked in the shower with them."

Her cheeks heat as she glares at me. "Well, I'm not one of them."

"No?" I reprimand myself for even saying this to her, but I'm unable to stop myself. I don't usually flirt, but something about her brings it out of me.

She intensifies the darts she's shooting at me with her glower. "No. Can ya please leave before I wee myself?"

I debate for a moment.

She adds, "I'm serious. I have to go."

"Fine," I grumble. I step outside the door, continuing, "But you're not showering alone."

"I need to get clean."

"Ya can shower with me or take a bath when you're done."

"Fine. I'll bathe." She waits, holding on to the counter.

I motion to the toilet. "Well, go on. Ya have to sit to wee."

"Can I have some privacy?"

"No."

"Ya don't expect me to use the loo in front of ya, do ya?"

"I don't trust ya," I admit.

"To wee?"

"To not jump in the shower."

"Well, trust is a two-way street." She huffs.

I shrug.

"Shut the door," she orders.

I debate again, then decide, "I'll shut the door halfway and stand against the wall. But this door is never to be locked. If ya disobey me—"

"Disobey ya? So you're going to be my ruler like him, huh?"

I freeze, my pulse creeping up.

Hatred fills her expression.

I tell her again, "I can't have ya hurting yourself. If ya lock the door, I'll bust it down. Ya won't have privacy the entire time you're here. Do ya understand me?"

She tilts her head, seething. "So I'm back to being a prisoner, only this time I'm yours."

I ignore the tightening in my chest, arguing, "It's for your own good."

She stares me down a moment, then gives in. "Whatever. Just let me go to the bathroom with a bit a privacy."

I give her a final look of warning, then shut the door halfway.

"Ya can shut the door all the way," she snaps.

"No, that's all ya get. Now go, or I'm coming back in."

She sighs, and several minutes pass. She admits, "This is stressing me out with ya standing right there."

"When I can trust that ya won't do something that'll result in a bad consequence, I'll give ya more privacy."

"Jesus, you're impossible," she mutters.

"Ya aren't the first woman to tell me I'm a grade-A asshole. Glad ya understand me," I claim.

She huffs, and it takes another moment, but then I hear her go to the bathroom. I wait until she flushes and then I walk back in.

She's standing, pulling her pants up. Disdain fills her expression, and she hurls out, "And ya really don't understand privacy."

"Guess the meek, scared woman I rescued is gone," I mutter, then realize what I said.

Her eyes turn to slits. She turns away, blinking hard.

"Sorry, I didn't mean—"

"Is that what ya want me to be? Meek? Scared? Worried you'll hurt me with every breath I take?" she asks, her voice low.

Guilt eats me. I shake my head. "No. Not at all."

"Ya sure?" she challenges.

"Aye."

"I'd rather know now if that's my fate."

"It's not what I want at all," I assure her.

Tense silence fills the air.

I decide it's best to change the subject. I try to keep my tone soft, but I don't really have a soft version of me. I remind her, "I don't need ya hurting yourself."

"I can wash my hands and stand." She reaches for the dispenser, pumps some soap onto her palm, and turns on the faucet.

I lean against the doorframe.

"This would be easier if ya weren't in the room. It's not a large space, and you're..." She glances over my body.

"I'm what?" I ask.

Her face heats again. "You're rather large."

"Yep, I sure am," I cockily state.

Her cheeks flame redder.

My lips twitch, and my grin grows larger.

"Ugh," she groans, putting her hands under the running water.

She finishes, and I hand her a towel.

"Such service," she chirps.

"See, that's a much better way to think about it," I tease.

She tosses the towel on the counter, then crosses her arms over her chest. "Ya can go now so I can take my bath."

I put the lid down and point to the toilet. "Sit."

"Why?"

"Are we really going to play this game?" I ask.

"What game?"

"Where ya ask questions about everything I tell ya to do."

She smirks. "I don't know. It depends, oh dear ruler of this cottage in the middle of nowhere."

I chuckle. It's another thing that doesn't happen very often. Most women bore me with their conversation and desire to please me for any cause. I rather enjoy her sarcastic rebuttals.

She rolls her eyes. "You're impossible." She sits on the toilet lid.

I reach around her, turn the bath water on, wait for it to warm, then plug the hole.

She announces, "I'm capable of taking a bath myself. Ya don't have to turn the water on for me either."

I ignore her. I grab the bath wash and squirt some in the tub so bubbles form.

"Ooh, you're getting fancy now. I must have done something good in my former life."

I glance at her. "Maybe ya did."

Her cheeks turn the color of her hair.

I add, "All right, time to take those clothes off again."

Her eyes turn to slits. "Like I said, I'm capable of taking a bath myself."

"So ya can slip getting in? I don't think so. Not only will ya have broken bones, but ya can add a concussion to that list."

"Are ya always such a Negative Nellie?"

"If that's what ya want to call it. But I told ya that I'd protect ya from Tommy. What do ya think will happen if ya end up in the hospital?"

Her face falls. She looks at the floor, mumbling, "Tommy and my da will already have everyone looking for me."

I don't tell her that her da is dead. It's on the tip of my tongue, but I'm unsure how she'll take the news. She's dealing with a lot, so I keep it to myself—for now. I soften my tone. "Which is why I'm going to help ya do this if ya want a bath, so don't fight me."

She closes her eyes and shakes her head, scrunching her face.

I add, "I'll try not to look."

Her eyelids fly open. "*Try?*"

I shrug. "I'm a guy."

Her eyes glow hotter. She orders, "Look at the wall."

I wait a moment to watch her expression turn redder, then turn.

A few seconds pass, and then she says, "Okay, look at my head only."

"This is kind of silly. I have seen ya naked a few times," I point out.

"Do ya really have to make this harder for me?" she sneers.

"Like I said, I'm a dude."

"A dude? That sounds more American to me. Are ya sure you're Irish?" she questions, assessing me.

Shit.

My father ensured my brothers and I could speak American and Irish. We've been in Ireland for a while now. Our accents come out as soon as we step over here, and we speak the lingo. But every now and then, I have to catch myself. The last thing I want her doing is finding out I'm an O'Connor. I'm unsure how she'll take the news that she's living with her family's archenemy.

"I watch a lot of American shows," I lie. I put my hands under her armpits and keep my focus on the top of her head, commanding, "Okay. Step over the tub."

She obeys. Once she's standing in the water, I say, "I'm going to lower ya down now."

She groans. "This is so ridiculous."

"It's not," I insist and help her until she's sitting in the water.

"Okay, ya can go now," she says.

I hesitate. Her hair's matted. I ask, "Do ya want your hair washed?"

"Yea, I'm going to do that. Don't worry. I see ya have some shampoo there. Good to know ya use it. And conditioner. Quite impressive. Then again, ya have some pretty thick locks, don't ya?"

"Glad ya noticed my stunning hair," I dryly say. I leave the bathroom and go out to the kitchen.

I grab the biggest glass I can find and return.

She's sunken down into the tub with her head back. Her hair floats in the water. The only thing popping above it is her nose and her mouth. Her eyes are shut. I stare at her for a minute and then sit on the toilet lid.

She opens her eyes and puts her hands over her chest. She squeezes her legs together, blurting out, "Jesus, what is wrong with ya?"

I hold the glass out. "Time to wash your hair."

"I can wash my own hair."

"Your hair is full of knots. It'll take a little more TLC than just a normal shampoo and condition." I open the drawer and grab a comb out of it.

She orders, "Just give that to me, and I can do it myself."

35

"Chill out," I say. I don't know why I'm pushing her on this, but I am. I grab the shampoo, put a palmful in my hand, then work it through her hair.

"This is ridiculous," she states again.

"Ya should get a better vocabulary. You're overusing that phrase," I taunt.

"And you're even more annoying."

"Sorry, petal." I scrub the shampoo into her scalp, massaging it.

She shuts her eyes.

"There ya go. Ya can admit it feels good," I tease.

Her eyes fly open.

"Relax. Shut your eyes again. Pretend you're at the hairdresser."

"Hairdresser? Jesus, how long's it been since I've been to the hairdresser?" she mutters.

Goose bumps break out on my skin. Whenever I learn about more things she's lost in her life because of Tommy, the anger resurfaces.

I finish shampooing her hair, turn on the faucet, put fresh water in the glass, and pour several over her head until it's rinsed out. Then I repeat everything with the conditioner. After I'm done, I take the comb and work the knots out of her hair.

She dryly states, "Such skills. Where did ya get them from?"

"My little sister. Well, she's older now, of course. My mom used to make us help out, and she always had stuff in her hair. She got gum in it a few times, and I was the only one home to help her."

"Gum?" Scarlet asks.

I chuckle, remembering. "Aye. There was this boy at school who liked her. He used to put gum in her hair."

"Another awesome thing that boys do," Scarlet mumbles.

"Yep. My brothers and I ended it. My oldest brother broke his nose. He didn't do it again."

She stays quiet.

I continue de-knotting her locks. I set the comb down. "Do ya want out now, or do ya want to stay in a little longer?"

She locks eyes with me. "I want to stay in."

"Okay." I turn the faucet on. I drain some of the colder water to warm it up again.

"Such service," she teases again, but there's some gratitude in her voice this time.

I turn the water off and state, "I'm taking the towels out of the bathroom. When you're ready to come out, yell for me."

She gives me another nasty look. "Ya really are annoying the hell out of me right now."

"Really?"

"Yep."

"Again, I don't need ya breaking bones."

"So ya claim is your excuse," she retorts.

I grab the towels and leave. I go back to the kitchen and check on the soup. I turn the heat off, stir it, and put the lid back on. I remove it from the hot burner.

Then I open the oven, take the bread out, put it on a bread-board, cut it up, and put a towel over it. I put the butter and knife on the table with the bread, fill two water glasses, and ladle soup into the bowls. I set both on the table and put towels over those as well.

I go back to the bathroom. "Dinner is ready whenever ya are."

She glances at me. "Dinner?"

"Aye. Aren't ya hungry?"

She thinks for a moment, then nods. "Yea, I am."

"When did ya eat last?"

She goes quiet and shrugs. "I don't know. It's..." She ponders some more. "It's been a few days."

I breathe through my anger. "Okay." I grab a towel and hold my hands out. "Are ya ready?"

"I can get out myself," she says and starts to move up, putting her hands on the sides of the tub.

I grab under her armpits and pull her out of the tub.

She groans. "Jesus!"

I haul her onto her feet.

She looks up. "If I fall, it'll be because of your jerky movements."

"Highly doubt that."

She rolls her eyes again.

I tighten my grip around her so her body presses against mine, and then wrap the towel around her. "I need to dry ya off."

"This is ridiculous. I'm getting ya all wet," she says.

"And that's a bad thing?" I challenge.

She opens her mouth, then snaps it shut. Her eyes widen, and a fetching shade of maroon sprawls across her cheeks.

I chuckle, then return to drying her off. When she's completely dry, I put the towel on the toilet and help her sit, ordering, "Stay here. I'll get ya fresh clothes."

She scoffs. "So dramatic."

I go into the bedroom and pull out fresh sweatpants and a T-shirt. I go into the bathroom and hand them to her.

"When you're done getting dressed, let me know. I'll help ya to the table."

"Aye, aye, sir," she sarcastically says.

I go back to the kitchen. I sit at the table and tap my fingers on the wood.

"Ya almost done?" I shout a few minutes later, right as she appears. I jump up, accusing, "I told ya to tell me when ya were ready."

"And ya haven't been listening," she says, quickly approaching the table.

I reach her right as she gets near the chair. I pull it out. "Sit."

"Ya can't do this every time I want to walk around. I'm fine."

"You're still drugged up."

"And whose fault is that?"

"Are we going to go over this again? And I did give ya a choice."

She tilts her head. "Is that your excuse for drugging me? Ya gave me a choice?"

"I did what I had to. Would ya rather be back at Tommy's?"

Tension fills the air.

She stares at the food.

I sit next to her and pull the towels off everything. Lines appear on her forehead as she studies everything.

"Don't tell me you're an Irish lass who doesn't like potato soup and bread?"

She looks up. "I do."

"Then why aren't ya digging in? Why are ya staring at it?"

Confusion fills her face. She looks back down.

I cautiously state, "I thought ya were hungry."

She bites her lip and nods.

"Then eat up."

"I'm allowed?" she blurts out, her greens glistening.

"Of course ya are. Why wouldn't ya be?"

She turns away, staring at the wall and blinking hard.

It hits me. Of course. Tommy probably ate in front of her and made her just watch.

I grab her hand. "Scarlet, whenever there's food, ya can eat. Ya don't need my permission. If I get food, ya get food."

She keeps her head turned away from me, closes her eyes, and breathes deeply a few times.

Her pain makes me want to kill Tommy even more.

She finally turns and lifts her chin but still stares at the soup. Then she meets my eye.

"Is something else wrong?" I ask.

She glances at our hands. "I can't eat if ya don't give me my hand back."

"Oh right. Sorry." I reluctantly remove my hand from hers.

She takes a bite, keeping it in her mouth for several seconds before chewing and swallowing it. She takes another spoonful, and once she swallows it, she says, "Are ya going to stare at me the whole time?"

"Nope." I take a mouthful of soup. Then I pull apart a piece of bread, butter it, and put it on her plate. I make one for myself too, then dip it in my soup.

We eat silently for a few more moments, then she states, "This is good."

"Ya sound surprised," I note.

She glances at me. "Ya don't really look like ya can cook."

I chuckle. "No? What do I look like?"

She blurts out, "Someone who can snap me in half."

My pulse skyrockets. I debate about what to say. She looks away.

I lower my voice, firmly restating, "I told ya I'm not going to hurt ya."

"Lots of men say they won't hurt people, women especially," she claims.

"Yea. Well, my word is my word." I point to the bread on her plate. "Have some before it gets cold. Ya need to gain some weight back."

Embarrassment floods her cheeks. She mutters, "I know. I look like a skeleton. I'm gross." She blinks hard again.

I lower my voice. "I didn't mean it as an insult. And there's nothing gross about ya."

She squares her shoulders and tears at the bread. She puts a piece in her mouth and chews slowly.

More tense silence follows until she declares, "The men in my family don't cook. How do ya know how?"

The uncomfortable sensation I always get whenever I think of my mother erupts in my belly. She left us when she didn't want to stay in my father's clan. He let her go, and she moved to California but never returned. But before she left, there were good times.

So I admit, "My mum said if you're Irish and ya can't make potato soup, then ya can't expect to survive in this world."

Scarlet laughs. It's soft, and I like it. I realize how much I love to hear her laugh. She declares, "Your mum sounds like a smart woman."

"She was," I say.

Scarlet's smile falls. She arches her eyebrows. "Was?"

I shrug. "Yea, I don't see her anymore."

"Why not?"

"She left us."

Scarlet's eyes widen. "I'm sorry."

"It is what it is."

"Who's us?"

"My brothers, sister, and Da."

"Sorry," she offers again.

I don't reply. We continue eating in silence. When we're done, I get up, and she tries to help me clear the plates. I command, "Just sit down."

"I'm not an invalid," she repeats.

I sigh, staring at her.

"Fine. Am I allowed to go sit on the sofa?" she asks.

"I'll help ya over there."

"No, I don't need your help to walk from the table to the sofa. I'm not going to fall. I'm not dizzy. I'm fine," she insists as she rises and takes her hand off the table.

I study her like a hawk waiting for its prey.

"Ya can't carry, guide, or do whatever every time I want to walk. I'm fine," she reiterates.

I hold my hands up. "Okay, but if ya get dizzy..."

"If I get dizzy, I'll stop. I won't make any quick movements. Ya have my word."

"And can I trust your word?"

She glares at me. "Of course ya can."

"I couldn't earlier," I toss in her face.

She puts her hand on her hip. "Maybe ya should let that go. Ya did drug and kidnap me."

I try to keep a straight face. "I prefer to say rescue."

She mutters, "Straight-up knight in shining armor, complete with your syringe."

I disregard the syringe comment, arguing, "Ya still lied to me." I don't know why I'm holding it against her. In all reality, I can't blame her for wanting to see sunlight after what Tommy put her through.

She gives me another exasperated look. "I'm going to the sofa now." She smirks, then crosses the room.

I hold my breath until she's safely seated.

She takes the blanket from the back of the sofa, hugs her legs to her chest, and puts the worn material over herself. She bats her eyes, declaring, "I guess I'll sit back and watch ya do the dishes."

"Ya do that," I tease, studying her until her cheeks heat again.

She takes a deep breath, quietly asking, "Why are ya staring at me?"

My pulse skyrockets. "I'm not."

Her eyes drift down my body until they reach my groin, then she gapes a brief moment before quickly turning away. Her chest rises and falls faster.

I glance down at the bulge in my joggers, realizing I have a raging hard-on.

Shit!

I go to the sink, muttering, "I wasn't staring."

"Seems to me ya were," she mumbles.

I do the dishes, wondering what I'm getting myself into. I figured she'd be a handful once she realized she's safe, but Scarlet's a bit more than I anticipated—in all the ways I don't need her to be.

My only goal should be to utilize her to make Tommy pay. But those green eyes and defiant attitude are everything I don't need to keep me on track with my plan.

3

Scarlet

*A*idan's broad back that stretches his T-shirt and rock-hard ass underneath his gray joggers aren't helping me. I can't tear my gaze off him while he does the dishes.

What kind of man does the dishes?

Definitely not ones like him.

But there he is, scrubbing plates.

Stop looking, I reprimand myself. Yet, I continue to fixate on all his body parts, which I shouldn't do.

I've just been with Tommy too long, and that's why I'm finding him attractive.

He drugged me.

But he got me away from Tommy.

Tommy will kill me when he hunts us down.

I sigh. Aidan seems nice. He's a little overboard about my safety, and I can tell he's got a crazy streak in him. It isn't any different than all the men I've ever known, but that's where the similarities end. He's only shown me kindness and tried to care for me, which confuses me.

Tommy's a cruel monster. There's no heart inside him. Every moment with him was torture.

His face pops into my mind, and I shudder, tugging the blanket tighter. I lean my head against the back of the couch and peek over the edge, continuing to stare at Aidan.

Why do I feel safe with him?

I'm not. Tommy will find us. This isn't permanent.

My inner voice warns that I don't even know who Aidan really is, so I shouldn't trust him.

All I know about this guy is his first name. He says he's friends with Alaina, but that doesn't make sense. My sister doesn't have friends. I rack my mind trying to think about who in our clan is named Aidan, but the ones I know don't come close to resembling the tall, rugged man standing in front of me.

They definitely wouldn't be doing dishes.

Why would he go against Da and Tommy?

Da's going to kill him if Tommy doesn't.

Something about that thought makes me sad. And the fear I can't escape of the consequences of being here with Aidan grows.

I sink into the couch and close my eyes. A shiver runs down my spine. I wish I could hide from the anxiety and trip down memory lane, but I can't.

My da didn't protect me. He fed me to the lions when I tried to run away. I just wanted to escape the clan, his ideas of what a woman in the clan's life should be like, and live like an average person would.

Yet I couldn't hide. He sent Tommy to find me in London, and within a day, I was right back in my father's house. And he was angry. He saw my actions as a betrayal. As a punishment, he forced me to marry Tommy. Now, Da's surely hunting me just like he did when I ran away.

I get lost in my thoughts, sinking deeper and deeper until Aidan's voice tears me out of them. "Scarlet, want me to take ya to bed?"

Adrenaline shoots through my core. I open my eyes, speechless, inhaling his cedarwood and musk scent. He's crouched on the floor next to the couch. His dark eyes peer at me. They swirl with concern and something else. Something I haven't seen since before Tommy, when men would look at me with interest.

The longer Aidan pins his gaze on me, the more the heat grows. I wonder if I'm imagining it.

He says, "Should I carry ya to the bedroom?"

My pulse skyrockets, and butterflies fill my stomach.

Jesus. What will he do to me in there?

What am I thinking? I have to stop these thoughts.

I'm married.

My body is disgusting right now. I look like a skeleton. No way he'd be attracted to me. He even admitted I need to gain weight.

But why is he staring at me like that?

He should be shot for those chiseled features.

"Scarlet, do ya want to sleep?" he asks again.

I force myself to sit up and blurt out, "Let's play a game."

Surprise fills his expression. "A game?"

I glance around the tiny space but don't see any board games or cards.

Aidan declares, "I don't think there are any games here, petal."

Petal.

Everything in my core heats up. I lick my lips. My heart races faster, and I pat the cushion beside me, ordering, "Sit down. I know a game."

He hesitates. "What kind of game?"

"You'll see. But what's your last name? I know it's not O'Leary," I claim, tilting my head.

His face hardens. "No, it's not."

My chest tightens. "Then what is it?"

"It's just Aidan."

"Ya aren't going to tell me your last name?"

"Not right now."

"Why?"

"Change the subject."

48

The hairs on my arms rise and I take a deep breath.

His expression stays hardened, and something tells me not to push him on it right now. So I ask, "Are ya scared to sit next to me? I won't break in two from your..." My eyes glance down to his groin and my face heats.

Jesus, that bulge is so big.

His lips twitch. He's not even slightly embarrassed. "My what, Scarlet?"

I circle my finger in front of his muscular pecs. "Your large self," I state, but it only embarrasses me further.

Arrogance washes over him. It might be the sexiest thing I've ever seen.

No, no, no. It's not sexy.

I've just been with Tommy too long.

His lips twitch as if he can read my mind, and he arches his eyebrow.

"Well, do ya want to play a game to pass the time or not?" I challenge.

He slides next to me, and more zings fly to my core.

Oh shit, this is bad.

Why did I tell him to sit next to me?

He rolls his head next to mine and stares at my lips, stating, "I'll warn ya, I'm not much of a rule follower."

My tingles grow more intense. "No? So I have to worry about ya cheating? Typical man."

His eyes meet mine. He firmly reprimands, "No, I'm not a cheater. Real men don't cheat at games or anything else."

"Anything else?" I squeeze my legs together. My heart pounds harder.

He gives me another expression that burns the blood in my veins, then admits, "I might, however, bend things to go my way." He grins and winks. Then he puts his large palm over my thigh.

I glance down, and more shame fills me. I look like I have a chicken leg. I'm so bony. But his touch just adds to the intensity of my adrenaline.

I need space.

I scoot my ass to the armrest, as far away from him as possible, and crisscross my legs, facing him. I rearrange the blanket over me and start, "Here's how ya play. I ask, 'would ya rather', and ya have to be honest with your answer."

"How do I win?"

"There isn't a winner, really."

"But this is a game?"

"Yea."

He declares, "All games have a winner and loser."

"Not all."

"Name one?"

I ponder his question. I can't think of any game that doesn't have a winner or loser, but I also don't want to admit it to him. Instead, I question, "So ya don't want to play, then?"

He stares at me, sniffs hard, then glances at my lips again. He lowers his voice. "No, I'll play. Show me what ya got, petal."

The sensations in my core I shouldn't be feeling grow. I blurt out, "Why do ya call me that?"

He arches his eyebrows. "Does it bug ya?"

I think about it for a minute and decide to be honest. "No."

"So ya like it," he cockily declares.

A warm flush deepens on my cheeks. I debate how to answer.

Before I can, he says, "It's okay. Ya don't have to admit it, petal."

Jesus, help me.

I'm married!

And beyond disgusting with my chicken legs.

I point at him. "Let's focus on the game. Ya have to answer all questions honestly."

He shrugs. "Okay, no problem."

I smirk and bat my eyelids. "Can I trust ya to be honest?"

He grunts. "I'm not the one with the history of deceit."

I ignore his comment, cursing myself for walking into that trap. I begin, "Let's start. Would ya rather drink only stout or whiskey for the rest of your life?"

"That's easy. Stout."

His answer surprises me. While all the men in my clan drink stout, whiskey's the number one go-to. I ask, "Not whiskey? Even top-shelf?"

He shakes his head. "Nope. Guinness all day long."

"Hmm."

"Ya don't like Guinness?" he questions.

I confess, "No. Tommy and my da drink whiskey. If I never smell it again, it will be soon enough. That and cigarettes."

Silence ensues, and pity grows on his face. Once again, I scold myself. *Why can't I just shut my mouth today?*

I clear my throat and declare, "Your turn to ask a question."

He recovers and asks, "Okay, if ya could only eat cola bottles or clove rocks for the rest of your life, which would ya choose?"

I gasp. "Taking away my sweets? Going right for my jugular."

He grins and points at me. "Pick."

"Cola bottles."

"Why?" he asks in surprise.

"They're soft."

"Ya don't like hard things?"

"Soft is nicer."

"Hmm, is it?" he teases.

"Yea. Soft candy is definitely better."

"In my opinion, soft is better only for special circumstances," he proclaims.

Something tells me I'm falling into a trap, but I still go there, stepping right into it. I ask, "Okay, when is soft better than hard?"

His eyes fall to my chest for a beat and then lift back to my face. "Women, for instance. Soft is good for a woman, but a man should be hard. Don't ya think, petal?"

Heat flies to my cheeks. I swat his arm, reprimanding, "Behave."

"See? Another example of what ya don't want soft," he declares.

I huff, questioning, "What would that be?"

He flexes, answering, "My bicep. Don't lie and say you'd want it to be soft."

I groan and cover my face with my hands while laughing and shaking my head. "You're so cocky."

He shifts on the couch and puts his arm over the back. I'm tempted to lean against it but force myself not to. He does have incredible arms.

Ugh! This is so bad.

He asks, "What's the next question?"

I lift my head out of my hands, inquiring, "What if ya had to choose between your eyes or your ears?"

His eyes widen. "Seriously? My sight or my hearing?"

"Yep," I answer, satisfied with myself.

He thinks about it, then replies, "I guess my eyes."

"Why?"

He shrugs. "I would use technology to record what people say and have it dictated on my phone screen to read. I can't think of anything I could use to help with my sight. So yea, I'd choose to lose my hearing to keep my sight."

I softly clap, impressed with his answer. "Bravo."

He taps his head. "I do have a brain."

"Well, aren't ya the Scarecrow after he went to the Emerald City?" I tease.

He grins bigger. "Are ya a *Wizard of Oz* fan?"

"I loved it when I was little."

He grins bigger. "Me too."

"Really?"

His face lights up. "Yep."

"Well, it's good to know you're not all hard muscle," I state, immediately regretting it.

What is wrong with my mouth tonight?

His cocky expression flares on his sharp features. He assesses me for a minute, then asks, "Are ya ready for your question?"

I compose myself and take a deep breath, squaring my shoulders. "Yep. Bring it on, kidnapper."

Amusement fills his face. "Is that what you're going to call me? Kidnapper?"

"Sorry. I should call ya my drug injector."

He groans. "Your disdain for how ya got here is getting old, petal."

"Is it?" I question.

He leans closer and drags his finger over my jawline as tingles fill every cell in my body. He slides his finger over my lips, then holds it there, asking, "What if ya got to keep your tongue or if I got to keep my tongue? What would ya choose?"

I swallow hard, mumbling against his finger, "What? How is it even a choice?"

"It's definitely a choice," he claims, then scoots closer and takes his finger off my lips, watching me intently.

"Is this a trick?" I ask.

"No. Why?"

Confused, I step into his trap and question, "Why would I let ya keep your tongue instead of keeping my own?"

A lewd expression fills him. My butterflies flutter harder. He says, "If ya let me keep my tongue, you'll get the benefits of it."

My entire body ignites with fire. I blurt out, "I'm a married woman. Ya shouldn't say things like that to me."

His expression falls and hardens. His voice turns cold as he says, "Ya were forced to marry that thug."

"How do ya know?" I question.

"Weren't ya?"

Shame fills me. I'm unsure why. All I can think about is Da telling the priest that I do and making a vow for me that made me a prisoner. But I still insist, "It doesn't change that I'm married. This isn't appropriate."

He sits back, and his chest rises higher with each inhale. He asks, "What exactly is not appropriate, petal?"

"Even ya calling me petal isn't appropriate," I declare, immediately regretting the words. I like it when he calls me petal.

A bit of hurt crosses his face, but he proclaims, "No, it's not inappropriate. Ya were forced to take a vow and should have no loyalty to him. You're free. So what's inappropriate?"

I motion between us. "Your seductive grin and sexy scent...that fire in your eyes... Well...they're not appropriate." My mouth turns dry, and I look away.

Why the hell did I just admit that to him?

He doesn't move, and I can feel his gaze locked on me. He declares, "Women forced to marry men they don't want and who abuse them aren't obligated to keep vows, and if I have to tell ya that 5,000 times, I will."

My heart feels like it'll pound out of my chest. I nervously laugh, "In what world? And I'm not an abused woman."

He crosses his arms. "Ya think what he did to ya wasn't abuse?"

Shame and mortification fill me. I insist, "I wasn't abused. I'm not a victim."

Aidan argues, "Ya were. And ya owe him nothing."

Anger mixes with my embarrassment. I shouldn't direct it at Aidan, but I jab him in the chest, accusing, "So ya think I'm yours to fuck?"

"I didn't say that," he claims.

"No? Ya might as well have."

"Don't put words in my mouth, Scarlet."

I bolt off the couch and race to the bedroom. I slam the door and lock it.

"Scarlet!" Aidan shouts, pounding on the door.

"Go away!"

He commands, "Open this door now."

"No!"

"I'll knock it down if ya don't," he threatens.

"Leave me alone, Aidan. For God's sake, just leave me alone." I slide under the covers, pulling them over my head, expecting him to kick the door in at any minute.

He pounds a few more times, but he doesn't make good on his threat for some reason.

I eventually drift off to sleep. I wake up in the middle of the night and have to go to the loo. I exit the bed and quietly open the door, tiptoeing into the bathroom.

I do my business, step out of the bathroom and stare at the couch. The moonlight streams through the window and onto Aidan's huge frame. His legs hang off the end. The tiny throw barely covers his torso.

Guilt eats at me. There's only one bedroom here. He'll have a backache tomorrow.

I go grab the top blanket off the bed. I return to the main room, remove the throw, and put the quilt over Aidan. Then I take the thin material and return to the bedroom, curling up under it. I pull the other blankets over me, wondering about everything Aidan insisted earlier.

Do I really not have to remain loyal to Tommy?

Am I an abused woman?

Neither of these thoughts bring any comfort to me. Fear of going against Tommy paralyzes me. My only hope is he'll give me mercy since Aidan kidnapped me and I didn't go willingly.

As much as I want to live in that notion, I know it's false. Tommy knows no mercy. This will be my fault. And when he finally finds me, there will be a new hell waiting for me.

4

Aidan

A rooster crows, and I open my eyes. Dull pain throbs in my lower back, and I groan, glancing around the tiny cottage. I move to get off the couch and realize that the quilt from the bed is covering me.

I freeze, staring at it. *I didn't put this on me. I had the crappy blanket.*

I lift the quilt to look for the throw, but it's gone. I get off the couch and go to the bedroom door, staring at Scarlet.

She's sleeping. Her slightly parted lips, and her red hair fanned over the pillow, make her look like an angel sleeping peacefully, even with the faint black circles still under her eyes.

She's gorgeous even though she's gaunt. I review the items in the kitchen so I know what I can make her for breakfast. She couldn't eat all the food I put in front of her last night, which is understandable. I'm sure her stomach shrunk from being starved.

She stirs, and I stay frozen. Then she settles back into the bed, hugging the pillow tighter. I carefully shut the door so it doesn't make any noise, then stare at the knob.

I can't believe she locked me out last night. It took everything I had not to kick the door in, but she was upset. I figured if I followed through with my threat, it'd make the situation worse. Plus, I didn't want to be like Tommy.

I tear my eyes off the knob and notice the fire is barely burning. I don't need extra heat, but Scarlet gets cold.

Because that bastard starved her and she has no fat on her body.

I stare at the fire, my fists at my sides, taking deep breaths full of anger. The embers dull further, and I leave the cottage, stepping out into the cold air.

Thick fog stretches over the yard, and my breath forms clouds before me with every exhale. I go to the woodpile and toss a few logs in the wheelbarrow.

A crackle comes through the woods. I spin, then relax when I spot a deer leaping through the trees.

I put my hands in my pockets, staring at it and gripping my phone.

Sighing, I decide I need to face the music. I turn on my cell even though I don't want to. I already know there'll be a slew of messages.

The screen lights up with dozens of texts, mostly from Brody and Alaina.

Brody: Where is she?

Brody: Ya need to bring her back.

Brody: Call me.

Brody: Why is your phone turned off?

Brody: This isn't okay, Aidan. I'm the boss.
Disobeying me will have consequences.

Brody: You're pissing me off now.

Brody: Goddamnit! My wife's going nuts. I need
ya to contact me immediately. That's an order!

It goes on and on and on. Then I open Alaina's messages, which range from angry to desperate.

Alaina: Where is she? Don't ya dare keep her
from me.

Alaina: *We can keep her safe here—more than ya can wherever ya are.*

Alaina: Bring her to me, Aidan. It's an order.

Alaina: Don't be like them and keep her away
from me. She'll want to see me. She has to be
asking about me.

Alaina: Tell her I love her and want to see her.

Alaina: Ya have to let me see her.

Alaina: I advise ya to get back here sooner
rather than later.

Alaina: Aidan, I'm begging ya.

I continue reading the threats and pleas until I finally send them a joint message.

> Me: Stop texting me. She's fine. I won't let anything happen to her. When I finish executing what needs to happen, you'll see her.

I immediately get replies.

> Alaina: Bring her back now, Aidan. This isn't okay.

> Brody: You've gotten your orders. Do not disobey us.

I groan, scrubbing my face.

"Everything okay?" Scarlet's voice rings through the air.

I turn.

She hugs her chest, and her lips quiver from the cold.

I point toward the cottage. "Get inside. It's too cold out here, and ya can get hurt."

She rolls her eyes. "Are we back to me being a weak woman who can't stand on her own two feet long enough not to break a bone?"

"It's not funny," I state, my worries from yesterday reappearing.

Her teeth chatter. "What are ya doing out here?"

"Getting wood."

"Looks like something else is going on." She glances at the phone as it buzzes with new messages.

I don't look at them, turning the phone off and sliding it into my pocket. I reiterate, "I need ya to go inside."

"I can help carry wood."

I scowl. "Absolutely not. Go inside, Scarlet, or I'll carry ya in."

"Ya really are annoying."

"Don't test me," I threaten.

"Ugh," she mutters, spins, and returns to the cottage.

Once the door shuts, I fill a wheelbarrow with as much wood as possible and roll it to the front porch. I take it all inside, then go back outside and get another wheelbarrow full. I shut and lock the door when all the wood is next to the fireplace.

Scarlet's in the kitchen. She calls out, "I'm assuming ya love an Irish breakfast."

I arch my eyebrows. "Aye, but I can make it. Why don't ya go rest?"

She puts her hand on her hip. "Aidan, I'm not going to just lie around all day. I'm fine."

I debate, unconvinced she has any energy to stand longer than thirty seconds. How can she when he almost starved her to death?

"I don't feel like fighting all day, but that's what we're going to be doing if ya don't stop this," she claims.

I cave. "Fine, but I'll help ya."

"No, sit down. How's your back, by the way?"

I don't tell her that it's sore. I lie, "It's fine."

"Ya sure? That couch is pretty small for ya."

"And we're back to how large I am," I tease.

Her cheeks flush. "You're impossible." She spins and grabs bacon out of the fridge. She unwraps it and looks over her shoulder, stating, "You're staring at me."

"Is that a bad thing?" I reply, even though I shouldn't after how she reacted last night.

She ignores me. "Why don't ya read a book or something?"

"Read a book?"

"Yea. I assume ya know how to read since if ya lost your hearing, ya would read what's on your phone."

I glance at the bookshelf. It's the only thing that's in here. I declare, "Yea, I'll pass on that idea."

Her lips twitch. "Ya don't like to read books?"

"Not really. I'd rather watch a movie."

"Why is that?"

I cross my arms and wiggle my eyebrows. "Ya could say I'm a visual guy."

She softly laughs. "Of course ya are." She puts the bacon in the pan, and the sound of it sizzling in the skillet hits my ears.

"Ya sure ya don't want any help?"

She turns and puts her hands on the counter. "Where I come from, men don't belong in the kitchen. Women do. And ya should know that since ya apparently are familiar with my clan. Yet I'm still unsure why ya would defy my da and husband."

My insides curl.

Her husband.

Her da.

Without thinking, I blurt out, "Your da's dead."

She gapes momentarily, then recovers, scolding, "That's not funny."

"Who said I'm joking?" My stomach churns more. I'm probably telling her at the wrong time, but I knew I'd have to tell her eventually. It should be one less worry for her, but I also don't know how she'll react. I study her carefully.

She blinks hard and seethes, "Don't ya dare lie to me, Aidan."

I step closer. "I'm not lying."

She steps away from the counter until her back hits the stove.

"Watch yourself," I warn.

She slides to the side. "Why would ya say such a horrible thing?"

I stand across from her. "Because it's true. Alaina killed him."

More surprise fills her expression. She gapes at me for a long time, then slowly shakes her head. "No. Alaina would never—"

"She did. He tried to kill her, and she got to him first. She slit him to pieces."

Shock fills her as she processes it.

I add, "Your sister did the right thing."

Scarlet raises her head and glares, seething, "If she killed my da, they would've taken her. You're lying!"

"No, your sister's safe."

"But the clan would've killed her."

"They didn't."

Confusion fills Scarlet's face. She carefully asks, "So she's in charge of the clan now?"

More rage fills me. Everything about the O'Learys irritates me. I inform her, "No. Your oldest brother Caleb is."

The color drains from her cheeks. "Caleb, not Alaina?"

I shake my head. "No. Your da named Caleb before Alaina killed him."

"I-I don't understand. Why would Alaina kill Da?"

I grunt. "Why shouldn't she? Look what he did to ya."

Scarlet looks away and puts her hand on her gut. I step closer to her. "Everything's fine. Alaina is fine. She's safe."

Scarlet's voice quivers. "Caleb will be looking for me. He's worse than my da. At least Da..." Her voice trails off.

"At least Da what?" I snarl, my mouth turning dry.

She stays silent and squeezes her eyes shut, but a tear runs down her cheek.

"Your da never treated ya the way ya should have been treated," I claim.

"Ya don't know how my da treated me," she snarls.

Frustration fills me. I don't know how she can be loyal to a man who forced her to marry the monster she did. It's so clear he never loved her. He didn't love her sister either. He only cared about his sons. Women were just disposable, and it didn't matter that they were his blood.

She asks, "So Tommy and Caleb are the ones hunting us?"

"Probably, but they're never going to find us," I declare.

Her hands shake. She insists, "Ya don't know that. They will."

"No, they won't." The trembling in her hands grows. I put my arm around her. "Scarlet, why don't ya go sit down? I'll make breakfast."

"No," she says, lifting her chin.

"It's okay. Just go sit down on the couch. You're upset."

"I'm fine," she snaps, then spins and goes to the fridge. She pulls more food out, and I watch her. She seethes, "Can ya stop staring at me?"

I don't move.

She grabs beans out of the cupboard and slams them on the counter. "Jesus! I asked ya to stop. Can ya do one thing that I ask?"

I sit at the table but don't take my eyes off her. I can't. No matter her outburst, it's impossible.

She stays busy in the kitchen, and the smell of bacon soon fills the air.

She removes it from the skillet, cracks eggs into the grease, and mutters, "And you're still staring at me." But her voice has less anger in it.

I want to ask her a lot of things, like how she feels now that she's had time to process that her da's dead. Or why she can't comprehend that she doesn't belong to Tommy. And I know she's fragile right now and confused, but my rationale doesn't make it easy for me to understand how she can still be loyal to them.

She finishes cooking, turns the stove off, and brings everything to the table. I grab plates and silverware, and we eat in tense silence.

She finally puts her fork down, swallows, takes a sip of tea, then asks, "Where's my sister?"

My chest tightens.

I might as well get it over with.

I reveal, "She's with my brother."

The questions pop into Scarlet's expression before she inquires, "Who's your brother?"

"Brody."

Her eyebrows furrow. She studies me. Then the color once again drains from her face. Her voice sounds raw as she demands, "Tell me your last name. Now."

I clench my jaw and stare at her.

"Aidan, tell me your and Brody's last name."

"I think ya know my last name."

Her eyes widen. She seethes, "Are ya an O'Connor?"

"Aye, petal, I am," I admit.

Her chair flies back so fast it hits the floor. She jumps up and moves toward the door.

I rise from my chair and reach the door before she does, stepping between her and it, asking, "Where do ya think you're going?"

"Away from ya."

"No, you're not. It's not safe."

She jabs me in the chest. "Don't tell me what's safe. You're an O'Connor."

"An O'Connor who removed ya from your prison."

"To be in yours!"

The hairs on my neck rise. "Ya know this isn't a prison."

She scoffs, then puts her hand over her mouth, turning from me. She mutters, "Jesus, I'm so stupid. How could I not put two and two together?"

"I need ya to calm down, petal."

"Do not call me petal," she snarls, spinning on me, red rage all over her cheeks.

"Nothing has changed."

She snarls, "Everything has changed. You're the enemy of my family. And Tommy...he'll...he'll definitely hunt ya down and kill ya. And me! What have ya done?"

Everything I've been holding inside boils over. I try to keep my voice calm but end up barking, "What have I done? I took ya away from that monster, and he'll be dead when I get done with him. Just like your da. Just like your brothers eventually will as well."

Her jaw trembles harder. Her eyes glisten, and the emotions in her expression are more intense than yesterday. Fear, loathing, and pure disgust are all directed at me.

I stay quiet, wanting to take away that look, but I can't.

"What's your brother doing with my sister?" she asks angrily.

"They're married."

Her head jerks backward. "You're lying."

"They are," I insist.

"He forced her?" she questions. Tears fall down her face. She swipes at them.

Disgust fills me. "No, we don't force women to marry us. And Alaina no longer is an O'Leary. She took an oath to be an O'Connor. It was her choice, and she now rules our clan with my brother."

Scarlet stares at me in disbelief, shaking her head. "Sure, and pigs fly, Aidan."

"I'm not lying, lass."

"Ya are."

"No, I'm not. I can show ya the messages from both of them if ya want."

Her eyes turn to slits. "Is that who ya were texting this morning?"

I slowly nod.

She holds her hand out. "I want to see the messages."

I take a deep breath and pull my phone out. I turn it on, pull up the chain of texts, and hold it in front of her face.

She tries to grab the phone, and I pull it back.

"You're not taking my phone, but ya can read the messages."

"Give it to me," she demands.

"No. Either read them like this, or ya won't see them at all."

She glares at me.

I scroll to the top of the messages and slowly move the screen as she reads.

When there are no more, she claims, "My sister wants to see me."

"Of course she does."

"Then let me see her."

"It's too dangerous. Getting ya here was enough of a risk. If we move around, it increases the chance that your brother and Tommy's men will find us."

Her face hardens. "I want to see my sister."

"Ya can't."

She gives me another look of hatred and finally says, "So I am your prisoner. Ya claim you're better than him, but you're not. He kept her from me, and now ya are too."

I hate myself for doing anything that resembles what Tommy did to her, but I know I'm right. I can't take her to Alaina right now. It's too dangerous. So I lift my chest and stand taller. "Well, then, lass, if that's what ya want to think, I guess that's what you'll think. Eventually, you'll see your sister again, but not until it's safe."

She shakes her head at me, then spins and goes into the bedroom, slamming and locking the door again.

I don't threaten her to open it again. I start to clean up breakfast, but then I see her plate, still full of food.

I pick up it along with her tea and take them to the door. I knock, calling out, "Ya need to eat. Open the door."

"Go away, Aidan!"

I position the plate over my forearm and bang on the door, warning, "I'll no longer threaten ya with knocking this door down. I'll spoon-feed ya if I have to. So don't play games with me, Scarlet. Open this door and take your food, now!"

Silence fills the air.

"You've got one more minute to get this plate and then your warning's over. Don't test me on this!"

The door opens. She shoots me darts with her glare, takes the food and the tea, then shuts and locks the door again.

Once again, I'm bathed in her silence. I don't like it, but there's no way I'm letting her see Alaina. I have my plan, and until I see it through, she's not leaving my sight.

I glance over at the bedroom, cursing myself and the damn door I'm stopping myself from kicking in.

5

Scarlet

I set the plate of food on the bed and pace the room.

Da is dead.

How is it possible?

And Caleb's running the clan?

The pit in my stomach grows. My brother has no boundaries. Da at least had some, but Caleb... He hates both Alaina and me. All my brothers do.

We were always just women in the family. It was the reason I ran away. I wanted to be more than that. I didn't want to run the clan like Alaina did, but I wanted my own life instead of only cooking and cleaning for men.

She warned me how horrible it would be if any of my brothers ever got into power. And I know she wanted to change things.

She admitted it to me once after she had had too much whiskey. The next day when I talked to her about it, she shushed me, told me never to speak of such matters again.

She was right.

If my father or brothers knew, they would've done something to hurt her. I know that now. But she did want to make changes. I know she did.

And my brothers, knowing they have no loyalty to me, will be worse than Tommy and my da. That doesn't sit well with me.

Did Da have any loyalty to Alaina or me?

Yes, he had to. We're his daughters.

He didn't.

He was my da.

"Ugh," I groan, not any less confused than yesterday. The debate continues.

I wish I could see things black and white the way Aidan does.

He's an O'Connor. He wants me to think certain things.

Maybe he's telling the truth and won't hurt me.

He's just as vicious.

He can't be trusted.

How could Alaina be married to Brody O'Connor and running the O'Connor clan with him?

It's not possible. She loves the O'Learys. She would die for them.

My stomach rumbles, and I pick up a piece of soda bread, nibbling on it. I go to the window and stare out at the sunshine.

Alaina killed Da?

I can't fathom it. I chew more soda bread and grab my tea. I return to the window, loving how the sunlight warms my skin.

Aidan lets me see the sun.

That doesn't mean he's a good person.

He's a monster too.

Is he?

I sip the tea, but it doesn't calm me. I can't stop thinking about how Aidan's an O'Connor. No matter what Da or Tommy have done, I'm still an O'Leary. Aren't I? And Aidan has to be as ruthless as anyone in my family.

There's no way I can trust him now that I know he's an O'Connor. His flirty, overly concerned act is only to trick me.

He could have been honest and told me yesterday when I woke up and asked who he was, but he lied.

What else is he hiding?

I finish the bread, then sit on the bed. I eat some of the egg, finish my tea, and push the plate away. I slide under the covers and contemplate what to do about all this.

I need to escape Aidan.

How?

My sister. She'll help me.

I return to pacing the room, wondering how to contact Alaina. I really am in the middle of nowhere. The cottage is surrounded by a small farm and woods. The only living things here are the chickens.

The door slamming hits my ears, and I return to the window. Aidan appears, walks over to the fire pit, and tosses a trash bag in it. He squirts lighter fluid over it, then strikes a match. He holds it in front of his face, watching it burn until it almost touches his fingers. He finally tosses it onto the burn pile and it bursts into flames.

The smoke moves toward him, and he steps to the side, crosses his arms, and stares at it, deep in thought.

I study him, unsure why I don't feel pure hatred toward him.

I should.

The men in my clan are bad, but so are the O'Connors.

Why would I betray my own clan for his?

Why would Alaina do that?

He's lying. He has to be lying.

Brody was on that message too though.

I put my hand in my hair, tugging at it, and it's as if Aidan can sense my frustration. He turns his head, locking eyes with me, and my core lights up.

Goddamnit! Why do I have to be attracted to him?

I'm not!

He's just a cocky, sexy, rugged man who thinks he can have any woman he wants.

He'd even take me looking as horrible as I do right now.

I step away from the window and move back in front of the mirror, cringing at how the sweatpants and sweatshirt fall against my body. I could be wearing a trash bag. If it wasn't for the drawstring in the pants, I wouldn't be able to keep them up.

No matter how much he feeds me, I wonder if I'll ever look like my old self.

It was so long ago.

Was it?

Will the dark circles under my eyes ever fade?

I study myself until I run out of disgust and only numbness remains. I step away from the mirror and return to pondering how I can get ahold of my sister.

She's my only option. Aidan's right about one thing; I'm still physically weak. There's no way I'd survive in the wilderness on my own. I don't even know where we're at, and there's no doubt that Caleb and Tommy are searching for me with the rest of the clansmen.

But my sister's smart. She's fierce and fearless. I know she'll come get me. Once she's here, she'll know what to do.

I pace until it hits me.

His phone. I need his phone.

Once again, the question of how plagues me.

I can't just reach into his pocket and grab it. And Aidan won't just hand it over.

I sigh. *I've got to get it.*

I pick up my plate, put the teacup on it, then leave my bedroom. I scrape the food into the kitchen trash, then wash the plate and cup. I set it on the rack to dry, and Aidan walks in.

He asks, "Did ya eat?"

Part of me likes the fact that he's actually worried about me eating. It's a relief after Tommy starved me for so long, yet I remind myself it has to be fake. There's no way this man, my family's archenemy who kidnapped and drugged me, could care about my well-being.

He'd take me to my sister if he cared about me.

Surely he would, especially when she's ordered him to do so.

I freeze.

Alaina gave orders to an O'Connor.

How is this possible?

"What's wrong?" he asks, shaking me out of my thoughts.

I recover and reply, "Nothing. I wish ya would've told me who ya were when I asked yesterday."

His face hardens. He steps closer, until he's standing across the counter from me. "Let's say I told ya when ya first asked me who I was, when ya were lying in bed. Ya were still drugged up, trying to process everything that happened, and a mess from what that monster did to ya. Would that have made ya any calmer, petal?"

My chest tightens. He's right, yet I'm not giving him a pass. I glare harder at him and cross my arms. "So that makes it okay that you're dishonest?"

"I didn't want to scare ya," he states.

He sounds sincere, but I can't trust him. As much as I want to, I can't.

I sarcastically laugh. "Ya want to talk about trusting me and me not lying to ya, but yet ya do the same thing. And while you're calling me out, you're telling me one lie after another. You're such a hypocrite."

His jaw twitches. He crosses his arms. "I've tried to do the best thing for ya."

"Have ya?"

He narrows his eyes. "Ya want to stand there and tell me I've treated ya poorly?"

"Well, ya drugged me, for one."

"When are ya going to let that go, Scarlet?"

"Probably never," I say.

He nods. "Good to know. Regardless, ya can stop talking about it. No need to keep shooting a dead horse. Like I said, I gave ya a choice, and I had to do what I had to do."

"What about the fact my sister wants to see me, and ya just ignore it? Ya won't let me see my family—the only person who actually cares about me and would take care of me."

He claims, "I care about ya."

My butterflies take off, but I continue to glare at him.

He adds, "And I'll take care of ya."

My flutters go nuts, and I scold myself. I put my hand on my hip, demanding, "What do ya want from me, Aidan?"

He stares at me, his lips tightly shut, not answering my question.

I scoff. "Thought so. More silence from the prison guard."

"Don't be so dramatic." His intense stare intensifies.

In need of a distraction, I wipe the little bit of water off the counter, toss the towel in the sink, then walk around the island.

He steps in front of me, declaring, "Ya need to get past who I am."

I look up. "The fact that you're a liar or an O'Connor?"

"I'm not a liar," he says.

I sarcastically laugh again. "Really? That's convenient for ya."

His expression hardens. "You're making this harder than it has to be, petal."

I ignore the tingles racing down my spine. I spout, "Why don't ya tell me what ya actually want from me? Ya could hand me over to my sister, but you're not, so tell me why. My sister, of all people, will protect me."

"She can't."

"Yes, she can."

"She didn't protect ya when your da married ya off to Tommy, did she?"

I reach up and slap him. I don't know where I get the energy, but a loud crack echoes in the room.

His face turns to the side. He sniffs hard, puts his palm on his cheek, and stays frozen for a moment.

My heart beats so hard, a sharp pain runs through it.

He slowly turns his head and scowls at me.

Fear fills me. As much as I hated Tommy, I never lashed out at him. I was too scared, and I don't know why I decided to do that to Aidan. I may not know much about him, but I know he's not someone to be messed with.

I cower, stepping back, and hit the counter.

He steps forward until there's no room between us, warning, "Don't ya ever do that again."

My insides quiver. I don't know what to do. I stare at his chest, afraid to see his anger.

He tilts my chin, and I can't avoid it. A crazed look lights up his dark eyes, and his voice turns so cold I shudder. He asks, "Do ya understand what I just said?"

I nod, unable to say anything, afraid now is the moment I'll see Aidan's wrath.

He's an O'Connor. It'll be worse than Tommy's.

I lean as far back as I can, until my back hurts, making me wince.

He slides his hand behind me, palming my spine, leaning an inch from my face. He warns, "Ya can get over these issues, and it'll be a lot nicer for us while we're here. Or ya can make your time miserable with me. Take your pick, petal."

Tense, fearful on my part, silence builds between us.

His phone rings, snapping us out of it, and it reminds me of what I need to do. He pulls it out of his pocket, continues staring at me, and snarls, "Alaina, we're not having this conversation again. Stop calling." He hangs up, then slides his phone back into his pocket.

I gape at him.

"Are we clear, Scarlet?" he asks.

"Ya could have let me talk to her."

"Why? So ya can tell her how horrible I am so she gets more upset?"

"No! I wouldn't do that!"

He snorts. "Sure ya wouldn't." He steps back, and it hits me how to get his phone. I take several deep breaths, then wrinkle my nose.

"Something wrong?" he asks.

I question, "Do ya think ya could shower?"

His eyes turn to slits. "I already did this morning."

"Ya stink like a bonfire." I put my hand over my nose, feigning that it's making me feel ill.

He studies me, then claims, "I burnt the trash. I don't smell that bad, do I?" He sniffs his pit, then arches his eyebrows.

"It reminds me of Tommy," I lie. Tommy smelled of tobacco and Aidan just reeks of bonfire.

He freezes.

I add, "Sorry. Ya-ya can stay smelly if ya want."

He shakes his head. "I'll take another shower if I'm that repulsive."

"Ya are. Sorry," I add again, offering a small smile.

He moves to the bathroom, then glances at me. "You're welcome to join me if ya want."

My adrenaline kicks in. I smirk. "Thanks for the offer, but no."

"Suit yourself." He goes inside the bathroom and shuts the door. I pray he doesn't lock it, and I'm relieved when I hear the shower turn on. I wait for a moment, then I step inside.

He sticks his head between the curtain and the wall. "Did ya decide to join me?"

My flutters ignite again and heat fills my cheeks. I smirk. "No, thanks, prison guard. I have to wee."

He pulls the curtain back a bit more, revealing his perfect pecs. "Ya sure about that, lass?"

"Positive," I say. But part of me wants to remove my oversized sweats and step in next to him.

Amusement fills his expression. "Ya sure you're here just to wee?"

I scoff. "Yep. Unfortunately, a girl's gotta do what a girl's gotta do."

"The offer is still open if ya want to jump in." He gives me one of his heated, arrogant looks.

How can he still look at me like that when he knows I'm aware he's an O'Connor and I'm an O'Leary?

I just slapped him.

He should be hurting me right now. That's what Tommy would be doing.

I don't understand it. It's all confusing. I sweetly coo, "Could ya please focus on your shower so I can go to the loo?"

He chuckles, then shuts the shower curtain. I watch his silhouette add shampoo to his hair through the flimsy curtain. I quickly reach for his pants, grab the phone, and slide it into my pocket. I pretend to go to the bathroom, flush the toilet, then wash my hands.

I shut the bathroom door, go into the bedroom, and lock the door behind me. My heart races and my hands shake. I pull out his phone, swipe the screen, and a security feature pops up.

Crap! What's his code?

I start punching in random numbers, but nothing works. It only takes a few minutes before he pounds on the door, ordering, "Scarlet, open this door."

"I'm getting changed," I lie.

"Ya have two seconds. I know ya took my phone."

I call out, "I don't know what you're talking about." I try a couple more codes, and then the phone locks.

"Jesus," I mutter.

There's a loud bang, and his foot comes through the door.

I shriek and back up to the bed. My knees hit the mattress, and I fall onto it.

He comes charging at me, cages his naked body over mine, and seethes, "Give me my phone. Now."

My chest brushes his hard pecs. Our breaths merge, and his eyes glow like an animal ready to tear its prey apart. I glance at his lips, then meet his leer, swallowing hard.

"Now," he demands.

With a shaking hand, I hold it out.

He rips it from me and glances at it. "Great, ya locked it."

My voice cracks as I confess, "I want to talk to my sister."

"If ya think stealing my phone will get ya what ya want, you're wrong."

"Please," I beg in a whisper.

He doesn't move, but his erection hardens against my stomach.

Time seems to stand still with the only sound coming from our breaths and the blood pounding between my ears.

I slide my hand onto his cheek, unable to stop myself. I manage to get out, "Aidan, please—"

"I guess I have to worry about ya more than I thought."

A new fear rises within me. I ask, "What do ya mean?"

He glances at my lips, stating, "There's no more privacy. I'm removing the bathroom door too."

"What? No! Aidan!"

"Ya want to slap me? Steal my phone? Trick me into showering?"

"Ya did smell," I argue.

"Did I?"

"Yea."

"Like Tommy?" he snarls.

I cringe, staying quiet under his angry scowl.

His disgust morphs into something so tempting I hold my breath. He asks, "Or maybe ya wanted me naked? On top of ya like this."

I open my mouth, but nothing comes out.

He threatens, "I'm going to warn ya one last time, petal. Don't lie to me. Don't slap me. Don't try to trick me. Stop pushing me."

"Pushing ya?" I whisper, my mouth watering. I glance at his lips, wanting him to press them down on mine.

He brushes them against mine and declares, "Last warning." He lifts his body off mine, stands before me, and doesn't say a word, breathing like a dragon ready to roar with fire.

Unable to stop myself, I drag my eyes up and down his large frame several times, taking in every inch of Aidan O'Connor.

He's nothing like my disgusting, aged husband.

Still, Aidan's a man women run from, and for different reasons than why they try to avoid Tommy.

Women don't run because they aren't attracted to him.

They run because they know he'll ruin them.

And I'm officially screwed.

There's nowhere for me to run and escape him.

6

Aidan

After I watch Scarlet check me out with her cheeks flushing the color of her hair, I leave the room and get dressed. Then I go out to the barn and sort through the tools. I find what I need and return to the cottage to take the bathroom doorknob off.

"You're being ridiculous," Scarlet accuses.

I don't look at her, focusing on my task and replying, "Yea? Well, I won't have to do stuff like this when ya can behave correctly."

She spouts, "I'm not a child."

I glance at her. "No, you're not. Which is why I should be able to trust ya, but I can't."

She scoffs, muttering, "Hypocrite." She storms into her bedroom, but the door is ripped apart, so she can't slam it this time.

I finish removing the knob, then go to the bedroom. I remove the broken wood, releasing the hinges from the frame. I take it to the bonfire pit, step on it a few times to break it further apart, then pour lighter fluid over it. I strike a match, staring at it, trying to calm down from the morning's events, but I'm still riled up.

Scarlet infuriates me. Yet there's something about her defiance that makes her intriguing to me. And that's dangerous. I need to remember she has O'Leary blood, which makes her unpredictable.

When the flame gets so close to my fingers, black forms on the tips, I toss it in the fire pit.

I've always been obsessed with fire. I like to do many things with it, including burn men when I torture them. And I wish I had somebody to do that to right now. Tommy or one of her brothers would be perfect.

Patience, I remind myself.

Tommy will endure much more than just my wrath before I take his last breath. I'll shame him in front of his entire clan before crossing him off my list.

The wood goes up in flames, and I wait until there's barely anything left.

Then I return to the cottage and assess what's inside the cupboards and fridge.

"What are ya doing?" Scarlet asks.

I curse Devin in my head. I gave him the task to make sure we had plenty of food, but there isn't much selection. Now I have to do something I don't want to.

I go into the hallway closet and pull a pair of handcuffs out of my bag. I walk toward Scarlet.

She glances at them. "What are those for?"

I grab her wrist and pull her into the bedroom.

She cries out, "Aidan, what are ya doing?"

I stop in front of the bed, ordering, "Get on the bed."

"What? No."

"Don't make me force ya on the bed," I warn.

She lifts her chin. It reminds me of Alaina in some ways. She asserts, "Do not restrain me to this bed."

"I have to go to town, and I don't trust ya to not try to run."

Her expression changes to fear. "Don't leave me here. I'll go to town with ya."

I shake my head. "Ya know that can't happen, petal. People will see ya."

She bursts out, "They're going to see ya. You're as large as a giraffe."

I refrain from chuckling. "Maybe so, but somebody has to go get food, and it won't be ya. Now get on the bed. I'm not telling ya again."

She gives me another angry, hateful look and finally slides onto the bed.

I take her wrist and cuff it to the headboard.

She protests, "This isn't necessary."

"Aye, it is. I'll be back as soon as possible." I leave.

"Aidan, get back here!" she demands.

I ignore her, grab my keys, and lock the cottage. My stomach flips. I don't like leaving her, and especially restrained when I'm not there, but I don't know what else to do.

I get in my car, and a pain shoots through my back. "Damn sofa," I mutter and turn on the engine, adding to my mental list to get some Deep Heat. I grab the baseball cap from the seat behind me and put it on, along with my sunglasses.

It's a forty-five-minute drive to get to town. The entire way, I can't stop wondering what she's doing. God forbid Tommy should show up when I'm not there. I'm confident he won't since my brother sent me an alert he's scouring Belfast, and I'm far from there. Yet it still makes me uneasy since I know anything is possible.

When I finally arrive in town, I go into the store and grab whatever I can find to add some pounds to Scarlet. I toss cheese, crackers, chocolate, potatoes, butter, bread, salmon, vegetables, sour cream, bacon, and rib eye steak into the trolley. Then I go to the dessert section and pick a trifle. When I get to the checkout, there's a stack of cards, so I toss those on the conveyor belt.

I pay, put the groceries in the trunk, and go to the only other store in town. I select a set of flannel pajamas, a thick jacket, and boots for Scarlet. My brother got her tennis shoes, but the farm's muddy, and he didn't get her a jacket.

Knowing Scarlet, I won't be able to keep her inside. I don't really blame her. Plus, fresh air is good for her. Once she starts getting some weight back on her, she won't be as fragile. I won't have to worry about her breaking a bone as much.

I pay for the items, return to the car, and head out of town. I watch the cars behind me, ensuring no one's following me, and relax once I'm back on the dirt roads and no other cars are in sight.

When I pull up to the cottage, I unload the car and put the groceries in the kitchen. I stick the boots and jacket into the hall closet and go into the bedroom.

Scarlet gives me a hateful look. "Was wondering when ya were going to get home. Thought maybe you'd just leave me here for weeks on end."

"Once again, you're being dramatic," I say, then take the key out of my pocket and unlock the cuff. I leave the other cuff attached to the bed.

She pulls her arm down and starts massaging her wrist.

"It wasn't that tight," I comment.

Her eyes turn to slits. "When you're the one who's restrained, ya can tell me how it feels."

I grunt. "That's the thing, petal. I won't ever be the one restrained."

She shoots me another death glare.

I ignore it, return to the kitchen, and unpack the groceries. I leave out the cheese, crackers, bread, butter, and ingredients to make twice-baked potatoes. I put the ribeyes on the counter. I turn on the kettle, slice the potatoes with a knife, put them all in the oven, then turn it on.

Scarlet comes out and steps next to me. She picks up the Kilmeaden cheese. "This is my favorite."

"Good. Ya can cut it up," I say, then open the package of bacon and put it on the skillet.

She grabs a knife, slices several pieces of cheese, and asks, "What are ya making?"

"Dinner."

"What are we having?"

"Twice-baked potatoes, ribeyes, onions, mushrooms, pepper sauce, brown bread, and butter. If you're good, I'll let ya have some trifle for dessert."

Her lips twitch. "That's a lot of food."

"Ya need to eat. You're too thin," I remind her.

Her face falls. "Do ya have to keep telling me how disgusting I look? I don't need a reminder. I see it whenever I look in the mirror or down at my bony body."

My chest tightens. "Do ya think I'm trying to insult ya?"

She doesn't reply and returns to focusing on the cheese.

I add, "I just want ya to get healthy. I don't want ya to get hurt. I thought we've been over this."

She remains silent.

I'm pretty sure she doesn't believe that my intentions aren't bad. So I try again. "Petal—"

"Can ya just drop it?" she asks.

I sigh and obey. I turn the burner on the stove for the bacon to cook. Then I wash my hands and grab a piece of cheese. I hold it toward her mouth, commanding, "Eat."

She looks at me. "You're going to feed me now too?"

I grin. "Maybe. If you're good." I wink.

The little flush in her cheeks erupts. My dick hardens. Something about it turns me on. I wish it didn't. It makes my time with her so much harder.

"Well, are ya going to eat your favorite cheese in the whole wide world?" I say, wiggling the cheese in front of her.

She smirks, "Now who's being dramatic?"

"Eat," I repeat.

She grabs it and pops it into her mouth.

I praise, "Good lass."

She continues slicing the food, and I open the cracker box. I start piling cheese on them and set everything on a board, along with bread and butter. Then I take it to the table.

The kettle whistles, and I fix two teas and take them to the table. I state, "Time to eat lunch."

Scarlet sits at the table and eats a few crackers and cheese.

I pull the cards out of my pocket. "Assuming ya know how to play?"

She glances at them. Her face lights up. "I don't know. What do ya Americans play? Maybe ya don't know how to play Irish games?"

I laugh. "Of course I know how to play Irish games."

"What about Lives?" she says.

"I'll slaughter ya in Lives," I declare.

She laughs. "Is that so?"

"Pretty sure. I'm quite talented," I claim.

She rolls her eyes. "We'll see about that."

I take the cards out of the box, shuffle, and deal. We play a few games, and I keep reminding her to eat more food.

"You're definitely going to make me fat," she mutters.

"I don't think ya have to worry about that," I claim.

She lays a card down, shouts, "Yes," and pumps her hand in the air.

I groan.

"That's game three. I win. Ya just lost," she boasts.

"Ugh," I groan again, tossing my cards on the table.

"Should have bet ya some money," she states.

"Too bad for ya," I tease, then get up. "Time to make dinner."

"I've been eating all afternoon," she claims.

"Aye, and you're going to eat all night," I assert and grab the steaks out of the fridge. I check on the potatoes and turn off the oven but leave them inside. Then I put on my flannel jacket and boots.

"Where are ya going?" she asks.

"To grill the steaks."

"Okay, I'll come outside too. I need some air."

"I figured you'd say that." I open the hallway closet and hand her the coat and boots. "Put these on."

She arches her eyebrows. "Ya got these for me?"

"Aye. You're not that much of a prisoner," I add.

She bats her eyelashes. "Good to know, prison guard."

My lips twitch, and I take the steaks outside. I set them on the tray, then I turn the grill on. I hold the match in my fingers just like I did at the bonfire, and when it gets too intense, I toss it onto the charcoal.

Scarlet startles me, asking, "Why do ya do that with matches?"

Unaware she was watching me, I turn and admit, "Fire's always intrigued me."

"What intrigues ya about it?"

"I'm not sure. The more I stare at it, the more obsessed I am with it," I confess.

"Really?"

"Aye. It's a tool."

She furrows her eyebrows. "How so?"

"It can be a weapon to hurt people, a way to eliminate things, a light in the darkness, or it can cook your steak."

She stares at the fire, and her expression changes.

I put the steaks on the grill, then shut it. "What's that look for?"

She hesitates, then replies, "My mom died in a fire."

I almost tell her that her da killed her mum, but I don't feel like rocking the boat tonight. Brody found out the truth. Alaina had a hard time with it, and I'm sure Scarlet will too. So I decide it's best to leave that for another time. Maybe it will be better for Alaina to tell her when I eventually let them reunite.

I reply, "Aye. I heard about that. I'm sorry for your loss."

She stays quiet, then walks over to the chicken coop. She opens it up, steps inside, and exits with a basketful of eggs. She shuts the chicken coop and beams. "Kind of cool we have these."

"Such a country girl," I tease.

She smiles. "I'm like a chameleon. Ya can put me in a five-star restaurant or the best crappy pub in all of Ireland, and I'll shine."

I chuckle. "I'm sure ya do, petal."

Her face stays lit, and I wish it was always like that.

"I'll take these inside," she states.

"Okay, lass." I finish cooking the steaks and return to the cottage.

Scarlet set the table and put the potatoes on a plate. A dish with onions, mushrooms, and pepper sauce sits next to them on the table.

I put a steak on each of our plates, and we sit down and eat.

She takes one bite of everything and announces, "I'm full."

"Ya can pick at it all night," I tell her.

"I really am full. I've been eating all day."

"I know. It's okay," I assure her.

She rolls her eyes. "I think ya like to take things overboard."

I shrug. "Maybe so. But humor me." I push my plate to the side and grab the cards again. "Ya know 21?"

"Duh. Who doesn't know 21?"

"Okay, then. Let's play 21. I'm pretty sure I'll beat ya at this game," I declare.

"Ya said that last time, remember?" She smirks.

I chuckle and deal.

We play until it's late into the night. Half the food remains on her plate, but I finally pick up our dishes and take them to the kitchen. I bring the trifle back to the table, claiming, "There's no way you're resisting this."

Her eyes widen. "More food?"

"Aye." I put a piece on a plate and put two forks on it.

"You're not going to make me eat the whole piece?" she teases.

"Oh, we can have more."

She shakes her head, takes a bite, and closes her eyes. "Mm, this is so good. It's my favorite."

"Is it?" I ask, happy I picked the right one.

She nods. "Yea." She takes a sip of her tea, then tilts her head. "Ya really are from America, aren't ya?"

My heart pounds a little harder. It's not something I ever talk about in Ireland, but I reply, "Aye."

"New York, right?"

"Correct."

"What's it like? I've always wanted to go there."

"Ya have?"

Her face drops. "Yea. Da would never let us leave Ireland though."

"Well, maybe I'll take ya there one day," I offer.

She pauses, licks her lips, then asks in a quiet voice, "Why do ya say stuff like that?"

"Like what?"

She locks her greens on me. "Like ya actually like me and our futures are together. Ya know you're an O'Connor, and I'm an O'Leary and your prisoner. So what's the point of saying that kind of stuff to me?"

My chest tightens. I admit, "Maybe I actually like ya."

She glances down at her body. "Yea, sure ya do."

"Do ya always disregard men when they say they like ya?" I question.

She doesn't flinch, answering, "Men haven't said anything to me in a long time. Did ya forget again that I'm married?"

My insides roil in anger. "Are we going to go through this again? We were having such a good night."

She tilts her head and sighs.

I point to the pie. "Eat your dessert."

She slowly takes another bite and we finish it in silence. She sets her fork down and puts her hand over her mouth, yawning.

I state, "Regarding your question about New York, it's fast-paced. Everything moves way faster than in Dublin or Belfast, but it's fun. It's a different energy."

She questions, "So ya like it better than Ireland?"

I shake my head. "No, not better. It's just different. I'm pretty sure you'd like it."

"Ya think so?"

"I do."

A tiny smile fills her face. She yawns again.

I glance at my watch. It's after one. I state, "I think it's time for bed." I get up, put the plate and forks in the sink, and go into the bathroom. I brush my teeth, step out, and let Scarlet get ready. I grab the set of pajamas I got earlier.

She reappears, and I hand them to her. She arches her eyebrows. "Why did ya get these?"

My gut drops. "Ya don't like them?"

She stares at them. "No, they look comfy."

"Thought it'd be better than ya sleeping in sweatpants."

"Thank ya," she says.

"Go put them on," I tell her and nod toward the bedroom.

She disappears, and I clean the kitchen.

She comes back out. The pajamas aren't as loose as the sweatpants, which makes me happy.

"Now ya look ready to go to bed. Although I'm pretty sure some sexy lace lingerie would look good on ya too."

Her face heats. "And there ya go again."

I chuckle, grab the Deep Heat from the side table, and go to the couch. "See ya in the morning." I squirt the cream in my palm and reach behind me, trying to slap it on my back, but the part that hurts the most, I can't reach.

Scarlet slides behind me and gently says, "Let me help ya." She puts her hands over mine, and I freeze.

I glance at her.

She won't look at me, focuses on my back, and orders, "Stop staring at me, Aidan."

I look forward and rub the rest of what was on my hands into my palms.

She massages my entire back with the Deep Heat, spending more time than required, but I don't complain. I'd sit here all night if she wanted to continue.

She announces, "All set," then rises.

"Thank ya," I say and pick up the afghan.

She grabs it from me and tosses it on the other end of the couch.

"What are ya doing?" I ask.

She bites her lip for a moment, and a nervous expression appears. She takes a deep breath and declares, "Ya can't sleep out here. It's ruining your back."

"Well, I'm not trusting ya to sleep out here alone."

She smirks. "Did I say I was giving up the bed?"

My adrenaline perks up, but I stare at her, waiting for her to finish her statement.

"Ya can stay on your side of the bed. No funny stuff, prison guard." She winks.

I softly chuckle and watch her disappear into the bedroom. I wait a few minutes, telling myself not to make any moves on her. The last thing my back needs is to return to this couch, and she'll surely toss me out if I try anything.

But my cock's already hard, and it's been a long time since I've had a woman, especially one I'm attracted to.

I continue lecturing myself as I go into the bedroom, wondering how I'll get through this night while keeping my word.

7

Scarlet

$\mathcal{T}$he floorboards creak from Aidan's weight. He sits on the mattress, and it sinks. I stare at the wall, my heart beating faster, the smell of his cedarwood and musk scent filling the air.

Why did I tell him he could sleep with me?

This was a horrible idea.

He slides in next to me, and the heat of his body penetrates me even through the flannel. He questions, "Are ya going to stay staring at the wall all night, petal?"

My pulse skyrockets. I slowly turn and stare at him. The moonlight shines through the window. I don't know why I didn't shut the shades, but I curse myself further. All his chiseled features glow as if he's a god of some sort. And his broad shoulders aren't helping my thoughts either.

My butterflies kick in. "Is this better than the sofa?"

"Yea, thanks. Appreciate your kindness."

"Especially when you're my prison guard," I tease.

His lips twitch.

He slides his hand up the mattress between us, and I hold my breath. He drags his fingers across my jaw, then over my lips.

"What are ya doing?" I ask.

"What does it look like I'm doing?"

"You're touching me," I murmur.

He mutters, "Aye. Kind of hard not to."

"Do I have to remind ya that ya promised to be a gentleman?"

"I don't remember a conversation where the word gentleman was used," he retorts.

I don't say anything.

"I'll be good." He moves his fingers off me and tucks his hands under the pillow, and a mix of relief and disappointment hits me. He asks, "So why do ya want to go to New York?"

I shrug. "I don't know. Saw it on TV. It always looked fun and different than Ireland."

"But ya love Ireland?"

"Of course I love Ireland. Don't ask stupid questions. Makes ya sound like a plonker," I state.

He chuckles. "Maybe I am a plonker."

"No, you're actually not," I blurt out before I can stop myself.

His gaze gets hotter. "Good to know ya don't think that."

The tension in my core grows. I squeeze my thighs together.

He questions, "What would ya be doing if ya didn't have to worry about any of this?"

My chest tightens. "About being here with ya? Or Tommy coming after me? Or maybe even worse, my brother," I admit, my stomach flipping.

Something passes over his expression. I don't know if it's pity, sadness, or anger. I study it until it disappears. He answers, "Aye. What would ya be doing if none of this was happening?"

I hesitate, then confess, "I'm in this situation because I ran away."

His eyes widen. "Ya ran away?"

I nod. "Yea. I went to London; that's where Tommy found me. He took me back home, and that's when my da forced me to marry him. But I tried to get away."

Shock fills his face. "Ya wanted to leave the clan?"

Anxiety blooms in my chest. So much fear hits me just from thinking or talking about it. I mumble, "If only I had been smarter."

"Why did ya run away?" Aidan asks again.

I swallow hard and curl farther into the pillow, revealing, "I wanted to have my own life. Alaina always knew she wanted to run the clan."

"Aye. She's good at it too," Aidan states.

I shake my head and admit, "I still don't believe ya that she's running your clan."

He grunts. "I promise ya I'm not lying. She is. She and my brother love each other, and he's proud to have her by his side. She's an asset to the O'Connors now. And the O'Learys never deserved her."

I gape at him, unable to understand how any man, especially one who holds power like he does within his clan, can state that my sister is an asset. And especially when she's an O'Leary.

Never once did I hear Da, my brothers, Tommy, or any man applaud anything Alaina did. And as much as she tried to gain power, she was fighting a losing battle. Even I thought that. But I always held out hope it would happen someday and things would change. But ultimately, I knew she'd lose, so I ran.

I admit, "I thought my life should be more than cooking and cleaning for men. I didn't want to be at their disposal. I knew my da would eventually marry me off. He was pressuring me more and more. In all reality, I should have accepted the man he wanted me to marry before I ran away. I'm sure he wasn't as bad as Tommy was." I blink hard, my voice shakes, and I squeeze my eyes shut, remembering too many bad things about what it was like to be with Tommy.

Aidan shifts on the bed, moving closer. He slides an arm under me and wraps his other one around me, pulling me into him.

I don't fight it. He feels safe, warm, and protective. And I don't know if I've ever felt that before. I mumble, "I should have known my worth instead of fighting it."

Aidan firmly states, "Ya *are* worth more than how the O'Learys treat the women in their clan. And I'm sorry for everything that has happened to ya. I wish ya would've gotten far away when ya ran and disappeared into thin air."

I say into his chest, "I should have been smarter. I should have known I couldn't escape my da. Alaina tried to protect me, but she couldn't."

Aidan's hand strokes my hair, and his lips move closer. His breath hits my forehead. He states, "If ya had run away, what would ya have done? If ya could have done anything in the world, what would it have been?"

I shake my head. "I don't know. I didn't get that far. I just thought there was something better out there. I assumed if I got away, I would figure it out. I had a couple thousand euros with me. Turns out I was foolish, wasn't I?"

He strokes my cheek. "No, ya weren't foolish, petal. Ya were in a shitty position. The odds were against ya. Even if you'd escaped, that money would've run out quickly."

"I would have worked and made more," I declare.

"Ya would have struggled," he insists.

"I wasn't afraid to struggle."

He asserts, "A woman like ya isn't meant to be in poverty, is she?"

"What does that mean?" I ask.

He pulls me tighter into him. "You're meant to be taken care of. You're meant for the finer things in life, not the harsh realities of poverty. And ya weren't meant to be ordered around all day like someone's slave."

"Ya tell me what to do," I point out.

He grunts. "I tell ya what to do to keep ya safe. There's a difference."

"Is there?"

"Of course there is."

"But ya always tell me what to do, not just to keep me safe," I argue.

"And ya love it when I do," he teases.

"No, I don't."

"Ya sure about that?" he challenges.

"Without a doubt," I claim.

"So ya never like it when I order ya around?"

"Nope. Never."

He glances at my lips, asking, "What if I ordered ya around in this bed? Would ya hate that?"

My cheeks heat. The fire in my core bursts into flames.

He drags his finger over the curve of my waist, and my butterflies take off faster. I hold my breath.

He closes the gap between us, presses his lips to mine, and slides his tongue into my mouth so fast I gasp for air. But before I know what's happening, I'm kissing him back.

My hands tug at his hair, and my body presses against his erection. He slides his tongue farther into my mouth, intensifying the kiss and fisting my hair with perfect pressure. It's also not gentle, but it's not too rough. And I thought after everything Tommy had done to me that the only thing I'd be able to manage ever again, if anything, would be gentle. I assumed I'd never want any man to touch me ever again.

Yet everything about Aidan is too much. It's like he knows how to touch me even though he barely has until now.

I whimper against him. My body begins to tremble. Emotions lodge in my throat, and I keep wondering how I can want him. It's not only because he's an O'Connor, I'm an O'Leary, and there's nothing that's supposed to be between us. After everything Tommy did to me, I shouldn't want Aidan to kiss me, pin me against his body, or even be next to me in this bed.

Still, I want all of it. So I kiss him back until he pulls me on top of him. His chest is bare. He's only in his underwear. He slides his palm into the back of my pants and grips my bare ass. His erection grows harder and harder, and I'm so wet between the legs it's almost painful not to have him slide it inside of me.

"You're a good kisser, petal," he mumbles.

I freeze, torn out of the moment. Even though he moves his tongue back in my mouth, I push away and retreat.

He tightens his grip around me, his palm freezes on my ass, and his other hand stays wrapped in my locks.

I whisper, "I'm married. We can't do this."

"Ya aren't," he declares.

"I am. The laws in Ireland and the church say I am," I state.

"Fuck the laws of Ireland and the goddamn church. Ya aren't," he firmly repeats.

I close my eyes, so confused, declaring, "But I know I am."

"Ya can't be forced to take a vow and have it be legitimate," he states, as if his word is the only thing I need to believe.

"I-I'm so confused," I confess. My voice cracks as I add, "If I don't keep my marriage vow, what kind of woman am I?"

He groans. "It wasn't your vow."

"But it was. My da had the authority to make it for me."

"No, he didn't," Aidan snarls.

I pull my hand away from him and stare at the ring on my finger.

He rolls me onto my back so fast I lose my breath. He grabs my hand, slides the ring off me, and tosses it across the room. He seethes, "Why are ya still wearing that? Ya are not his."

My gut drops and quivers.

Aidan says through gritted teeth, "Ya don't want to be his, and ya never have. Admit it to me."

He's right. Everything about that statement is right. Yet I can't seem to get the words out. All I can do is cry. Tears stream down my cheeks, and I repeat, "I'm so confused. Nothing makes sense. I want to believe ya, and I want that to be my reality, but every time I've thought things aren't true, my life's proven me wrong."

He sighs. He tugs me back into him. I press my head against his chest, my tears streaming down his pecs. He quietly states, "I know you're confused. I'm not trying to add to that. We don't have to do anything tonight. We'll wait."

My breath hitches. I glance up at him, asking, "Wait?"

He looks at me with so much certainty, I shudder. Tingles light up my core, conflicting with the anxiety I feel. He declares, "I will have ya, petal. I want ya, and I know that deep down ya want me too. There's something here between us. So yea, we'll wait. But ya are *not* his. I will continue to remind ya until there's no more confusion and you're a hundred percent adamant that ya are not his and were never meant to be."

I sniffle.

He adds, "And I'm telling ya right now, I will kill him. But before I kill him, ya will be free of him, and ya will be mine."

8

Aidan

*S*carlet sleeps on my pec, her breath teasing my chest. I stroke her hair for the millionth time. All night, I've been unable to stop my mind from going a mile a minute.

The rooster crows, and she doesn't even stir. I gently slide her off of me and silently curse my erection. As much as I want her, I know it's not right. At least for the time being. She's too confused, and I don't want her to regret me. Yet now that I've kissed her, I know there's something between us. She felt what I did, and now, there's no turning back.

I grab my clothes and leave the bedroom, quietly getting dressed. I put the flannel jacket on and grab two boxes of matches out of the cabinet.

There's too much building up inside of me right now. The only way I can think to calm myself is through fire. So I put on my boots, and I leave the cottage.

Thick fog covers the yard. I cut through it, find the bonfire pit, and toss some logs into the hole. I squirt lighter fluid over the wood, and one by one, I light matches, letting them burn down farther than I normally do. My fingertips soon turn black from the soot.

The numbness is always there. My fingers have been calloused since I was a child and I struck my first match. My mom used to get upset with me. She'd always argue with my father about it, but it's like Dad knew I needed it. He always told her that it was part of me and to let it be.

I light another match and watch it burn. I can hear my mom shrieking at me to stop, our eyes locked as she gave me her horrified stare.

I toss the match into the bonfire as well as the empty box. I pull a fresh one out of my pants, open it, and strike another.

I don't know how to get Scarlet to realize she owes no loyalty to Tommy. I don't understand why she's so confused and doesn't realize she's not bound to him. What her da and Tommy did wasn't legal. That's not how Ireland or any church in it works.

Yet because of her da's power over her, she believes it's real. She thinks there's legitimacy to it, and there's not. Even with him dead, she still can't accept what he did was wrong and doesn't tie her to anyone.

And I hate that she's confused for so many reasons, not just because I can't have her right now. Her torment and pain flash behind my eyes, replacing my mother's stare.

My fingers burn through the numbness, and I toss the match into the pit. I reach for another one.

Scarlet's voice tears me out of my thoughts. "Aidan, what are ya doing?"

I spin.

She has on her coat and pajama bottoms. She hugs herself from the cold. It's still foggy outside, and I can't see the cottage behind her. I order, "Go inside. It's freezing out here."

Her eyebrows furrow. Her eyes dart between the matches in my hand and the fire pit, and finally come to rest on my face. "Aidan, I asked what you're doing."

The uncomfortable pull in my chest I always feel whenever anyone catches me doing this ignites. I answer, "What does it look like I'm doing, petal?"

She frets, "It looks like you're about to burn your fingers off."

"I won't. Now go back inside."

She defies me, stepping closer and curling her fingers over the back of my hand that holds a match. She quietly asks, "Why are ya doing this?"

I stare at her, unable to explain it, just like I never could to my mother or father when he took me aside and privately questioned me all those years ago. My brothers don't understand it either, but everyone has come to accept it. It's been a long time since anyone questioned me about why I have to have matches when stressed out. And no one's ever touched me while I'm in my fire zone.

She doesn't take her eyes off mine, questioning, "Is this something ya do often?"

I don't lie. "Aye."

"Why?"

I shrug and repeat, "Go back inside. It's freezing. I'll bring more wood inside in a minute."

"Come with me," she whispers, her eyes full of worry.

My voice grows firmer. "Scarlet, I need to do this right now, and I need ya to go back inside. Do ya understand me?"

She studies me for another moment, and I think she'll defy me again, but she finally takes her hand off mine, then turns and disappears into the fog.

The cottage door shuts, and I return to the bonfire, cursing myself. I'm not embarrassed she caught me, or shameful in any way, but I wish I knew how to explain it. I wish I understood why I'm compelled to stand here and light boxes of matches, but I don't.

I continue with my routine, but my rage doesn't dissipate the way it normally does. My questions don't stop swirling in my head about how to make Scarlet understand she's not held to any vow with Tommy, and no answers come. It only frustrates me more.

When I'm out of matches, I toss the empty box into the pit and return to the cottage.

I need more.

I open the cupboard where Devin stocked cases of the Maguire & Paterson's.

Scarlet reaches for my shoulder from behind me. "Aidan, you've burned enough."

I grab two more boxes and shove them in my pockets. I spin toward her, ready to return outside.

She puts her hands on my cheeks and pulls my head down so I can't avoid her, ordering, "Aidan. Stop."

The fire in my stomach matches the one in the pit outside. It's like she can see my goddamn burning soul, and I know it's burning. I know where I belong when I finally leave this earth. And she's not the first woman to realize where I'm going, but she's the only one who seems to accept it without any fear.

My heart beats harder, but my cock throbs, and I curse myself. I should have slept on the couch last night. The back pain would've been worse, but that's at least manageable. This is torture, adding to my already tormented state. I demand, "Step aside, petal."

She lifts her chin. "No."

"Why don't ya start breakfast? I'll be in later."

She doesn't move, shaking her head. "No, you're not going back out there."

I scoff. "Is that so?"

"Aidan..." She blows out a frustrated breath.

There's pity in her eyes, and that evokes anger inside me. I bark, "Ya don't need to feel sorry for me, lass. This is just how I deal with things."

"What are ya dealing with?"

"What do ya think I'm dealing with?" I blurt out before I can think about it.

Her eyes turn to slits, and she studies me until my cock's throbbing harder, and every ounce of blood in my veins flows through me quickly, burning how my fingertips feel.

I step forward, and she takes several steps back until she's against the refrigerator.

Her breath hitches.

I reiterate, "I said to stay inside."

She squares her shoulders, pushing me. "What is bothering ya, Aidan?"

I shouldn't say it, but I do. "You've made it pretty clear where your loyalties lie."

Her expression drops.

I instantly hate myself.

This is why I need to be outside at the pit and not in here.

I add, "When I'm like this, petal, I say things I regret. I'm choosing the wrong words right now, and I'm not trying to hurt ya, but if I don't go outside, I can't guarantee I won't."

"Ya told me ya wouldn't hurt me."

My chest tightens. I admit, "Not physically. But I can't guarantee I won't say stupid shit. Now, please stay inside while I do what I need to do."

She puts her hands back on my cheeks, asking, "You're doing this because of me?"

I freeze, breathing harder, as time seems to stand still. My heart pounds so fast I hear it.

She stands on her tiptoes, tugs my head down, and presses her lips to mine. For a moment, I'm unsure what to do.

She retreats an inch, studying me, then moves her lips back against mine, sliding her tongue into my mouth.

I kiss her back, but not as intensely as the night before.

She pulls away and looks at me again.

I murmur, "Don't kiss me again, petal. You're playing with fire right now, and I assure ya, it'll burn ya hotter than any of these matches."

"So now you'll hurt me?" she challenges.

My pulse skyrockets, pounding hard against my ears to the point I feel dizzy. My one fist curls behind her back, and I refrain from tugging on her hair.

I release a breath and growl, "I'm warning ya. I'm in a mood, and I need to go outside."

She doesn't listen. She keeps her fingertips pressed against my skull and brings her lips back to mine, flicking her tongue back into my mouth.

I lose the fight inside me. I grab her ass and pick her up, pinning her between the fridge and my body. Her legs wrap around my waist, and I kiss her as if it's the last kiss I'll ever give anyone.

The fire in the hearth flickers, and something gleams from the corner of my eye. Anger fills me again. I retreat and turn my head, breathing hard and accusing, "Why is that on the counter?"

Her breath matches mine. She furrows her brows again and admits, "I-I didn't know what to do with it."

"Ya felt the need to bring it out here?"

"I didn't put it on my finger! Even though I know Tommy will kill me if he ever found out I don't have it on!" she cries out, and her conflicted expression returns.

I hate that ring. It represents all the shit Tommy put her through and the problem between us.

"I thought ya didn't want it on my finger."

The comment makes me angry. "Do ya want it on your finger?"

She lowers her voice and blinks hard, answering, "No."

"Then why is it on the counter, reminding us of what he did to ya?"

She glances at the ring, then back at me. "What do ya want me to do with it, Aidan? Tell me. Do ya want me to go throw it in the garbage? Hide it in the vent? Should I bury it in the yard? Toss it down the loo? What?"

"I want ya to tell me ya don't ever want to see it again," I seethe.

She looks at me, swallowing hard. For a brief moment, I think she'll tell me she can't do it, that maybe she wants to see that representation of everything wrong in her life or that Tommy's hold over her is too strong for her to even consider escaping it. But then she lifts her chin and proclaims, "I want ya to get rid of it and never let me see it again."

Relief fills me. I kiss her, then gently set her down, still worried she's too damn skinny. But in the last few days, she seems to have gained more strength than when we first arrived.

I make sure she's steady on her feet, and I reach for the ring, ordering, "Put your coat on."

She looks at me in question but obeys. She zips it, and I grab her hand and lead her out of the cottage and through the blanket of fog.

We get to the bonfire pit, and I put the ring in her hand, stating, "Hold this."

She wraps her fingers around it.

I pour lighter fluid all over the fire, which erupts in flames. I instruct, "Toss it in."

She stares at the blaze, frozen with fear.

"I'm not doing it for ya," I quietly state.

She takes a deep breath and then tosses the ring into the flames. It lands on one of the logs.

I hand her the box of matches. "Light one."

"The fire's already hot."

"I don't care, light one," I insist.

Her hands shake, so I put mine over hers and help her light the match.

Unlike my fingers, I know hers aren't used to the heat, so I only let it burn a second before I order, "Toss it."

She does.

"Again," I say.

She looks at me. "Why?"

I take a match out of the box and hold it out to her. "Light it, petal."

She takes another deep breath and obeys.

"Again."

She doesn't question me again.

We get through two boxes of matches, but a fire of this caliber won't melt gold or destroy the diamond. And I want all of it out of sight forever.

So I pick up the shovel and put it in front of her. I wrap my hands around her body, position her fingers on the shovel, and dig into the pit. We dump the ashes over the log, and when the ring is buried under the hot embers so deep it isn't visible, I toss the shovel to the side.

I spin her into me, asserting, "There's no vow for ya to keep. A promise not made from free will isn't valid. From here on out, ya do what ya want, not because of what ya were forced to be tied to."

She swallows hard and slowly nods her head.

I tug her into me and lead her through the fog and back into the cottage, determined to make her mine and finish Tommy off sooner rather than later.

9

Scarlet

*T*he heavy weight of the ring no longer strangles me. I stare at my bare finger for the first time, still in shock it's gone and will never again be a noose around my neck.

Aidan leads me into the cottage, and I glance up at him, unsure and nervous about what happens next. There are no more excuses between us. It doesn't matter what blood flows through our bodies. I want Aidan. I know he wants me. There's no escaping it in this cottage with no one else around. No matter how forbidden we are to each other because of our families, it's a moot point.

I expect Aidan to kiss me, take me to the bedroom, or make another move, but he doesn't. He steers me to the kitchen and states, "We need to make breakfast."

"Oh?" I ask, trying to hide my disappointment.

Maybe I'm wrong. Perhaps he doesn't want me and only wanted me free of Tommy's grasp?

Is it possible I imagined everything between us?

"Yea, ya need to eat. Ya need your energy." He releases me and starts pulling items out of the fridge.

He places eggs and bacon on the counter, grabs the soda bread and butter, and sets a tin of baked beans on the counter. He asks, "Can ya open these for me?"

"Sure," I affirm and find the opener in the drawer, still trying to cover up my confusion.

We silently make breakfast with tension building between us, but I wonder if it's only on my part. Aidan continues to give me his intense stare but doesn't touch me.

When the food is ready, we sit at the table. He fills my plate, then sets it before me, ordering, "Eat." He prepares a plate for himself and takes the seat next to mine.

My thoughts continue to race about whether he really does like me or if it was a cruel part of his plan.

Not that I know anything about what he ultimately plans on doing with me. Yet I know he has one.

"Why aren't ya eating?" he questions.

"Oh," I say, realizing I'm playing with the eggs on my plate. So I take a bite, then sip my tea, and concentrate on my food. If I don't eat, Aidan will get angry. I manage to eat half of the food, then shove my plate away, announcing, "I'm full."

He glances at it. "Can't ya get any more bites in ya?"

"No." I shake my head.

He takes the last bite off his plate, chews and swallows, then wipes his mouth with his napkin. He tosses it on the table, glancing at my half-empty dish again, then claiming, "Okay. Ya did a good job, petal."

Petal.

Relief hits me, and I reprimand myself. *It's just a word.* Still, butterflies fill my belly. He locks his gaze on mine, and more tension builds between us.

I finally can't take it anymore. I rise and take the empty dishes and silverware to the kitchen. I scrape my food in the trash and wash our dishes while Aidan keeps his focus on me. I don't look at him, but I can feel it.

When I finish, I wipe my hands on the towel, set it down, and announce, "I'm going to shower."

He says nothing.

I get to the bathroom door, clutch the frame, then spin. I take a deep breath, find my courage, and ask, "Well, are ya coming with me?"

A dark expression fills Aidan's face. He drags his eyes over my body, staying quiet.

"Okay, guess not," I mutter, trying to hide my disappointment.

He scoots his chair back so fast it tips over. A loud crash fills the air, and he lunges toward me.

My heart races faster than I can ever remember, but he steps to the side and enters the bedroom.

Rejection fills me. I blink hard but stand in front of the bedroom doorway, unsure of what to say.

121

He goes to the window, shuts the blinds, then adds some logs to the fireplace. He steps in front of me, questioning, "Well, are we going to take that shower?"

Tingles race down my spine. I go into the bathroom, then turn on the faucet in the tub. Then I spin into Aidan's chest, frozen, unsure what to do next.

He tilts my chin up, staring down at me. I swallow hard, and he reaches for the bottom of my shirt and pulls it off me. With one hand, he pins my wrists above my head and drags his fingers down one of my arms.

I shudder, my breath hitching.

He continues trailing his fingertips down my body, over the curve of my waist, which suddenly makes me feel self-conscious. I blurt out, "I used to have a curvy waist."

He pauses, leans his face closer to mine, then slowly releases my wrists. He puts that hand on my cheek and declares, "You're beautiful, petal. This size, ten sizes bigger, whatever. Do ya understand?"

My heart beats faster. I blink hard and take a deep breath.

He gives me a chaste kiss, then unties my pajama bottoms. They fall to the floor. He reaches behind his back, tugging his T-shirt off.

Blood pounds hard between my ears. My core lights on fire, and even though I've seen him without clothes before, he still takes my breath away.

He drops his pants, then reaches behind me and adjusts the knob so the water comes out of the showerhead. He tests the water, then takes my hand, ordering, "Get in, lass."

I obey.

He steps beside me, shutting the shower curtain. He positions me in front of the water so it cascades down my back. It barely touches him, yet his body is always warm.

He reaches around my waist, tugs me into him, and presses his lips to mine. His erection grows harder against my stomach.

I tremble in his arms, kissing him back, in awe that for days I've wondered what it would feel like to have him, to be with him like this, and it's finally happening.

I expect him to take me here, but he doesn't. He pulls back, washes my hair with the same attention he gave me the first day I got here, rinses it, then gently works conditioner through the wet locks. He slides soap all over my body, and every part of me throbs, wanting him.

He washes himself quickly. He shampoos his hair and spins me out of the water momentarily. He holds me tight to his hard frame while he rinses off, then positions me back under the water. He asks, "Are ya warm?"

I nod, reach up, and lace my fingers behind his neck. I say, "You're probably not. Ya haven't really gotten any water. I'm stealing it all."

He grunts. "I'm fine, petal. Are ya ready to get out of here?"

Confusion fills me again. I thought he'd want to have sex in the shower. I blurt out, "Ya don't want to have me here?" My face heats as hot as the water.

He studies me, firmly answering, "No. I want ya in the bed the first time I take ya. I'll take a rain check for the shower." He winks.

"Oh..." New butterflies fill me as well as relief.

Aidan reaches around me and turns off the water. He grabs the towel, dries off my hair, then makes sure my entire body gets toweled off.

He quickly does the same for himself, then leads me out of the bathroom and into the bedroom. The glow of the fire lights up the room. He moves me toward the bed and orders, "Lie down."

I don't think I've ever been so nervous. I've never had a man like Aidan. Tommy was old and disgusting. Before Da forced me to marry him, I dated some guys, but looking at Aidan, I realize they were only boys.

He studies me, and I clench my thighs together, trying to look confident and not squirm. His assessment doesn't last long. He quickly cages his warm, hard body over me.

"Aidan..." I whisper, unsure what I'm even saying.

He cups my cheek, tracing my jaw with his thumb, ordering, "Tell me ya want me, lass."

The nerves in my belly kick in, but I take a deep breath and nod, admitting, "I do."

"Say it, then," he demands.

"I want—"

His tongue flicks into my mouth so fast I gasp. It takes me a moment to recover, but I urgently meet his pace. He kisses me until I'm out of breath and I'm grinding my hips underneath him.

He dips his mouth to my breasts, giving attention to each one until my nipples are hard and I'm moaning, arching my back, my legs spreading wider.

From time to time, his eyes meet mine, dark, heated, full of something so tantalizing I can't understand it, except that it turns me on even more.

He stays quiet except for the occasional grunt, focused on every inch of my skin. He makes his way down my torso until my skin's on fire from his touch, and I'm writhing.

When he reaches my hips, I'm already wet. A plethora of zings rushes through my body. He commands, "Look at me."

A fire burns so hotly in his eyes, I swallow hard.

He slides a finger inside me, and I inhale sharply. He circles it, then adds another, and his thumb glides over my clit while he studies me intently.

My voice cracks. "Aidan..."

"I want to see and hear what ya sound like coming, lass," he declares, then takes his tongue and flicks it under his thumb.

"Jesus Christ!" I cry out.

His lips twitch and his eyes turn to slits. He keeps his gaze on me, his fingers positioned the same, and teases me with small flicks of his tongue.

I blink, trying to keep my eyes open, but the sensations are too powerful. Every time his tongue hits my clit, combined with his thumb pressing part of it and his fingers curling inside me, a burst of endorphins ignites inside me.

He teases me for a long time until I'm begging, "Don't stop, Aidan. Please, don't stop!"

He softly chuckles, then reaches for my mouth, shoves his thumb inside it, and sucks on my clit.

I arch my back off the bed, tug on his hair, and my entire body erupts in convulsions, and incoherent sounds fly out of me. I circle my pussy into his face, frantically trying to get every bit of what he's giving me.

A tidal wave of pleasure seizes me. I get dizzy, crying out his name, shaking, not wanting it to stop, and not remembering anything ever feeling so good. And it continues until I can't handle it anymore and the sensation becomes too strong. I push at him. "Aidan, I can't take anymore," I whisper, barely able to speak.

He lunges over me, sliding his tongue into my mouth, full of my orgasms. His large palm grips my lower thigh, lifts my leg higher, and he pushes inside me until there's no more space.

I cry out as he groans, then mutters, "Fuck, petal."

He freezes for a minute, breathing hard, and right as I start to get used to him, he begins a slow thrusting pattern.

I match his thrusts, and he increases his speed. I continue moving in tandem with him, gripping my arms around his shoulders and holding him as tight to me as possible.

My whimpers turn louder. I close my eyes, dizzy with adrenaline pounding me at the same pace he does.

He buries his face in my neck, sucking on the curve, sliding his hand behind my head and fisting my hair. He tugs my head back and then drags his teeth against my neck.

"Jesus!" I cry out. My insides spasm forcefully.

He mumbles into my neck, "Aye, petal. Like that, lass."

"A-a-Aidan!"

I barely hear him declare, "Fuck, your pussy's tight."

More adrenaline beats into me.

He puts his face in front of mine, his hand on my chin, and holds it, demanding, "Open your eyes."

I lock them on him, shuddering further at the crazed expression within them.

He thrusts faster, his breath ragged.

A tidal wave of pleasure and sensations I've never felt rips through me. And I can't look at him anymore. My vision blurs, turning white. Sweat coats my skin as heat annihilates me.

"Fuck," he mutters through his teeth. His erection spreads my walls wider and pumps into me with accelerated force.

We cling to each other tighter. Our sweat merges, and he buries his head in my neck as his body violently convulses against me until everything is over, and it's just our ragged, hot breath on each other's skin.

10

Aidan

I roll off Scarlet and tug her into me, stroking her back and kissing her forehead. "Are ya all right?"

She looks up, pinning her greens on me. "Yea. I'm good. Are ya not good?" She furrows her eyebrows.

My lips twitch. I give her a chaste kiss, replying, "I'm really good."

A smile plays on her lips. "Ya are?"

"Aye. How could I not be?"

She bites her lip briefly, studying me, then states, "Okay, as long as ya are."

I rest my palm over her ass cheek. "Why are ya questioning this?"

She shrugs, sighs, and rests her head on my chest. She glides her fingers between my pecs, and silence fills the air. She closes her eyes.

Within minutes the sound of her soft breath hits my ear. She curls farther into me, asleep. I stare at her for a long time and, at some point, pass out.

When I wake up, she's on top of me, her legs straddled over my hips, her pussy touching the tip of my cock. I rub her back and tuck her locks behind her ear, questioning, "What are ya doing, petal? You're playing with fire, waking me up like this."

She smirks. "What are ya going to do about it, Aidan?"

I chuckle, warning, "Is that a challenge?"

She gives me a look that makes my cock harden.

I flip her on her back.

She shrieks, laughing, then asks, "Do ya not like me on top of ya?"

"'Course I do." I flip on my back and pull her back over me. I tighten my arm around her and push her hips down so her pussy consumes my cock.

She inhales sharply.

I state, "I like ya on your back or on top of me. Any other concerns over this subject?"

She smiles.

I lift my hips, driving my cock as far into her as possible, and her walls throb against me. Then I lean into her ear, murmuring, "And I really love it when ya squeeze your tight little pussy on me." I grab her hips and circle her over me.

"Is that..." Her eyes flutter. "Jesus, Aidan." Her face flushes deeper.

I move her hips faster over me. "Is this what ya wanted, waking me up like this?"

"I-I-" She briefly shuts her eyes.

"Ya what, petal?"

"I think I'm still sensitive from earlier," she confesses, keeping her eyes shut.

I grunt, warning, "Ya haven't seen anything yet, lass."

She opens her eyes and blurts out, "Right there. Don't... Don't stop. Oh Jesus."

Christ, this woman.

Her insides throb with a new intensity against my shaft. She brings her lips toward my ear. Her hot breath tickles my neck. She whispers, "Tell me ya like it as much as I do."

I move her face in front of mine, assuring her, "Aye. I like it more."

Her lips twitch and her spasms intensify. She breathlessly asks, "So good, right?"

"Aye, lass," I say through gritted teeth. The last thing I want to do is come too early. But I'm fighting it.

She whimpers, her body squeezing me harder.

Goddamnit, I silently curse myself, but fuck, she feels good.

I slide my hand between us, pinching her tit. She gasps. Her mouth hangs open, and she arches her back farther, leaning her head back and shifting her hips faster over me. I fist her hair and catch her eyes rolling as I tug her head back. Her body convulsions intensify, and she moans louder.

"Ya want me to go easy on ya?" I taunt, trying to catch myself from blowing my wad inside her.

She meets my gaze, blinking several times, and shakes her head.

I order, "Then tell me to make ya come."

She blinks in confusion. "I am. Oh Jesus," she blurts out, her body shaking harder.

Fuck's sake. I love it when she comes. But I'm not ready to, and it's too intense for me to hold back much longer. "Tell me to make ya come again…and say please," I bark, slowing my thrusts down, trying to avoid making this end sooner than it should.

Her challenging stare appears. It's barely audible, but she manages to demand, "Make me come again, Aidan. Please."

I push her off me, tugging her thighs over my shoulders so her pussy's on my face. "Ride me," I order, then I slap her ass and grab her hips, moving her at my desired pace. Then I take a nibble of her clit, knowing it's still sensitive from a few hours ago.

"Oh fuck," she cries out.

I reach up, grab the handcuff, and secure her wrist in it. Then I put her hand on her other nipple and instruct, "Play with yourself and ride me, petal."

She glances down at me. Her cheeks turn fire-engine red. Her skin glistens. Her scarlet hair falls over her shoulders toward me. Her lips part and her pink nipple peeks between her fingertips. Her greens glow like hot embers, and it's fucking perfect. Nothing and no one has ever looked so fucking, goddamn perfect.

"You're too fucking hot, lass," I announce, slapping her ass again, and she inhales sharply. I bark, "I gave ya an order, lass. Ya better start riding my face!"

She hesitates, then circles her pussy over my mouth, tracing her nipple with her fingertip and gripping the headboard with her restrained hand.

I shove a finger into her forbidden zone and thumb up her pussy.

"Aidan," she cries out and stops moving. An expression fills her face, and I'm unsure how to take it.

I state, "Tell me if ya want me to stop."

She swallows hard.

I try not to challenge her, but I have a hard time not making it sound like one. "If ya want me to stop, now's the time to tell me no, lass." My heart pounds harder. I stop moving, waiting for her to answer.

She stares at me, breathing hard.

"I listen to 'no' and 'stop'," I inform her.

She continues to stay still, her hand frozen on her nipple, and swallows hard.

I slowly inch my fingers out of her.

She says, "Don't stop! I want it," and sinks back on me.

I slide my forearm over her thighs, holding her still. "Ya sure?"

She nods, a new expression forming in her greens. It all makes my blood pump faster. Everything about this woman turns me on.

She leans closer, locking her greens on me, asking, "Do ya want it all with me, Aidan?"

My cock twitches. "Is that a question?"

She nods. "Yea."

It amazes me she would ever question any part of me wanting her, but I tell her, "I want everything with ya."

"Do ya?" she asks, and it comes out vulnerable.

I kiss her inner thigh and she shudders. I state, "I do. And ya should never question that again."

She gives me a sultry gaze, then rocks her hips, saying, "Then ya better give it to me."

I groan, take my forearm off her thighs, add another finger into her forbidden zone, and watch her arch her back. I curl my thumb inside her pussy, commending, "That's it, petal. Now ya better ride my face and show me how much ya like to touch yourself."

She keeps her gaze on me, which makes it all better. Then she takes her fingertips and squeezes her nipple, slowly moving her body over my hand.

"Good lass," I praise, then latch my mouth onto her clit.

She moans, shuts her eyes, and her lips part wider. I slap her ass again, and she whimpers. Then I circle my fingers inside her faster and suck her harder.

She cries out, "Aidan. Jesus, Aidan."

I slap her again. The crack echoes in the air.

She whispers, "Yes. Jesus Christ. Yes."

"Other nipple," I order, wanting to see how swollen she made it. I've never seen such pink nipples as hers.

She moves her hand over the other, and I groan with delight. I have to stop myself from pulling my fingers out of her and moving up to suck her rosy buds.

Another time, I tell myself.

She begins to play with the other nipple, and I continue a pattern of slapping and rubbing her ass while I work her with my fingers and mouth.

The sounds of pleasure fill the room, and I'll be damned if they aren't the most addicting sounds I've ever heard, but I keep denying her a full-blown orgasm.

She begs, "Aidan, please. I need to come."

I don't give it to her. My eyes dart from her expression to her nipples to her white knuckles gripping the headboard. And the way her back arches and her hair falls is perfection.

"Aidan, please," she begs, and a tear rolls down her cheek and drips onto my forehead. Her body's barely able to stay upright. She's doing everything she can, but the tremors intensify, and I know she's on edge.

I stop slapping her, grip her hips, and keep her body circling over me. I take her swollen clit into my mouth and show her no mercy, sucking, flicking, and biting while her hoarse voice cries out.

She releases her tit and grabs the headboard. Then her eyes roll, and an earthquake releases within her so strong she can barely hold on.

Her walls spasm against my thumb. I keep my mouth suctioned on her while ferociously flicking my tongue on her clit. Her sounds turn into long, delicious moans. Her greens flutter, and there's no way she can focus on anything.

More sweat rolls down her glistening skin. Her back arches and her breasts push between the headboard bars. A pool of her juices drips onto my chest, sliding down to the mattress.

I pull my hand from inside her, move her body off me, then quickly pin my body behind her trembling frame. I tug her hair so her head rests against my neck. I kiss her and murmur in her ear, "Ya make me so fucking hard, petal."

Her chest rises and falls heavy.

I dip down and suck her swollen nipple, and she whimpers louder. I slide my knee between her legs, widening them, and I look her square in the eye, asking, "Do ya want me in ya?" I press the tip of my cock into her wet pussy.

She nods.

I kiss her again, and she slides her tongue into my mouth. I let the kiss deepen for a moment as I inch inside her and then pull out, declaring, "I want all of ya, lass. Is that what ya want?"

She whimpers, pushing her hips toward me, whispering, "Yea."

"Do ya know what that means?" I question.

She swallows hard and nods.

"Have ya done it before?"

Something passes over her face, and I hate myself for the question. Of course she has. *He* made her do it. I quickly say, "We don't have to do it."

She takes her free hand and bends it so it's behind my neck, holding me close to her face, asserting, "I said I want all of ya. Don't stop, Aidan."

"Are ya sure?" I double-check.

She nods. "Yea. Don't ask me again. Give me all of ya." Her eyes flutter again. I kiss behind her ear, and she murmurs, "Take all of me, Aidan. Please. I want it, I swear."

It's all I need to hear. I shove my cock inside her pussy, thrusting a few times, groaning. "Such a good lass, being so wet for me." I tighten my hold on her locks and put my hand on her clit, circling her, even though I know it's super sensitive, but it'll make my entry easier on her.

She whimpers harder, shaking, closing her eyes, admitting, "You're merciless."

"Yea, petal, I am," I declare and circle more quickly.

"Jesus," she moans, another orgasm hitting her.

I pull my cock out of her pussy and slide it past her hard ridge.

"Oh fuck," she cries out, her voice cracking.

"Shh," I murmur, kissing her cheek, holding still for a moment so she can adjust to me, then asking, "Ya okay, lass?"

She opens her eyes, pinning them on me. "Mm-hmm."

"I need to hear it, petal."

She swallows hard, giving me a provoking look. "Ya feel good, Aidan. Don't stop."

I slowly inch in and out of her, holding my arm tight around her waist, my other hand circling her clit. She never stops making incoherent noises. I curse myself for not hitting the record button on my phone. It's the most beautiful sound I've ever heard, and she sounds nothing like I imagined.

My sweat mixes with hers so much that my forearm slips on her stomach. I tighten my grip and thrust deeper.

She moans as another orgasm rips through her. Then she comes down from it and orders, "Faster, Aidan."

"Shh," I coo again, adding, "I want to see ya like this for as long as possible." Then I slide my tongue into her mouth.

She urgently flicks against it, circling her hips faster. But I pin my forearm tighter, holding her to my body, reprimanding, "You're not in control, petal. I am."

"Please. I don't know how much more I can take," she admits, shaking harder.

My lips twitch. "I do, lass. There's a lot more for me to give ya."

"I need ya to come, Aidan," she claims.

I peck her on the lips. "Shh. Just enjoy it." I return to slowly thrusting, sliding my hand off her clit and inching three fingers into her pussy, curling them inside her.

She mumbles, "So full..."

"Ya feel amazing, petal." I nibble on the curve of her neck.

She moans. "So goo— Oh God, Aidan!" she cries out as another earthquake shoots through her and she turns limp against me.

I release her hair and put my hand over her wrists, wrapping my fingers over the bar, then speed up my thrusts, knowing I can't hold out much longer either.

"Oh God...Jesus... Yea," she whimpers.

"Is that what ya want, lass? Me like this?" I taunt, flicking my fingertips inside her.

"Yea. I...oh...oh...oh!" she shrieks.

There's no more control left in me. I explode within her, pumping my seed deep inside, violently pinning her between the headboard and my body as we convulse into the other for what feels like forever.

My vision turns blurry, and an ocean of adrenaline annihilates me.

Time stands still until my focus returns, and we're both breathing hard, still pinned against the headboard.

I kiss her cheek and announce, "Let's shower. Then it's time for ya to eat again."

She arches her eyebrows, her chest still heaving, trying to find oxygen.

My lips twitch. "Let's go, petal. Ya need your energy if you're going to be around me."

11

Scarlet
One Week Later

*A*idan's chest rises and falls, taking in fresh oxygen. He's insatiable. Or maybe it's me. All we've done is fill our days and nights being consumed by the other. When we aren't in bed, we're playing cards or cooking, and then we're unable to keep our hands off the other again.

He always surprises me. Whenever I think I know exactly what he's like, he shows me another side of him in the bedroom or outside of it.

We've done it all over the property. Inside, outside, even in the car, even though he only drove me down the road, since I complained he had me trapped in the cottage.

The rooster crows, and Aidan does what he always does after sex, tugging me into him, kissing my head, and sliding his palm over my ass.

A few moments of silence pass. I glance up, lift my head off his chest, and ask, "Aidan, what happens after this?"

His lips twitch. He turns to me and drags his knuckles over the curve of my waist. I shudder as tingles race under his touch, proving once again that it doesn't matter how much I have him. My body always reacts to his.

He teases, "I feed ya. I get a few minutes for my dick to recover. Then I do whatever is necessary to make ya moan. Ya know, the one that I love so much."

I bite my smile.

He adds, "Actually, I'll make ya do it several times, lass." He wiggles his eyebrows.

My cheeks heat. I laugh, then nudge him, stating, "I mean, what's the long-term plan for us? After we leave the cottage?"

"Who said we're leaving?"

I sit up. Vulnerability hits me, but I find the courage to assert, "Ya know we can't stay here forever. Just tell me what ya see for us."

His face falls. "Ya don't have to worry about that, lass."

My stomach churns. "What do ya mean I don't have to worry about it?"

"You're safe. I'll keep ya safe."

I take a frustrated breath and confess, "That isn't what I'm asking. Where does this go, Aidan? How does this work? Not just between us. Obviously, ya know what family I belong to, and I know who yours is, along with the issues, so...?"

"Well, ya can't return to the O'Learys," he snaps.

I jerk my head back, admitting, "I didn't say that, even though it feels weird."

"It feels weird not to return to the people who threw ya to the wolves?" he hurls, his eyes darkening.

I cross my arms over my naked breasts. "Ya aren't being fair right now."

He glances at the ceiling, then blows out a breath of air.

I put my hand on his cheek, softening my voice. "Hey."

He meets my gaze, and hatred is all over his expression. He states, "I can't stand the thought of what they've done to ya. The notion that you'd want to go back there—"

"I don't want to go back. I just said it's weird. Surely ya can understand that if ya thought about having to leave your family and everything ya ever knew," I point out.

He grunts. "My family would never treat anybody the way your family treats its own blood."

I stay silent, my heart racing, my mouth turning dry. I know he's right, but it's still hard. I grew up with the O'Learys, not knowing any different. And now Aidan's showing me a different world, even if it's just him and me.

I've never had a man treat me like he does, and maybe it'll change if other people are around. But in our own little world, he's nothing short of amazing, more than anyone I could ever imagine having. So I try not to think about how it will be outside our bubble. And the thought of him changing how he treats me almost kills me, but I don't want to be naive and think it couldn't happen.

He scoots me off him and sits on the edge of the bed, declaring, "I need to go into town for more food."

I slide beside him, announcing, "Then I'll go with ya."

"Ya know ya can't go with me, Scarlet."

It's the same fight we've had several times. "Aidan, I don't want to stay here."

He puts his hand on my thigh. "I'm sorry, lass, but ya have to. It's too dangerous."

I insist, "No one's going to know it's me. I can wear a hat and sunglasses just the way ya do."

He shakes his head. "There's no way I'm taking any risk with ya."

"What if somebody comes here and you're not here? I don't know how to protect myself. Surely ya know that."

He closes his eyes for a moment and admits, "I don't like leaving ya, Scarlet, but ya can't come with me. This is the best scenario."

"Well, it's not the best scenario. I could go with ya. No one's going to recognize me. Nobody knows us here."

"Ya don't know where his men are," Aidan states firmly.

I get up and go over to the window, hugging myself tightly and staring out into the yard. The sun's bright, and it's a beautiful day out. Yet I suddenly feel nothing of the happiness I had previously.

He comes behind me and puts his arm around my waist, kissing the top of my head. He murmurs, "Don't be mad at me."

Don't back down.

I need to know.

I spin into him. "Where does this end, Aidan? Surely there's something more for us besides this cottage."

He grins. "Ya don't like the cottage or what we're doing in it?"

I tilt my head, glaring, and put my hand on my hip. "Ya know what I mean."

His face turns serious again. He scrubs his hand over it and states, "Ya don't need to worry about what's going to happen. Tommy will be dead."

"How's he going to die? Who's out there hunting him to kill him? At least tell me some details."

Aidan challenges, "Why do ya need to know details? What will it change?"

My stomach flips. "Why are ya avoiding my questions? Just tell me what I want to know."

He clenches his jaw and looks out the window over my head.

More anger hits me. I don't want to be left in the dark the way I've been my entire life. Everything with Aidan is different. I want to keep him, but I also want to be on an even playing field. That has to start with honesty and trust. If he doesn't trust me to inform me about where we're going and how he's taking Tommy out, then what do we really have?

I tug his face toward me so he can't avoid me. I try again. "Tell me, Aidan. Is somebody hunting Tommy the way he's hunting me?"

He sniffs hard. "Tommy's day is coming."

"Why can't it come now? Why? Why doesn't somebody from your clan go kill him? Surely, ya have the clout to order that," I suggest.

Aidan gives me a look like I'm ridiculous, replying, "Aye, I do, but it's my job to kill him."

I squint at him. "What do ya mean?"

Hatred seethes from his voice. "When Tommy takes his last breath, he'll look at me. But before I do, he will pay, and he'll pay dearly."

Something about the way Aidan says that makes me more anxious. My pulse shoots up, and I inquire, "How's he going to pay? Isn't death enough?"

Aidan shakes his head. "No, petal. It's not enough. He's going to suffer for everything he's done to ya and for what he's done to others."

It's the first time Aidan's ever mentioned anyone else. I ask, "What others?"

He stays quiet.

I add, "Why do I feel like this is personal?"

"It is personal. He hurt ya."

"But who else did he hurt that ya know?"

Sadness fills Aidan's expression. Then the hatred covers it up again. He announces, "No one ya knew, lass. But I'll tell ya this: Tommy's going to lose everything, and he's going to pay more than just through death."

"Why does it matter? Just go kill him," I order.

Aidan locks eyes with me and puts his hand on my cheek. "I know what I'm doing, and I know why I'm doing what I'm doing. Ya have to trust me."

Several tense moments pass. I finally admit, "It's hard to trust somebody when they won't be clear about why they chose to add more risk to our lives."

"I'm not adding more risk," he claims.

"How is Tommy being alive not adding more risk?"

Stubbornness fills Aidan's expression. It's the first time I've really seen it.

"Don't be hardheaded," I state.

His hardened expression never changes. He kisses my forehead and steps back. "I need to go to town and buy more food." He pulls out a pair of joggers and a T-shirt from the dresser. He slides into his pants and tugs the T-shirt over his head.

"I'm coming with ya," I repeat, grabbing clothes from the small closet.

"No, you're not," he states.

I continue to get ready, asserting, "I am. I'll wear this hat." I grab one off the dresser and put it over my head. I spin. "Where are the sunglasses that ya bought me?"

He shakes his head. "You're not listening, and I'm not changing my mind, so get it through your skull, Scarlet. You're staying here. I'm going to town, and I'll be back as soon as possible."

"No, I'm—"

The sound of a car pulling onto the gravel stops me dead in my tracks. My gut drops.

Aidan lunges toward the window, ordering, "Get down, petal."

I don't question him. I crouch next to the wall, slightly trembling. Since we've been here, this is the first time anyone else has approached the cottage.

Please don't be Tommy.

Please don't be Tommy.

Please don't be Tommy.

Aidan mutters, "What the..." then he barks, "Goddammit."

"What's wrong?" I whisper.

He takes my hand and pulls me up. "Stay in the bedroom. It's my brothers."

"Your brothers?"

"Stay here, Scarlet," he repeats and leaves the bedroom.

"I bet it's one time ya wish ya had a door," I toss out, unhappy that he's fighting me about going to town or won't tell me what he means by making Tommy pay. I don't understand why he won't send someone to off him, and I still want an answer to my question about what happens when all this is over.

Will it ever be over?

Yes.

Do I want it to be if it means losing Aidan?

I'm not naive. I know we're in close quarters with no one else to interrupt or cast judgment upon us. Once we leave here, that will end. I don't know where that leaves us or how Aidan will handle it. I have nothing to lose at this point in my life. And I can't claim he doesn't since he's an O'Connor and I'm an O'Leary.

146

The floorboards creak from Aidan's footsteps. He barks, "I told ya no one was to know I was here, Devin, including Tynan."

"Aye. Thanks for your support, bro. Glad ya don't trust me," a man sarcastically states.

"It's not about that," Aidan scolds.

The sound of more footsteps entering the cottage hits my ears, and the door shuts. I step next to the doorframe and peek out of it.

"What are ya doing here?" Aidan questions.

His brothers stand in front of him. Both are as gorgeous as he is, with similar height and build.

One of them says, "Ya got to get back to Belfast. We need ya there."

"I can't go back to Belfast right now, and ya know that," Aidan states.

"Tommy's blown up two warehouses. He's sent several messengers that he wants his wife back," the other brother announces.

Fear fills me as goose bumps break out all over my skin. I step out of the room, fretting, "He knows I'm with Aidan?"

The three men jerk their heads toward me.

"I told ya to stay in the room," Aidan scolds.

I put my hand on my hip and lift my chin. "When it concerns me, I have a right to be here."

"Ya don't," he claims.

Anger fills me. The last thing I want is to be left out of decisions that involve me. That was how I grew up. If my life's taught me anything, it's that I need to be smarter going forward. And while

I trust Aidan with almost everything in my life, our current issue makes me uneasy. If he wants to keep me in the dark like I've always been, how can I ever fully trust him? I glare at him, then pin my gaze on his brothers, seething, "Since ya two seem to know who I am, why don't ya tell me which ones ya are?"

Aidan points, snarling, "That's Devin, and that's Tynan. And they were just leaving, weren't ya?"

Devin insists, "Ya can't stay here. He's coming this way with men. Dozens of men."

I gape, my insides quivering so hard I have to grab Aidan's forearm to keep me from falling.

He protectively slides his arm around me, and I sink into his hold. His jaw twitches, and the room turns silent.

"Jesus. Not ya too," Tynan says in disgust, glancing at my hand and scowling.

"Shut up," Aidan warns, his fist curling at his side.

Offended, I snap, "What does that mean?"

Tynan's face hardens like Aidan's. He glances at his other brother and shakes his head. "First Brody, now him. What is it with these women?"

"Mind telling me what you're going on about? I'm standing right here," I hurl.

He looks back at me, mumbling, "Nothing."

"Well, it sounds like ya meant something," I push.

"God, you're just like her too," he adds, studying me.

"Shut up. Don't ya dare disrespect Scarlet," Aidan threatens, tugging me tighter into him.

I seethe, "Are ya talking about my sister?"

Tynan's scowl deepens.

Devin keeps his eyes on Aidan. "We need ya in Belfast. Maybe ya should turn her over to Alaina. She's going crazy on all of us anyway. You're defying orders, and ya know there's going to be consequences."

Aidan's fingertips press into me harder. He grits through his teeth, "It's not happening."

"Alaina can take care of her. You're needed in Belfast," Devin repeats.

"Is there anything else ya came to tell me?" Aidan questions.

Devin steps closer. "You've created a bad situation. We need to sort it out and fast. Tommy and his men are on your trail. They're destroying our assets on the way, and the longer this goes on, the more damage he'll do."

Aidan's voice turns cold, stating, "Then our men should step in and do what they're supposed to do."

"Everyone is doing the best they can. Ya know what our numbers look like right now," Tynan claims.

"Then do your job and get more recruits into Belfast. Let off some bombs in Dublin. I don't care what it takes, just do it," Aidan orders.

"Ya know the challenges."

Aidan takes a deep breath, asserting, "This is a conversation ya should have with Brody. He's the one who needs to make sure our men can handle stuff like this. If we can't, we've got a problem."

"He's working on it," Tynan states.

"Well he should work faster," Aidan claims.

Devon's eyes turn to slits. "It's all of our problem, and ya know it."

Aidan's voice turns so cold I shiver. He declares, "Nothing is my problem right now. My only concerns are to protect Scarlet and make Tommy pay. Until that happens and he's crossed off my list, all of ya need to sort it out."

Tynan reiterates, "Turn her over to Alaina."

"No," Aidan says. He spins into me. "Petal, go into the bedroom."

I square my shoulders. "No, this is about me."

His eyes light hotter. He points to the bedroom. "I said to go in the bedroom. I need to talk to my brothers. Alone."

I retort, "Maybe I should go to Alaina's."

His face falls, and hurt explodes all over it. He lowers his voice. "Is that what ya want, lass?"

I blink hard, trying to make a point but unable to tell him yes. I do want to see my sister, but the thought of not being near Aidan is too painful.

He studies me, and I turn my head, continuing to try to not allow my tears to flow. He says, "Fine. Ya stay here, we'll go outside. Do not come out. I'm warning ya," he threatens.

Relief hits me that he's not telling me to go to Alaina's since I tossed it in his face. One thing I know is Aidan's a proud man. He's only going to let me push him so far. And I don't know what he'd do to me if I did step outside, but something tells me not to, so I don't argue.

He motions for his brothers to follow him.

I go to the window, watching them argue. I can't hear anything. Devin and Tynan finally get into their car.

Aidan crosses his arms and waits until the vehicle disappears. Then he spins, locking eyes with me.

My insides quiver with fear, confusion, and frustration.

Tommy's coming.

I swallow hard and put my hand on my stomach, feeling ill. I've always feared the day he would find me, and his men are as ruthless as he is. If they are coming after us, it's only a matter of time before they find us.

Aidan returns to the house and steps inside.

I blurt out, "If Tommy's coming, ya should turn me over to Alaina and do whatever ya need to protect yourself."

He grunts. "I don't need protection from that thug. And it's not happening, petal. You're staying with me. Unless ya changed your mind and no longer want me?" He gives me a challenging stare.

Tears well in my eyes again.

He steps in front of me and tilts my chin, warning, "Don't ever suggest to leave me unless that's what ya really want. Understand?"

A tear escapes and I nod.

He swipes at it and tugs me into his chest, holding my head firmly against his pecs. He murmurs in my ear, "We're staying together. But we don't have much time, so get ready." He kisses my head, releases me, and goes into the bedroom. He grabs a duffle bag and tosses clothes into it.

Tommy and his men are coming.

I freeze, watching Aidan pack.

He looks up, stating, "Ya wanted to leave this cottage. Well, ya got your way. Whatever ya want to take with ya, make sure it gets packed. We're leaving in five minutes, petal."

12

Aidan

hatever food and water we can take, I toss into the trunk next to our bags. Scarlet runs into the chicken coop, and I pull out a map, staring at the path of how to get up north to the mountains.

Tommy's men are coming south, so we need to pass them while avoiding them. Tynan told me where he heard they were coming from, so I decide to veer west to get there. It'll take a few hours longer, but the less chance we have of running into any of the O'Learys, the better.

I double-check I have my gun and knives in the car where they're easy to access, and Scarlet strolls across the yard, carrying a basket full of eggs.

She's gained some weight, but she still needs to be stronger. I'm ready for this to all be over and I wish I could implement my plan, but until she's healthier, I have to be patient.

She steps in front of me, her face full of worry. "Do we have everything?"

I glance at the basket of brown eggs, teasing, "We're going to have a hard time cooking those in the car."

She tilts her head, squinting from the sun. "Funny."

I reach for her cheek and stroke my thumb over her lips, admitting, "Just trying to make ya smile, lass."

Her mouth curves, but it doesn't erase the worry. She frets, "I don't like that he knows I'm with ya and that he's now chasing us."

"We'll be fine," I assure her and open the door. "Get in, petal."

She obeys.

"Put your seat belt on," I order and shut the door. I go around to my side of the car, slide inside, and turn on the engine. I pull out onto the dirt road, and silence fills the air for several miles.

My senses are on high alert. I keep looking in the rearview mirror, feeling paranoid that someone's following us even though there are no cars anywhere.

I knew it was only a matter of time before Tommy found out I was with her. He probably put two and two together since it doesn't take much to know that when one O'Connor is missing, they're probably involved.

Scarlet blurts out, "Aidan, what do ya have up your sleeve?"

I glance at her. "We're going to the mountains."

"That's not what I meant, and ya know it."

My chest tightens. "Why don't ya be clear, lass?"

"Really?" she hurls, glaring at me.

I'm not going to give Scarlet any leeway. If she has a specific question, she'll have to ask me. So I state, "I'm not a mind reader."

Her face hardens and it reminds me of Alaina's. My brother was right about one thing. She's just as stubborn as her sister. She asks, "What do ya plan on doing to hurt Tommy before ya kill him?"

"Ya don't need to worry about that."

"Stop not answering my questions. This involves me. I have a right to know," she claims.

"Ya have a right to know? Why do ya have a right to know?" I question.

She blinks hard.

I sigh and I grab her hand. "I'm sorry, petal. That didn't come out right. I don't like ya worrying about this stuff."

"Just tell me, Aidan. I want to know."

I don't want to tell her everything. She doesn't need to know. It's not going to affect her. But I need to give her something, so I admit, "A man like Tommy values his ego more than anything else, so I'm going to destroy it."

"How?" she questions.

I turn down another dirt lane and glance at the GPS to ensure I'm going west, even though it'd be a lot faster to just keep going north. I confess, "By making it clear he has nothing he thinks he ever did, now or in the past."

"How?" Scarlet's eyes slowly turn into a glare. The hairs on my neck rise, and she fumes, "By using me?"

My stomach tightens. I claim, "I'm not using ya, petal."

"What would ya call it?"

"This is why we shouldn't get into this," I declare.

"Aidan, you're scaring me."

"Ya don't need to be scared," I reassure her.

"Tommy isn't someone that ya fuck around with. Ya know this. Why do I have to remind ya about this fact?"

Anger fills me. I'm not scared of Tommy. I assert, "Why don't ya leave Tommy to me?"

Her lips quiver. She lifts her chin and continues to pin her challenging stare on me. "Ya don't know who you're messing with, Aidan." She blinks hard.

"Do ya think I'm scared of him?" I ask.

She points at me. "You're being arrogant. It's going to be your downfall."

I snort. "No, I'm not. And I'm not going to tell ya again. This is nothing for ya to worry about. Change the subject. This matter is closed."

I focus on the road even though I can feel her glaring at me with too many rageful emotions. I hate every moment of it. And I don't want her to feel like this toward me.

Over the short time we've been together, if anything's clear, it's that I have deep feelings for her. I'd do anything to protect her, including going up against Tommy. But I won't back down from what I set out to do. When my mind's on something, I follow through. And Tommy's not going to be any exception.

I pick up her hand and kiss the back of it. "Would ya rather be spanked or whipped, petal?"

She continues looking out the window. I kiss her hand again, then lean close to her ear. "I asked if you'd rather be spanked or whipped? Are ya not going to play your game? It's a long ride to sit here pissed at me."

She finally caves, letting out a frustrated breath. She turns in her seat, asking, "What are ya whipping me with? Your pants? Your belt?"

"What about a flogger?" I ask.

She arches her eyebrow. "I don't know. I've never been whipped by one."

"But ya like to be spanked," I say, winking at her.

Her lips twitch, and that's what I want to see.

"Your turn. Ask me a question," I tell her.

She props the side of her knee on the seat and asks, "Okay, would ya rather lose a leg or an arm?"

"Ouch. You're always into bodily harm, aren't ya?"

"Ya just asked me if I wanted to be spanked or whipped," she points out.

"Totally different from losing a limb," I declare.

She laughs. "Well, sorry, but ya have to choose. Are ya losing your leg or an arm?"

I think about it. "Probably an arm."

"Why?" she questions.

I shrug. "I can still walk and run. They have those fake arms. I'm pretty sure I could learn to use that. They're pretty far advanced as far as I know."

Amusement lights up her face. "Have ya studied this? Worried that you're going to lose a limb?"

I chuckle. "No, I can't say I have, but I'm sure an arm would suit me better. So if I had to choose, I'd prefer to keep both my legs."

"Okay, fair enough," she says.

The road turns from gravel to pavement. There's still no one around, and it's all farmland. I accelerate and think about my next question. Then I ask, "Would ya rather have sex on a train or a plane?"

A little flush heats her cheeks, and she smirks. "I think a train."

"Yea? Why is that?" I question.

Her flush grows more intense. "A train's always vibrating, right?"

"Ah, so ya like vibrators. Noted," I tease.

She scoffs. "Maybe. Maybe not."

Toys are one thing I haven't gotten to use with Scarlet since we've been in the cottage. But I make a mental note to get some as soon as possible. I declare, "When all this is over, we'll go shopping."

"Shopping?"

I nod. "Aye. Get ya a vibrator. Then come home, sit ya up on the counter, let ya spread your legs, and put a show on for me."

She softly laughs and puts her hand over her face. "You're so dirty."

"I think ya love me dirty."

She stares at me, the green in her eyes shining brighter.

"So, you're not into plane sex, huh?"

"I didn't say that," she claims.

"But definitely a train."

She shrugs. "I mean, if I had to choose, I'm assuming."

"Because you've never done it on either?"

Her face heats hotter. She puts her hand over it and peeks through her fingers, groaning.

"No need to be embarrassed."

"Have ya?" she asks.

I admit, "Aye. I'm a mile-high club member."

She rolls her eyes. "Of course ya are."

I lean closer and wiggle my eyebrows. "But I saved the train for ya."

"Is that so?"

"Definitely. We'll have to book some tickets as soon as possible," I add.

She bites her lip and shakes her head.

A few minutes pass, and she snaps her fingers, claiming, "I know the next question."

"What's that?"

"Would ya rather choose five years in prison or ten years in a coma?"

It doesn't take me long to answer, "Five years in prison."

"Really?" she says in surprise.

"Yea, if I'm in a coma, I don't know what's happening."

Her smile falls. She mutters, "It's got to be better than prison." She turns and looks out the window, and tension fills the air.

I lower my voice. "Hey, did I say something wrong?"

She shakes her head and quietly mutters, "No."

"What's wrong, then?" I ask.

She takes a couple of deep breaths and turns to me. "I was in Tommy's prison. I'd rather be in a coma."

All the hatred I feel for that piece of shit comes back, curling in my gut. I sigh. "He's going to pay, petal."

"I'd rather ya just kill him, though, instead of whatever this plan is that ya have. I don't have a good feeling about it, Aidan."

I run my fingers through her hair and glide my thumb over her temple, assuring, "I told ya not to worry about this."

"But I am."

"But ya don't need to," I insist.

A car approaches us, and I take my hand off her, putting both on the steering wheel and telling her, "Put your glasses and hat on."

She obeys.

"From now on, ya got to keep them on at all times, okay?"

"You're being a bit paranoid, I think."

"No, I'm not. It stays on," I insist.

"Fine," she groans.

I drive another mile, and more cars come into view. Some are behind me, and some come toward us. It all makes me more anxious.

"Ya need to ask me a question, Aidan," she asserts.

I concentrate on the road, pondering momentarily, then ask, "Would ya rather eat a sheep's testicles or a cow's balls?"

"Ooh, that's disgusting," she cries out.

I chuckle. "Hey, you're the one with the crazy questions. Which one's it going to be, princess?"

"Oh, now I'm a princess?"

I laugh. "Yep, you're whatever I want ya to be."

"Is that so?"

"Definitely. Now, are ya eating sheep testicles or cow balls?"

Her face turns slightly green, and she wrinkles her nose. "Er, I guess cow's balls."

"Why is that?"

She shakes her head. "I don't know. We eat red meat, and I don't think I've ever eaten sheep."

"Sheep's red meat," I say, then pause, questioning, "Is it red meat?"

"Ummm…yea, I think it is," she says.

I lean my head closer. "Why don't we know if a sheep is red meat? Why am I questioning this? It's red meat, right?"

She scrunches her face, laughing. "I don't know, Aidan. I've not thought about it because who actually eats sheep?"

"A baby sheep is a lamb, and we eat those. That's red meat."

"Duh! You're right. Why don't I think of a lamb as a sheep?" she questions.

Both of us look at each other, then start laughing. She declares, "We've been in the cottage too long!"

I add, "We sound super unintelligent right now."

"Don't ever tell anyone about this conversation!" She laughs.

"Nope! My lips are sealed!" I agree.

She looks out the window and then turns back toward me. "Okay, next question. Would ya rather shag a man ya can't see or hear, or would ya rather shag a man ya can't see or smell?"

"I'm not shagging any man," I claim.

She smiles. "Okay, fine. Would ya rather shag a woman that ya can't see her face or hear her speak, or would ya rather shag a woman that ya can't see her face or smell her?"

"Well, what's she smell like?" I question.

"Whatever ya want her to smell like," Scarlet says.

"And what's her voice like? Is it shrieky? I really can't stand a shrieky voice," I admit.

Scarlet bursts out laughing. "No, it's not shrieky. Again, her voice is beautiful. She smells delicious. So would ya rather shag a faceless woman without being able to hear or smell her?"

I groan and scrub my face. "I don't think I can answer this question."

"Ya have to," she states.

"Yea, but let's take ya, for instance," I tell her.

"What do ya mean?" she questions.

"Well, I love to hear how ya sound when I'm shagging ya. And I certainly love how ya smell, especially that pussy of yours."

Her face turns maroon. She slaps my bicep. "Aidan."

I shrug. "Just telling the truth, lass. I can't answer that question."

"Ya just lost a point," she claims.

"I thought there weren't any points and nobody wins or loses this game." I remind her of what she said the first time we ever played it.

"Well, starting now, there are points," she announces.

"Wow, that's convenient for ya."

She shrugs. "Oh, well, if you're not going to answer questions, then I'm going to have to make some rules up."

I tease, "You're merciless. Ask me another question."

She thinks, then asks, "Would ya rather be branded with my initials, or would ya rather have a knife cut my initials into ya?"

"Ooh, we're getting serious now if I'm going to be wearing your initials. Is that something ya want from me?" I question, but I'd do it for her if she wants.

She arches her eyebrows. "I didn't say that. It's just a what-if question."

"Really? Are ya sure ya don't have some deep-down desire for me to carry your initials? Maybe your full name on me. Like, where do ya want it? Just don't tell me to put it on my dick. That's probably the only place I won't put it."

"So you'd put it on your balls?" she questions.

"No, not there either. Balls and dick go together."

"But you'd brand my name on your ass?" she asks.

I think about it. "Aye. If ya really felt a deep need for me to do that, then I'd take one for the team."

"Really? Ya would?" she says in shock.

"What can I say? I'll do a lot to please ya, lass," I tease and wink.

She laughs. "Okay, well, what's it going to be? Are ya branding my initials on ya? Or am I taking a knife and cutting them into ya?"

"That's easy. Branding."

"Why was that easy?"

I admit, "Branding's hot. It's got fire attached to it. Ya know how I am with fire."

Her face turns serious. She nods and puts her hand on my thigh. "I guess I should have known the answer before I asked ya, huh?"

I put my hand over hers. I don't know how, but she accepts my crazy obsession with fire. Several times I'd needed to go out to the pit. She always came out with me. Even when I told her to go inside, she always stayed there. Sometimes she stepped back and just watched. It was an odd comfort that soothed me, knowing she was there. I'm still trying to figure out why.

She orders, "Okay, ask me a question."

I turn onto a major motorway, getting slightly nervous but knowing we have do it. I ask, "Would ya rather eat human ribs or human rump roast?"

"So now I have to be a cannibal?" she blurts out, wrinkling her nose.

"Aye. So what's it going to be, lass? Will ya gnaw on some ribs or dig into a rump roast?"

She shakes her head. "Both sound equally gross."

"But ya got to pick. It's for dinner."

Her face scrunches in disgust. She puts her hand over her stomach. "The thought of that is just...ugh."

I chuckle. "Pick."

She thinks about it briefly and says, "Fine, I'll take the rump roast."

"Ah, ya like all things ass, don't ya?"

She tilts her head and gives me a little smirk. "Funny. But let me ask ya, Aidan, would ya rather die from drowning or burning? And I feel like I already know the answer, but go ahead and answer it."

"Fire."

"Yea, already knew that."

I question, "How about ya?"

She doesn't hesitate. "I'd rather drown via suffocation."

Her answer shocks me. I'm so in tune with fire that I can't even consider that somebody would want to die any other way. I ask, "Why?"

She takes a minute and answers, "I feel like suffocation would be quicker. Fire would probably hurt way more. I think you'd be dead within a matter of minutes via drowning. Plus, my mum died from a fire." She turns quiet.

My chest tightens. I pick up her hand and kiss it. "Ya okay?"

165

"Mm-hm."

I catch something in the mirror. Goose bumps pop out on my skin. I put my hand on her shoulder, ordering, "Scoot down a little bit."

She frets, "Why? What's wrong?"

"Just scoot down, petal."

She obeys.

I switch lanes, and a red vehicle follows. My heart pumps faster. I drive the normal speed for a few minutes, then get out of the lane and pass several cars, going faster than anybody should on this road.

The car doesn't follow. I breathe a sigh of relief. "I think we're okay."

"Ya thought someone was following us?"

"Aye, but I think we're fine." I glance back in the mirror again. The red car is still several behind mine, not making any moves to pass.

To be safe, I make another aggressive move, passing another dozen cars until I can't see the red vehicle.

Scarlet questions, "Are ya sure they're not following us?"

"No, they aren't," I declare. But for the rest of the way, I stay more vigilant, knowing I could be wrong at any moment.

13

Scarlet

$\mathcal{S}$now lightly dusts the mountains. We keep traveling higher up, making our way around the dangerous curves. It's making me nauseous, so I shut my eyes and lean back against the headrest. Yet it doesn't help it go away. I turn toward Aidan and ask, "Where will we stay?"

He glances at me quickly and then puts his eyes back on the road, gripping the steering wheel with both hands to take the tight turn.

My stomach rolls again, and a sharp pain shoots through it. I wince.

Aidan answers, "We'll find somewhere."

The hair on my neck rises. "Like a B&B or something?"

He grunts. "No, petal. We can't stay anywhere with people. We'll have to break into a cottage."

"But what if somebody catches us?" I question, and my stomach rumbles loudly.

He glances at me again. "Ya need to eat. Grab something from the back."

I groan. Aidan keeps making me eat whatever I can pull from the bags that doesn't need to be cooked. My stomach feels full, so I state, "I'm not hungry."

He arches his eyes, accusing, "Then why is your stomach rumbling?"

I shrug, confessing, "I don't know. It just does that sometimes."

"Eat," he orders again and grips the wheel tighter as we hit an ice patch and skid toward the edge. He veers us back into the other lane.

My heart pounds harder. I decide it's better not to argue with him when we're in these treacherous conditions. I remove my seat belt, grab a piece of candy from the bag, and sit back in my seat.

He demands, "Put your seat belt back on. These roads are horrible."

I don't argue and obey.

The snow picks up, forming a blanket in front of the vehicle. Aidan turns down a side road, but all I can see is white.

"How do ya even know there are places up here?"

"We'll find something. Stop worrying," he declares.

His assurance doesn't calm my fear. I sit back and turn the heat up, wishing the snow wasn't so thick and I could see.

Fog forms around the edges of the window. We drive farther toward the top of the mountain, and Aidan declares, "There's a place."

"I don't see anything," I admit, leaning toward the window.

He slows the car, and a tiny cottage barely comes into view.

My chest tightens. I inquire, "How do ya know no one's here?"

He stops the car and glances around. "No one's around here. No tracks on the ground, and there isn't any smoke coming out of the chimney. From the looks of it, I'd say no one's been here for a while."

I blurt out, "But ya can't be sure."

"See that tarp?" he points.

More nausea hits me. I inhale deeply and squint, confessing, "I don't see anything."

"There's a tarp over there, and I bet it's covering wood for the fireplace. So I'm ninety-nine percent certain no one is here."

"What if the one percent is the truth?"

His lips twitch. "Since when did ya become a pessimist?"

"I'm not. I'm a realist," I declare.

"Is that what ya tell yourself?"

"Yea."

He chuckles, then announces, "There's only one way to find out."

I continue to fret and reply, "Say you're right and they're gone. What if they come back and we're here?"

"My gut says they won't." He pulls into the small driveway, then parks as close to the cottage as possible. He orders, "Stay in the car until I tell ya." He gets out, leaving the car running.

A gust of air fills the interior, and I shiver. Another sharp pain shoots through my stomach. I mutter, "Ouch," and put my hand on my abdomen.

Aidan walks around the house and must figure that it's safe. He pops the trunk, then returns to the front door. He jiggles the doorknob a few times, then steps in front of the window. He puts a cloth around his hand, leans away, and punches through the glass.

It startles me, and I jump in my seat. My heart races faster. I'm sure someone will catch us breaking in, but it's a silly thought. Aidan's right that no one is anywhere near here.

He reaches in and unlocks the cottage, then comes back to the car. He opens my door, commanding, "Go into the house. I'll join ya inside in a minute."

"How do ya know they're not coming back?" I repeat again, still worried.

"Chance we have to take, petal. Now, go inside."

"There's a lot to unpack though. I'll help unload the car," I offer.

He hands me the basket of eggs. "No. Go inside and try to stay warm." He leads me over the slippery ground until I'm inside the cottage. It smells musty, as if no one's been here for years. It's not quite as cold as outside, but it's pretty close.

A fireplace and a small kitchen are in the main room, and there are two other doors. I peek into the rooms and find a bed that fills most of the space of one and a tiny bathroom in the other.

I try to turn on the water, but nothing comes out. I yell, "There's no water."

Aidan brings the duffle bag inside and sets it down. He replies, "They probably turned it off so it wouldn't freeze. I'm not surprised. We'll have to use the water we brought with us sparingly until I can figure out how to turn it on."

"Oh. Okay."

He shuts the door, goes to the fireplace, and tosses some wood into it. He sprays lighter fluid over it and strikes a match. The flames erupt, and he steps back, staring at it a few moments, then glances around.

A gust of wind blows through the broken glass. I point and ask, "What are we going to do about that?"

He shoves the bookshelf across the room until it's in front of the hole. He asks, "Is there a broom and dustpan in that pantry?" He nods toward the kitchen.

I open the door and find both. I reach for them and freeze as another sharp pain hits me.

"Petal, ya okay?" Aidan calls out.

I fill my lungs with air, grab the items, and force a smile. I spin back, take them to the window area, and hand him the dustpan. I sweep the glass, and he holds the pan until it's full.

"I'm going to get the rest of our stuff and toss this glass. I'll be right back." He leaves the cottage.

I step in front of the fire, trying to get warm, rubbing my hands together.

He brings all the groceries inside and then returns to the cold.

I go to the kitchen and put the little food we brought into the cabinet.

He returns with the dufflle bag and tosses it into the bedroom. He reappears and steps behind me, sliding his hands over my waist and kissing my neck.

I look up. "Don't be starting that. We've got work to do here."

He chuckles. "Work can wait."

I jab him with my elbow. "No, I think you've got to wait."

He groans and dramatically says, "You're killing me, petal." He leaves and gets to the door, stating, "I'm going to go outside and get more wood."

"Good idea. It's cold in here," I admit.

Aidan makes several trips until a big stack of wood sits inside the cottage. He adds more to the fireplace and stares at it.

I go into the bedroom and unpack the clothes. Then I find more blankets in another closet and pile them on the bed, sure that it'll be freezing since there's only one fireplace, and it's in the other room.

Another pain shoots through my stomach. I grab my side and have to sit on the mattress. Nausea hits me. I close my eyes, squeezing them tight.

Aidan's voice cuts through the air. "Scarlet, what's wrong?"

I open my eyes and start to lie. "Nothing. I'm—" Another pain rips through me. I take a deep breath.

Concern fills Aidan's expression. He sits beside me, gaze drilling into me as he says, "It doesn't look like nothing. What's going on?"

I admit, "I'm just... I feel a little sick."

"Ya need to eat," he declares.

"I'm-I'm not hungry."

"Lie down. I'll make ya some food," he states, pulling the cover back.

I don't argue. The pain in my stomach feels worse, but I also suddenly feel hot.

He puts his hand on my forehead, stating, "Your cheeks are flushed, and ya feel like ya have a fever." He looks at me in concern.

"I'm fine. Maybe I do need to eat," I say to appease him.

He stares at me with worry but finally says, "I'll be back with some food." He leaves the room, and I hug the pillow to my face, breathing in the musty odor. It makes me feel sicker.

Another pain shoots through my abdomen. I close my eyes, not sure what's happening. Surely, this can't be from not eating. I've been starved before. I know what that ache is like, and this isn't anything close to it.

Aidan's gone for a few moments and returns with buttered bread. He declares, "I've got to figure out how to turn the electricity on. There's no way to cook right now. Start with this, and I'll make ya something hot once I sort our situation out. I bet a nice cup of tea will make ya feel better."

I sit up and glance at the bread, but it only makes me feel sicker. I turn away. "I can't eat anything right now," I say weakly, swallowing down bile.

Aidan puts his hand on my forehead again. "You're burning up, petal."

"I don't feel good," I confess and then cringe as another sharp pain hits my stomach.

Aidan tugs the blankets back and pulls my shirt up, questioning, "Where does it hurt?"

I continue to grip my lower gut, not answering.

Aidan studies me and puts his hand over different parts of my stomach. And when he gets to my lower right abdomen, I wince in pain.

"Fuck," he mutters.

"What?" I ask.

"Ya could have appendicitis."

My eyes widen. I shake my head. "No, I'm...I'm sure it's just the flu or something."

"Ya have all the symptoms, petal. Have ya had your appendix out?"

"No," I say in horror. The thought of anything being removed from my body sounds scary to me. I've never had surgery, nor do I want to.

Aidan gets up and rubs his hand over his face, pacing the room. Another pain shoots through me, and I curl into a ball, trying not to cry, but I begin to whimper from the intensity of it.

"Goddamnit," he says.

"I'm sorry," I cry out.

He comes over to me and pulls me into him. He kisses the top of my head. "Ya don't have to be sorry. I have to take ya to the hospital."

Fear fills me. I blurt out, "What? No. I can't go to the hospital. We've talked about this. Remember? If anything happened to me, ya said I wouldn't be able to go."

Aidan claims, "We have no choice. If I don't take ya, ya could die."

"Die? I'm not dying!" I proclaim.

He picks me up before I can say anything else. He carries me to the car and sets me down in the passenger seat. He buckles my seat belt and puts a blanket over me. He shuts the door, then gets into the driver's side. He turns the engine on, and another pain shoots through me.

I cry out, "Jesus, it hurts. So bad!"

He puts his hand over mine and kisses it, suggesting, "Just try to breathe."

"Do ya even know where the hospital is?" I question.

His expression doesn't give me any confidence.

"Ya don't, do ya?" I panic.

"No. But don't worry, petal. I'll find it."

"How?" I ask.

He puts his hand over my forehead. "Just try to go to sleep. Rest is the only thing ya can do now. Put your seat all the way back."

I do it so I'm in a more comfortable position. Then I close my eyes, holding my stomach, trying to fight nausea.

Soon, sweat coats my skin. It feels like we're on a never-ending journey. I don't know how long we're in the car. Maybe it's an hour, possibly two.

Aidan finally turns off the car, softly murmuring, "Petal."

I open my eyes and look at him, revealing, "I feel so bad." Another pain hits my stomach.

"Aye. I know ya do, lass. Stay still. I'm coming to get ya." He exits the car, opens my door, and sweeps his arms underneath me. He carries me into the emergency room and shouts, "I need a doctor. I think there's something wrong with her appendix."

Everything turns blurry. There are faces of nurses and doctors, and I barely hear what they say. The pain is so intense. I'm constantly crying and gripping my stomach.

When a doctor pushes on it, I almost jump off the bed.

"Don't hurt her," Aidan cries out.

"I'm not trying to," the doctor declares. "Suit up," he orders his staff, then Aidan, "Ya have to leave. We're taking her to surgery."

"What? No," I protest, reaching for Aidan. Then I fret, "I don't want to have surgery. Please don't let them put me under!"

He crouches in front of me and puts his palm over my cheek. "Ya don't have a choice, petal. If ya don't have surgery, you'll die."

"I...I don't want to go. Please don't leave me," I beg, even though I'm scared of dying.

He kisses the top of my head. "You'll be okay. I'll be right here when ya get out."

Yet he can't hide the concern in his expression. A fear I've never seen before appears in his eyes, making me more fearful.

A medical team transfers me to a gurney and rolls me away from Aidan.

I cry out, "Aidan! Don't leave me!"

"I won't, petal! I'm right here."

"Aidan!" I call out the entire way down the hall.

"Ma'am, ya have to calm down," a nurse advises.

Yet I can't. I'm afraid I'll wake up from surgery, Tommy will be at my side, and Aidan will be dead.

The nurse forces a mask over my face, and I soon black out, falling into the darkness.

14

Aidan

$\mathcal{T}$ime moves slowly. Every second Scarlet's in surgery, I hate. I want her safe and healthy, yet I also gave the hospital an alias, claiming I lost our identification cards. They couldn't refuse us, and so far, it appears that no one knows who we really are, but I'm not resting easy.

At any moment, Tommy and his men could catch wind that we are here. We're almost two hours away from the cottage in the mountains that we broke into, and I can't stop debating about what to do.

It might not be safe to return to the cottage. Scarlet was right. Somebody could have found out that we broke in. Plus, I left all of our stuff there, which could give Tommy a heads-up that we're not too far away.

I turn on my phone and search for what's in the town that we're in. There's not much. It's small, like the previous one we stayed in. But that's the thing about small towns. They have locals, and locals talk—especially if someone threatens them the way that Tommy and his men will if they come here.

I finally cave, realizing I need a different plan. I can't do this alone. Not now, with Scarlet in the shape she's in. So I call my brother.

Devin answers, "Did ya come to your senses?"

"I didn't call to talk about that. I have a situation." I grind my molars.

"What's happened?" he questions.

"Scarlet's appendix almost burst. We're at the hospital, and she's in surgery."

The line goes quiet. Devin finally states, "That's a dangerous position to be in."

"Aye, I know. That's why I'm calling. I need ya to find me a new location, and no one's to know, not even Tynan. And I expect ya to keep your word this time. Do ya understand?"

Devin groans. "This isn't anything to mess around with, Aidan. Ya should hand her over to her sister."

"No, and that conversation's over. Can I trust ya to do this favor for me and have my back or not?" I spout.

He grunts then affirms, "Aye, of course, ya can."

"Text me when ya have the new location." I hang up, not wanting to discuss or argue any further about what he thinks I should be doing.

I'm not turning Scarlet over to Alaina.

I pace the hospital floor as time slowly crawls by. The doctor finally appears. He scratches his bald head, informing me, "She's out of surgery and did great."

Relief fills me.

Then the doctor states, "She's going to need to stay for a few days."

The hairs on my arms rise. I shake my head. "Yea, we can't do that. So what's the option to release her sooner?"

He furrows his brows, his eyelids turning to slits. He scolds, "She's just had a major operation. She needs to be monitored. Ya have no choice. She's here for at least two days, possibly three, depending on her recovery."

I cross my arms. There's no way we can do that. But there's also no point arguing with him. He's never going to see it my way. It's better to keep my mouth shut until I know how to get her out of here without causing a stir.

The doctor adds, "She can return to her normal activities within a few weeks, but she needs lots of rest. It might take a while for her to get back to her normal energy level. But we did the surgery laparoscopically, so she'll likely recover quicker."

"Good to know," I say.

The doctor peers up at me and hesitates. Then he continues, "It's really important that she gets her rest and is monitored. Don't try anything stupid."

"Did I say I would?" I ask.

He arches his eyebrows, declaring, "I know your type."

Insulted, I ask, "What type is that?"

"The type that's going to do whatever ya want, and ya could put her life in danger, so don't do it," he warns.

I stay quiet, clenching my jaw, not tearing my gaze off his.

He adds, "They're trying to wake her up now."

"When can I see her?" I ask.

"After the nurse finishes, you'll be able to go in. Shouldn't be too much longer." He spins and walks away.

My anxiety starts to increase again. I walk over to her room and stare through the window at the nurse trying to wake her up.

I ignore the doctor's orders, bust through the door, and pull a chair up to the other side of the bed.

The nurse's eyes widen. She declares, "Ya can't be in here while I'm doing this."

"I promised her I'd be here when she wakes up. She'll freak out if I'm not," I insist.

"Do I need to call security?" the nurse threatens.

I shoot her my most intimidating look, asking, "Do ya really want to do that? Do ya think it's smart?"

She lifts her chin, glaring at me.

I put my palm on Scarlet's cheek and wrap my fingers over her hand, softly stating, "Petal, it's time to wake up. Come on, lass."

She stirs. Her lips slightly part.

I keep stroking her cheek, pushing, "Come on. Wake up."

She blinks.

I praise, "That's a good lass. Ya can do it."

She finally opens her eyes and then her face turns green. She squeezes them shut, moaning.

The nurse shoots something into her IV, ordering, "Easy there."

"What did ya give her?" I ask.

"Anti-nausea medicine."

Scarlet's face returns to a normal color. She takes a deep breath. She closes her eyes again.

I add, "You're going to be okay, petal. Ya did well." I pick up her hand and kiss it.

She opens her eyes again, mumbling, "My stomach hurts," and tries to sit up.

"Whoa," the nurse says, holding her down to the bed. "No fast movements. Ya don't want to rip your stitches."

"It hurts," Scarlet admits.

The nurse nods. "Yea, you'll be sore for a while, but every day you'll improve. If ya need anything, just push that button."

She gives me another disapproving look, leaves the room, and shuts the door.

Scarlet turns to me, swallowing hard. "We can't be here, can we, Aidan?"

"Ya don't need to worry about anything. We're fine."

"What if..." She swallows hard, continuing, "What if they know we're here?"

"They don't. Now let me worry about things. Just close your eyes and rest some more."

"But, Aidan—"

I put my finger over her lips, ordering, "Shh, close your eyes, petal."

She's still worried, but she finally drifts off.

A text comes in from Devin with a new location. A bit of relief fills me that one problem is solved. Then I pace the room again, knowing our time is running out. The longer we stay here, the more we put ourselves at risk.

But I'm also worried about Scarlet. I know the doctor's not totally wrong. It is a risk for me to move her. Yet we don't have any other options.

I research everything I can on appendicitis recovery. Then I send my brother another text.

> Me: Bring our doctor to the new location and whatever meds she'll need. Hurry.

It takes a moment before I get a reply.

> Devin: Three hours.

I glance at my watch. Three hours pass, but it's not until close to midnight when I finally decide it's quiet enough in the hospital and safe enough to move her without causing any commotion.

I wake her up, kissing her forehead. Her green eyes flutter open, glowing in the dark. She asks, "Is everything okay?"

"Shh, it's fine, petal. But it's time to leave."

"Why, what's happened?" she says worriedly.

I shake my head adamantly. "Nothing's happened. But we need to be cautious."

She tries to move, but I hold her down. "Whoa, lass, ya heard the nurse. No sudden movements."

"But I have to get up if we're going to go."

"No, ya don't. I'll carry ya. Now listen, I'm going to put the blanket over ya. Ya stay quiet in my arms. Okay?"

She gives me a look.

I don't know how to take it. But I kiss her forehead again, then glance one more time out the door. The hallway's clear. I scoop Scarlet up in my arms, then wrap the blanket around her.

She winces slightly.

"I'm sorry," I murmur.

She curls into me, and I tug the blanket to cover her head. Then I go to the doorway and wait until the nurse turns the corner.

I quietly step out, carry her down the hall, and open the staircase exit door. I carefully move down the five flights of stairs, and when I reach the exit, I crack open the door, glancing around my surroundings. When one of the security guards turns and walks the other way, I leave the staircase and exit the first door to the outside.

I step into the back lot. The area is barely lit, and I stay in the shadows as I carry her around the building until I get to our vehicle.

I place her into the car, put the seat back, and get her settled.

She reaches for my cheeks.

I kiss her on the lips, reassuring her, "Everything's fine."

She wrinkles her forehead. "Where are we going? Back to the same place?"

I shake my head. "No, a new place."

"Where?" she asks.

"A place my brother secured for us, and our family doctor from Belfast will be with him too. Don't worry, I just need ya to rest on the way there, okay?"

She slowly nods her head.

"That's a good lass," I praise. I kiss her again, then secure her seat belt across her.

She winces, and I decide it's better to leave it off, as much as I don't want to.

I shut the door, go to the driver's side, and turn on the engine. I pull up directions in my phone to the place that Devin secured.

It's another hour and a half out of town, and the roads aren't well lit. There's barely any traffic, but I stay vigilant, ensuring nobody's following us.

It's the most paranoid I've been in a while. Word might get out about us being at the hospital. I hope it doesn't. I don't need Tommy anywhere up here.

I curse myself for leaving everything in the cottage. I call Devin.

He answers, "Where are ya?"

I reply, "We're just leaving. I left our stuff at the last cottage. I need ya to go get it so we don't leave a trail."

"Where's the cottage at?" he asks.

"I'll send ya the coordinates. We broke in, so you'll have to look for a place with fresh tracks in the snow and broken glass."

He groans. "Ya got to be kidding me."

"No, I'm not," I reply and hang up.

I pull over to the side of the road, shoot him the location, then return to driving.

I continuously watch my rearview mirror to ensure that it's us and only us going to the new place. A few times, some cars pull in behind me. It puts me in a predicament with Scarlet in the state she's in and no seat belt secured around her.

I don't want to speed up, so I slow down both times, waiting for them to pass, and eventually, they do. By the time I get to the new cottage, Scarlet's asleep. She's been out for a long time, and I don't wake her. I slide my arms under her and carry her into the house.

She stirs.

"Hey, we're here, petal. Everything's okay," I assure her, kissing her on the forehead.

The doctor opens the door, and I nod at him as I step into the new place. He shuts and locks the door and then points toward the bedroom.

I carry Scarlet inside and put her on the bed. I sit next to her and push her locks behind her ear. "This is Dr. Murphy. He's been in our family for years. He'll take good care of ya."

She grabs my shirt. "Aidan, don't leave me."

"I'm not leaving ya, lass," I reassure. "I'm just going to step to the side, okay?"

She grips me tighter, begging, "Just stay here."

"It's okay. He won't hurt ya," I assert, stroking her cheek.

"I can come on this side of the bed," the doctor offers.

Scarlet turns her face toward him, and fear overtakes her expression.

I repeat, "Ya don't need to be scared, lass."

She looks at me, takes a deep breath, and winces.

"Careful there. No sudden movements. Ya got a lot of stitches there. Do ya mind if I look?" Dr. Murphy asks.

More anxiety riddles her face. She shakes her head. "No, I'm okay. I don't need any help or anything. I just need to rest."

"Scarlet, ya got to let the doctor look at ya. I'm right here. Everything's fine."

She squeezes her eyes shut.

"I'm going to lift your gown now," the doctor states.

She squeezes my hand tighter.

He lifts it and pulls the dressings off her wound. "They did a good job. Do ya want to see your scar?"

She swallows hard, slowly opens her eyes, and looks down at her stomach. "Will it disappear?"

He answers, "Eh, there will probably be a little one. It'll start to fade though."

She bites her lip.

He says, "Everything looks fine. I'm going to clean it to keep it sanitized and then put another dressing over it, okay, lass?"

She releases an anxiety-filled breath, stating, "Okay."

I stay close to her, stroking her forehead.

He covers it, then pulls some pills out of his bag. "This is for pain. It'll also help ya sleep. I'll leave the directions with Aidan, but I think right now everything is fine. I'll stay here for a few days during your recovery, if you're okay with that?" He glances at me.

"Aye. Please," I reply, wanting to have medical attention for Scarlet should she need it.

He rises and hands me the pill bottle. "Let me get a glass of water. She should take one right now." He leaves the room.

"See, he's nice. Ya don't have to worry about anything."

"He won't tell anyone we're here?" she frets.

"No, like I said, he's been our family doctor in Belfast forever," I insist.

She bites her lip, scrunching her face.

Dr. Murphy returns to the room with a glass of water and hands it to me.

I hold the glass to her lips, and she drinks the water.

Then I hold the pill to her mouth. "Here, lass."

She allows me to put it in and she swallows it.

The doctor says, "I'll be in the other room if ya need me." He leaves.

I lie beside Scarlet, putting my arm around her shoulders, and she rests her head on my chest.

It doesn't take long before she's asleep again.

I study her sleeping form, glad we're out of the hospital and that the doctor is here, but I can't relax. Every part of my instincts says that Tommy's coming and we can't stay here long.

Yet I don't know where we'll go once we have to move again. I'm running out of hiding places, and Ireland has never felt smaller.

15

Scarlet
Four Days Later

*A*idan dotes on me, barely letting me move about except to go to the loo. He even refuses to let me go to the main area to eat at the table. He brings everything to the bedroom.

My stomach still hurts when I try to sit or walk around, but every day I feel better. Plus, Aidan's kept me on a strict schedule with my pain medication, so that's helped numb things a bit.

He's always close by, even though I can tell he's got a bit of cabin fever. Yesterday, I could see the crazed look in his eyes. He kept fidgeting as if something was on his mind, but he wouldn't tell me.

I finally ordered, "Aidan, get a box of matches and go outside."

He gave me a shocked look.

I added, "You're making me nervous. Whatever is going on that ya refuse to let me in on is bothering ya. So go do what ya need to do."

He continued to study me.

"Why aren't ya moving?" I questioned.

He asked, "Why don't ya have a problem with it?"

"With your obsession with fire?"

He nodded. "Aye."

I walked over to the desk, tugged the chair to the window, and sat. I replied, "I don't know. And I won't claim to understand it, but I can tell ya need it. So go. I'll watch ya from here."

He took a deep breath, then slowly exhaled before leaning down, pecking me on the lips, and said, "I'll be right back, but ya shouldn't have scooted that chair over here."

I chirped, "I'm not an invalid. Now go. I'll be here, so no need to rush."

He softly chuckled and spent the next hour outside. There wasn't a fire pit in front of the window, but he created a makeshift one on the ground several feet from my viewpoint. Occasionally, he'd look up, as if needing to know I was still there, watching him. Even from that distance, his eyes blazed with chaos. When he returned, his antsy-ness wasn't fully gone, but a lot of it had disappeared.

I glance out the window now, staring at the spot where he burned one match after another. The sun beams across the yard and through the glass. I rise and go to the window, closing my eyes and enjoying the warm brightness. It's something I'll never stop appreciating after what Tommy put me through.

After a few minutes, I turn and freeze. Aidan's duffle bag is on the desk.

How did that get here?

I furrow my brow, trying to recall if it's been in the room before, but I'm sure it hasn't. It was chaotic when we left the mountain cottage, yet I thought we had left everything there.

A door slams, and muffled voices fill the air. I step out of the room and come to a halt.

Devin states, "Those coordinates ya gave me sucked."

Aidan retorts, "Sorry ya had to use your brain."

Devin grunts. "Next time ya send me on a mission like that, give me more information."

"There wasn't exactly an address," Aidan offers.

Devin crosses his arms and narrows his eyes, advising, "I don't think ya should stay here long. It's not safe."

"Scarlet's still recovering," Aidan declares.

Devin scowls. "As I said, it's not safe. Tommy and his men are moving back north. At some point, they're going to find ya. Ya need to return to Belfast."

"We're not going to Belfast. Not yet," Aidan says with more determination.

Dr. Murphy clears his throat, stating, "Scarlet's recovering well. A few more days here would be ideal before ya move her."

"But she can go?" Devin asks.

"Aye. Still, travel isn't ideal."

"We're not moving until she's had more time to recover," Aidan insists.

My insides quiver. While the thought of a long car ride isn't appealing, and I'd much rather stay in the warm cottage, I'm not stupid. I know Devin has a point. And nothing's changed; Tommy is hunting us. So I interrupt, "If Tommy's coming toward us, then we need to go, Aidan."

The three men turn.

He declares, "Ya don't need to worry about this."

I cross my arms. "Stop saying that."

"Ya heard Dr. Murphy. It's not ideal," Aidan asserts.

I lift my chin. "A few more days and Tommy will be here. We won't be alive if he and his men find us."

Aidan grunts. "I'll kill that bastard."

"What? With dozens of his men around him? Ya underestimate him, Aidan. I know what he's capable of, and neither of us needs to experience it."

"I know what *I'm* capable of, petal."

"It's not about your skills. We have to go," I argue.

"We're not going."

Devin chimes in, "Take her to Alaina and Brody's. With the change in circumstances, ya know it's the best option."

Aidan's face darkens. "We're not going there."

"Why not? Why are ya refusing?" Devin asks.

Aidan's voice turns more determined. "It's not an option. Drop it."

Devin angrily fires back, "Then what are ya going to do? He's increased the number of his men. How do I get it through your thick skull?"

Dr. Murphy pipes in, "Devin's, right. If he's increased the number of men, ya don't have much of a choice."

Aidan scowls at him, then declares, "No offense, but this isn't your concern. Your job is to be the doctor."

Dr. Murphy's jaw clenches. He stays quiet.

"All of them are right," I declare.

Aidan turns toward me again, scowling in disapproval.

I lift my chin, ordering, "I want to talk to ya. Alone."

He stays planted.

"Now, Aidan," I insist and point inside the bedroom.

Tension fills the air. Nobody says anything, and the crackling fire is the only sound.

"Aidan," I plead, not taking my eyes off his.

He finally caves and obeys, coming into the bedroom.

I shut the door. "Ya need to take me to my sister's, and then ya need to finish Tommy off."

"You're not going there," he claims.

"Why? Why won't ya let me go? What's so bad about Alaina and Brody's that ya won't listen to everyone else who only have your best interests at heart?"

"It's not that it's bad."

"Then what's the issue?" I ask.

"I'm not getting them involved in this."

"What do ya mean you're not getting them involved? They're both our families. They already are part of this, so why are ya fighting me and everyone else about this?"

He keeps his mouth shut and looks above my head.

"Don't ya dare ignore me," I warn.

He slowly looks down, meeting my gaze. "I'm not ready to take ya to Alaina."

"Why?"

"I'm not ready to have her decide what's to happen here. I know what I've set out to do, and until I finish it—"

"Until ya finish it? What if ya don't have a chance to finish it? Because if ya don't take me there, they will find us. He has too many men. He won't stop until he gets what he wants. And what he wants is both of us dead."

"He's not killing us."

I lose control of my voice, shrieking, "What's scarier is he might not even kill me!"

Aidan's eyes turn harder. "Do ya think I won't protect ya? I'd die protecting ya."

I blink hard. "Aidan, this isn't about that, and ya know it."

"What's it about, then?"

"I don't want to be back in Tommy's grasp!"

"Ya aren't! Ya never will be again!"

"Stop being pigheaded," I cry out.

He crosses his arms. I step closer and reach up, but then wince from the dull throb in my gut.

He spins me and lowers his voice. "Sit down. Ya shouldn't be standing up."

I obey because it is hard to stand up. And then I can't help it. A tear escapes. I swipe at my face.

He sighs and sits next to me, putting his arm around me. "I'm doing what's best for ya. Ya have to trust me."

"Then tell me why ya won't take me to Alaina. I haven't seen my sister..." I stop and look down, but I can't help the tears that fall. I sniffle and force myself to meet his gaze. "I haven't seen her in years, not since I tried to hide out with her in London. I thought I would never see her again. I want to see her. Why can't ya take me there? I could see her, and we'd be safe. We wouldn't be running anymore. Then ya can go kill Tommy."

"It won't be enough."

"Why can't it be? He'll be dead. There's nothing else that's more important than him being dead."

"He's got to pay."

"You're being stubborn," I state.

"No. There are bigger things at play."

"Like what?"

"Ya don't need to worry about this, petal."

"Stop telling me not to worry about things."

Aidan snaps his mouth shut, then grinds his molars.

"You're really going to sit here and stay silent?"

Devin opens the door. "Ya got to get out of here. Now."

My stomach flips. "Why? What's wrong?"

"They're thirty minutes away. We're leaving now. All of ya, go."

"You're joking," Aidan says.

"No, I'm not." Devin scowls, grabs the duffle bag off the dresser, and shoots Aidan another nasty look before leaving the room.

"Fuck," Aidan mutters, then rises and grabs my boots. He holds one next to my foot. "Scarlet, let me help ya."

"Aidan, we have to go to Brody and Alaina's. There's no other place," I restate.

He slides my boots on my feet, staying quiet, then picks me up.

"What are ya doing? I can walk."

"I know, but ya can't walk fast. Let's go." He takes me to the car and sets me in the passenger seat.

Devin and Dr. Murphy are in the other vehicle, waiting.

Aidan pulls out on the road, and Devin follows. The phone rings, and Aidan puts it on speaker.

Devin orders, "Ya have to go to Alaina and Brody's. There's no other choice."

Aidan stays quiet.

I grab his hand.

He glances at me.

Devin firmly asserts, "There are no other options, bro. Ya got to go."

Aidan shuts his eyes briefly, shaking his head and clenching his jaw.

I quietly say. "Aidan. He's right. Please."

His expression hardens. He states, "Fine. We'll go to Alaina and Brody's. Call him and tell him we need escorts as soon as possible. And give him our coordinates."

"Done," Devin says and hangs up.

Aidan tosses his phone into the cupholder.

I squeeze his hand. "Thank ya."

He looks at me. "Everything's going to change now."

A new fear hits me. "What do ya mean?"

He repeats, "Everything will change."

"Meaning what?"

He gives me an upset look.

I fret, "Why don't ya spit it out? What is going to change?"

He turns down a road and accelerates. "Us."

My stomach quivers. "Ya aren't going to want me anymore?"

He answers, "No. Did I say that?"

I demand, "Ya better start talking, then. I'm not a mind reader."

He hesitates.

"Aidan!"

He blurts out, "You'll see, petal. Alaina will take over. Brody too."

"What does that have to do with us?"

"Everything."

I still don't understand what he's getting at, and fear pummels me.

He turns down a road and adds, "It's no longer just the two of us."

His statement only makes my chest tighten. The air in my lungs turns stale. I stammer, "What do ya... What are ya trying to tell me, Aidan? You're talking in cryptic sentences right now."

He scrubs a hand over his face and grips the steering wheel so tight his knuckles turn white. He announces, "I've disobeyed orders. There will be consequences for me when I return."

The blood drains from my face. "Is your brother going to torture ya?"

He grunts, muttering, "No, but your sister might."

"Brody won't allow that!" I insist, even though I've never met him.

Aidan shakes his head. "Ya still don't understand."

"Then fill me in!"

He takes a sharp right turn and accelerates. He glances at me and says, "When I said your sister rules my clan with my brother, I meant it."

I've tried to wrap my head around this since Aidan first told me, but it's mind-boggling. I declare, "Your brother can override whatever she wants. He won't allow her to do anything to ya. You're a man."

Aidan's nostrils flare. "It doesn't work that way. My clan is way more progressive than the O'Learys. We value women, and no one values your sister more than my brother. When I tell ya that he gave her power to rule beside him, I'm not exaggerating. She has as much authority as he does. And she's not going to forgive and forget I didn't bring ya straight to her."

"He's your brother. He won't allow her to torture ya!"

Aidan grunts, insisting, "She isn't going to torture me, petal. But there will be consequences, and your sister isn't one to overlook things."

More panic hits me. "Are ya saying I won't be with ya anymore?"

He sighs. "I don't know what's going to happen, lass."

I sit back in my seat, staring out the window, with new tears falling. I turn back to him. "Are ya telling me this is it for us?"

He glances at me. "I don't know what I'm saying."

"I feel like ya do, but ya just don't want to say it," I angrily spout, feeling like he's somehow rejecting me. I knew Tommy would pull us apart should he find us, but I didn't think we had to worry about our siblings. And I still don't understand how my sister can have the power Aidan insists she does.

He sighs and states, "Forget I said anything."

"No, I'm not going to forget ya said anything. Ya obviously meant something by it," I accuse, letting my fear turn to anger.

He accelerates faster, and the phone rings again. He groans and mutters, "And so it begins." He hits the answer button.

A familiar voice I never thought I'd hear again seethes, "Aidan, where is my sister?"

My heart squeezes. I blurt out, "Alaina?"

"Scarlet? Scarlet, are ya okay?"

"Yea, I'm...I'm fine. We're...we're coming to ya. Tommy and his men, they're..."

"They're forty minutes away. We have a tracker on ya now."

"How do ya have a tracker on us?" Aidan questions.

Alaina snarls, "I ordered Devin to put it on your car."

Aidan's eyes turn to slits. "My own fucking brother betrayed me?"

Alaina scolds, "Someone had to make sure that ya did the right thing and brought my sister to me before ya get her killed."

"So he ratted me out?" Aidan spouts.

"No, I tracked him up in the mountains doing your dirty work. Both of ya are in trouble," she threatens.

"Is it even true? Are Tommy and his men even close?" Aidan questions.

"Of course they are. They're always close. Ya should know that, but ya underestimate him and his resources. And you're being reckless with my sister," she accuses.

My stomach flips. Alaina's mad. If she has the power that Aidan claims, who knows what his consequences will be when we get there. So I blurt out, "Aidan's taken excellent care of me. He rescued me from Tommy."

"He better have taken excellent care of ya," Alaina warns.

"Alaina—"

"We'll talk when ya get here. You're to come straight here, understood?" she interjects.

Aidan confirms, "Aye. We're on our way. Send the escorts as soon as possible. If they're this close, we can't take any chances."

"Which is exactly why ya shouldn't be taking any chances with my sister, but that's all you've been doing, isn't it?" Alaina fires at him.

I try again, "Alaina, he hasn't. Please. Ya don't know—"

"Ya don't have to protect him," she seethes.

I grab Aidan's hand, but he pulls it away and puts it on the steering wheel. He clenches his jaw.

"I'm not," I tell my sister.

Her voice softens. "Scarlet, are ya okay?"

"Yea, I'm fine. Aidan's taken excellent care of me," I reiterate.

"Ya had an operation?" she asks.

"Yea, but I'm recovering really well. Honestly, I've been in great hands," I tell her and put my hand on his thigh. He doesn't look at me, keeping his eyes on the road.

She snaps, "Aidan, you'll bring my sister right to us. No more disobedience."

I cringe. When she uses that word, it's never good.

Aidan picks up the phone. He replies, "Right now, Alaina, you're not in charge. I am. Once we get back, ya can have your little power trip. For now, keep it to yourself and focus on sending out the escorts." He hangs up and tosses his phone in the cupholder.

"Ya shouldn't have done that! She'll be angrier!" I scold.

He glances at me, snarling, "Do ya think it matters at this point?"

"I-I...I don't know! But let's not infuriate her more!"

He sarcastically chuckles. "Your sister has me on her chopping block. I'm already in the shitter."

My pulse continues skyrocketing. "Maybe it does matter!"

He shakes his head. "No. It doesn't."

Several minutes pass, with tension building between us, and neither of us says anything. He turns onto a two-lane road and passes several cars.

The phone rings again.

Aidan glances at it and answers, "Ya fucking rat."

"I had no choice," Devin claims.

"Ya always have a choice."

"No, ya don't."

A black car tries to pass us, then the driver looks at Aidan and slows.

Aidan grumbles, "That our escort?"

"One of them," Devin answers.

"We'll finish this conversation in Belfast, ya rat," Aidan states, then hangs up.

Silence fills the air once again. I put my hand on his, but he pulls it away again. Blood pounds between my ears. I quietly ask, "Do ya no longer want me?"

"Don't say stupid things."

"Then why won't ya let me touch ya?"

He takes a moment and swallows hard. He finally glances at me, his eyes full of the crazed expression I've only seen a few times, and I'm suddenly scared. He declares, "Ya don't get it, petal."

"I'm trying to," I claim.

He glances back at the road.

"Aidan, tell me nothing is going to change between us," I order, my voice shaking.

"I can't."

Hurt fills me. I manage to get out, "Because ya don't want me anymore."

His voice turns firm. He asserts, "That's not true. But ya don't know what this will do to us."

I blink hard, insisting, "Nothing has to change between us."

He scoffs. "That's where you're wrong, lass. Everything's about to change."

16

Aidan

*S*carlet's confused, but I'm unsure how to explain to her that nothing will ever be the same between us. Once Alaina and Brody are in the picture, I'll be powerless under their rule, and so will Scarlet.

I pass the guards and pull up to Brody and Alaina's house. As soon as I open the car door, they appear on the steps. She runs down and yanks open Scarlet's door before I can get to it. She cries out, "I thought I'd never see ya again."

Scarlet gets teary and swings her legs out of the vehicle.

I bark, "Careful, you're still recovering."

She freezes.

Alaina turns her head and fumes, "I'll take over from here, Aidan."

"Like hell, ya will," I declare, even though she's the one who gets to call the shots now.

"Don't piss me off more than I already am," she seethes.

Scarlet glances between Alaina and me with worry on her face. She tries, "Don't be mad at Aidan."

Surprise fills Alaina's expression. She states, "He kept ya from me."

"He did what he thought was best," Scarlet refutes.

"Ya don't need to stick up for me, petal," I declare.

Alaina's glare shoots darts at me, and she snarls, "What did ya call my sister?"

I cross my arms and lift my chin, answering, "Petal. Not that it's your business."

Her emeralds turn to hot fire. She steps in front of me, threatening, "Don't ya dare—"

"I'm going inside. Not interested in this scuffle," Scarlet announces.

Alaina steps between my petal and me. "Let me help ya up out of the car."

Scarlet shakes her head. "I'm fine."

"Ya just had surgery," Alaina says, reaching in to help Scarlet out of the vehicle.

I step on the other side of her and pick her up, tearing her out of Alaina's grasp.

She cries out, "Aidan, what are ya doing? Let go of my sister!"

I shoot her a dirty look, warning, "Don't come between your sister and me."

Another shocked look fills her face, then she looks at Scarlet in question.

Scarlet's cheeks heat.

Alaina's eyes widen further. She shakes her head, declaring, "Tell me that ya two aren't—"

I brush past her, carrying Scarlet into the house.

She protests, "Aidan, I'm fine. I can walk."

"Steps aren't good for ya. They could rip your stitches," I point out.

She groans. "They won't. I'm fine."

I hold her tighter to me, my heart thumping faster. I murmur in her ear, "I don't want things to change between us."

She blinks hard, whispering, "Then don't let them."

"Put her down. Now," Alaina orders.

I freeze, clenching my jaw, staring in my petal's green orbs.

Alaina growls, "I said now."

"Ya better start listening to my wife," Brody demands.

I grunt, turning toward my brother. "Ya should stay out of this too." I slowly put Scarlet on her feet, holding on to her.

Disapproval fills his expression. He announces, "There are consequences to be paid."

"Tell me something I don't know," I mutter.

Scarlet blurts out, "Aidan rescued me. He took care of me. Be nice to him. He doesn't need any consequences!"

Alaina steps forward and puts her arm around Scarlet. In a concerned tone, she states, "You're just confused right now. I think they call it Stockholm syndrome. In a few days—"

"I don't have Stockholm syndrome!" Scarlet seethes.

Alaina points at me and snarls, "Ya took advantage of my sister, and now she's confused."

"He did no such thing!"

"Ya don't have to try to protect me, petal. Your sister's going to think what she wants," I state.

Alaina snaps, "Do not call her that!"

I scoff. "Jesus. Never pinned ya as a busybody."

"Don't disrespect my wife," Brody barks at me.

I scowl at him. "Don't get involved in this."

"Don't get involved in this?" He steps closer, fuming, "Ya defied our orders. Ya kept Scarlet away from Alaina."

I eliminate the gap between us, lower my voice, and remind him, "The O'Learys are not supposed to be together. Your wife is supposed to show no mercy toward any O'Leary. Or did ya forget about the vow that she took?"

Scarlet's eyes widen. "What are ya talking about?"

"Nothing. Don't listen to him," Alaina interjects.

I spin on her. "So the vow ya made to the O'Connors isn't real?"

She glares at me with her most intimidating expression, but I don't miss the hint of fear in them.

Brody steps in front of me, jabbing my chest. "Don't talk to her that way. Show some respect!"

"So it's not real?" I repeat.

"I'm warning ya," Brody threatens.

I continue, "Ya want to get mad at me for keeping Scarlet safe and both of ya out of trouble. And I'm the one in the hot seat. Jesus. Have both of ya listened to yourselves lately?"

"Safe? She had her appendix out!" Alaina shrieks, which is the first time I've ever heard her voice rise so high.

"That wasn't Aidan's fault," Scarlet insists.

"Like hell it wasn't," Alaina proclaims.

I sarcastically laugh. "Really? It's my fault that her appendix almost burst?"

Brody shakes his head. "Alaina, take your sister upstairs. Show her where she can stay. Aidan, don't ya dare move."

"I'm not leaving Aidan," Scarlet states.

"He's got work to do," Alaina snarls.

"Nonnegotiable work," Brody adds.

Fear fills Scarlet's expression.

I put my hand on her cheek, ordering, "Go with your sister."

"What? No. Aidan, come with me," she demands.

"He's not going anywhere with ya," Alaina announces.

Scarlet turns her head toward Alaina, seething, "Don't—"

I put my finger over her lips, forcing a smile and commanding, "Go with your sister. Ya have a lot to catch up on."

Tears fill her eyes. "When will I see ya again?"

I fight the emotions building in my chest, answering, "As soon as possible."

"That's not an answer, Aidan," she sniffles.

"Everything is okay," I reassure her.

Alaina steps over and wraps her arm around her. "Come on, Scarlet. Let me show ya where your room is, and ya can rest."

"You're not being fair," Scarlet argues.

Alaina huffs. "Ya can tell me all about how I'm not being fair once we get to your room. Come on." She moves Scarlet forward.

She turns her head. "Aidan—"

"Go on, petal," I order and wait until she gets to the lift. The doors open, and they step inside. We lock eyes until the metal cuts off my view of her. I turn back to my brother.

Brody shakes head. "What the fuck were ya thinking?"

"Really? You're going to lecture me? After all the shit ya did with Alaina, you're lecturing me for saving her sister?"

"Don't even try to act like the hero."

"I'm not trying to act like anything."

"We told ya to come back. We gave ya orders."

"Aye. And ya can't always follow orders when you're doing what needs to be done, now, can ya?"

Brody crosses his arms, but instead of his face turning angry, an eerie calm passes over it.

I've not seen my brother control himself like this before. I'm not used to it. It makes me uncomfortable.

Devin walks in, and Brody snaps his head toward him, accusing, "About fucking time ya got here."

Devin holds his hands in the air. "I was following him just like ya told me to."

"Just like I told ya to?" Brody repeats, shooting him a nasty look.

"Why are ya pissed at him? He's a rat, after all," I state, scowling at Devin.

He shakes his head. "You're both impossible."

"Well, you're both on cleanup duty," Brody announces.

Fuck.

I knew it was going to be bad. Cleanup duty's the worst. It means I'll be at the warehouse all night, possibly even for several days, and I won't get to see Scarlet.

As soon as I stepped foot in here, I knew they'd keep me away from her as a punishment, and this is only the start. Alaina isn't going to let me anywhere near her anytime soon.

Devin argues, "Why am I on cleanup duty? I didn't do anything wrong."

Brody scowls. "Ya knew where he was, and ya helped him. Ya didn't tell me. How many times did I ask ya if ya knew where he was?"

Devin clenches his jaw, lifting his chin, staring our brother down.

Brody warns, "Both of ya need to shut up and get to the warehouse. Until further notice, you're on probation."

"I can't be on cleanup duty. Tommy's still out there, and I need to end things with him," I declare.

Brody shakes his head, announcing, "I'll handle Tommy."

I seethe, "He's on my list."

"I don't give a shit. Ya lost your privilege to take him out when ya disobeyed Alaina's and my orders."

"He hurt my woman. He's on my list. I will take care of him," I insist.

"Your woman?" Brody murmurs with disapproval.

"Aye. Ya got a problem with that?" I hurl, clenching my fists at my side.

"Ya kidnapped her, and now she's your woman?"

"I rescued her," I state.

"Well, we'll see how she feels about ya once she's free of ya and doesn't have to be under your close watch. I bet she'll feel different when she's not subjected to ya in close quarters, doing God knows what, while I was ordering ya to get your ass back here."

I cross my arms. I step closer to my brother, warning, "Don't ya dare get involved between Scarlet and me."

"Too late. Now go get your ass to the warehouse."

I almost argue further but stop. There's no point right now. I just need to do what I'm supposed to and take my punishment.

"I suggest ya get moving!" Brody warns.

I leave with Devin and get into the car. I snarl at him, "You're such a fucking rat. I still can't believe it. I never in a million years thought that you'd be one."

He groans. "What was I supposed to do?"

"Not be a rat," I reply and gun the engine.

He retorts, "Ya know what? If it weren't for me, Tommy would've caught ya. So stop being a dick. And thanks for getting me involved in your fucking punishment."

"Whatever. Fucking rat," I mutter.

"Oh, go fuck yourself!" He slouches down, pulls his hat over his eyes, and adjusts the seat so it's flat.

"Really? You're going to pretend to go to sleep?"

"Nope. I'm drowning out the sound of your stupid fucking voice. Now, shut the fuck up," he demands.

I mutter, "Rat," and accelerate the vehicle, driving faster than the speed limit the entire way to the warehouse. I pull into the garage, get out of the car, and Devin and I cross the main room.

The stench of death seeps out of it. Devin buries his nose into his arm, declaring, "Fuck's sake."

I open the door and groan. There are at least a dozen dead men, all with different causes of death. Some were shot, others stabbed, and a few were burned.

The charred corpses make me want to strike a match so badly, I start itching my thigh.

Devin taunts, "Didn't bring any matches?"

"Jesus. Shut the fuck up," I warn again, then walk over to one of the burned ones, grab his arm, and tug him toward a bigger area.

"Figured you'd take that one," Devin mutters and chooses a guy with a bullet hole in his head.

The door opens, and Tynan strolls inside.

I ask, "Why are ya here?"

He scowls. "Thanks to your stunt, Alaina thought it was best to remind me who's in charge and not get any ideas about loyalty and where it should lie."

"Loyalty, eh?" Devin quips.

Tynan fumes, "Aye. She wants to make sure I remember my first loyalty is to her and Brody and not either of ya." He gives us another nasty look.

"Fucking bitch," I mutter and motion to the chair, ordering, "Just sit down and watch, then. Ya shouldn't have to deal with this shit because of what me and your rat brother did."

"I'm not a fucking rat," Devin barks.

"Really? Seems to me like ya are," I accuse.

Tynan's eyes turn to slits. "You've been gone a long time, brother. Things are different."

My gut drops, and my chest tightens. "What are ya talking about?"

He points to the ceiling in the corner. "Alaina and Brody made some big changes since they got to town. One of them is that all of our moves are watched."

"Control freaks," I snarl.

Tynan shakes his head, relaying, "They're also listening, so I'd be careful what ya say, because you're going to get in more trouble."

I look up at the camera, and more anger fills me. I hurl, "You've got to be kidding me. We're not even allowed to dispose of bodies without being recorded?" I turn back to my brothers, acknowledging, "There's no way Dad would ever approve of this. This is reckless. All it has to do is get into the wrong hands, and we'll all get locked up."

Tynan shakes his head. "Nah. Alaina has Brody erase it daily unless there's a reason she needs it to prove a point. She covers her tracks. Ya know how smart she is."

My gut drops. I do know how intelligent she is, but I still glance up at the camera and state, "I don't know if I'd call her smart. More like a pain in my ass." I kick the corpse in front of me. Ashes fly in the air.

"Don't have a fucking tantrum," Devin states.

"Shut up, rat," I bark, then put my middle finger toward the camera.

"Don't make it worse for all of us," Tynan mutters.

Pissed, I shake my head but turn back toward the bodies. I point to the pile and order, "Go pick your guy. Let's get this over with."

I refocus on my corpse, determined to quickly finish so I can return to Scarlet, but every part of me knows one thing: Alaina's not going to forgive and forget.

This is only the start of my punishment, and there's no way she'll make it easy for me to see, much less touch, her sister.

The truth only makes me more determined to figure out how to defy Alaina further. Nothing is going to stop me from being with Scarlet.

Nothing.

Not Alaina, nor Brody, and definitely not Tommy.

And no matter what my brother says, Tommy's on my list. I'll be damned if he takes him out instead of me being the one to do it.

But I'm going to have to figure out how to get back into his good graces, and that includes Alaina's too.

Yet nothing has ever felt more impossible.

17

Scarlet

"This is your bathroom," Alaina states, opening another door. I step inside the large interior, glancing around. It's the most luxurious thing I've seen since I was in my father's house. Lit candles create a soft glow against the teak wood. Roses float in an oversized jacuzzi tub. White, fluffy towels are draped over heated racks.

A bad feeling moves through me. I swallow the lump forming in my throat.

Alaina frets, "What's wrong? Ya don't like it?"

I pin my gaze on hers, asking, "Did ya really kill him?"

Confusion lights up her features for a moment. Then her face pales. "Ya don't know what was going on. There wasn't a choice. Tommy kidnapped me and then Da arrived to kill me."

A shiver runs down my spine. I state, "I'm not mad at ya."

"You're not?"

I shake my head. "No. After what he did to me, making me marry Tommy, I'm just sad ya didn't slice him to pieces sooner."

A sense of understanding mixed with guilt crosses her face. It's something maybe only I'd understand. At the end of the day, he was our da. No matter how awful, we can't escape the lifelong brainwashing to love, honor, and respect him. So I step forward and pull her into me, admitting, "I'm grateful ya killed him first."

She hugs me and then retreats, questioning, "Do ya want to talk about it?"

I consider it for a moment. Then I shake my head, replying, "No, not right now."

She hesitates, then adds, "Whenever you're ready to know the details, I'll fill ya in."

I blink hard, claiming, "I don't need to know the details."

"Ya might change your mind."

"I don't think so."

Silence fills the air. I glance around again, unsure why I still feel uncomfortable when I know it's safe here and doesn't harbor any of the dangers my father's house would.

Alaina states, "Ya should take a bath and relax."

"I can't because of my stitches," I reveal.

"Oh. Sorry. I should have known that," she says.

"It's okay. I'd love to take a shower though," I admit.

"Sure. I filled the dresser and closet with clothes for ya. I think I picked stuff you'll like, but we can switch it out if ya want."

"That won't be necessary. Whatever is in there is fine. Thank ya," I state.

She studies me.

"What did I say?"

A tiny smile appears on her lips. She answers, "I never thought I'd hear ya say that."

"Meaning?"

She arches her eyebrows, holds her hand over my forehead, and teases, "Are ya sick?"

I jerk my head back. "No. Why would ya say that?"

She softly laughs. "Ya always used to say you'd rather be caught dead than in something that wasn't designer."

The dark room Tommy kept me naked in flashes through my mind, and a chill seeps into my bones. I mutter, "That was before I was forced to be Tommy's prisoner."

She freezes, then a pitying look overtakes her features. "Jesus. I'm...I'm sorry. I wasn't thinking."

I lift my chin. "It's fine. I'd like to shower now."

She lowers her tone. "Okay. I'll wait in the bedroom until you're done. Then we can talk more." She pats me on the shoulder, then moves toward the door.

"Alaina!"

She spins back. "Hmm?"

I cross my arms. "Ya can't keep Aidan from me."

Hatred fills her face. "I can and I will. He took advantage of ya. And he disobeyed our orders."

"He did not take advantage of me. Ya don't know what you're talking about, so don't ya dare accuse him of anything of the sort!"

She pins her eyebrows together. "He did. And I know you're confused right now. You've been through a lot. It's my fault. I didn't protect ya."

"Ya had no choice. Nobody could have protected me against Tommy and Da."

"No! I should have kept ya safe!"

"It was impossible."

Alaina squeezes her eyes shut. "I should have."

"Don't do this," I order, not wanting to see the guilt all over her face since it's true. There's nothing in the entire world she could have done to stop Da from forcing me to marry Tommy. The last thing I want is for my sister to take the blame for things she shouldn't.

"I should have," she repeats.

"Ya couldn't. But the person who did protect me was Aidan," I declare.

Her guilt turns to anger. "Once you've had a few days away from him, you'll have time to think. You'll realize he should have brought ya to me right away. He shouldn't have kept us apart."

"That's not true," I insist.

"It is," she declares.

I lean against the counter and point out, "Why can't ya give him credit for rescuing me? He did something even ya couldn't do."

The guilt returns, swirling with her rage. It tears at me, but I'm not going to sit back and watch her make Aidan suffer. Her voice shakes, which I've rarely heard, as she claims, "I tried to find ya. I would've done anything, but I didn't even know ya were alive. Tommy told me he killed ya."

I squeeze the edge of the quartz countertop. "I know, but Aidan was the one who found me. He was the one who took care of me."

"He disobeyed my orders."

"So what?"

"When I give an order, it's his job to obey. Ya know how this works."

I hurl, "Da wasn't always right. Neither are ya."

Her face hardens. "You're just confused."

"I'm not," I snap.

Tense silence fills the space between us.

I blurt out, "I love him, Alaina," before I can even think about it.

Her eyebrows furrow. She firmly repeats, "Like I said, you're confused."

"I'm not confused! And stop being a hypocrite! You're married to Brody O'Connor and run his clan with him. Ya made an oath to show no mercy to any O'Leary. If I hadn't gone through what I have, I'd say you're the confused one! But I'm not judging ya, am I?" I cry out.

She turns and walks to the window, crosses her arms, and stares across the lawn. She states, "A lot happened. And our family, the O'Learys..." She swallows hard, her face darkens, and a shiver runs down my spine. She adds, "We should have never been born into their blood."

"But we were," I point out.

She spins to face me. "Yea, we were, and choices had to be made. So my allegiance is no longer with them, but neither is yours, is it?"

I stay silent. I've not had time to think about where my loyalties lie, but I don't need to. After what they put me through, I owe them nothing. And the only person I want to be with is Aidan...an O'Connor.

Alaina asserts, "It doesn't change the fact that he disobeyed orders. He could have brought ya to me. We could have been back together."

"What about ya and your vow? Aren't ya supposed to show me no mercy?" I fume, upset that she's angry at Aidan when he's the one who found me, and I'd still be in Tommy's grasp had he not.

"Ya don't need to worry about my oath. Brody and I will protect ya. When it's time, we'll make it clear to the world that ya no longer have an allegiance to the O'Learys."

I stay silent, and the tension only grows stronger and stronger.

Alaina finally steps toward the door. "I'll let ya shower. We can talk when ya get out."

"No, don't bother. I want to rest," I announce, not wanting to talk anymore. I know my sister. She's stubborn. There's no point talking until I can think about how to convince her to leave Aidan alone.

She softens her tone. "Don't be mad at me."

"Don't punish Aidan. He doesn't deserve it," I state again.

She glances away, then back at me. "Rules need to be followed. Ya know Brody and I can't allow disobedience."

"I'm so sick of all your clan bullshit," I blurt out.

Her eyes burn like fire. "It's not bullshit. There are reasons things are the way they are."

"Yea, well, where's that gotten us?" I question.

She hesitates.

"Ah, it's all water under the bridge now that you're in power," I accuse.

She scrunches her face. "Don't say that. What they did to ya will never be water under the bridge."

"But you're okay ruling how Da did?"

"I don't rule how he did," she snaps.

"Don't ya? Seems to me that ya do."

She glares at me with her emeralds, retorting, "No, I don't. Things *are* different now. You'll see."

"Why? Because you're at the top, and ya get to order everyone around? And then if they don't do exactly what ya want, ya get to punish them even if they did the right thing?"

"It's not like that," she claims.

I huff. "Sure it isn't."

"What he did wasn't right!"

My stomach pitches, and my mouth turns dry. I seethe, "What wasn't right, Queen Alaina? Rescuing me from another night with Tommy?" My lip quivers and my eyes fill with tears. I turn to avoid her pity-filled stare.

She puts her hand on my shoulder. "Scarlet—"

"Don't!" I warn, shaking her hand off me and wiping the tears off my cheek.

She stays quiet.

I add, "I need to shower. Please leave."

She doesn't move.

"Now," I demand.

She sighs, then steps toward the door. She gets two feet into the bedroom, then spins and softly states, "I promise ya things are different now."

"Keep telling yourself that," I say, then shut the door and lock it. I put my hands on the counter, staring at my reflection, trying to stop my insides from trembling with anger and sadness.

Thanks to Aidan, I've gained some weight. Not that my sister would give him any credit. I'm still skin and bones, and I wish she would have seen me when he rescued me. Maybe then she'd get off her high horse.

I push off the counter, turn on the shower, and wait for the water to warm up. Then I step under it. When I'm done, I dry myself, comb my hair, and then go to the bedroom. I open the dresser and put on a pair of designer leggings and an oversized shirt.

I stare at myself in the full-length mirror. The clothes are my old size and slightly big on me. In the past, I would have loved this outfit. Now, it feels foreign.

After a few moments, I force myself to stop assessing my body. I crawl into bed and try to figure out how to get Alaina off Aidan's back, but no answers come. I toss and turn, trying to sleep, hoping that Aidan will be there when I wake up, but I can't get any shut-eye.

Several hours pass. I give up, get out of bed, and leave the bedroom. I go down the hallway. Most of the doors are shut. I don't open any of them. I peek into the ones I can until I step in front of one that's cracked open. A soft light glows from the inch-wide opening, so I push the thick wood forward and freeze.

Large screens fill the wall, and three are turned on. Devin's on the first, Aidan's in the middle, and Tynan's on the last. Alaina stands in front of it, her arms crossed, eyes narrow with calm rage.

Concrete walls form the backdrop wherever the men are, and they're cutting up bodies with saws.

I put my hand over my mouth, swallowing bile. I manage to blurt out, "What the hell is this?"

Alaina spins, her eyes widening. "Ya shouldn't be in here, Scarlet."

I stare at the screen Aidan's on. It looks like he's working on a body that's been burned. I glance back at my sister. "What is this?"

"Their punishment."

"Their punishment?" I question.

"This is clan business. Ya shouldn't be in here."

"Don't give me 'it's clan business.'"

"It is, and nothing has changed regarding clan business. You've never had an interest in it, and I'll be damned if ya start now. Ya don't need to know anything about this. Pretend ya didn't see it and go back to your bedroom. I'll be in soon, and we can talk."

I narrow my eyes on her. "No. We can talk here. I'm not returning to my bedroom. I'm not your child. And I'm an O'Leary, so I'm not under your jurisdiction."

"Watch it," she warns.

"Or what?"

"Scarlet—"

"Ya say you're different from Da, but it sure as hell doesn't look like it from where I'm standing."

Her face hardens. She insists, "I am. You'll see."

I stare at the screen again, then demand, "Bring him home, now."

"No, he has a job to do," she asserts.

I blink hard. My voice cracks. "I swear to God, Alaina, if ya don't bring Aidan home soon, I'll never talk to ya again."

"Ya don't mean that. You're being emotional, and you're confused."

"Stop telling me I'm confused!" I yell for what feels like the hundredth time.

She picks up a remote and clicks a button. The screen turns black.

"Who are those dead men?" I ask.

She stays quiet.

"Tell me," I seethe.

She squares her shoulders. "They're O'Learys who Tommy had hunting ya."

My stomach churns.

"This isn't your concern," she softly adds.

More anger fills me. I hurl out, "Do ya think ya can just turn it off, and I'll drop it or forget about what you're making him do?"

"Making him do? This is what he does. This is what our people do."

"Our people. The O'Connors, ya mean?"

She shakes her head, deeply exhaling. "I know ya don't understand this."

"I don't care about the O'Learys, and I don't care about the O'Connor clan business. I care about Aidan, and I'm telling ya right now, Alaina, ya better bring him home. If ya don't, I'm leaving."

"Yea? Where will ya go, Scarlet? Did Aidan not tell ya Tommy and our brothers are hunting ya down?"

More bile rises in my throat. I hold on to the doorframe, and tears stream down my face.

She lowers her voice. "Ya know what they're capable of, so don't make stupid threats."

I swallow the lump in my throat, asserting, "I want Aidan home now, Alaina."

"Brody and I will take care of ya. We'll protect ya, and we'll make sure Tommy dies," she insists.

I stare at her, trying not to cry, but I can't. She's always been stronger than me. I only remember once in my life seeing Alaina cry. But the tears stream down my face, and I swipe at them, declaring, "I don't want ya to protect me. I want Aidan to protect me, and I won't tell ya again. If ya try to keep him from me, I swear to God, Alaina, I'll find a way to kill ya myself." I turn and leave the room. I continue down the hall and go down the stairs.

"What are ya doing? Ya shouldn't be racing down the steps with your stitches," she cries out.

I spin on the landing. "And ya shouldn't interfere in my life when ya have no right."

"No right? I'm your sister!"

"That means nothing," I say.

Hurt fills her expression. She claims, "Ya don't mean that!"

"I love him!" I exclaim.

She gapes at me.

I look away, my insides quivering.

Why the hell did I just say that again?

She lowers her voice. "Ya don't love him, and ya don't need him. I'll take care of ya."

Rage fills me. "If you're going to keep the one person from me that I trust, the one who's done more for me than anybody in my entire life, then I want nothing to do with ya," I snarl and continue down the stairs, wincing from the strain in my stomach.

She yells, "He took advantage of ya!"

"He didn't! Stop saying that!" I shout back and continue moving through the house.

"Ya can't know something is real when you're forced to stay with them," she claims.

"He didn't force me to do anything!" I seethe, then turn the corner and run into Brody.

"Whoa, ya all right there, lass?" he asks, grabbing my shoulders.

I cringe but jab his chest, stating, "I don't care what your laws and rules are. Ya and my sister better bring your brother back to me now, not later." I push on his chest, shove past him, find a loo, and lock myself in it.

I sit on the bench and put my hands over my face, trying to calm my emotions.

I need Aidan with me. How am I going to get it through to Alaina?

I told her I loved him.

Do I? Is it possible?

I've never been in love with anyone before. It even shocked me when it rolled out of my mouth. But if this isn't love, I don't know what is, yet I also don't know what this means. It's not like I had any examples of it growing up, except for when my mum was alive.

I stay locked in the loo, ignoring Alaina's orders to come out, trying to decipher all the new questions forming based on my admission. The biggest one won't stop nagging me.

Does Aidan love me, or are my feelings one-sided?

I stare at my reflection in the mirror, still disgusted by my too-thin body, wishing I had answers I'm unsure I'll ever get—especially if my sister has anything to do with it.

18

Aidan

he steel blade cuts through the torso of body number four when a loud beep cuts through the air. My brothers and I turn off our saws. Alaina's voice comes blaring into the warehouse. "Aidan, clean up and get back to ours."

Panic hits me. I glance up at the camera in the corner, asking, "What's wrong? Is Scarlet okay?"

I'm met with silence.

"For fuck's sake, Alaina!" I bark.

"She's fine. Clean up and get back here," she orders.

Tynan tosses his saw. "Good. I have a date tonight."

"Where ya going?" Alaina questions.

He freezes, and his eyes dart to the camera.

She demands, "Get back to work."

He groans.

"I can hear ya," she taunts.

I'd laugh if I weren't so pissed at her. But not a moment has passed without me angry over Alaina's determination to keep Scarlet from me. And too many thoughts plague me.

What is my petal thinking?

Has Alaina convinced her to stay away from me?

No. Scarlet has her own mind.

What if Alaina has some sort of power over her and Scarlet no longer wants me?

I go into the bathroom, strip out of my clothes, and scrub all the bodily fluids and soot off me. When I finish, I grab a pair of joggers and a T-shirt off the shelf. I put them on and then get into the car.

I don't follow most of the traffic laws, accelerating through red lights and stop signs while going above the speed limit. My antsy-ness to see Scarlet grows the closer I get to their house, and I can't shake the feeling that Alaina will give me some other shit job to keep me away from my petal.

When I pull up to the house, I jump out of the car and race up the steps. I pass the guard and enter the foyer, yelling, "Scarlet!" I run up the staircase.

"Quit your yelling," Brody barks.

I spin on the landing, demanding, "What room is she in?"

He narrows his eyes. "She's not up there."

"Don't lie to me," I seethe.

"I'm not."

The hairs on my arms rise. "Then where is she?"

He glances down the hall, then pins his gaze on me and takes a deep breath.

I lunge down the steps until I'm in front of him. I jab him in the chest, repeating, "Where is she?"

He bats my hand away from him. "What do ya think you're doing?"

"Don't mess with me, Brody. Where's Scarlet? I'm not going to ask ya again," I threaten.

He crosses his arms over his chest. "She won't come out."

My heart beats faster. "What do ya mean she won't come out? From where?"

"From the loo."

"The loo? Why? Is she sick?"

He glances down the hall again, then scrubs his face, admitting, "She and Alaina have been going at it all night."

"What do ya mean?"

He shakes his head. "I don't know. They're both upset."

"What did your wife do to her?" I accuse.

Anger fills his face. "Don't speak about her in that tone."

"Goddamn ya," I say, running down the hall.

He follows. "Aidan."

"Mind your own business, Brody," I warn and continue until I spot Alaina. She's sitting next to the bathroom door with her head against the wall. I snap, "What the fuck have ya done to her?"

She jumps up. "I haven't done anything to her."

"Then why isn't she coming out of the bathroom?" I ask.

She glares, accusing, "This is your fault."

"My fault? I've been doing your dirty work."

She scoffs. "*My* dirty work? Those were O'Learys ya were chopping up. O'Learys we killed for hunting my sister. But ya wouldn't know that, would ya, because ya kept her from me and put her at more risk."

"I didn't put her at more risk."

"Ya did."

"Enough, both of ya," Brody barks.

Alaina and I look at him.

He lowers his voice, saying, "A stór."

I shake my head. "Both of ya get out of here."

Alaina protests, "No, I'm not leaving."

"Alaina, let Aidan handle this," Brody orders.

She jerks her head toward him, her eyes widening.

He softens his tone and holds out his hand. "Leave them be. Let's go."

She hesitates, looking at the door.

He puts his arm around her waist. "Come on, nothing bad's going to happen to your sister. Take a breather."

She finally caves and gives me another hate-filled glare. Then Brody leads her down the hallway. When they're no longer in sight, I knock on the door. "Petal, open up."

A moment passes.

"Petal, I said open up."

The lock clicks, and the door swings open. She tosses her arms around my neck, then winces.

"Easy, you're going to hurt yourself," I gently reprimand.

She puts her hands on my face, and tears fill her eyes. "I thought I wasn't going to see ya again."

"Shh. Don't say that kind of stuff. I'll always find ya," I vow.

She shakes her head and swallows hard. I glance in the loo, asking, "Why are ya in here?"

"I-I... My sister and I were fighting, and I told her I wasn't coming out until she brought ya home."

I arch my eyebrows at her. "Ya locked yourself in the loo to get me out of that shit job?"

Her lips twitch and she sniffles. "Yea, I guess I did."

I grin and slide my hands over her cheeks and kiss her. I quickly retreat, praising, "I knew ya were a good lass."

She tilts her head. "I am, aren't I?"

"That ya are, but can we get ya out of the bathroom now?"

She glances behind her. "But the bench and I were getting to be friends."

"I can't blame the bench. I love your ass too," I tease.

She beams and shakes her booty.

I pat it and chuckle. "Let's go somewhere a little more comfy, okay?"

"All right." She lets me lead her down the hall, and I find a sitting room. I shut the door, lock it, and we go over to the couch. I pull her onto my lap and hold her head to my chest, kissing the top of it. "Are ya sure you're all right?"

"Yea."

"You're feeling okay?" I ask, concerned about her health.

She glances up. "Yea. I'm just happy to see ya. I..." She gets teary-eyed again, blinking hard.

"Ya what, petal?" I ask.

She shakes her head, agony painting her features. She states, "I seriously thought Alaina would keep ya from me. She threatened it, saying she and Brody would protect me, but I want ya to protect me. I don't want anybody else to. I want things to be how they were. I...I don't want them to change."

I tug her closer to me. "Shh. I don't want them to change either."

"But ya warned me they were going to. Ya said, now that we're back, they would, and look what happened within the first few minutes of us arriving."

I nod, admitting, "Aye. It's not ideal, and I'm going to have to deal with Alaina's wrath for a while. Brody's too, so in fairness, it's not just your sister's fault."

"She shouldn't have made ya do that. It was disgusting," she blurts out.

I freeze. My pulse skyrockets. "What do ya mean, petal?"

"The bodies ya were chopping up," she states.

The hairs on my neck rise. "How do ya know what I was doing?" I question. I know she knows I'm not a saint, but I don't want her to know the depths of what I do.

She sits up and lifts her chin. She swallows hard, then confesses, "I caught Alaina watching ya and your brothers on the TVs. Ya were sawing a guy's torso in half."

My breath catches. I stare at her, speechless.

"Say something, Aidan."

"I don't want... Alaina shouldn't have let ya see that."

"Well, she didn't exactly say, 'Come on in and watch,'" Scarlet admits.

"There should never have been any possibility of ya seeing that," I angrily declare as more rage builds in me.

Scarlet shrugs, asserting, "I snuck up on her. I didn't know where I was going, and I walked down the hallway and opened the door. It's not her fault. She didn't want me in there."

"She shouldn't have let ya see it," I repeat.

Scarlet sighs and puts her hand on my cheek. "Did ya shower? Ya have different clothes on."

I glance down at my shirt. "Aye. Before I left."

"Where were ya?" she questions.

"Somewhere I'll never tell ya for your own protection."

"But this is a place ya go to often?" she asks.

I shake my head. "I'm not going to give ya any more details, Scarlet. Ya shouldn't have seen it. Alaina and I will have words about this."

She closes her eyes. "No, it was my fault. Please, we don't need any more problems. We need to get ya back on her good side. And I don't want to be here without ya, Aidan."

My heart swells as relief fills me. I don't know why I thought she would lose her feelings for me, so I confess, "I don't want to be here without ya either."

She opens her mouth and then shuts it.

I slide my hand over the side of her head. "What's wrong?"

She shakes her head. "Nothing is wrong. At least, I don't think so." She bites her lip.

"Your expression tells me otherwise, so want to fill me in?"

She hesitates again, then says, "I realized something while ya were gone."

"What?" I ask.

Nerves fill her expression. She furrows her eyebrows and turns toward the window.

My anxiety reappears, and I wonder if I was wrong. What if she did lose some feelings for me? I move her chin back toward me. "What is it? Ya have me worried now."

"Worried?" she questions.

"Aye. Please don't tell me ya realize that your sister's right and that ya shouldn't be with me. I can assure ya that Alaina's wrong. In fact, she's so wrong..."

"I love ya," Scarlet blurts out, and her cheeks flush.

The blood pumps through my veins hotter. I study her.

She blinks a few times, opens her mouth, and shuts it. Her cheeks turn redder. She looks away. "Sorry, maybe I shouldn't have said that. I don't know what I'm saying. Just forget I said it."

"Why should I forget ya said it? Do ya mean it or not?" I question.

She stays quiet.

My chest tightens. "Scarlet, did ya mean what ya just said?"

She slowly turns her head and meets my eyes, nodding. "Yea, I do."

I swallow the lump in my throat.

She adds, "I'm sorry. I shouldn't have said anything. And ya don't have to say it back. I just... I shouldn't have said it. I'm sorry."

My heart races faster. "No, don't apologize. And I love ya too."

"Ya do?" she asks, then bites her lip again.

I take a deep breath. "Aye, and I've never said that to anyone before."

"Ya haven't?"

"No."

Her lips turn into a small smile. "I haven't either."

"No? I would've thought ya would've said it to dozens of lads," I tease, but I'm also serious. It's shocking to me that she's never said it to anyone.

She answers, "No, I haven't, Aidan."

Her truth only makes me happier. I state, "Well, good. Let's make it so I'm the only one ya ever say it to."

She softly laughs and puts her arms around my neck, lacing her fingers together. "Okay." She kisses me, sliding her tongue against mine, and we spend a few moments lip locked. She finally pulls back and asserts, "We need to leave here, Aidan."

"We can't, petal. Not now. Your sister's right. Tommy's after us. It's unsafe for ya to be anywhere but here."

"There has to be somewhere we can go. I can't... I don't want to be here without ya. And I don't want Alaina at your throat."

"I'll be fine," I declare.

"Ya were the one who saved me. She didn't. Neither did your brother. But you're getting punished for it. It's not fair."

I grunt. "I'll take their punishments. As long as we're okay, I'll deal with it. And I *will* kill Tommy. I don't care what Brody says."

"What do ya mean?" she questions, pinning her brows together.

I groan. "I shouldn't have said anything."

"What do ya mean ya shouldn't have said anything? What does that mean, Aidan?"

"Nothing. Brody said he was going to kill Tommy. I told him that Tommy's on my list."

"Your list?"

"Aye. When I put someone on my list, they're mine to deal with," I admit.

"Ya have a list?"

I curse myself. I need to shut my mouth. I keep digging myself deeper and deeper into the hole. I mutter, "I've said too much."

She adds, "Aidan, I don't care how he dies, whether it's by your hand, Brody's, or whoever's. I just want him dead so we can be free."

"We will be," I insist.

She continues, "I don't want to stay here with Alaina and Brody forever. I know ya don't either. But I do want to be with ya forever."

I lean forward and peck her on the lips. "I'll take forever."

She smiles, then states, "The only way we can do that is to get rid of Tommy. So it doesn't matter who kills him, does it?"

"It does matter. He's on my list," I say.

She scrunches her face. "Why do ya have to be so stubborn?"

"Because this is who I am. When I say I'm going to do something, I do it. And if a man is on my list, he's going to look at me when he takes his last breath, especially when he's hurt my woman."

She turns her head, looking at the window again, her jaw trembling.

"Why do ya look so frightened?" I question.

"I'm scared."

"Ya don't need to be scared anymore. You're safe," I reassure her.

"I'm not scared for my safety. I'm scared that you'll do something stupid, get hurt, and I won't see ya again."

"Ya don't need to worry about that. Nothing has changed. I was always going to kill Tommy."

"But—"

I put my fingers over her lips, claiming, "Petal, this isn't negotiable. I don't care what my brother says. I'm going to hunt him down and kill him."

She blinks hard.

"Ya have to stay here with your sister and Brody. After I finish him off, we can start our life together."

A tear slips out of her eye. She begs, "Just let Brody do it. Please. I don't have a good feeling, Aidan."

"I'm sorry, but that won't happen, lass. And I won't lie to ya. I don't want to have any lies between us."

She closes her eyes. I pull her back into me and kiss her head, stroking her hair.

She pushes away from my chest, pleading, "Please don't go anywhere right now. I can't handle it if you're gone tonight, Aidan."

I grin. "Okay, lass, ya win. But I think it's time ya showed me to our bedroom."

"Are ya tired?" she questions.

I lean into her ear and murmur, "No. I'm pretty sure there are some things I can do while you're lying on your back and getting your rest."

Her lips twitch. "Like what?"

I wiggle my eyebrows, teasing, "It's top-secret stuff. I can't discuss it. I can only show ya."

A fire ignites in her greens. She widens her eyes and states, "Then I think I'm due for some rest."

19

Scarlet
A Month Later

The scents of cedarwood and light musk flare in my nostrils. Aidan's warm torso presses against my back. His hot breath and lips tickle my neck. He murmurs in my ear, "I've missed ya, petal."

Am I dreaming?

His tongue flicks against my lobe, and my skin crackles with electricity. I blink a few times, then turn my head, whispering, "Are ya really here?"

His mouth grazes my cheek as he answers, "Aye, lass, I'm here."

It's been five days since I saw him. Alaina and Brody haven't forgotten their mission to teach him a lesson, which means sometimes he's gone for days. And every second that passes while he's gone is torture.

He kisses me again, demanding, "Tell me ya missed me."

I spin in his arms, admitting, "All I've thought about is ya."

Approval lights up his expression. "Good."

I ask, "Are ya home now?"

"For a bit."

Disappointment fills me and I pout. "How long are they going to keep ya working like this? It's not fair."

He puts his fingers on my lips. "Let's talk about it later."

A moment passes, and he intently studies me.

Butterflies fill my stomach. I put my palm on his cheek and nervously ask, "Why are ya staring at me like that?"

He grabs my hand, pins it above my head, and slides his tongue into my mouth.

I flick against it, needy, hungry, desperate to have him, and widen my legs. He's my addiction, and it's been too long since he's touched me, controlling my body and displaying his dominance over me.

He laces his fingers with mine. His erection slides over my pussy, taunting me at a slow speed. He nibbles my ear, fists my hair, and drags his teeth down my neck.

A shiver runs down my spine. I arch into him, whimpering.

He slides over my clit faster, murmuring, "I'm going to make ya come all night."

"Jesus," I manage to get out.

He chuckles slightly. "Glad to see ya missed me as much as I missed ya."

A slow tremor moves through my cells, and I breathe out, "I have."

He dips his head to my chest, and his wet tongue circles my nipple.

Hot blood rushes through my veins. The longer he's been gone, the more I've craved feeling him all over me.

He sucks my other breast, then presses his erection harder against me, gliding faster.

Adrenaline explodes throughout my body. I shudder underneath him, and he grabs my thigh, tugs it up, and slides into me.

"Oh Jesus," I cry out.

He thrusts a few times, then flips onto his back, pulling me with him. His forearm locks me close to him, and his fingers slide through my hair, holding my head firmly.

Within seconds, we're in sync with each other.

"Aidan," I whimper again.

He grips my hip and moves me faster over him.

"Oh Jesus," I mutter again.

He groans. "Fuck. I missed ya. Ya have no idea how hard I've been thinking about ya, petal."

"No, I'm the one who...oh...oh..." I close my eyes as a wave of dizziness hits me.

"That's my lass," he praises, pushing deeper into me.

"Aidan! I... Oh holy mother of God!" Endorphins explode in all my cells, giving me a high I've been aching for ever since he left.

He groans, muttering, "Christ, I've missed ya squeezing your pussy around me." He keeps me moving until the tremors slow, then he flips me on my back again. He widens my thighs and thrusts even deeper inside me, which only creates more toe-curling sensations.

"Aidan! Right there! Oh...don't...oh!"

"I'm not stopping. I know what ya need," he growls, thrusting faster into me and taking me from one orgasm to the next.

Sweat coats our skin, merging together. The air fills with the scent of our arousal and incoherent sounds.

Stars and white light fill my vision. More adrenaline floods me, and I call out, "I-I can't take anymore!"

His voice turns gravelly. He declares, "Ya can. And ya will. Now, tell me to keep going."

"I...I..." Another wave of adrenaline pounds into me.

"Tell me," he demands.

"Pl-pl-please!" I cry out.

"Nothing feels better than ya, petal."

"Oh God," I moan, then all the sensations accelerate to the point I can't control anything. An earthquake explodes within me. My entire body turns to an onslaught of tremors, and I can't stop whimpering.

He grunts. "You're going to make me come too soon."

I wrap my arms around his shoulders tighter. "Come...Aidan. I-I-I want...need..."

"A little longer, petal," he says through gritted teeth.

"I want... Oh shit!" Another tremor of euphoria hits me.

"Fuck," Aidan growls, and his body convulses violently against mine.

My high intensifies too quickly. I get dizzy again, and this time, all I see is black. My body turns limp.

When our tremors subside, he studies me, breathing hard, holding himself up by his forearms. His hot breath tickles my neck.

I try to catch my breath as his face slowly comes back into focus.

He pecks me on the lips, then rolls over, pulling me with him.

I curl into his body, his arm around me, my leg pretzeled around his, and my head resting on his chest. His heart thumps in my ear, the rapid beating slowing over time.

He strokes my hair and asks, "What have ya been doing since I've been gone?"

"Going crazy," I admit.

He groans. "Ya and me both. But tell me what ya filled your days doing. Have ya been eating right?"

I roll my eyes. "Don't worry. Between Alaina and Brody, I'm getting stuffed full of food twenty-four seven."

He softly chuckles, then runs his hand over the curve of my waist and hip, resting it on my ass cheek and softly squeezing. "Aye. It feels like you've gotten a little bit more meat on ya."

I laugh. "A long time ago, that would've insulted me."

He kisses my forehead again. "Ya know I don't mean it as an insult. Ya know I love ya no matter what. I'm just worried about ya being healthy."

"I am healthy. I'm fully recovered from surgery and no longer the frail woman ya rescued," I declare.

"No, ya aren't," he agrees.

"So let's not have this conversation again."

His lips twitch. "Yes, ma'am."

I kiss him. "Good lad."

He chuckles. "Besides eating, what else have ya been doing?"

"Walking around the estate with Alaina's bodyguards following me. They won't even stay in the shadows. I'm on her property, so I don't know why she has to be so paranoid."

He lowers his voice. "She's as paranoid as me. That's one thing I can give your sister credit for. And those are my orders as well."

I lift my chin off his chest, tilting my head, questioning, "Your orders? That's ridiculous, Aidan. I'm on the estate. It's their house. Who's going to dare breach their territory in that way?"

He strokes my cheek. "I'm not taking any chances with ya, petal."

I groan. "You're both overreacting."

"Nope."

"Well, can ya at least tell the bodyguard to back off a bit? I mean, he's literally breathing down my neck."

Aidan's voice darkens. "What do ya mean he's breathing down your neck?"

I laugh. "Wrong choice of words. Don't worry. No one's doing anything inappropriate."

"He better not be," Aidan warns.

"Everything is professional. So how long are they going to keep ya working like this?"

He kisses my forehead. "My punishment is over."

I tilt my head up. "It is? But ya said ya were only home for a little while," I point out.

His expression hardens.

"Aidan, don't keep me in the dark!"

"Don't worry. Things are going to change."

"How?"

"I won't be on shit jobs anymore."

"But you'll still be gone?"

Silence fills the air.

I push, "Why will ya be gone?"

"I won't be gone from ya all the time."

"But you'll be gone for some of it?"

He studies me again.

I confess, "This is driving me nuts, Aidan. I hate it. I'm worried the entire time you're gone."

"I've told ya, ya have nothing to worry about," he insists.

"Then tell me why you'll be gone if they said your punishment is over."

More tension builds between us.

"Aidan—"

"Tommy is still out there."

My stomach drops. "I know, but Alaina told me he went into hiding. There were too many O'Connors after him."

"That's right." Aidan clenches his jaw.

"What aren't ya telling me?" I question.

His expression shifts and that crazed look appears in his eyes.

It scares me. I add, "Please don't go silent on me!"

He deeply exhales. "My only job going forward is to find and kill Tommy."

My chest tightens. "So you're going to be gone a long time?"

"Not a long time."

"How do ya know? No one has been able to find him, according to Alaina."

In his this-conversation-is-over voice, he declares, "I will. Let's talk about this later. Tell me what else you've been doing."

I sigh, lay my head back on his chest, and slide my fingers between his pecs. "Nothing. I need to get out of here, Aidan. The walls are starting to press in on me. Will things ever get normal so we can leave this compound?"

He sits up and pulls me with him, giving me a quick kiss. Then he states, "Aye, we will. And I bought ya a present for tomorrow night to start our normalcy."

"Tomorrow night?"

"Aye." He grins.

"What's going on tomorrow?"

He motions to the wall. "Your present is hanging in the closet if ya want to look."

I arch my eyebrows. "Ya bought me clothes? Ya don't like Alaina's outfits she got me?"

"Didn't say that." He wiggles his eyebrows and adds, "It's not just any clothes. It's a dress."

I blurt out, "I don't think I've ever worn a dress in front of ya."

"Well, it's about time ya did," he says, then runs his hand over my inner thigh.

Zings erupt under his touch. I tease, "So are we going to get dressed up and have dinner in the house?"

He shakes his head. "No, I'm taking ya out."

My stomach fills with butterflies as I take in what he said.

"Ya don't want to go out, petal?" he questions.

"Of course I want to go out. But Alaina says I can't leave."

Annoyance fills his voice. "I already took care of Alaina. And I'll be with ya, so we're going out."

I start to protest, "But Tommy—"

"He's in hiding. Let him come out of it. It's time we started forming some sort of normal life, and I'm taking ya out."

"Is this where ya use me as bait?"

He sighs. "I'm not using ya as bait."

"You've always planned to use me to get to him," I remind him.

He tugs me closer to him and slides his palm on the side of my head. "Ya want to know the truth?"

My pulse skyrockets. "Yea. I do."

He collects his thoughts and then admits, "At first, I did want to use ya to make him pay, but it's not about that anymore."

A bite of anger pinches in my chest. I attempt to keep my voice calm as I tilt my head. I assert, "Ya need to explain that, Aidan."

He stares at me momentarily, then confesses, "I love ya. So while it will burn Tommy enough to make him come out of hiding to find me, this isn't about that. It's about us having a life and going on a proper date. But when he does come out, I'm ready to kill him. Then all this will be over."

"But isn't it dangerous for me to be out there with ya?"

"No. Plus, this needs to happen."

"Now I'm confused again. That sounds like ya have ulterior motives again," I declare.

He stays silent.

My anger reignites. I demand, "What needs to happen, Aidan?"

His face hardens further. He asserts, "I'm showing all the O'Learys, and O'Connors too, for that matter, that you're mine. No one's ever again going to disrespect or touch ya."

"How does that keep me safe? If they know I'm here..."

"We're in Belfast, petal. We're not in Dublin. The O'Connor clan surrounds us. There are men who will die to protect ya because your sister, Brody, and I gave them orders. Now, is there any reason ya don't want to go on a date with me?"

My lips twitch, and butterflies fill my stomach. "No. And it is time ya took me out on a date. You've been slacking a bit."

He grins. "Slacking? I'll show ya slacking!" He flips me on my back and tickles me.

I shriek. "Stop! I'm going to wee my panties!"

"Ya aren't wearing panties," he says and tickles me more.

"Aidan!" I cry out.

He finally stops and kisses me. His face turns serious. "I've always wanted to take ya on a date."

"Well, ya better make sure ya put everything into it. I have high expectations. I need to be impressed," I tease.

He chuckles. "Oh, don't ya worry. I got lots up my sleeve, petal."

"Do ya, now?"

He slides his tongue back into my mouth, kissing me deeply until I'm breathless, then he murmurs, "I also got ya shoes."

I arch my eyebrows. "Shoes, huh?"

"Not just any shoes," he states.

I tilt my head. "Well, what kind of shoes are these?" Mischief fills his eyes. "They're a very high pair of stilettos, and I have lots of plans for them."

I laugh. "Do ya have a stiletto fetish?"

He kisses me again, grinning. "Definitely. Now, let's get some sleep. I'm keeping ya out late tomorrow night."

20

Aidan

*a*laina waves her hands in the air. "I still don't like this."

I groan. "How many times do we have to go over this? He'll come out of hiding, then I'll kill him."

"I still haven't given ya permission to take that away from me," Brody interjects, walking into the room.

I glare at him. "Enough with the power trip. He's on my list, and ya know it. I did my time and finished your punishment. Ya told me it's over, now let's move on."

Alaina insists, "We'll find Tommy soon enough. Scarlet needs to stay here. Ya can go out after."

I shake my head. "No. She needs to get out of this house. You're driving her nuts."

"No, I'm not," Alaina claims.

"Ya are."

"Can ya two ever stop fighting?" Brody asks but pins his glare on me.

I sniff hard and cross my arms over my chest. I declare, "Like I said, my punishment's over. Neither of ya have found Tommy. All ya did was help push him into hiding."

"Because he's scared, Alaina states.

"Aye, and that's why this is necessary. Once he gets word I'm with Scarlet and taking her out in public, he'll show up in Belfast. He'll have to in order to save face, then I'll kill him."

"Something could go wrong," Alaina states for the hundredth time.

I push, "So ya aren't confident in our men?"

Her face hardens. She stays quiet, glaring at me.

"Well, is there a suspected breach I should know about with the men we've lined up for tonight? Because we went over it, and ya insisted they were the strongest in the clan."

"They *are* our strongest in the clan," Brody assures.

I push Alaina harder. "Is there something that Brody and I don't know about that you've kept from us?"

"Watch it," Brody warns.

"Hey, I'm not the one going back on plans. We all agreed on this and all the safety measures," I point out.

"It's my sister," Alaina says.

"And it's my woman. I would never let anything happen to her," I assert.

She presses her thumb and pointer finger on her upper nose, squeezing her eyes. She mutters, "I just got her back."

I soften my tone. "Aye, and you'll see her tomorrow morning at breakfast like ya do every day. I promise. Ya need to stop creating issues when we've already gone through all this with a fine-tooth comb."

Brody steps closer to her and puts his hand on her back. He quietly asks, "Ya all right, a stór?"

She opens her eyes and assures him, "Yea." She redirects her gaze to me, then softens it further. "We shouldn't take risks we don't need to."

I peer closer at her. I question, "Are ya sure you're okay? Ya look a bit pale."

"I'm fine. Let's not detour from the topic."

"Ya really do look a bit ill," I state, studying her more closely and suddenly concerned about her health.

She lifts her chin. "Nothing is wrong with me. I just don't like the thought of my sister anywhere that Tommy or his men could show up."

"There's no risk, Alaina," I insist. "It's a win-win. Scarlet leaves the house for the night, and we lure Tommy out of hiding. If any of his men have the balls to step in front of the O'Connors, they'll die, just like the lot we took out over the last month."

"Anything could happen," Alaina points out.

"It won't. I won't let it, nor will the men we've instructed to stand guard."

"Ya don't know Tommy."

"I'll be damned if I let him keep Scarlet locked up anymore."

Hurt fills Alaina's expression. "She's not locked up!"

I cross my arms. "She is! You've made her a prisoner in your castle."

"Don't be dramatic."

"You're being a control freak."

"I'm not a control freak," she insists.

I mutter, "Of course you're a control freak."

"Don't talk to my wife like that," Brody warns.

I snap, "We've been over this. All of us agreed. The plans aren't changing. I'm taking Scarlet out tonight."

"It's not necessary," Alaina states.

"Why is everything a fight with ya?" I accuse.

"Watch your tone," Brody reprimands.

"Your brother is as bad as a child," Alaina grumbles to Brody.

I huff. "*I'm* a child?"

"Goddamnit! Enough!" Brody barks.

Silence fills the room, and tension builds in the air around us. Alaina shoots daggers at me with an angry look, and I glare back at her. Things have gotten a lot better between us, but when it comes to Scarlet's safety, she still thinks she's in charge.

No matter how much Scarlet tells her that she needs to stay out of our relationship, or Brody comes to my defense, which he more often than not is starting to do, she still thinks it's her job and that she knows what's best for Scarlet. But Scarlet's my woman, and I'm the one who will make the calls on her protection and security.

So I announce, "I'm taking Scarlet out. She can't stay a prisoner here."

"She's not my prisoner. Stop using that word," Alaina cries out.

"Why are ya all arguing? Did something happen, or is it another round of Alaina versus Aidan?" Scarlet asks, stepping inside the room.

Brody answers, "Another round."

"Ya two need to stop," she orders, putting her hand on her hip.

My heart beats faster, and my breath catches. I drag my eyes over her body several times, then whistle. "Wow. Ya look incredible."

"Ya have drool ya might need to wipe off your face." Alaina smirks.

I ignore her and study Scarlet some more.

The cocktail dress I bought her is black with gold multi-shaped cutout mirrored glass all over it. The back dips low, and it's sleeveless. When I saw it, I knew she'd look great, but it fits her like a glove, showcasing her curves, which have started to return.

My erection strains against my zipper. But that's the thing about my petal. She can wear nothing, sweatpants, or get dressed up, and she's always the most beautiful woman in the room.

She holds the gold handbag close to her, and I glance down at the matching six-inch stilettos. All the thoughts of what I want to do to her in those shoes fill my head.

"Up here," she teases.

I drag my eyes back up her body and say, "Ya really look amazing."

Her face slightly flushes. "Thanks. So do ya."

"Ya do look amazing," Alaina inserts.

I step next to Scarlet and put my arm around her waist, asking, "Are ya ready?"

She beams. "Yea."

Alaina starts, "Scarlet, I think—"

"Don't ruin this night for your sister," I warn.

Alaina shuts her mouth and furrows her brows until rows of tiny lines fill her forehead.

My brother steps next to her, tugging her close to him. He glances at her and murmurs, "Let them go and stop stressing. Aidan's right. We've got things covered. Our men know what to do, and they're our best."

Her worried expression doesn't change. It almost makes me feel sorry for her.

Brody lowers his voice further. "It's not good for ya to stress out about stuff. Remember what the doctor said?"

"Is something wrong?" Scarlet frets.

Alaina's lips twitch. She gives Brody a half-frustrated, half-excited expression, tilting her head.

"Well? Is it?" Scarlet pushes.

Alaina scolds Brody. "I thought we weren't telling them until later."

Brody shrugs, grinning. "Oops."

She laughs softly. "Who's more excited about this, ya or me?"

"About what?" Scarlet questions.

"Aye. Get on with it," I state.

They stay quiet.

Scarlet blurts out, "Secrets don't make friends!"

"Aye. What she said," I second.

Brody nods at Alaina, saying, "Tell them."

They slowly turn their heads toward us. She announces, "I'm pregnant."

"What?" Scarlet shrieks so loud my ears hurt. She lunges at Alaina and pulls her into a hug.

"Easy there, petal," I tease, putting my palm over the side of my head.

"Sorry. How far along are ya?" she questions.

Alaina's expression brightens. "Two months."

"Two months! How long have ya kept this from me?"

"We only found out a few days ago."

"A few days! We could have been planning baby things!" Scarlet states.

Alaina laughs. "We have plenty of time."

Scarlet asks, "What are we having?"

Alaina's beam lightens further. "We don't know. The ultrasound isn't for a few more weeks, and Brody and I can't decide if we want to find out the sex or not."

Scarlet gasps. "What? Ya have to. We have to be able to plan."

Brody declares, "We can still plan."

"How? If ya don't know, we can't plan pink or blue! This is important to know," Scarlet excitedly states. She tosses her arms around Alaina again and adds, "This is so awesome. I'm going to be an aunt!"

Alaina squeezes her back. "Yea, and that's why I must ensure you're okay."

Scarlet groans. "I'm fine. Aidan won't let anything happen to me."

"Agreed," I concur, then pat my brother on the shoulder. "Congrats. Ya tell Dad yet?"

"Nope. He's coming in next week. We thought we'd tell him in person," Brody says.

I nod. "You'll make his year." I pull Alaina into me and hug her as well. "I'm happy for ya. And don't worry, your baby's favorite uncle will be me."

She groans and smirks. "I'm not sure how I feel about that."

"You're elated," I reply.

She laughs.

In a firm voice, Brody asserts, "It's important we find a way to reduce Alaina's stress. The doctor clearly stated it's not good for her or the baby."

"I'm fine," she insists.

He gives her a reprimanding look. "As of now. But we want to keep it that way."

Scarlet pulls away. She lifts her chin and squares her shoulders, aiming her gaze at Alaina.

I hold my laughter in. My Scarlet is just as feisty as her sister, and she doesn't hold back. I suppose the only reason I'm no longer in the punishment zone with Alaina is due to Scarlet constantly sticking up for me. And when they told me yesterday that I was done with the punishments, I have to say I was relieved. I hate being away from Scarlet.

She scolds, "Yea, ya need to stop worrying. Aidan wouldn't ever let anything happen to me. And ya said yourself that your best men would be watching us."

Alaina doesn't look convinced.

I restate, "Nothing's happening. And this conversation is becoming a broken record."

"Let them go. Besides, I have plans for you tonight," Brody declares.

Alaina glances up at him.

He grins. "Your dress is upstairs."

She arches her eyebrows, and her lips twitch. "And what are we doing?"

"Not going anywhere near them," he asserts, staring at her until her face flushes.

"I guess we're ready to go, then," Scarlet chirps, glancing up at me.

I give her a quick kiss. "That we are. Don't wait up for us."

Alaina says, "Why don't ya check in—"

"Absolutely not!" I huff.

"Scarlet, call me—"

"Stop acting like my mum. I'm not practice for your baby," Scarlet scolds.

"Practice..." Alaina's eyes widen, then she rolls them. "Ha ha. Funny."

"It was good, wasn't it?" Scarlet looks at me.

"Sure was, petal." I put my arm around her. "Let's go." I ignore Alaina's continued protests and lead Scarlet out of the house. We get into the car, and our driver pulls out of the driveway.

Scarlet releases a heavy breath. "Never thought we'd get out of there!"

"Your sister has issues."

She snickers. "Yea, but she means well."

"Agreed," I state and tug her closer to me. "How's it feel to be free?"

Scarlet glances out the window. "Good. So this is Belfast?"

"Aye. Have ya never been here?"

She shakes her head.

"Never?" I ask, surprised.

"No. Da always forbade us to come here. He said it was unsafe."

The mention of her da makes my gut flip. She says it as if he was trying to protect her. In some ways, he was, but he didn't have her or Alaina's best interest at heart.

Her da would've been more worried about his daughters being kidnapped and him not being able to save face. It's how Tommy will feel after he learns I'm with Scarlet and we're no longer hiding.

I hug her closer to me and kiss the top of her head.

"What do ya think of Belfast?"

She doesn't take her eyes off the window. "It's different."

"Aye. Do ya miss Dublin?" I question.

"Why would I?"

"Ya grew up there. I would think this would feel a little foreign, even though it's still Ireland."

Sadness fills her expression. She shrugs, claiming, "Dublin doesn't hold anything for me. The only place that does is wherever you're at."

My chest tightens. I normally ask her what she's thinking about when her expression turns sad, but it often leads to a bigger trip down memory lane. I don't want to spoil our night, so I make note to ask her about it later. I simply say, "Agreed."

She snuggles closer to my chest, and we don't say much. By the time we get to the restaurant, the sun has set, and it's dark outside. The driver parks in front of the building, and I get out of the car. I reach inside to help her out and lead her toward the front door.

A few feet away from the entrance, her body stiffens. I glance down at her, and her face is green. Her hand is over her mouth. "What's wrong, petal?"

She swallows hard, closes her eyes, and takes a deep breath.

"Petal?"

She turns her head toward a man smoking a few feet away. "Nothing." She lifts her chin and moves toward the door.

The valet holds the door open, and we step inside. I guide her to a quiet corner and question, "What just happened?"

The color on her face is still slightly off. She shakes her head. "Nothing."

"That wasn't nothing."

She hesitates.

"I need to know what just happened," I firmly assert.

She opens her mouth, then snaps it shut. She takes a deep breath.

I wait.

She finally states, "I don't know. The smoke... I... Well, I haven't smelled it since *him*." She looks away, blinking hard.

I tug her into me. Her heart pounds against my chest. I wrap my arms tight around her and murmur, "He's not here, petal."

"I know," she mutters into the curve of my neck.

I add, "If ya don't want to stay, we can go."

She pulls her head back. "What? No!"

"Are ya sure?"

"Yea. Don't let that ruin our night."

I study her, trying to decide if I should take her home. Maybe this is too much for her first trip out of the house.

She blurts out, "Aidan, I'm sorry. I-I won't let it happen again. Please! I don't want to go back yet."

"There's nothing to be sorry about. I just want to make sure you're okay."

"I'm fine. I just..."

"Just what?"

She doesn't answer.

"Tell me," I order.

She blinks hard and releases an anxious breath. She admits, "I had a flashback."

"Of what?"

She looks away and whispers, "Don't make me talk about it. Not here."

Anger fills me. I can't wait to kill that bastard, but no matter what I do to him, it'll never be enough to make him fully pay for what he did to Scarlet. I attempt to keep my cool, debate about what to do, and finally pull her back into me. "Okay. But if ya want to go at any time—"

"I don't!"

"But if ya do, tell me. You're allowed to change your mind."

She nods, smiling. "Okay. But I won't. Can we go to our table now and have a date like a normal couple?"

I study her for another moment.

"I'm fine. Don't become Alaina. Please."

I chuckle. "Ouch. Ya know exactly what to say."

She chirps, "That's why ya love me so much."

"Aye. I do. More than you'll ever know." I peck her on the lips and spin, then lead her to the hostess stand.

There's another couple in front of us, so I lean into her ear, murmuring, "Ya really are a knockout."

Her face flushes and a twinkle sparks in her eyes. She challenges, "What are ya going to do about it, Aidan?"

I smirk, vowing, "Oh, you'll find out."

She warns, "Don't make promises that ya can't keep."

"Have I ever made a promise I haven't kept?"

She smiles and shakes her head. "No, you've not."

"Okay, then, don't let your guard down," I tease.

She laughs.

The hostess addresses us. "Good evening. Do ya have a reservation?"

I nod. "Aidan O'Connor."

Her eyes widen. "Oh yes, Mr. O'Connor, it's nice to see ya. And ya." She looks toward Scarlet.

Scarlet beams. "Thank ya. I love your lipstick. Do ya know the color?"

The hostess chirps, "Why thank ya! It's Ravish Red."

"It's really great on ya," Scarlet compliments.

"Thank ya. And I have to say that your dress is amazing. Can I ask where ya got it?"

"Aidan got it for me," Scarlet replies, looking up at me with pride in her eyes.

My dick goes from a semi to a fully loaded erection. I groan inside and keep her close to my body. I answer, "Sorry. It's my secret."

The hostess's face falls slightly, but she forces a smile. "I understand. Ya did a terrific job picking it out."

I nod. "Thank ya."

"Right this way." She grabs menus and leads us to the back of the restaurant and into a private room. I pull out Scarlet's chair. She sits down, and I take the seat next to hers.

The hostess sets the menus down and declares, "Your server, Patrick, will be in shortly. Is there anything I can get ya in the meantime?"

"No, we're good," I state.

She nods and leaves.

Scarlet glances around and says, "This is super private. Ya must have pulled out all the stops."

I wiggle my eyebrows. "Stick with me and you'll see what I'm capable of when I get to spoil ya."

She softly laughs. "Well, I have no plans of tossing ya out anytime soon." She picks up the menu and reads it over.

My pulse skyrockets. If I get my way, she's never getting rid of me. And tonight's the first step of making that happen.

21

Scarlet

"This is a gorgeous room," I state, glancing around. The dim lights create a romantic flair. An eggplant-colored tablecloth matches the curtains that cover the wall where the entrance is. A low fire dances in a fireplace set in the side wall, and cream candles flicker in the center of the table.

"Glad ya approve," Aidan declares as he picks up my hand and kisses the back of it.

My butterflies kick off again.

So this is what it's like to be on a date with Aidan.

The door opens, and a short, bald guy enters the room. His red cheeks make him appear winded, as if he's been running all over the restaurant. He booms, "Welcome to Club Fifty-Eight. As ya may or may not know, this is Chef Kilpatrick's fifty-eighth restaurant and the dearest to him, as he's from Belfast."

"Didn't know that, mate," Aidan admits. He rolls his head toward me. "Did ya know that?"

I hold back my giggle. "Nope."

Patrick grins, adding, "Most don't. And you're in luck tonight."

"How's that?" Aidan asks.

Patrick answers, "We have one of the best-tasting menus our chef has ever created. And some great wine to go with it."

"That's a big statement. It better be amazing, Patrick," Aidan warns.

"Aye. It will be. Would ya like to hear the wines we recommend for this evening?"

Aidan slides his arm around my shoulders, glances at me, and arches his eyebrows.

I nod. "Yes, please."

Patrick announces, "We have a 2015 Masseto Toscana IGT red wine. It's a bold and structured Merlot with a 98/100 rating."

"Ohh. Sounds like a winner," I chirp.

"Ya had that two weeks ago and didn't care for it," Aidan reminds me with amusement in his expression.

"I did?"

"Aye. When Alaina tried to cook that Irish stew for dinner."

"The one she burnt?"

"Yep."

I wrinkle my nose. "Okay, we're passing on that one. But it sounds impressive."

Aidan chuckles. "What else do ya have, Patrick?"

He replies, "We also have a 2019 Tenuta San Guido Sassicaia Bolgheri red wine. It is another bold and structured wine but a Cabernet Franc - Cabernet Sauvignon blend. It boasts a 97/100 rating."

"Anything else?" Aidan asks.

Patrick's eyes light up. "Aye, and it happens to be my favorite. It's a 2016 Vieux Chateau Certan red wine. It's savory and a classic Bordeaux blend red, also with a 97/100 rating. Of course, I would rate it higher."

I softly laugh. "Well, I guess I have to try that one, then."

"Good choice. If ya don't like it, I'll replace it for ya, but I'm sure you'll love it. And for ya, sir?"

"I'll have the same," Aidan states.

"Very well, sir. Are there any allergies I should be aware of?"

"No," I answer.

"Not me. Ya can put anything in me. I'm a human garbage disposal," Aidan states.

I laugh and agree, "He is."

Patrick chuckles. "Wonderful. Are ya ready to hear what's on the tasting menu?" Patrick questions.

Aidan says, "Aye."

Patrick declares, "Our bread is paired with cuinneog butter. We'll start with potato brandade, trout roe, and chive, followed by chicken liver parfait, hazelnut, and Seville orange."

My stomach rumbles.

"Did ya eat today?" Aidan asks, his forehead wrinkling.

"Of course. That sounds great, Patrick. Please continue."

"The crab and prawn bisque sprinkled with almonds is to die for!" he boasts.

"I love bisque. Bring it on!" I exclaim.

Patrick continues, "Our Wicklow venison is dressed with chicory and artichoke. Then I'll bring out the monkfish cooked with peppercorn and more artichokes."

"Chef loves artichokes, huh?" Aidan asks.

"Ya can say that," Patrick agrees, then adds, "Next is salt-aged beef, pied du mouton, and foie gras."

"Now we're talking. Can't go wrong with beef," Aidan claims.

"No, sir. The rhubarb, blood orange, and ginger dish that follows will clean your palate to prepare ya for the salted caramel, chocolate, and malt dessert," Patrick informs us.

"That's a lot of food!" I blurt out.

Aidan pats his stomach, declaring, "We'll get it all down."

I laugh. "I shouldn't be surprised ya picked a huge menu."

"Don't worry, lass. The servings are smaller, but it will leave ya satisfied. Promise," Patrick vows.

Aidan's eyes dart over my body, and he murmurs, "Tell him I always satisfy ya."

I giggle and elbow him in the chest as my cheeks heat.

"Ouch. Don't kill me before dinner."

Patrick clears his throat, and his cheeks turn redder. "Would ya like time to review the menu, or would ya like the tasting?"

I reply, "We'll do the tasting. Thank ya, Patrick."

"Very well. I'll return with the wine." He scurries out of the room.

Aidan slides his hand between my crossed thighs.

Zings race to my core. I squeeze my legs tighter and state, "You're going to give Patrick a heart attack."

"Nah. I'm sure he's seen a lot in this room," Aidan replies.

I glance around, admitting, "It is very private."

"Are ya into reverse voyeurism?"

I arch my eyebrows. "Reverse?"

"Aye."

"Doesn't that fetish involve sexual acts?"

"Aye. Voyeurism is the act of watching others when they are naked or during sexual activity."

"Are people having sex or eating naked out there?"

He grins. "Nope. But I can't guarantee what will or won't happen in here tonight."

I laugh. "Then I wouldn't be the one into voyeurism, would I?"

"That's why I called it reverse voyeurism. Maybe ya want to be watched?"

Anxiety creeps into my chest. I shake my head. "No. Are ya into that?"

"Nope. But if ya were, then I'd make it happen," he claims.

The door opens, and Patrick appears with the bread and a bottle of wine. He sets the basket down and announces, "2016 Vieux

Chateau Certan, my favorite, but if ya find any fault with it, the bottle's on me. Who would like to try it?"

Aidan motions to me. "Ladies first."

Patrick pours an ounce into a glass and hands it to me.

I swirl it, then take a deep sniff and groan. "It smells so good. Is that cherries?"

"Very good!" he praises.

I take a sip, and the velvety liquid rolls over my tongue. "Mmm. This is delicious."

Patrick beams. "Glad ya approve." He fills two fresh glasses and states, "I'll be back with your first course." He disappears, and the door shuts behind him.

Aidan holds his glass in the air, grinning. "To your freedom. And the fact you're madly in love with me every second of the day."

I laugh and nudge him. "You've been waiting to say that all night, huh?"

"Aye. Sláinte."

"Sláinte." I clink my glass to his and take another mouthful.

Aidan does the same and then sets his glass down. He butters two pieces of bread and then sets them on our plates. "Eat while it's warm."

I stare at him.

"What, petal?"

I tilt my head. "Are ya ever going to stop worrying about me eating? I'm almost back to my normal weight."

"I just want ya to enjoy it while it's warm. Plus, I'm a gentleman, so lasses first."

I snicker. "Are ya?"

He leans into my ear. His hot breath sends tingles down my spine. He claims, "Only in public."

I laugh.

He picks the bread off my plate and holds it in front of my mouth. "Try it so I can too."

I take a bite, chew it, and swallow.

He watches me the entire time, then asks, "Well?"

"It's delicious."

He puts half his piece in his mouth, places his hand over his stomach, leans back, and groans.

"So dramatic," I tease, then take another bite.

He swallows, takes another swig of wine, and states, "I love bread."

"So you've said before."

"No. I *really* love bread." He grabs another piece and butters it.

I take a sip of wine and ask, "Would ya rather be hit by a bus or a big lorry?"

He answers, "Big lorry," then shoves more bread into his mouth.

"Why?"

He chews, swallows, and answers, "No screaming kids."

"Ya don't like screaming kids?" I tease.

He shakes his head. "More like I don't like to torture children. Ya probably don't believe me, but I love kids."

"Ya do?" I ask in surprise.

"Aye. That's why we're going to have loads of them."

I scoff. "Ha ha. Funny."

His face turns serious. "I'm not joking, lass. Unless ya break my heart and tell me ya don't want any."

I gape at him.

"Did I say something wrong?" he asks.

My butterflies kick up again. I shrug. "I guess I just haven't thought about it."

He pins his gaze on me, questioning, "Ya never thought about having kids, or ya haven't thought about having them with me?"

I open my mouth and then shut it.

His face falls. "Aye. Ya don't have to say anything. Your answer is clear. Guess I'm not the father ya imagined for your children."

I put my hand on his arm. "Aidan, that's not it."

"No?"

I shake my head. "No. I..."

He arches his eyebrows and waits.

I collect my thoughts and confess, "When you're gone, all I obsess about is how this will end."

"How we'll end?" he says in a hurt voice.

"No! How it'll end with Tommy. I..." I look away, blinking hard.

Aidan slides closer to me and turns my chin toward him. He gently asks, "Finish your thought, petal."

My voice shakes as I say, "Sometimes when you're gone I have these visions." I swallow the lump in my throat, wishing my heart wouldn't race so badly.

"What visions?" he prods.

I squeeze my eyes tight.

"Petal, please tell me."

I refocus on him and admit, "That Tommy kills both of us. Only he kills ya first, and I have to watch it." My stomach flips, and I put my hand on it.

"That's not going to happen," Aidan firmly asserts.

I continue, "I don't want it to."

"It won't. We're going to live a long time," he insists.

"How do ya know?"

"Because I do."

Silence settles between us for a moment.

He tucks a lock of hair behind my ear. His eyes twinkle, and he says, "So once I kill Tommy, there won't be any excuses. You'll want to have my babies, right?"

A tiny laugh escapes my lips.

"No?"

I slide my arms around his shoulders, lacing my hands behind his neck. I move an inch in front of his lips and announce, "Ya can keep me barefoot and pregnant if ya want."

His face lights up. "I can?"

I nod. "I love kids. I can't wait for Alaina and Brody's baby to arrive." I kiss him, and he immediately deepens it.

Patrick clears his throat, breaking our kiss. He says, "Sorry to interrupt. Potato brandade, trout roe, and chive." He sets a plate down.

"That smells divine," I state.

"It is." He picks up the bottle of wine and tops our glasses off. "Is there anything else I can get for ya?"

Aidan looks at me, and I shake my head. He answers, "We're good, Patrick."

"Okay, I'll be back soon."

"Tell ya what, why don't ya bring everything out except the last two dishes? Then we can try it all at the same time, and ya don't need to keep coming back so much," Aidan states.

Patrick's lips twitch. "Very well, sir. I'll tell the chef."

"Thank ya."

Patrick leaves, and Aidan puts some food on his fork. He holds it in front of my mouth, and I bite into it.

I chew it, swallow, and declare, "So good."

Aidan pops a bite into his mouth and nods. "Aye."

We eat and drink in silence for a few moments.

Aidan asks, "Would ya rather be locked in a room with Alaina or Brody?"

I choke on my wine.

"Shit. Sorry, petal," he says, rubbing my back.

I finish coughing, take a sip of water, then wipe my mouth. I answer, "Alaina, hands down."

"Seriously?"

"Yea. No doubt about it."

"Why?" he asks.

"She's my sister. And she's amazing when she's not worried about my safety. Plus, she's a total badass."

"So's Brody. He's an O'Connor. All O'Connors are badasses," Aidan claims, then winks.

I roll my eyes. "Alaina's a woman. The only female in power in any clan I know of."

"Aye. I'll give ya that."

"Admit she's amazing even though she gets on your nerves."

Aidan groans.

"Ya can't deny it, can ya?" I push.

He scrubs his face, then confesses, "Fine. Ya win. Alaina is a total badass, but don't ever tell her I said it."

I laugh. "I won't. I wish I could be a badass like her."

Aidan laces his fingers through mine and kisses the back of my hand. "Ya are a badass."

I scoff. "Not in the least."

He shakes his head. "Ya go head-to-head with your sister. No one else does."

"She's my sister. I'm allowed."

"But ya don't have to. It still takes guts. Plus, ya don't back down from me." He feeds me another bite, then takes another one for himself.

I study him, then ask, "Why doesn't it bug ya?"

"What?"

"When I stand up to ya? I never could have done that to anyone in my father's clan. They would have punished me, but ya never make me feel scared or like I can't," I admit.

His eyes narrow. "One, ya should be able to speak your mind even if I disagree."

I take a deep breath. No man's ever thought that where I come from. Definitely not Da, Tommy, or my brothers.

Something passes in Aidan's expression, but I'm unsure what. He continues, "And all the women I've dated have always been scared of me."

I gape at him. "Really?"

He nods. "Aye. And I would rather go head-to-head in an argument with ya than not know what your opinion is, even if I disagree."

I stay quiet, processing his statement. Then I ask, "Why were they scared of ya? You've never hurt me in any way."

He stares at me a moment, then lowers his voice. He claims, "I think ya understand me, even if ya don't really understand the cause of me."

I put my hand on his cheek. "Are ya talking about your obsession with fire?"

"Aye. But not just that. Ya seem to accept me and my quirks. No one else ever has."

My heart swells and hurts that he hasn't felt unconditional love before. Of course, I never have until him either.

Patrick enters the room carrying a large tray. He sets six courses down until the table is full of steaming dishes.

"Wow! This looks amazing, but it's a lot," I declare.

"Don't worry. I'll finish whatever ya don't," Aidan states.

Patrick tops our water and wine off, points at each dish, tells us what each one is, then leaves the room.

Aidan fills my plate with a bit of each dish, then serves himself.

I try the bisque and groan. "I think I've died and gone to heaven!"

Aidan chuckles, tries a spoonful, and nods. "Pretty good. But I think I'll have to take ya to Baltimore."

"Baltimore? Where is that?"

He chuckles again. "South of New York City. They have the best bisque I've ever tasted, along with grapefruit-size crab cakes."

"Don't tease me!"

He puts his hand in the air. "I swear."

"Then you're definitely taking me!"

"I will," he promises, then takes another mouthful of the creamy, rich soup.

I take a forkful of the monkfish and hold it near his mouth.

He bites into it. I wait for him to swallow, and he says, "That might be my favorite."

"Really?" I take a bite and shrug.

"Ya don't like it?"

"Not as much as the bisque. Ya can have the rest."

He pushes his soup in front of me. "Then ya take this."

"Deal."

We eat in silence, trying all the dishes.

I ask, "Would ya rather never see Brody, Tynan, or Devin again?"

He freezes and stares at me.

"What?"

"That's not a fair question, lass."

"But ya have to answer it."

"Sorry, can't."

"Hmm."

"What's your *hmm* for?" he questions.

"I thought you'd say Devin."

He jerks his head backward. "Really? Why?"

"Because ya kept calling him a rat."

He grunts. "Aye. That wasn't cool, but in fairness, he didn't have much of a choice. Your sister really is smarter than us lot."

Shocked, I ask, "How so?"

He shrugs. "She's got her finger on the pulse. No matter what, she just seems to know what's happening."

"Except where Tommy is," I blurt out.

Tension fills the air. Aidan finally states, "I will kill him."

I nod, but my chest tightens.

"Ya don't believe me?"

"It's not that," I claim.

"I sense ya doubt my abilities," he states in a hurt voice.

I put my hand on his thigh. "I just want it over. I want ya in one piece and him dead."

"And that's exactly what will happen," Aidan insists.

"What if it doesn't?"

"It will."

More silence follows.

Aidan holds a bite of beef to my lips, and I eat it but barely taste it, wishing all this was over.

He sighs, pushes his chair back, then tugs me onto his lap. He slides his palm over my cheek and says, "Let's think about other things. This is our night out. Don't let that bastard steal it."

I release an anxious breath and then nod. "You're right."

"Of course I am," he says and winks.

I softly laugh.

His face turns serious. He studies me until my butterflies kick in.

"What?" I ask.

Something passes in his expression I've never seen before. I don't know what to make of it. He takes a minute and keeps staring at me.

"Aidan—"

"Do ya want to get married sooner rather than later, or do ya want a long engagement?"

"Wh-what do ya mean?"

"Just what I asked."

I gape at him.

He drags his knuckles down my cheek, then neck, then over the side of my breast. Tingles race down my spine. He asserts, "I'm selfishly hoping you'll say yes when I ask ya an important question."

My pulse skyrockets. I manage to whisper, "What's the question?"

22

Aidan

$\mathcal{M}$y stomach flips into overdrive. I've never been so nervous in my life. My petal stares at me, her green eyes questioning, holding her breath. I pull my thoughts together and admit, "I know I don't always articulate things the right way, and it's important to me that I say the right thing right now."

"What are ya talking about? Ya always say things perfectly," she declares.

I nervously chuckle. "Is that so?"

She puts her hand on my cheek. "Yea. Think about when we play Would Ya Rather. Ya don't beat around the bush."

"What do ya mean?" I question.

She answers, "People tend to choose their answer, but then they can't tell me why they chose it. Not ya. There's always a reason for your choice."

"So that makes me able to speak coherently?"

"Duh. Anyway, ya were saying?" she prods with excitement in her eyes.

My heart beats faster. I clear my throat and tug her closer to me. "So I was saying..."

The door opens, and Patrick booms, "I have your palate cleanser and dessert."

This guy has the worst timing.

I turn my head, shooting daggers at him with an annoyed look.

He freezes several feet from the table. "Oh, I'm sorry. Am I... I'm interrupting again, aren't I?"

"Aye, ya are," I agree, frustrated. This is the most important moment in my life and everything I planned to say, I suddenly forgot. My pulse continues skyrocketing, and the blood in my veins heats to the point I'm going to break out in a sweat. The last thing I need is Patrick interrupting like this.

Scarlet babbles, "It's okay. We were just talking about things. Aidan thinks he can't talk right... I mean, articulate things, but I was telling him how he can. And, of course, he doesn't really believe me because I can see it in his eyes, and I know when I see that look that he's humoring me, but—"

I put my finger over her lips. "Let's let Patrick set the stuff down and go away."

She arches her eyebrows, and her cheeks heat.

My dick hardens. I love it when she turns that expression on me.

Scarlet mumbles, "Oh. Yea. Right. Umm..."

I make a quick decision. "Patrick, could ya box that up for us? We're going to be leaving soon."

"Oh, is everything all right?" he questions.

I give him an exasperated look, wondering if he suddenly became daft. I concede, "Everything's fine. Do ya mind?" I motion toward the door.

He finally takes the hint. "Oh, right. Sorry. I'll just box these up for ya. Do ya want any more wine before I leave?"

I groan. "No, Patrick. Just box it up, please, and get the fuck out of here."

"Aidan!" Scarlet exclaims, but amusement fills her expression.

I soften my delivery, announcing, "Patrick, you're interrupting a moment."

He puts his hand over his mouth. "A moment! How special! Should I bring champagne?"

Oh shit. Maybe I should have thought about champagne.

"Sir?" he questions.

What am I thinking? Scarlet hates champagne.

In a firm voice, I order, "No, Patrick. I'll get the box at the hostess stand on our way out. And I'll pay the bill there too."

"Okay. Well, it's been great serving ya."

Scarlet states, "You've been a really lovely server. We really appreciate everything you've done tonight. And the food was great. All the recommendations, the wine, and every dish was just delicious. I'd definitely give ya a high rating on the survey." She pats my shoulder. "Don't worry, I'll make sure I'm the one to fill it in and not Aidan—not that he'd mark ya down. Well, I hope he wouldn't mark ya down. But don't worry, I'll do it. And if your boss wants to hear me sing your praises, I'd be more than happy to—"

I put my fingers over her lips again.

She looks at me, then mumbles against my fingers, "Oops. I'm doing it again, aren't I?"

I can't help but chuckle. It's one of the reasons I love her. The fact that she's nervous right now makes me love her even more, but it also calms me in some weird way.

Patrick finally states, "Very well, then. It was lovely meeting ya as well."

"Ya too," I add to be nice.

"Yea, really lovely," Scarlet adds.

"Now move along," I order, pointing toward the door.

Patrick gives us a final nod, then exits and shuts the door.

Scarlet says, "Sorry. I think I've been out of public for too long."

"You're fine, petal," I assure her. I reach into my pocket and pull out a ring, curling my fist around it.

Can't forget the diamond.

What was I going to say to her?

Focus!

Scarlet takes a deep breath, and nerves reappear on her face. She blurts out, "So we were talking about Would Ya Rather—"

"No, we weren't," I say.

"We weren't?"

"No, I was talking to ya about something else."

"Oh?" she questions, and her cheeks heat further. She bites her lip again.

I stroke her spine, confessing, "You're making my dick too hard, petal."

A nervous laugh escapes her. She asks, "Isn't your dick always hard when I'm around ya?"

I grin. "Aye. That's why it's very important that ya service it regularly."

She laughs hard and puts her forehead against my shoulder, muttering, "Aidan."

I drag my knuckles down her spine, and she shudders. I tease, "Do ya not want me to be dirty now? I thought ya liked it when I was dirty."

"Wasn't there a point to this conversation?"

"Is ya servicing my dick not something to discuss?" I challenge, then curse myself for going off on a tangent instead of asking her. But I blame her. She's the one who got me off topic.

She leans into my ear. Her lips brush against my lobe.

Everything inside me heats hotter.

She seductively asks, "What kind of dirty things do ya want to say to me right now?"

I should cut this off and get to the point before I chicken out, but I can't. I slide my hand under her dress until my palm is on her ass. I answer, "Maybe we should talk about your pussy and how wet it is just thinking about what I'll do to ya."

"Oh? Is it now? How do ya know it is? Can ya smell it? Can ya feel it? I don't think so. Your hand's not on it, and neither is your nose, so how exactly do ya know my pussy's wet, Aidan?" She pulls back and bats her eyelashes.

"Oh, ya naughty little vixen," I state.

She continues giving me that look, challenging, "What was it ya wanted to articulate?"

I groan, admitting, "You're too sexy for your own good. And bad. Very, very bad!"

"Am I?" She innocently widens her eyes.

Why can't I remember my speech?

She traces the tip of her tongue around my lips, then teases, "Where do ya want my tongue right now?"

Fuck my speech.

"Ya know what's funny?"

"What?" she whispers.

I continue, "I have a really expensive jewel in my hand, but I can't seem to get anything out to ask ya what I wanted to. So it might stay in my hand and have to return to my pocket."

Her face turns serious. She sits straighter, lifting her chin and squaring her shoulders. "I can be quiet."

"But can ya? I'm not sure ya can, and if ya don't, then I can't remember what to say," I warn.

She pretends to zip her lips and toss the key over her shoulder.

Ask her.

Nope. It's time to show her who's boss again.

I put my face in front of hers, my mouth inches from her succulent lips. I drag my eyes down her and then stroke her cleavage.

Her breath turns hotter.

I force myself to drag my gaze back to her emeralds, which shine brighter. Her cheeks deepen to maroon.

She opens her mouth, and I arch my eyebrows. She shuts it again and smiles, tilting her head.

"What was it ya just want to say?" I challenge.

She shakes her head.

"Really? Okay. Well, I wanted to ask ya if ya like necklaces."

She furrows her forehead, and I don't miss the disappointment forming on her expression, which makes me happy. She recovers and says, "Oh, um...necklaces are nice." She forces a smile.

I relax a bit.

She'll say yes.

She'll say yes.

I know she'll say yes.

But if she doesn't say yes...

She's going to say yes!

I take my fingertips and trace her collarbone. She shudders and her eyelids droop.

"I mean, ya do have this necklace on." I tug at the chain.

She opens her eyes and swallows hard. "Do ya not like it?"

"No, it's fine," I affirm.

"But ya have another one for me?" she questions, unable to fully cover up her disappointment.

I tuck a lock of her hair behind her ear. Then I take the ends and twirl my finger around them. I ask, "Did I ever tell ya how much I love your hair?"

Confused, she answers, "Uh, no."

"Oh, well, I do," I declare.

She slides her hand through my hair. "Well, I like your hair too."

"Do ya now?" I state, squeezing the ring in my fist tighter.

She nods and proclaims, "I do. I like how it's longer. Kind of messy. Gives ya that rugged look."

"Rugged, huh? Is that what ya like? Rugged?"

Her lips twitch. "I like ya, and you're rugged, so I guess so."

"Really? What else do ya like about me?"

She softly smiles. "I like everything about ya. You're a real man."

"Am I? Well, I feel like you're a real woman."

"What makes me a real woman?" she asks.

"Wouldn't ya like to know?"

"I do," she states.

I slide my hand along her head and fist her hair back. I murmur, "Maybe I shouldn't give ya a necklace. Maybe I should give ya something else."

Her body stiffens.

Then I kiss her neck until she whimpers. I move my lips over her jawline to her ear. "Maybe I should give ya something that sits on a different part of your body."

"Like what?" she whispers.

I move my hand to the front of her and slide it under her panties, gliding my fingers inside her.

She softly moans.

I pump them a few times until she mumbles, "Oh Jesus. Aidan, are we going to do this here?"

I taunt, "Ya don't want to come right now?"

Her insides clench my finger.

"I think ya do," I assert.

"Aidan."

"Do ya want to go home, or do ya want to get naughty with me right now? Or maybe in the car, where the driver can hear us? Or, we could go into the bathroom at the back of the restaurant..."

I let her move her head so she's looking at me. She answers, "Wherever ya want, Aidan."

"And that's why I love ya, precious petal. You're always up for a challenge."

"And ya aren't?" she retorts.

"Didn't claim that," I answer.

She scrunches her face. "So why do ya have me on your lap talking about jewelry? Is this a new turn-on for ya?"

I push, "Why? Does jewelry turn ya on?"

She shakes her head, babbling, "No, I don't know why I said that. I just, well, I don't know. Ya started talking about jewelry and then ya started touching me, so I just, I don't know."

Amusement fills me. I tease further, "No need to get all frazzled."

"I'm not frazzled. You're the frazzled one."

"Am I?" I ask, suddenly very, very calm and not nervous anymore.

"Yea, ya seem very frazzled."

"How's that?" I say, sliding another finger into her.

She inhales deeply.

I grab her hip and move her over me.

She blurts out, "Jesus. Why are ya doing this to me right now?" She takes over, circling her hips faster.

I hold her firmly, not letting her move, claiming, "I didn't tell ya to move." I thrust my fingers a few times.

She pouts. "Ya aren't being fair."

"It's not fair? Is this fair?" I ask, sliding my thumb over her clit and adding, "By the way, ya can't come right now."

Her eyes widen. "What?"

"I said no coming, or I won't give ya your jewelry."

"What jewelry? I'm so confused. Is there jewelry or not? And I don't care if ya give me jewelry."

My gut sinks. "Ya don't care if I give ya jewelry? Ya don't want gems and metals and blingy things that represent that you're mine?"

Her hot breath hits mine. "Aidan, you're confusing me."

"Am I?"

"Yea. I...I don't know what's going on here."

"My fingers are in your pussy. My thumb's on your clit. The last time I checked, that made ya feel pretty good. But ya don't know what's going on? How are ya confused?" I taunt, working her harder, then slowing down.

She closes her eyes. "Uh, I'm... Please let me come. Please."

"No." I continue to drive her up and then back down until my palm's soaked.

Her voice cracks as she says, "Oh my God."

I stop.

She pins her emeralds on me, begging, "Aidan, stop teasing me. I-I can't handle it."

I lean into her ear. "Then tell me what piece of jewelry ya really want from me."

She freezes.

"Tell me," I demand.

She looks at me and swallows hard. "I don't expect anything from ya, Aidan."

"I didn't ask what ya expected. I asked what ya wanted."

"I want ya, no matter what that looks like."

Her answer couldn't be more perfect. I give her a kiss on the lips, sliding my tongue against hers and speeding it up to the point where we're both urgently flicking against the other. As a reward, I work her pussy so hard she erupts in an earthquake, coming on my lap and crying out against my lips, "Oh Jesus Christ! Aid— Oh fuck!"

Her body convulses harder against mine, and I hold her tight against me, murmuring, "Shh. Ya don't want the restaurant to hear."

"Aidan," she moans in my ear, her body still shaking.

I kiss her neck and wait for her to calm down. Then I pull my hand away from her pussy and shove my fingers in her mouth. I demand, "Suck."

She obeys like the good lass she's always been, perfectly utilizing her tongue and lips.

My cock throbs against my zipper. "I think it's time I told ya what I want." I pull my fingers out of her mouth.

She blinks a few times, staying quiet and catching her breath.

I peck her quickly on the lips, then stare at her, stroking the side of her head. She takes a deep inhale and waits.

Nerves quickly fill me again. I stall, asking, "Is there anything else ya want to ask me first?"

Confusion clouds her expression.

"No Would Ya Rather questions or maybe another game ya have up your sleeve?" I ask.

She shakes her head again.

"Well, I have a Would Ya Rather question I've been dying to ask ya."

She tilts her head and furrows her eyebrows. "What?"

I hold the ring in front of her. "Would ya rather marry me and wear this forever or keep things as they are between us?"

Her eyes dart to the ring and then back at me, glistening over. She tosses her arms around me, pulls my head toward her, and presses her mouth to mine.

We kiss for a long time, and when I retreat, I state, "Ya haven't answered me, petal. What option are ya picking?"

"What do ya think?"

"I'm not going to assume or put words into your mouth on this issue."

She tilts her head and smiles, stroking the side of my head.

My stomach flips. "You're making me feel a bit ill right now."

"Aww, poor Aidan," she coos.

"Not funny. Ya have to choose," I push.

She softly laughs. "Maybe I should slide my tongue over your cock first."

I groan. "Don't tease me, lass."

She pouts. "Aww. Ya don't like a bit of your own medicine?"

I fist her hair and tug on it. She gasps, and I lean over her face. "Would ya rather marry me or keep things as is, petal?"

Her face lights up. "Are ya serious right now?"

"Of course I'm serious. Do ya really think I'm going to joke about this?"

"But weren't ya a few minutes ago?"

"Scarlet—"

"Are ya really asking me to marry ya? Because if this is a joke—"

"Do ya think I'd put a ring in front of ya and joke around about this?"

"I... I'm just checking."

I kiss her lightly, then affirm, "I'm asking ya to marry me. I'd never joke about it, nor have I ever spoken those words. So stop giving me a heart attack and answer my question, petal."

Her face turns serious. Her eyes water until a tear escapes, and she says, "Of course I want to marry ya."

"Ya do?"

She laughs. "Aidan, stop asking me. I love ya. That isn't a question."

Relief hits me. I grab her hand and slide the ring over her finger, stating, "If ya don't like the ring, I'll get ya another one."

"What are ya talking about? Don't be silly! I love it. It's perfect."

"Is it? Because I really want to make sure—"

She puts her ring finger and the middle one against my mouth. She glances at the diamond, then back at me, claiming, "It's the most perfect ring I've ever seen."

Happiness sears through me.

"Ya sure?"

She groans. "Aidan, stop doubting things." She kisses me and curls into my chest, staring at her ring. "It's beautiful. I love it."

I relax, admitting, "I had a better speech planned. But I warned ya I'm not good with words."

"But ya are good with words. Ya said everything perfectly. Ya don't have to think twice about it. Just tell me ya love me again."

I tilt her chin up and stare at her for a moment. "I love ya more than anything on this earth. And I want to be with ya forever. The day ya become Mrs. Aidan O'Connor will be the happiest day of my life."

She slowly smiles, blinking away more tears. "That's good, my love. Because I can't wait for that day either."

23

Scarlet

*T*he dull morning light peeks through the blinds, glinting off my diamond. It sparks to life as I wiggle my finger, which I've been doing for a while.

I'm still in shock. I can't believe I'm going to marry Aidan. The happiness I've felt since he gave it to me won't seem to go away, which I'm not complaining about.

He stirs, kissing the back of my neck, and murmurs, "Future Mrs. Aidan O'Connor, are ya going to stop looking at that ring or what?"

I turn to him, answering, "No. Do ya want me to?"

He grins. "Nah, as long as ya remember that I'm the one that gave it to ya."

I climb my fingers over his pecs. "How could I ever forget that?"

"Maybe I should make ya remember," he claims, then slides his hand through my hair and kisses me. His erection pushes into my pelvis, and I slide my arms around him.

A loud pounding on the door makes me jump, then freeze.

He orders, "Just ignore it," then returns to kissing me.

The knocking gets louder.

Devin's voice hurls out, "Dad's here. Time to get to breakfast."

Aidan's body turns stiff, as does mine. He buries his head into my pillow.

Devin yells, "Let me know you're awake, or I'm going to come in there."

Aidan warns, "Ya come in here, and you're going to leave with a broken neck."

"Whatever. Get your ass out to the breakfast table," Devin orders.

Aidan groans softly.

My anxiety builds in my chest. "Your da's here? I thought he wasn't coming for another week."

Aidan answers, "He must have come early. It's typical for him to surprise us, so I should have anticipated he'd arrive sooner rather than later."

I stare at him. The air in my lungs expands.

He strokes my cheek and questions, "Why do ya look pale all of a sudden, petal?"

"Your da... Is he... Is he anything like mine?"

Aidan's eyes widen. "No. Not in the way you're thinking. Ya don't have to fear him."

I swallow hard, wishing I had some water for my suddenly dry mouth. "But what will he think about us? Well, me? I'm an O'Leary."

Aidan puts his thumb over my lips. "Shh. Ya have nothing to worry about. Brody's married to Alaina. My dad knows the situation ya were in. Honestly, there's nothing to fear. My dad will welcome ya with open arms."

"How? I don't understand how that's possible. He surely won't forget I'm the daughter of his enemy."

His lips twitch. "Because he already worked out all of it with Alaina. Don't worry. You'll see. Besides, I'll be with ya the entire time. Ya have nothing to worry about."

I release an anxious breath. He pecks me on the lips, then rolls out of bed. He pulls the covers back, ordering, "Time to get up, my sexy, soon-to-be wife. Breakfast is waiting."

I groan, curl into the pillow, and pull my knees to my chest, whining, "But I'm still tired. Ya wore me out too much last night."

He challenges, "Are ya complaining?"

"Nope!"

He chuckles. "That's why I need to get some food in ya, so I can wear ya out later today."

I laugh.

He reaches forward and slides his fingers over the side of my body, tracing the curve of my waist and hips. Then he pats my ass. "Time's a ticking. Come on."

I groan again and get up, stating, "Let me take a quick shower."

"No. If my dad's at the breakfast table, we need to go. Devin wouldn't have come to get us if it wasn't necessary."

"But I want to look presentable when I first meet your da."

"Don't worry, petal. You're beautiful, all done up or not. Just toss on some joggers, and let's go downstairs."

"No way. I have to put something nicer on." I go over to the closet and fumble through my clothes.

Aidan gets dressed, and I'm still naked. He asserts, "Ya just need clothes, lass. Here." He grabs a pair of leggings and an oversized sweater. "Toss it on. Let's go."

"But this looks too..." I stare at the clothes.

"What's wrong with them?"

"This outfit is way too casual to meet your da."

He shakes his head. "Honestly, petal. Ya need to trust me on this. Put the clothes on." He shakes them in front of me again.

I cave. "Ugh. Okay, fine." I step into the leggings, put on a bra, and toss the oversized sweater over me.

Aidan wiggles his eyebrows and teases, "No panties. Just how I like ya."

I slap the back of his chest. "Do ya want me to take them off and put some panties on? Then ya can concentrate at breakfast better while your da's next to ya."

"Hell no. Ya keep those panties off. That's a direct order."

I laugh. "Is that so?"

"Aye." He pats my ass, then slings his arm across my shoulders. He leads me out of the closet.

"Can I at least brush my hair?"

"Ya look fine."

"Aidan, come on. I don't want your da to see me for the first time with my hair a mess like I just got out of bed."

Mischief fills his grin. "But ya did just get out of bed. *My* bed." He puffs out his chest.

I elbow him.

"Ouch! You're getting too dangerous with that move of yours," he declares.

"Seriously. I'm going to the bathroom." I shove out of his grasp and rush past the doorway. I pick up his toothbrush and call out, "Ya should brush your teeth first too."

He enters the room. "So I can eat breakfast and drink coffee?"

"Yea." I put toothpaste on his toothbrush and hand it to him. Then I put some on mine, and we brush our teeth and swig mouthwash.

"There. Let's go," Aidan states.

"Not yet!" I grab my hairbrush and pull it through my locks. I reach for makeup.

He grabs my hand. "Ya don't need makeup. It's breakfast."

"I'm sure Alaina will have her makeup on."

"There are lots of times Alaina doesn't have her makeup on."

"Yea, but your da's in town. It's different," I declare.

"Seriously, petal. You'll see. Come on." He drags me out of the bathroom before I can put on makeup, and we leave the bedroom.

"Aidan, please let me put a little bit on so I can look more presentable," I protest.

"You're fine. Beautiful as always," he asserts, then spins and scoops me up in his arms.

I shriek, "What are ya doing?"

"I'm carrying ya downstairs so ya can't go back."

"Aidan!" I laugh and slap his chest.

"It's going to take a lot more energy to make a mark on my body," he boasts.

"Ha ha, funny."

He kisses me on the forehead and walks down the stairs. I lace my hands around his neck, saying, "Ya really can put me down."

"Yea, I know, but I'm not going to."

"Honestly, you're being dramatic."

"Rather be dramatic than ya go back into the bedroom and put on a ton of makeup. My dad will love your natural beauty anyway." He drags his eyes over my body.

My cheeks heat.

We get to the bottom of the stairs, and I order, "Okay, time to put me down. I don't want ya to carry me into the breakfast room."

"What will ya give me if I put ya down?" he taunts, continuing to walk down the hallway.

"What do ya want?"

"I think ya should get creative and figure out what I want."

I roll my eyes. "Let me guess. It's something sexual and has to do with your cock. Maybe my mouth around it?"

"That's a good start, lass," he teases.

I lean closer to his ear, lower my voice, and add, "Or maybe ya want my mouth around your balls."

"Hmm, those are both good options. Ya have permission to do all of it."

I lick his lobe, then suggest, "Or maybe ya want my hot pussy dripping over your hard cock. Would that be better?" I retreat and bat my eyes.

"Vixen."

"I'm your vixen." I smirk.

"Aye. Ya are. Don't forget it. And I'm holding ya to all three of the above," he declares.

I giggle. "Of course ya are."

He stops walking and then gives me another peck on the lips. "Are ya ready to meet my dad?"

My anxiety builds again. "No," I admit.

"Honestly, petal, there's nothing to worry about. He'll love ya."

"Please set me down," I beg.

Aidan softly chuckles. "Okay. Your wish is my command." He puts me on my feet but keeps his arm around my waist, tugging me close to him. He opens the door to the breakfast room and guides me inside.

My gut fills with butterflies as Brody states, "Ya can't light that up. Alaina can't be around smoke. Plus, we have a no smoking rule in this house."

An older man, who I assume is Aidan's father, with a smoker's voice, grumbles, "That's not a rule. That's just a stupid idea that ya have in your head."

"No, it's not a stupid idea, and they're our rules. Our house, our rules."

"I bought ya this house."

"Ya gifted us this house. And remember, you're on my turf now."

Tully shakes his head, asserting, "I gave ya a little bit of power, and look what's going to your head."

"Call it what ya want. No smoking in here," Brody restates as he leans back and slides his arm around Alaina.

"It really is best for the baby, Tully. But we have a porch out back that ya can use. I even had the staff put ashtrays out there for ya," Alaina adds in a sweet tone I barely ever hear her use.

Tully puts his cigar down, and his voice softens. "Since you're pregnant, I'll smoke on the porch."

Alaina beams. "Thanks, Tully."

"Dad, you're early," Aidan states and stops guiding me toward the table.

Tully turns. Wrinkles line his face, but his eyes are kinder than I imagined. He looks me over, then rises, saying, "I'm assuming you're Scarlet?"

"Yea." I hold my hand out.

He glances at my hand, then chuckles and coughs, turning his head into his elbow.

Devin mutters, "Ya might want to stop smoking those killer cigars, Dad."

Tully ignores him, stops coughing, then steps forward. He tugs me into his arms. "Glad to see you're safe and alive."

Embarrassment washes over me, but I'm also overwhelmed. I thought he'd be cold like my da was, and I didn't expect a hug. My da never hugged any of us. The thick scent of his previous cigars flares in my nostrils, but I'm grateful it's not cigarette smoke.

When he releases me, I offer a smile, still nervous. I reply, "Yea, thanks to Aidan."

Tully glances at Aidan, and his expression turns stern. "Heard you've been a little busy."

Before Aidan can say anything, I interject, "If Aidan hadn't rescued me, I'd still be with Tommy. Who knows, I might be dead by now. He saved me. Please don't be mad at him."

Tully turns his head and looks at Alaina. "I see your sister's got a bunch of your balls, huh?"

She laughs and then lifts her chin with pride. "She sure does. Never really realized it until lately."

"What do ya mean? I'm nothing like Alaina," I declare.

He shakes his head. "Ya sure are. But don't worry about it." He motions to a seat. "Please, sit down. Let's have some breakfast. I'm starving. Are ya hungry?"

My stomach growls, and I put my hand over it, answering, "I guess so."

Aidan pulls my chair out. "Sit down, petal."

We both take our seats, and food gets passed around the table.

When my plate's full, Alaina asks, "What is that around your finger?"

I glance down at my ring and then at Aidan, unable to stop beaming.

"Is that what I think it is?" Alaina inquires.

The room turns silent.

Aidan tugs me closer to him and announces, "Aye. I asked Scarlet to marry me. She agreed. We're going to get married as soon as possible."

"What?" Alaina shrieks.

Brody puts his hands over his ears. "Since when do ya shriek, Alaina?"

"Oh, sorry." She smirks and gets up. She comes around the table.

I rise, and she hugs me.

"So we get to plan a wedding, and we get to plan for a baby. This is going to be so much fun."

I laugh. "I don't remember the last time I heard ya use the word fun, Alaina."

"Is that a bad thing?"

"No, not at all."

"Good. We can have some fun. We're going to do some baby shopping today anyway. Just ya and me."

Excitement fills me. "You're going to let me out of the house? Awesome!"

The excitement on her face dulls. "Not exactly."

"Meaning?"

"Meaning, we have a baby consultant coming to the house, and her team's bringing a ton of things over for us to look at."

I groan. "You're not going to let me out of the house again, are ya?"

"It's just easier this way," she claims.

I tilt my head and stare at her with my hand on my hip. "Really? Is that the excuse you're going to use?"

She smirks. "Yep, and since I'm pregnant and the one who's tired, ya have to go by what I say."

"Since when does anybody not have to go by what ya say?" I tease.

She reaches over and hugs me again. "Oh, I'm so excited for ya. Congratulations. Even if it is Aidan you're marrying." She smirks at him.

He booms, "Well, aren't ya chipper this morning, Queen Alaina."

"Well, I kind of have to be nice to ya now."

"Do ya?"

She shrugs.

"We'll see how long it lasts," he states.

Alaina rolls her eyes, squeezes me again, and returns to her seat.

Tully rises again and pulls me back in his arms. "Another O'Leary coming into the O'Connor clan. Starting to like how ya ladies give up your family allegiance."

I freeze, and panic fills me. I thought any loyalty I felt toward the O'Learys was over, but it feels weird all of a sudden.

Tully challenges, "Are ya questioning coming into the O'Connor clan?"

I open my mouth, but nothing comes out. I look at Alaina for help.

She interjects, "Give her a minute to process, Tully."

For the first time in a while, I'm relieved that my sister's my sister.

Tully studies me another moment, then declares, "You'll get used to us, lass. You'll be happy you're an O'Connor and that we're caring for ya." He winks and sits down.

I glance at Alaina again.

She nods for me to take my seat and shoots me a look like I shouldn't worry about anything, but I have anxiety that won't go away.

Devin asks, "So ya want to get married sooner rather than later?"

"Yep, soon as possible. Scarlet and I talked about it last night," Aidan answers.

"Ya know you're going to have a problem," Devin proclaims.

Aidan's eyes turn to slits. "And why is that, little brother?"

Devin sits back in his chair with his arms crossed and a satisfied look on his face. He glances at Tynan and shakes his head. "They always think the youngest ones are the dumbest, but we're actually the smartest, aren't we?"

Tynan nods arrogantly. "Yep. One of these days, they're going to realize it."

"What the fuck are ya talking about?" Aidan barks out.

Devin puts his gaze back on him. "Did ya forget about the fact that Scarlet's already married?"

Aidan's face shows his anger. "She's not married. They forced her, and she never even said her vows. Her da said them for her. So she's not married."

Devin adds, "That's the case, true. However, that's not how Ireland or the church see it."

"Are ya trying to start trouble?" Aidan hurls.

"No. I'm trying to get ya to use your brain. There's a marriage license on file."

"How do ya know they filed it?" Aidan asks.

"Of course they would've filed it, dumbass. Ya think Tommy wasn't going to claim the daughter of the clan as his?"

My stomach flips. I grab Aidan's thigh, fretting, "Is this true? We won't be able to get married?"

He tugs me tighter to him. "Of course we're going to be able to get married. Don't listen to my asshole brother. I'll take care of it."

"But how? He's right. I'm not legally divorced."

"Or widowed," Devin mutters.

"She will be soon," Aidan claims.

"But I'm not right now," I point out again.

"We don't even know for sure if it's on file. Plus, everything can change in life. Don't worry about this, petal. I'll take care of it," Aidan insists.

The room turns quiet for a while.

He murmurs in my ear, "Honestly, ya have nothing to worry about. I will figure it out and take care of whatever needs to happen. I'll start right after breakfast, okay?"

I release an anxious breath. "Okay."

"Ya spend the day with your sister planning for the baby and whatever else ya want to plan for the wedding."

"Ya don't want to do that with me?" I question.

He kisses me on the forehead. "Whatever ya want me to be involved in, I will. Whatever ya want to do with your sister is fine. But I'm going to take care of the legalities because I won't marry ya in a ceremony and not have things legal. Do ya understand me?"

"What if ya can't undo it?"

His eyes darken. "No matter what I have to do, I will legally marry ya. Now, don't worry about this."

I swallow hard and nod. "All right. If ya are sure—"

"I'm sure." He glances at my plate. "Finish your breakfast. I don't need ya to turn into skin and bones again."

24

Aidan

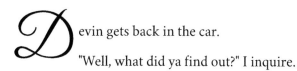 evin gets back in the car.

"Well, what did ya find out?" I inquire.

He shakes his head. "The registrar said that ya have to go to Dublin to find out if Tommy filed the paperwork."

"Why can't they tell us here?"

He shrugs. "Different government, different system. But she asked me if it's the same Scarlet O'Leary who married Tommy."

I groan and put my hand over my face. "Goddammit."

"You're never going to escape that one," Devin states.

"Shut the fuck up."

"Well, she was married to him."

"She was forced to marry him. It wasn't her choice," I bark.

Devin puts his hands in the air. "That may be so..."

"It's not 'that may be so.' It's the truth," I declare.

He keeps his hands where they are. "Yea, I get that. Sorry. Wrong choice of words."

"Ya should be sorry, ya fucking rat."

"Are we back to this again? I thought ya were past that situation."

I grip the steering wheel tighter and growl, "I don't want to go down to Dublin today."

"We can't go to Dublin anyway. Somebody else will need to go. Ya know ya can't show your face there with everything going on."

"I'll show my face wherever I fucking want," I claim.

He shakes his head and points at me. "Sometimes you're dumber than I think ya are."

"Shut up," I order again.

"We've got to send one of our guys down there. If ya show up in Dublin, there will be issues, so focus on what ya can. Ya have to find Tommy right now and take care of him. And ya know ya can't take any undue risks."

I hate that my brother's right. I stay quiet for a while.

He adds, "I don't know why ya want to get married anyway. It's a stupid ritual."

I turn my head and scowl. "That's because you've never met the woman who's supposed to be yours forever."

He grunts. "No one's supposed to be anyone's forever. That's just a fallacy."

"You're a moron." I shake my head.

"Not as big of one as ya are. You're not only getting married, but you're also marrying an O'Leary."

I smack him across the head.

"Jesus. What the fuck was that for?" he hurls.

I jab his chest. "Don't ya ever talk about my woman that way again."

"I just stated a fact. She is an O'Leary."

"She's not an O'Leary anymore."

"Oh, sorry. She's an Ahern."

I smack him again, this time harder.

Fire erupts in Devin's eyes. "Goddammit. I swear to God, Aidan, if ya don't stop..."

"You'll what?" I taunt.

His face hardens. He shakes his head harder. "You're losing it over a woman."

"Ya need to grow up," I tell him, then turn on the car. I pull out of the parking lot in the opposite direction of the house.

"Where are ya going? I told ya we can't go to Dublin today. Don't be stupid," Devin restates.

"I'm not going to Dublin," I say and continue down the road.

"Then where are we going?" he questions.

"To pay Father Michael a visit."

He groans. "He's going to pray those stupid prayers he reserves specially for us. Don't make me sit through all of that."

"Yea, well, maybe it'll be good for someone to pray for your soul," I state.

He grunts. "That's funny coming from ya. Pretty sure he should pray for your soul more. You're the one who will be burning in flames before ya even get there."

I ignore his remark about my pyro habit, but the itch to burn something suddenly fills me, and it pisses me off.

Devin knows exactly how to get under my skin.

For several minutes, all I can think about is fire. I haven't lit a match in a while. Something about Scarlet has calmed me in certain ways, but right now, I'd do anything to light a match and then toss it on my brother. I snarl, "You're lucky your blood."

"Whatever."

I veer through the busy Belfast streets, avoiding cars and going through traffic lights.

"Jesus, why do ya have to go so fast? You're making my breakfast churn. It's not like Father Michael will be doing anything except praying all day."

"Stop being a pussy."

"I'm not a pussy."

"How do ya know his schedule anyway?" I question.

Devin snorts. "Because that's what he always does."

"And ya keeping tabs on Father Michael? Is there something ya want to tell me?"

Devin scowls. "Shut up. Every time we have to go there, he's kneeling in front of the candles and reciting the rosary. It doesn't take a genius to know what he'll be doing."

I lean closer and taunt, "Or, maybe ya are keeping tabs on him."

"Put your money where your mouth is, then! I guarantee ya a hundred pounds that he's praying and saying a rosary when we get there."

I don't take my brother's bet. I know damn well Father Michael will be doing just that. I continue through the streets and pull up to the church. I park and get out of the car.

Devin stays where he is.

I open his door. "What are ya doing?"

"I'm not going in. This is your gig, not mine," he retorts.

"Aye, ya are. Get your ass out of the car."

He grumbles, "Why do I have to go in?"

"Because someday you're going to have to do this, ya dumbass. And ya need to learn how to do it."

He scoffs. "Bullshit. I'm never getting married."

"Dad will have something to say about that," I state.

"I don't care what Dad says. I'm not getting married. Marriage is for losers who aren't part of this century and have no balls."

"No balls?" I question.

He nods. "Aye. Losers without balls because a woman snagged them for life."

I step back and snarl, "Get your ass out of the car before I beat it."

He slowly gets out, but he's not happy with me. That's okay though. I'm not happy with him either.

Feeling antsy, I put my hand inside my pocket and grip my lighter.

We enter the church, and Devin nudges me. Arrogance washes over his face. He points to Father Michael, who, sure enough, is kneeling in front of the candles.

"Stay here," I quietly say. I go to the front of the church, kneel next to him, then take my lighter out and ignite several candles. I toss a bunch of cash into the box.

Father Michael turns toward me. "Well, if it isn't Aidan O'Connor."

"Father," I say, nodding my head in reverence.

He puts his rosary down and then makes the sign of the cross.

To appease him, I do the same.

He puts his hand on my shoulder. "Dear Lord, please protect this man's soul. He knows not what he does."

I hold in my comments as the silence ensues, and Father Michael keeps his eyes shut. It's the same damn prayer he always gives me. He knows I'm going to hell, yet he always prays to God to save me.

"Amen," he adds.

"Amen," I repeat.

He stays frozen, surely praying harder for me in his head.

When he finally opens his eyes, I announce, "I have a private matter I need to talk to ya about."

"Aye, I'm sure ya do or ya wouldn't be here," he states in disapproval, then adds, "Ya should be coming to church on Sundays and Holy Days."

I ignore his comment. I get up, go over to the front pew, and nod for my brother to join us.

Father Michael booms, "Well, Devin O'Connor. I didn't know I would be graced with your presence as well." He makes the sign of the cross and then puts his hand on Devin's shoulder and prays, "Dear Lord, please make this young lad find his way and see the ways of his sins."

Devin grunts, and I give him a dirty look.

Father Michael opens his eyes and arches his eyebrows. "Is there something else ya want me to pray for ya over?"

Devin's face hardens. He shakes his head. "Nah, that works. Let's not change things."

Satisfaction overtakes Father Michael's face. He says, "Amen."

Devin doesn't echo the sentiment.

Father Michael crosses his arms and glares at my brother.

I nudge him.

"Amen," Devin grumbles.

Father points to the pew. "Please, lads, sit. Something's obviously on your minds."

"Not my mind. I was pressured to come inside," Devin confesses.

"Shut up," I say.

"Please watch your language in the house of God," Father Michael reprimands.

I make a note to keep my comments to myself, especially when I need him to do what I want him to do.

We all sit down, and Father Michael asks, "Now, what can I do for ya?"

I take a deep breath and say, "I'm getting married."

"Well, congratulations. It's about time. Does your da know?"

I nod. "Yea, he met her this morning."

Father Michael's eyes lighten. "And who is the lass?"

"Let's get to that in a minute," I state.

Curiosity fills his expression. He squints at me.

I announce, "We're getting married as soon as possible."

"Ya must love her very much, then."

"Aye. I do," I admit.

"Well, marriage classes are starting—"

"No, we're not doing classes," I interject, narrowing my eyes.

He objects, "Everyone has to take classes."

"Let's not beat around the bush. I know there's an expedited process."

He gives me a challenging stare and glances around to ensure we're alone. He states, "Aye. For special circumstances I can accommodate. However, there's a big donation for that."

"Aye. I'm not daft. How much?" I ask.

"Well, it depends."

"What do ya mean it depends?"

320

"How fast ya want it to happen, what her previous situation is, and her current religion. There are a lot of factors that come into play."

"For a fucking priest, ya sure do know how to take people for their money," I blurt out.

He scolds, "Do not use that language in the house of God."

I sit up straighter. "Sorry."

He gives me another disapproving look and asks, "So I'm not going to ask ya again, Aidan, who is the woman?"

My stomach flips. I hate having to admit who Scarlet is. Not because I'm ashamed of her but because of the situation. I know this is going to get more complicated. But I answer his question. "Her name is Scarlet."

His eyes narrow. "Scarlet, what?"

"Scarlet O'Leary."

His head jerks backward. "Ya mean Ahern?"

"No, O'Leary," I say.

"Didn't she get married to Tommy Ahern, the O'Leary under-boss?" he asks.

I fist my hand next to my thigh with my lighter in it, stopping myself from flicking it. "She was forced to get married. It wasn't legal."

"But she's married, correct?"

"She isn't. It wasn't of her own free will," I repeat.

His face softens. "Aye, I'm sure it wasn't. However, ya got a problem on your hands, lad."

"I know what problems I have on my hands. How much is it going to be for ya to expedite our marriage classes?"

"It's not about the money."

"Sure it isn't," I snap.

"Watch it," he warns again.

I sigh. "What's the problem, then?"

"Before ya get married, she needs to be divorced. Or widowed," he adds, with hope in his voice. Father Michael may be a man of the cloth, but he hates the O'Learys as much as we do.

"I'm taking care of that," I claim.

He nods. "Good. It's best for everyone. The people of Ireland don't need that man around, and neither does your soon-to-be wife."

"Agreed. So ya do your part and I'll do mine. How do we get this done?" I question.

He studies me for a while. Then, without emotion, he says, "It's going to cost ya fifty thousand pounds."

"Fifty thousand pounds? Are ya insane?" Devin blurts out.

"Ya need to watch the level of your voice in the house of God," Father Michael scolds him again.

Devin crosses his arms. "That's highway robbery, and ya know it."

"Is it? Seems to me ya can either go through the classes the way you're supposed to, at the time that you're supposed to, or ya can pay the small fee for a luxury—"

"Small fee? That's not a small fee," Devin claims.

"Be quiet," I say through gritted teeth.

Father Michael turns to me. "I think I misread the situation. I meant to say sixty thousand pounds."

"Are ya a blackmailer too?" Devin asks.

"Goddammit, Devin, get the fuck out of here," I order, annoyed.

Father Michael threatens, "I'm not going to warn ya again, Aidan. Ya need to watch your language inside this church. Have some respect for our creator."

I scrub my face. "I'm sorry. Devin, leave."

"Gladly." The sound of my brother trudging out of the church and then slamming the door fills the air.

"That will be another ten grand for him slamming that door. That's an old door. He probably broke it."

I look back at the heavy wooden door. I assure him, "The door is fine."

"Is it now?" Father Michael asks, arching his eyebrow.

My chest tightens. The longer I'm here, the higher the price will get. I know how Father Michael operates, so I hold my tongue.

He studies me. "Are ya sure ya want to marry an O'Leary?"

My gut tightens. "She has no allegiance to the O'Learys. She was forced to marry that thug. I would think ya, of all people, would have some sympathy for the situation."

A look of pity crosses his face. "Aye, I do have sympathy for her and that situation. However, facts are facts. You're bringing a lot of problems into your life."

I retort, "Nothing I'm not taking care of. And ya should watch your mouth. Do I need to remind ya that Brody is married to Alaina, her sister?"

Father Michael stays quiet, but he doesn't stop giving me his challenging stare. And I've got to give it to the guy. He knows how to play a lot of sides. He doesn't back down or look scared, but he still maintains his saintly priest's routine perfectly.

I assert, "Fifty thousand. I'll have it to ya by tomorrow."

"I think it went up to seventy," he claims.

In a firm voice, I insist, "No, fifty thousand. I'm not going a penny higher."

He arches his eyebrows. "I thought ya wanted to get through the marriage classes without waiting and attending all seven sessions."

I shake my head. "There are other churches around here. There are other priests. My guess is that you'd prefer to have fifty thousand pounds in your church versus another church. A lot of things ya can do with that amount of money."

"Aye, but it's going to be seventy," he declares, sticking to his guns.

I take my chances and rise. I hold out my hand. "Good to see ya, Father Michael. I guess I'll report to my father that we need a new family priest."

He rises and glances at my hand. "Who else are ya gonna go to? I'm the priest for the O'Connors. No one else. Your da will tell ya that."

"It might be time we got another priest. And come to think of it, I don't need to tell my dad. Brody and Alaina are in charge of Ireland now, with full authority. And I know neither will look favorably upon this. Especially Alaina...ya know how she is." I stare him down and wait.

He stays quiet, not flinching.

"I'm walking out the door in three seconds. Three...two..."

"Fine. Fifty thousand pounds. I need it by tomorrow. Cash."

"I know the drill," I reply, patting him on the back. "Good doing business with ya, Father. I expect our one session to take place two days from now."

"Two days!" he exclaims.

"Aye. I'm marrying her as soon as possible, and I don't want anything holding it up."

He asks, "What about the fact she's still married? I can't marry ya if that isn't taken care of. That's illegal and on paper. It's a different set of rules and laws. No amount of money will buy ya out of that."

I scoff. "We'll see about what money can and can't buy. Ya do your part, and I'll let ya know when the nuptials can take place."

25

Scarlet

"**S**hould I be nervous? What's he going to ask me at this meeting?" I question Alaina.

She waves her hand in front of her face. "Nah, it's not like we follow our religion, and neither do the O'Connors. Getting married in the church is more for show."

"That's exactly why I'm nervous. What if he asks me things about Catholicism I don't know and then he won't marry us?"

"He won't."

"I didn't have to have any meeting with Tommy. I still don't understand why this is necessary," I say.

Alaina's expression darkens. She states, "Ya were forced to marry him. Nothing was done the right way."

I stay quiet, remembering how horrible it was standing before three men in my white dress. I wish I could erase the memory, but I'm unsure how.

Alaina slides her arm around me. "Really, ya don't need to worry. I've met Father Michael and he's a lovely man."

I release an anxious breath. "Okay."

She admits, "But if it makes ya feel any better, I was a little nervous before my meeting too."

"Ya were?"

"Of course I was," she insists.

"Nothing makes ya nervous."

She gives me one of her knowing looks and chirps, "That's what ya think, but that's not the truth. There are lots of things that give me anxiety. You're one of them."

I smirk. "Ha ha, funny."

Since finding out a few days ago that she's pregnant, things have gotten slightly less tense. She's gotten off Aidan's back, and they seem to have come to some sort of truce. Although, we'll see how it is later today because I know I have another fight on my hands.

I question, "What will the priest have me do?"

"Well, when I got it done, I was in America, but all he did was discuss some things I'd have to do during ceremonies. And, of course, they want ya to get involved in the church based on our influence in the clan."

"I don't know anything about the church to volunteer for anything," I fret.

"Don't worry about it. Just tell him you'll do it. Ya don't have to do anything ya don't want to once you're married."

"That seems dishonest," I say.

Aidan enters the room. "What's dishonest?" He leans down and gives me a kiss on the head.

Alaina states, "I'm explaining to Scarlet how the church works in this family."

Aidan grunts. "Don't add any morals into it, petal. Now, Father Michael confirmed he'll be here in the next hour."

Here's where the fight starts.

I rise. "Aidan, I want to go to the church. I don't want to do it here."

"We don't have security set up," Alaina states.

I cross my arms. "Then get it set up."

She tilts her head. "We were doing so well. Do we have to fight today?"

"I have to get out of here, Alaina. Ya can't keep me prisoner. We've talked about this."

"I'm not keeping ya prisoner."

I look at Aidan. "Please, whatever ya have to do, let's go to the church."

"Out of all the places ya want me to take ya, ya want to go there?" he questions.

I nod, challenging, "Yea. Is that a problem?"

Alaina interjects, "Yea, it is a problem. There are a lot of logistics that go into making sure that you're safe."

"I didn't ask ya. I asked my soon-to-be husband," I smirk.

She shuts her mouth but her emerald eyes shoot me a disapproving look.

I refocus on Aidan. "Please."

Aidan looks smug as he says, "Aye, my dear soon-to-be wife. I will make sure that it's set up. It might take a few hours though."

"I don't care how long it takes. I want to get out of here and go to the church to meet with the priest. I don't want to do it here," I restate, lifting my chin higher.

His lips twitch. He kisses me and then assures me, "I'll take care of it."

"Ya two are going to be the death of me before I even have my baby," Alaina curses.

I accuse, "Since when are ya the dramatic one?"

Aidan states, "Let me take care of some things." He steps toward the exit.

Alaina starts to follow.

"Nope, I have this handled, Alaina. Ya just rest."

"I'm not an invalid," she says.

I burst out laughing.

She wrinkles her forehead. "It's not funny! I'm pregnant, not physically hurt in any way!"

"That's exactly what I used to tell Aidan all the time."

He freezes in the doorway and turns around, lecturing, "Brody said ya needed your rest. He said ya needed to stay de-stressed. Let me handle this, Alaina."

She opens her mouth and then shuts it.

I state, "Ya have the baby to think about." I put my hand on her stomach. "Hey, little baby. It's Auntie Scarlet. Tell your mum that she needs to keep out of my business."

Alaina gives me another disapproving look.

Aidan slaps the side of the doorframe. "On that note, I'll take care of things and be back. Enjoy your time together, ladies." He shuts the door.

Alaina crosses her arms. "Ya don't need to be taking risks."

I firmly assert, "Conversation's over. Now, are we going to look through this baby book or not?"

She tilts her head.

I hold up the book. "Come on. We have decisions to make."

A tiny smile forms on her lips as she relents. "Okay, fine."

We sit on the couch and look over all the books the baby planner had left us for the next few hours, deciding what we'll order for the nursery.

Aidan returns to the room, announcing, "We're all set."

"How many men do ya have out there?" Alaina questions.

He answers, "Brody took care of it with me. Ya don't need to worry."

She crosses her arms. "I asked ya a question, Aidan. I expect an answer."

He sighs. "We've got two hundred men surrounding the church for over a mile. The police have been notified as well. It's taken care of."

Alaina stares at him in silence.

"Is there anything else, Alaina?" he questions.

"No, be safe." She hugs me and asks, "What time will ya have her back?"

Aidan growls, "When we're back."

She looks at Aidan. "Ya know this makes me uncomfortable."

He rolls his eyes. "I'll text ya."

"Thank ya."

Aidan guides me out of the house, and we get into the car. The driver takes us through Belfast, and I look around in awe, still mesmerized by the surroundings and how different it is from Dublin.

We don't say much. We get to the church, and my anxiety starts to grow again. I fret, "What if I say the wrong thing?"

Aidan grunts. "Ya can't. I paid him. It's all good. Don't worry."

"So there's nothing I can say wrong?"

"No, just don't ask him any Would Ya Rather questions. I don't want to be here all day."

I stifle a giggle. "But it might be entertaining."

He grunts. "Not with Father Michael. Trust me on this." He gets out of the car, reaches for me, and leads me into the church.

I catch my breath, glancing around, then exclaim, "Wow. This is beautiful."

The windows are made of stained glass and a large crucifix hangs over an altar. A man wearing a dark robe is kneeling in front of an assortment of candles. His head is half bald, just a ring of white hair around the bottom of his skull. It's similar to Tommy's, except this man's is cleanly cut instead of grown out.

Aidan leads us to him, kneels, and takes out his lighter. He ignites several of the wicks, tosses some cash in a box, then nods for me to kneel next to him.

I obey.

He hands me the lighter, puts more cash in the box, and holds out three fingers.

I light three of the candles, and silence ensues.

Father Michael finally turns, booming, "Aidan O'Connor." He sets his rosary down and makes the sign of the cross, then prays, "Dear Lord, please protect this man's soul. He knows not what he does. Amen."

Aidan states, "Amen. Good to see ya too, Father Michael. This is my lovely bride-to-be, Scarlet."

Father Michael's eyes narrow on me. There's a slight disapproval in them.

I blurt out, "I have no ties to the O'Learys."

Aidan puts his arm around me. "He already knows that, and there's no question about it, is there, Father?"

Father Michael straightens his shoulders. "No, there is not." He makes the sign of the cross again and then says, "Dear Heavenly Father, we ask ya to protect this woman and make her the best O'Connor she can be. Amen."

"Amen," Aidan states, then nudges me.

"Amen," I softly repeat, my anxiety building.

Father Michaels rises, leading us through the church and into a side room. He sits down at the desk and motions to the two chairs. "Please have a seat."

Aidan pulls mine out, and after I'm seated, he takes his.

Father Michael questions, "How active were ya previously in your church?"

I wince, confessing, "Not very."

Disapproval fills his expression. "Why weren't ya active in your religion?"

"Is this necessary?" Aidan questions.

"I'm just trying to understand why a lass of her stature isn't more active in her church."

"She just told ya she wasn't. No need to keep beating a dead horse."

I stifle a laugh. I can always count on Aidan to protect me, even in a situation with a priest.

Father Michael sits back in his chair and drums his fingers on the armrest. "There are a lot of committees in our church. The health of our institution should always be a concern of yours. Are ya committed to making it a top priority?"

Just say yes to everything, Alaina's voice says in my head.

But instead of doing what she told me, I blurt out, "I'm sure that's important, but I'm not sure how I can help. I'm really a nobody."

"Oh, I can assure ya, ya are not a nobody, Miss O'Leary. Especially after ya become Aidan's wife."

"Do not call her Miss O'Leary," Aidan barks, his face hardening.

Father Michael clears his throat. "Miss Scarlet, you're going to be married to an O'Connor—a man who's nearly the head of the O'Connor clan. This is your church going forward. Ya and your sister—and I really would like to see more of Alaina, besides at baptisms and marriages—have a responsibility and duty as heads of the clan to help ensure the health of our church. Are ya committed to doing that?"

"Aye, she is," Aidan states.

Father Michael scowls at him. "I didn't ask ya. I asked her. Do I need ya to leave the room?"

"I'm not leaving my wife."

"Soon-to-be wife," Father Michael corrects, arching his eyebrows.

I grab Aidan's hand. "It's okay. I can answer. Yes, I'm committed. I don't know what I can do, but ya can help me figure that out after we're married." I give him my most dazzling smile.

He seems to like my answer. "Very good, then, and I assume ya know about how the ceremony works since ya got married previously?"

My gut flips.

Aidan scolds, "I told ya she was forced. Let's not discuss it ever again."

"Well ya still need to deal with that situation," Father Michael adds.

"Next topic," Aidan orders.

The two men pin their challenging stares on one another.

I jump in, "I really don't know what to expect. Do I need to know all that before I get married?"

"Well, it'd be good if ya two started attending church."

"We're not going to start coming to church, Father. That wasn't part of the deal."

"Deals can be tweaked."

"The fifty thousand pounds I gave ya did not include that, and there will be no tweaking," Aidan states, his eyes narrowing on him.

"Fifty thousand pounds!" I shriek.

Father Michael winces, covering his ears.

"Sorry, but that's a lot of money," I blurt out.

His cheeks heat. "It would be good for the congregation to see your faces."

Aidan insists, "Not happening. And our deal is already negotiated. You're not getting any more either."

"This isn't about the money."

Aidan scoffs. "Sure it isn't."

"I guess if we're talking about money, if ya wanted to make another donation, I could talk with the bishop about annulling Scarlet's previous marriage."

My chest tightens. "What would that do?"

"An annulment would make it so it never existed."

I stare at him and blink hard.

Never existed?

But it did.

Aidan tightens his arm around me. He interjects, "Scarlet and I will discuss that privately and get back with ya."

Father Michael nods. "We're looking to build a new library for the school. It would be a wonderful gift to your future bride to have it named after her."

Aidan grunts. "I'm sure you'd love that. Now, if you're—" Aidan's phone rings. He glances at it and then freezes.

"What's wrong?" I question.

He picks up the phone, answering, "What's going on?"

A moment of silence follows.

Aidan booms, "What do ya mean he's alone?"

The hairs on my arms rise.

Aidan states, "Scarlet is with me. The police better be holding them back with our men."

My chest tightens.

"Aidan," I quietly say.

He glances at me, then tugs me closer, stating, "He's got balls coming on our turf, especially our religious turf. Make sure he's unarmed. Don't ya dare let him go."

My heart races so fast it feels like it will beat out of my chest.

Aidan grazes his fingers over my biceps. He stares at me, then states, "You're sure he's unarmed?" He kisses the top of my head and then says, "That's fine. I'll meet ya outside." He hangs up the phone.

I fret, "It's Tommy, isn't it?"

He nods.

Father Michael declares, "We can't have trouble here. This is the house of God."

"We won't, and I'm assured he's secure. Our guys and the police have stopped his men farther back. But he wants a word, and they aren't going to leave unless he gets it. In order to avoid it getting ugly, I need to go out there, and ya know it," Aidan informs, locking eyes with Father Michael.

"Scarlet will stay inside with me," Father says.

I blurt out, "No, I'm going with Aidan."

His eyes widen. "Ya aren't going with me, lass."

"I need to face him. I want to show him he has no more power over me. Please," I beg, suddenly needing to face Tommy.

"Absolutely not."

I grab his arm. "Please? I need to do this."

"We've not talked about this before, petal. Where is this coming from?"

"I don't know, but I may not have another chance. Let me face him if you're saying it's safe."

"Things aren't always a hundred percent reliable," Father Michael comments.

Aidan turns his head toward him. "It is safe. My men have assured me."

"Then please, let me go with ya, Aidan. Don't deny me this," I plead, lifting my chin.

Aidan ponders it a bit more.

"Please?" I quietly beg.

He finally nods. "Okay, petal, but we aren't staying out there long. If I tell ya to go back inside, ya need to listen to me."

"I will," I assure him.

We leave Father Michael's office, and Aidan ignores his protest. He cracks open the church door and says, "Stay here for a minute." He steps outside and assesses the situation.

My insides quiver, and I almost chicken out.

What am I doing?

It's now or never.

I don't need to do this.

I do!

Aidan returns. "Are ya sure ya want to do this? This isn't necessary."

"I have to," I tell him, my nerves skyrocketing.

A mix of understanding and disapproval crosses his face.

I put my hands on his cheeks. "If you've ever given me a gift, this will be it," I claim, once again unsure why I'm pressing him to face Tommy.

Aidan sighs. "Okay, petal." He kisses me, then leads me out into the cold air. A burst of wind swirls around us, and the closer we get to the wall of men, the more Tommy's pungent smell of tobacco fills the air.

I put my hand on my stomach.

Aidan stops. He mutters, "Are ya okay, petal?"

I force myself to overcome the nausea and square my shoulders. "Yea."

He waits.

"Let's get this over with," I say.

He hesitates another moment, then leads me to the middle of the wall of men. He snarls, "Ya have a lot of nerve coming here, Tommy."

Several men step aside. Two hold Tommy by the arms, so there's no way he can fight them.

My insides shake harder, and maybe it's because Aidan is next to me, and I've never seen Tommy not in control, but he looks pathetic.

He's aged since I saw him last, and represents a shell of the man I remember. While I'm sure he's still stronger than me, there's no doubt Aidan would kick his ass.

The wind picks up, and more tobacco scent swirls around us. I swallow hard, trying not to get dizzy.

Aidan tightens his hold on me.

Tommy's bloodshot, beady eyes narrow on me. He threatens, "Ya got a lot of nerve sleeping with the enemy, especially when you're my wife."

"I'm not your wife. Ya forced me to marry ya. I didn't say those vows."

"Your da said them for ya. That's good enough."

"It's not," I seethe, filling with a wave of anger I haven't ever allowed myself to feel.

Aidan pushes me a tad behind him. "Ya do have balls coming here, Tommy. And your days are numbered. But ya said ya had something to say to me? So go ahead, say it."

Tommy's lips curl into a sinister smile. "I came to give ya and my whore a warning."

"She's not yours! She never was!" Aidan barks.

Tommy's arrogance rises. "That's funny since I marked her pussy way before ya did."

My knees lose the ability to hold me up. Fire explodes on my cheeks. I wobble.

Aidan tightens his arm around me, not taking his eyes off Tommy. He threatens, "The only pussy who's going to get marked is ya when I show ya my wrath."

Tommy snorts, locking his eyes on mine.

The air in my lungs turns stale. I do my best not to flinch.

Aidan orders, "Ya have two seconds to say whatever ya want. Then you're going back. Unless you're ready for a bloodbath? " Aidan points over Tommy's head.

More O'Connor men and police litter the entire area, creating a human wall. Men I recognize as O'Learys are posted up on the other side. It's clear the O'Connors outnumber them.

Tommy keeps his leer on me and snarls, "I'm going to get my wife back. Ya will be mine again, Scarlet. And ya…" He refocuses on Aidan. "I'm gonna feed her your balls."

26

Aidan

*R*age fills me. I push Scarlet back, ready to end Tommy's life now, right here in front of everyone.

Devin and Tynan step in front of me. Devin orders, "Time to leave, Tommy."

"That'll be the last threat ya ever make to my woman," I threaten.

"Caleb!" Tynan calls out, and the wall of men moves forward, pushing Tommy farther away. Another slew of cops appears from around the corner of the building, stepping behind our men.

When they're out of earshot, I snarl at my brothers, "I didn't ask ya to insert yourselves."

Devin points out, "Scarlet's green. What were ya thinking by bringing her out here? Alaina and Brody will kill ya."

I glance at her and tug her closer. I shouldn't have let her come. As much as she begged me, I knew it was a bad idea, and Devin's right. Her expression tells me that I made the wrong decision. I demand, "Time to go to the car, petal."

"I need to breathe fresh air," she claims.

I move her toward the car and open the door. "Get in. We can roll the windows down."

She obeys, still shaking, and I slide in beside her, holding her close. "I'm sorry. I shouldn't have let ya out there."

The car takes off, and she inhales deeply. She turns toward me, stating, "I told ya I needed to do that."

"It wasn't safe. I made a bad decision. I won't make any judgment errors again. And that's the last time you'll ever see that bastard."

"I don't need to see him anymore. I..." She closes her eyes and then sticks her head out the window. She adds, "I just need fresh air."

I rub her back. I had forgotten what the tobacco smell does to her. She stays near the window for a while until we're almost home. She finally rolls it up and rests against my chest.

"Are ya okay?" I question.

She nods. "Yea, but Tommy...he's...he's out for blood."

"Aye. We always knew that, and nothing's changed," I reassure her.

"But how did he get here? How did he get on your turf?"

"Because we let him. Remember, we wanted to pull him out of hiding."

She closes her eyes.

"Are ya sure you're all right?" I question.

She locks eyes with me. "Yea. I don't know why, but I needed to do that."

I kiss her forehead. "Ya were amazing, petal."

"I-I was?"

I hold her chin. "You are the most incredibly brave woman I've ever met. Ya had more courage than most men, to be honest."

"Really?"

"Aye, lass. Ya did." I tug her onto my lap, and she curls into my chest. I stroke her hair and kiss her head a few times until my phone rings.

I answer, "What's the situation?"

Caleb replies, "We're moving him toward the border, but there's nothing we're going to be able to do once we get there. Their men are lined up. Unless ya want us to attack."

I want to tell him to go ahead with it. I'm ready for this to be done, even though Tommy's on my list. But Brody will kill me, and I know it's not the right thing for the well-being of our clan. We can't risk more of our men losing their lives because of my dumb decision. So I order, "No, make sure there's no bloodbath." I hang up.

The car pulls through the gates and down the long driveway. It parks in front of the steps.

I get out of the car and help Scarlet out, then guide her inside the house. I go directly to the den, where Alaina seems to spend most of her time now.

She looks up. "What's wrong?"

Scarlet jumps in before I can. "Nothing's wrong. Have ya made any more decisions with the baby?"

Alaina asks, "Why are ya home so soon?"

I'm not ready to get into it with Alaina. Right now, I need to figure out my next steps with Tommy. He's too close not to go after him. So I interject, "Because it was over. Where's Brody?"

Alaina pins her glare on me. "He's in his office. Is there something ya need to tell me, Aidan?"

"No," I lie, then kiss Scarlet on the head and leave the room.

I'm sure I'll receive another punishment from her, but at this moment, I need to deal with Brody, not her.

I enter my brother's office. He has his phone to his ear, and he scowls at me. He orders, "Don't ya dare make a move without my permission." He hangs up, crosses his arms, then accuses, "What the hell were ya doing putting Scarlet in that situation?"

"She said she needed to confront him."

"Are ya thick? Alaina is going to have a fit."

"Aye, I know, but let's not talk about that right now. We need to focus on Tommy. He's out of hiding. He's going to cross the line again."

He seethes, "Ya could have created a bloodbath in Belfast with Scarlet as the first victim!"

My insides flip, but I don't flinch, retorting, "It was a controlled situation, and she needed to face him."

"That was careless of ya. I thought ya loved her."

I lunge at him, gripping his shirt and taking him by surprise. I push him against the wall and warn, "Don't ya ever question my love for her."

"What the fuck, Aidan!" Devin shouts, grabbing my shoulder.

Tynan pushes himself between Brody and me, shouting, "Jesus Christ, Aidan!"

Brody turns his scowl on my brothers. "And ya two didn't think to stop him?"

Tynan crosses his arms. "Why are we getting blamed for his decision? We were outside dealing with Tommy. He's the one who stepped outside with Scarlet."

"Oh, I see I have another rat brother," I mutter.

"Shut up," Tynan says.

Alaina orders, "All of ya shut up." She flies into the room and lunges at me. She slaps me so hard my face jerks toward the wall.

The sting floods my cheek. I sniff hard and make a fist at my side, forcing myself to not retaliate.

She snarls, "Ya put my sister in front of that monster?"

I slowly look at her. "It was her decision."

Scarlet cries out, "Ya never listen, Alaina. I needed to do it."

Alaina jabs my chest. "Ya could have gotten her killed or kidnapped."

"That wasn't going to happen. We had them outnumbered," Devin says in my defense.

Scarlet steps next to me and declares, "I didn't tell her, Aidan. She got a phone call."

"It's fine, petal," I assure her, pulling her toward me.

Alaina shakes her head. "How dare ya take that risk."

"I told him I needed to confront him. Why can't ya ever listen and realize what I need instead of what ya think I need."

Alaina gapes at her.

"Ya don't have any idea what he put me through!" Scarlet adds.

Alaina asserts, "There's no reason ya needed to confront him. He's a monster, and he's dangerous. Ya know this."

"Yea, well, you're not me, are ya? Ya weren't the one forced to marry him and have him on top of your body every—" Scarlet cuts herself off and turns her head, squeezing her eyes shut.

I hold her tighter to me. I pin my gaze on Alaina. "This conversation's over. It was her decision, and she was safe," I insist, even though I know it was a stupid move on my part.

Alaina shakes her head at me, and she blinks her eyes. They start to glisten, and her voice trembles as she says, "Ya are not to play with fire when my sister is involved."

"I'm not playing with fire."

"I explained the situation. Why can't ya listen for once?" Scarlet accuses.

Brody interjects, "Alaina, I need ya and Scarlet to leave the room."

Alaina snaps her head toward him. "What are ya talking about?"

"Let me handle this," Brody orders, giving her a look he rarely does.

She opens her mouth, then snaps it closed.

He steps forward and puts his hands on her cheeks. "We need to think about the baby. Take your sister and go to a different room, please."

She finally caves and pulls Scarlet out of the room with her.

When the door shuts, I announce, "I'm going after Tommy. This needs to be over, and ya know it."

Brody stays silent.

"This is what we wanted. To get him out of hiding," I add.

Brody walks over to the window, puts his hand through his hair, and stares across the lawn.

Tynan interjects, "I agree with Aidan. It's what we wanted to happen."

"Agreed. Time to follow through," Devin adds.

Brody spins toward us. "I'll tell Alaina we're leaving."

"No, ya aren't going anywhere," I declare.

Brody jerks his head back. "Who do ya think ya are to give me orders?"

"Someone has to stay here with Alaina and Scarlet. Ya know that."

"We have men."

"No, we need one of us here. The three of us will take care of it," I claim, motioning to our brothers.

"But ya make bad decisions when I'm not with ya," Brody accuses.

"This isn't the time to throw shit in my face. The longer Tommy's out there, the more risk there is, not just to Scarlet but to Alaina and your baby. And ya know that. But we can't leave them without one of us here. And you're the best option to stay here," I hurl out.

"No. I'll stay. The four of ya go. And ya made a horrible call today, Aidan," Dad's voice booms.

I spin.

He points at us. "Get your arses out of here, and don't fuck it up. There's too much on the line, and you're wasting time."

We stare at him.

Dad orders, "Don't fuck it up. Now, get moving. You're leaving within the next hour."

I exit the room.

Brody follows me toward the den, muttering, "Ya really are a plonker."

"Don't start again," I warn.

"Alaina doesn't need the stress."

I freeze and bark, "Goddammit! This isn't about Alaina! Stop making this about her! Did ya ever think this was about Scarlet and what she needs?"

He turns to me.

I add, "Ya have no idea what he put her through. It was her call. I realize there were risks, but they were minimized. Now get over it." I shove past him and enter the room.

Scarlet rises and meets me halfway.

I ignore Alaina's glare and announce, "I need to talk to ya, lass."

She doesn't say anything, and I guide her out of the room to another one, then shut the door. I sit on the sofa and pull her onto my lap, announcing, "I need ya to plan the wedding. When I get back, this'll all be over."

She pins her eyebrows together, fretting, "When ya get back? Aidan, where are ya going?"

"To take Tommy out."

"I don't feel good about this."

I put my fingers over her lips. "Petal, we need this to be over. When it is, his head will be sent to the registrar, and we'll be free to marry."

She shakes her head.

I question, "Ya don't want to marry me now?"

She cries out, "Of course I do! It's all I want!"

"Good. Then ya do your job and plan everything ya want for our wedding. I'm going to go do mine."

27

Scarlet

"What were ya thinking, Scarlet?" Alaina accuses.

I put my hand over my face and groan. "Jesus Christ. Alaina, just stop."

"Stop worrying about ya?"

"Yes!" I uncover my face. "Ya have to stop. I can't take this anymore. It's not your concern!"

"I'm your sister. It's my job to take care of ya!" she insists.

"No, it's not! And this isn't about ya. It's about me. Now either shut up and help me plan my wedding and let me help ya with your baby stuff, or I want nothing to do with ya."

Her eyes widen, and her hurt tone fills the air. "I'm sorry. I-I know what he put ya through."

Anger fills me. It's like seeing Tommy unleashed all my emotions, and I can't hold them back anymore. I cry out, "No, ya don't know what he put me through. And ya don't have a right to stand here and claim ya do."

"She's right." Tully's voice booms into the room.

I glance toward the door. He steps in front of us, adding, "Alaina, none of us know what Scarlet's been through. It may not have been the call ya would've made, but it was made."

"She could have died," Alaina states.

"She didn't."

Tense silence fills the air.

Tully adds, "Now, ya two can sit here and fight while they're gone, or ya can start planning the fun things. And it'll be good for ya to do something non-work-related for once, Alaina."

After a moment, she cautiously asks, "Are ya unhappy with anything I've done, Tully?"

"Of course not. Do ya think I wouldn't have called ya if I didn't approve of how ya were running things here?"

More nerves appear in her expression. It hits me how much pressure she has on her.

I put my arm around her. "You're amazing, Alaina. Truly. But Tully's right. Ya need to have some fun in your life."

"I do have fun," she protests.

Tully and I stare at her.

She tosses her hands in the air. "I do!"

Tully orders, "Then take a breather and have some with your sister. Enjoy this special time ya both have." He takes his cigar out and his lighter.

"Ya can't smoke in here," I remind him.

He groans. "I forgot. Sorry, lass." He points at both of us. "Ya two are sisters. Ya only have each other. You've left everything ya know and entered our family. We're happy to have ya, but ya need to make sure ya work this out. And, Alaina, I know as leaders we think we know what's best, but sometimes we don't. We get so caught up in making decisions, we forget people need to do things we don't understand."

She stays quiet.

"On that note, I'm going to smoke my cigar on your porch," he adds, shaking his head and leaving the room.

More tension fills the air.

Alaina grabs my hand. In a soft voice, she says, "I just want to make sure you're okay. When ya were gone, ya don't understand how much I missed ya. Every day I worried about ya. And...and for months, I thought ya were dead. I...I grieved ya. And it was my fault." Tears fall down her cheeks.

I pull her into a hug. "Ya have to stop blaming yourself. It wasn't your fault."

"It was."

"Ya couldn't have done anything to stop what happened with Da and Tommy."

She insists, "I could have. When ya were in London, I should have sent ya away from there. I should have done something."

"And they would've found me. Ya know they would've. It would've only temporarily put off what happened."

"We don't know that."

I sigh. "We do. But this isn't your battle, Alaina. It's not your scar to carry, and it's not your nightmare to relive."

She tilts her head and squeezes my hand tighter. "Are ya having nightmares?"

My pulse creeps up. I reprimand myself for mentioning them and try to play it off. I shrug, admitting, "Only when Aidan's not with me."

Sympathy and guilt take over her expression. "I'm sorry."

"Please stop apologizing. I don't want to keep doing this, but I needed to confront Tommy," I admit.

"But why? I don't understand."

I groan. "Ya, of all people, should understand, Alaina. Ya don't back down from anybody. You're the strong one. Maybe for once in my life, I wanted to be strong."

"You're the strongest person I know," she states.

I sarcastically laugh. "No, I'm not. I've always been your little sister. I'm the one who took the back seat. I was never brave like ya."

She claims, "No, ya are, Scarlet. Ya just don't realize it."

I take a moment to gather my thoughts, then state, "I'm tired of ya punishing Aidan for making decisions on our behalf or letting me do what I need to do. I'm tired of the fighting and constant battle between ya and him. I love him. I want to marry him. He rescued me. Nobody else did. And I'm not saying that so ya feel guilty, but why can't ya trust that he has my best interests at heart?"

She blurts out, "I don't want Tommy ever in front of ya again."

"He's not going to be," I say in a firm voice, lifting my chin. I hate that Aidan's leaving, and he has to chase after him, putting himself in a dangerous situation. Yet I realize Tommy needs to be stopped.

Her angry expression lightens, and she blinks hard.

My sister is more emotional than normal, but I can't keep having her all over Aidan's ass and trying to control me. So I slowly shake my head. "Ya may be in charge of the clan, but we're family. Ya need to figure out how to separate this. What happens between Aidan and me is not your business."

"Everyone in the clan is my business," she objects.

I shake my head. "No. Our decisions aren't yours to make. He's going to be my husband, and if I tell him I need something, he'll decide whether to give it to me or not based on whether he thinks he can keep me safe. Ya need to accept it. And our marital decisions aren't clan business."

Her expression tells me she's struggling with accepting my statement.

I add, "Maybe ya should discuss this with Tully and have him help ya decipher this."

She closes her eyes and puts her hand on her belly. Her face turns pale.

I fret, "I'm sorry. Did I hurt the baby by saying that?"

She grits her teeth and takes short breaths, muttering, "Morning sickness. I'm feeling a little..." She swallows hard. She places her hand on the back of the sofa.

"Come sit down," I direct and lead her around the furniture.

We take a seat. "Can I get ya crackers or something else? Bread? What will help ya?"

She answers, "I just need to breathe for a minute."

I wait for a while.

She finally smiles. "Okay. It passed."

I stare at her. "Are ya sure you're okay?"

She nods. "Yea, it's normal. The doctor assured us."

"Okay, well, do ya want to plan some things with me for the wedding?"

Her face lights up. "Yea, I'd love to."

"Good." I slide my arm around her. "Because ya know you're my matron of honor. If ya want, that is," I quickly add.

She softly laughs. "Of course I want to!"

"Good, but ya can't glare at Aidan the whole time."

She laughs harder. "I promise. I won't glare at him on the wedding day. Well, maybe I shouldn't promise that. I mean, if he starts anything with me—"

"Alaina," I reprimand.

She holds her hands in the air. "I'm teasing."

I arch my eyebrows to make sure.

"I am. I'm actually happy for ya. I can see how much Aidan loves ya and how happy ya are when he's around."

"I am. And I'm happy ya found Brody too."

"He's so good to me, Scarlet."

I smile. "Yea, I can see that. It's weird, isn't it? Us with O'Connor men?"

She nods. "Yea, but thank God we are. I'm so glad I'm not an O'Leary anymore." Disgust fills her expression.

Her sentiment is mine. I admit, "I can't wait to be an O'Connor."

"Agreed."

I rise. "Ya might not be hungry, but I am, so let's get some food."

She stands, and we stroll to the dining room.

Tully's inside and booms, "Ladies, glad ya could join me. I was getting lonely." He winks, gets up, and pulls two chairs out.

We sit and spend over an hour eating with Tully, discussing the wedding and the baby.

The confusion I always feel around Tully returns. I realize how much I really like him. It's odd. My da was so cold, and Tully holds the same power he did. I expected him to be the same, but he's not. He's funny and nothing but warm to Alaina and me.

I blurt out, "Why are ya so nice to us?"

He freezes for a moment, then takes a cigar out and runs his thumb over it.

"Ya can't smoke that in here," Alaina reminds him.

"Calm down, darling. I'm not," he claims, then looks back at me.

"Sorry, I shouldn't have asked ya that."

"Lass, ya can ask me whatever ya want. And to answer your question, it's not your fault ya were born into that situation. What your family did to ya was wrong. I can't imagine doing anything like that to my blood. But both of ya made a choice. Ya chose to leave the clan. Ya chose to not accept their ways. And I'll tell ya this. I'm more than happy to bring ya into the O'Connor clan and that we're going to take care of ya for the rest of your life."

I blink hard, but a tear escapes, and I swipe at it.

He adds, "You're good lasses. Ya both have amazing talents and traits, and it's a shame that your own blood couldn't recognize all your gifts."

I scoff. "I think ya have me confused with my sister. Alaina's the one with all the talent."

She protests, "No, I'm not!"

Tully chuckles. "You're a spitfire, Scarlet, just like your sister. Ya got more of her in ya than ya know. And aye, ya lasses are different, but ya both can do whatever ya set your minds to. And we probably shouldn't bring this up, but I need to say something about ya confronting Tommy."

My gut drops. "I'm sorry. Please don't be mad at Aidan. I begged him."

Tully holds his hand up. "Scarlet, I'm not going to lecture ya."

"You're not?"

"No. That took a lot of courage. More balls than most of our men would have, and I hate to admit that."

I stay quiet, my stomach flipping.

He asks, "Did ya get what ya needed from it?"

357

My stomach quivers, thinking about staring at Tommy earlier today. I slowly shrug, confessing, "A part of it, I guess. I don't know. I still don't understand why I needed to do it, but I did."

Tully glances at Alaina. "Do ya mind leaving us alone for a moment?"

She looks at him in surprise but doesn't argue. "Sure." She leaves the room and closes the door.

My nerves skyrocket. I ask, "Am I in trouble?"

He chuckles again. "Lass, ya need to stop thinking you're in trouble or that I have anything but good intentions for ya. Okay?"

I release an anxious breath. "Okay."

He hesitates for a moment, studying me.

I admit, "You're making me really nervous, Tully."

He carefully chooses his words stating, "There's a therapist I'd like ya to talk to."

My mouth turns dry. "A therapist?"

He nods. "Aye. She's helped some women I know who dealt with similar things ya did."

I insist, "I'm fine. I'm with Aidan. Everything's good. I'm protected."

He keeps his intent gaze on me.

I lift my chin higher, my insides quivering harder, my chest tightening, and suddenly more emotional than I want to be. I start blinking and have to look away.

He gets up and sits next to me. "Scarlet."

I turn to him.

He continues, "Lass, you've been through a lot. I'm glad ya confronted Tommy, but I want ya to talk to a therapist."

"It's not necessary."

"Humor me. Just one time. If ya talk to her and want to meet again, then great. If ya never want to see her again, then that's your call. But humor an old man and give her one session."

"It's not necessary," I restate.

"I think it is, lass," he claims.

More tears fall. I swipe at them, wishing I could control them. My voice shakes as I declare, "I'm fine."

"No one's saying you're not fine. But I believe it will be helpful for ya to talk to her."

"I don't want to discuss Tommy or anything he put me through."

"Ya don't have to if ya meet her and don't want to talk, but at least sit down with her," he pushes.

I ponder speaking about things with a stranger, when I've barely told Aidan.

"Give her five minutes," he says.

I tilt my head. "So ya want me to have therapy, but have ya ever had it?"

"No. Do I need therapy?" he questions.

"Probably. I'm sure you've done a lot more bad stuff than I have."

His lips twitch. "I can assure ya, I've done way worse things than ya have, but this isn't about anything you've done. It's about what's been done to ya."

359

I turn my head again, my face heating, clenching my jaw, hating the shame filling me.

Tully declares, "If ya talk to her once, I'll never ask ya about this again. I'll leave ya alone."

His offer sounds nonthreatening, but I still can't contemplate if I can talk to a stranger about anything related to Tommy and me.

Tully adds, "Everything will be confidential. She won't even tell me, if you're worried about that."

"I should have been able to stop things," I blurt out, staring at my hands.

He grabs them and squeezes. "Nothing he did to ya was your fault. Ya couldn't have stopped him. But this is why I want ya to talk to my friend."

"She's your friend?"

"Aye."

I tilt my head. "What kind of friend?"

"What do ya mean?" he questions.

"I don't know. Is she your girlfriend? Or do ya have a bunch of mistresses? What's your personal life like, Tully?"

His face freezes.

I continue babbling. "And what's your type? Do ya date really, really young women? Do ya date older women? I'm just curious."

Amusement and a bit of uncomfortableness cross his expression.

But once I start, I can't stop. I ask, "Ya do date, right?"

He chuckles really hard.

"What's so funny?" I question.

"Scarlet, ya really are a spitfire. But let's get back to the thera-pist. Will ya meet with her?"

I take another moment, then ask, "It means a lot to ya?"

He nods. "Aye. It does."

"Then I'll tell ya what, Tully. I'll meet with your friend for one session. I won't guarantee anything past that, but ya have to play Would Ya Rather with me."

He arches his eyebrows. "What's that?"

"I ask ya a question and then ya have to answer. It's harmless. Don't worry."

He arches an eyebrow. "Why do I feel like I'm being tricked?"

"No one can trick ya, Tully. Don't be scared," I taunt.

He takes the cigar and tosses it on the table. "Okay, fine. Let's play this game of yours. Then I'm setting up the meeting."

My stomach churns at the thought of the therapist, but a deal is a deal. So I ask, "Would ya rather date someone your age or forty years younger?"

"Do I really have to answer that?" he questions.

I stifle a giggle. "Is it hard to answer?"

He nods. "Aye. I can't answer that."

"Ya have to answer it."

"I can't. I love all women. That's the problem, Scarlet. All ages."

"Ya find women your age as beautiful as women in their...what? Twenties? Thirties? I don't know your age."

He picks up his cigar and taps it on the table. "Aye. There's an intellectual stimulation for me as well as physical."

I lean closer. "Intellectual like ya want a professor, maybe? She could wear those cute cat-eyed glasses." I wiggle my eyebrows.

He chuckles, and his face turns a little red. "I wouldn't be opposed to that. Do ya have someone in mind for me?"

"No, but I can stay on the lookout for ya if ya want."

He chuckles again. "Aye, ya do that for me. Let me know when ya find her."

"Okay. I will! Now, would ya rather date two women at once or one woman? Or"—I glance behind me, even though we're alone, then lower my voice— "would ya rather have them both at once?"

His face turns red, and he chuckles again. He declares, "One."

"Really!" I exclaim.

"Why do ya sound surprised, lass?"

"I don't know. I kind of expected ya to have a harem."

He laughs so hard it turns into a cough. I hand him a glass of water, and he takes several mouthfuls. Then he asks, "A harem? Ya think I have a harem of women?"

I shrug. "I think ya could pull it off. Maybe ya could keep the cigars out of the bedroom though. That'd probably choke them to death."

He groans. "What's with everyone in this house hating on my cigars?"

"It's gross. Ya should quit. Your cough is bad," I point out.

He scrubs his face. "All right, Scarlet, I'll take your advice into consideration. Now, I'm sorry to tell ya this, but your game is over. I'll set up a time for my friend to come over, but right now, I'm going to the porch and smoking my cigar in peace. You're killing me, spitfire."

I grab his cigar. "But this would be a really great time to quit. Think about it. Ya could be over your addiction before the baby comes. Maybe even before our wedding!"

He rises and grabs it out of my hand. "Never happening. I'll die with a cigar in my hand."

"Yuck. That's so gross!"

Arrogance washes over him. "The women who love me have never complained." He winks.

I groan and put my hand over my face.

He puts his hand on my shoulder.

I look up.

"I'm glad you're going to talk to my friend."

"Only for five minutes," I insist.

"Or maybe more," he says and winks.

He starts to leave, and I blurt out, "Will ya give me away for the wedding?"

He freezes.

"Sorry, maybe I shouldn't have asked that. I don't know why I did." My face heat again.

He turns, grinning. "Of course I will. I'd be honored."

"Ya would?"

"Aye. Really honored. It's been nice having more daughters in the family. Now I really do need to get to the porch."

I point to the door. "Go on, then. Get on with it."

He leaves, and I sit back in the chair. I take a few deep breaths. I'm not looking forward to talking to his friend, but part of me wonders if maybe it could help me.

28

Aidan
Two Weeks Later

wo grueling weeks have passed since I've seen Scarlet. I'm starting to lose track of the days. We've been on Tommy's trail, and there's been bloodshed on both sides.

Four of our men are dead, while dozens of theirs no longer breathe. Yet every time we think we have Tommy, he manages to escape.

My brothers and I are running on barely any sleep, and it's making me antsier than ever. I'm back to craving fire several times a day.

We stop at a petrol station and all get out of the car to stretch our legs. Brody goes inside to pay cash, and I put the pump handle into the tank. Once the attendant turns the fuel on, I take the matches out of my pocket. I light it up and stare at it.

Devin snaps, "What the fuck are ya doing?"

I continue staring at the flame. "It's fine."

"We're surrounded by petrol, ya daft fucker."

I take my eyes off the match and glance at him. "So what?"

Tynan blows it out. "So you're going to blow up the whole station. Stop being a crazy dumbass."

I take another match out, but Brody booms, "Aidan, go for a walk."

I turn and lock eyes with him.

He motions for me to go.

I don't fight him and trudge down the street. I don't get very far before I can't handle it anymore. I light another match and focus on the flame, letting it burn longer against my fingers than normal.

Devin comes up behind me, asserting, "Ya got to keep it together, Aidan."

"I am keeping it together," I claim.

"You're starting to make bad decisions."

"No, I'm not."

"Ya are. But we're close," he assures me.

I grunt, toss the match, and stomp it out with my boot. I light another, grumbling, "I don't understand how he keeps getting away. It doesn't make any sense."

Devin firmly assures, "We're going to end this. We're close."

The car pulls up next to us and Brody orders, "Get in."

I let the flame continue to burn.

"Aidan, now!" Brody demands.

I wait a few more seconds until I can feel it, then toss it on the ground and slide into the front seat.

"God, I miss SUVs," Tynan mutters.

"Stop bitching," Brody asserts.

Devin grunts. "Easy for ya to say. Ya aren't stuck in the back like a sardine."

Brody grins at me. "Only makes sense the weaker of the pack is in the back."

"Shut up, ya fucker," Tynan shouts, then slaps the back of Brody's head.

"Watch it!" he warns.

We head to an abandoned house our intel told us Tommy's currently using as his hideout. Excitement would normally fill me, yet it's nowhere right now. There have been too many failed attempts. And every day I'm away from Scarlet pulls me further into the place I can't escape. I know I'm moving into an out-of-control zone, and soon, no amount of fire will calm me.

In the past, I didn't have Scarlet. It was only me to worry about, and no one else was affected. I could work through it for months if needed. Now, I don't have that luxury. I'll lose Scarlet if I can't escape it, and I don't want her to ever see me when I get where I'm currently close to being. And one fear I always have digs into me harder than normal.

When this is over, what if I can't get out of it?

The drive is long. My brothers and I barely talk. Devin and Tynan take a nap in the back.

Brody asks, "Have ya talked to Scarlet?"

"Aye, but only briefly," I admit.

"She doing okay?"

"She's fine. She's happy, healthy, and safe. Well, she said she'll be happier when I return."

"Good. Ya don't need to worry about her, then," he claims.

"Are ya not worried about Alaina?" I question.

His expression hardens. "I'm always worried about Alaina."

"Aye. Well, it's the same for me. I'm always going to worry about Scarlet. So ya shouldn't be making these statements when ya know ya feel the same way."

He grips the wheel tighter and nods. "Point taken." He turns down another dirt road.

I grumble, "Tommy sure as fuck has a lot of places in the middle of nowhere. I can't wait to bury this bastard."

"Ya and me both. Especially with Dad in Belfast making all the decisions now. I feel like I'm going to come back and all the authority he gave us will be gone."

I snort. "I'm sure Alaina's keeping him in check."

Brody's lips twitch. "Aye, that's true."

The afternoon light turns to darkness. A few more hours pass, and I get more anxious. "Where is this place?"

"It's supposed to be up here," Brody answers, pointing at the screen on the car.

I stare at the map. There's nothing around. It's just a few roads. We pass several fields with scattered trees.

Brody pulls over. "We're walking the rest of the way. That's got to be it." He points.

Smoke comes out of a chimney a quarter mile away. A tiny patch of forest surrounds it.

My adrenaline kicks up. I mumble, "That's got to be him."

"Aye."

I turn and hit Tynan's and Devin's knees. "Wake up."

They stir.

"One of us needs to stay here with the car. I'm not taking any more chances," I declare, thinking about the other night when our car was too far away.

"Tynan, ya can stay. I'll go," Brody orders.

"Nah, I missed out on the action last time when ya made me be the lookout. Ya told me I could be part of it this time, and you'd do the boring part."

"That's true, ya did," Devin adds.

Brody groans. "Fine. I'll stay on car duty."

We leave the car and skirt along the edge of the woods, staying in the shadows as best as possible. When we get closer, we assess the situation.

There's one man outside the house, but I assume he's got at least one more inside with him, if not more.

I remove my gun, put on the silencer, and continue forward. When I can't go any farther without the risk of being seen, I lie on the cold, wet ground and crawl through the small open space.

As soon as I get close enough, I point my weapon and shoot. The bullet hits him in the head, and he drops to the ground.

I wait to see if there's any motion inside the house. Even with the silencer, there's a significant pop. The old cottage resembles a lot of Tommy's other properties. It's run down, and the windows have boards over them, which might have further muted some of the sound.

When everything remains silent, I motion for my brothers. It only takes them a short time until they're next to me. I nod at Devin, and he goes up and kicks the door in.

"What the fuck?" a man's voice barks in surprise.

He steps outside, and I shoot him, then rush inside. Footsteps fill the air, and I shoot at a silhouette I believe is Tommy, but he turns the corner, and I miss.

I run after him, and there's a bang. I turn the corner and find another door.

"Goddammit! He's outside," I yell and tug it open.

My brothers stay close on my heels. We get outside, and an engine roars inside a barn that's seen better days.

Tynan calls out, "Brody!"

Their car peels out of the structure, and I shoot, but they're too far away.

Brody pulls up and we get in.

I demand, "Don't lose him!"

Brody steps on the accelerator.

I close my fist on my matches. "Where are they?"

"There!" Devin shouts.

"Faster," I order.

"Foot's all the way down," Brody states.

My adrenaline shoots higher. It takes several dirt roads before we finally get closer. I lean out the window with my gun.

"Don't waste the bullets. We're running out," Brody warns.

I hold myself back, wanting to shoot, but I know he's right.

Tommy's guy takes a sharp turn, and the car slides on the wet road, slowing them down. It allows us to get closer, and Brody bangs into the back of their car.

It skids across the dirt, but the driver regains control. He gets a few feet ahead of us and veers to the left.

"Hold on," Brody shouts. He slams into them again.

They fly off the road and down a hill. The vehicle rolls three times and then crashes into a fence.

"Got 'em!" I shout.

Brody pulls over, and the four of us get out, rushing toward them.

Smoke surrounds the crash. The car's upside down. Tommy's guy gets out of the car and limps several feet.

I take my gun and shoot him in the back.

He falls to the ground.

I continue moving toward the vehicle and find Tommy trapped inside.

Blood surrounds him. He pins his beady eyes on me, then shuts them.

I slap his face. "Wake up, ya fucker."

He blinks hard, then mumbles, "I'll see ya in Hell."

I yank open the door, grab his shoulders, then tug him out until he's lying in a puddle of mud. Bright red soon swirls against the brown.

His tobacco stench fills my nostrils, and all I can think about is how Scarlet couldn't breathe and how his body was on top of her against her will. And I know there's way more shit he did to her she's never even discussed.

He taunts, "What are ya waiting for? Don't have the balls to finish me?"

I lean in close to his face and declare, "Ya deserve so much worse. There's nothing I can do to ever make up for what you've done. But know this, ya bastard. For the rest of eternity, she's mine. She was never yours."

I can barely hear his voice, but he declares, "She was mine first."

I spit on him, seething, "She never chose ya. She chose me. Deep down, ya know that." I should make him suffer longer, but I lose control. Unable to stop, I grab the remaining remnants of his hair, pull his neck as hard as possible, and slice his throat with my knife. Then I keep slicing until his head is separated from his body. I lift his head in the air by his scraggly hair and spin, holding it out to my brothers like a trophy.

They erupt in shouts.

"Grab the case," I order.

Tynan goes to the trunk and brings a steel box to me. I put Tommy's head in it.

Tynan secures it and takes it back to the trunk.

Devin hands me a box of matches. "I've been saving these for ya."

The craziness that fills me whenever I'm in these moments ignites. I nod gratefully to my brother. He knows it's the only thing that helps calm me.

Brody steps next to me and hands me a can of lighter fluid. He orders, "Finish it."

I douse Tommy's body in the fluid and light the match. I hold it in my fingers until I feel the burn, then toss it on him.

His body erupts in flames.

For over a half hour, I stand there watching him burn until he's nothing but a charred corpse, making wishes I know will never come true.

I hope Scarlet can forget about him and think about nothing whenever the name Tommy is mentioned. Yet I know that'd be a miracle. Even in his death, he didn't get as much wrath as he deserved. And my petal will always carry the scars.

Brody finally puts his hand on my shoulder. "That's it, Aidan. Time to go home."

29

Scarlet

*M*aureen closes her notebook. "You're doing well, Scarlet. Why don't we call it a day?"

I swipe my cheek and nod. "Okay."

She asks the same question she does every time we meet. "Would ya like to schedule a time to meet in a few days?"

I don't need to think about it anymore. Tully was right. Talking to Maureen makes me feel better, even if it's hard while doing it. But it seems to be helping me. My nightmares have drastically reduced. It had been several days since I had one until last night.

I just finished working through it with Maureen, and she helped me process some more things. So I give her the same answer I always do, "Sure. But I'm not sure when Aidan's back from work. I might need to reschedule."

She replies the same as always, "Not a problem. Why don't I come back in two days? Same time?"

"Sounds good. I'll walk ya out."

We both rise and stroll through the hallway. When we get to the foyer, the front door flies open. Aidan lunges in.

"Aidan, you're back!" I exclaim, rushing over to him.

He pulls me into his arms, picks me up, and kisses me on the head.

I cry out, "I missed ya so much."

"I missed ya more, petal."

"Is it..." I pull my face out of his chest. "Is it over?"

His answer lies in his eyes. His voice grows darker, and he affirms, "Aye, there's nothing to worry about now."

Relief fills me. Another round of tears falls.

He takes his thumb and brushes my cheek. Then he leans down and kisses me. He pulls back, studying me.

Maureen clears her throat.

We glance over at her.

I chirp, "Oh, sorry. I don't mean to be rude."

Maureen laughs. "I take it this is the famous Aidan."

"Aye. And can I ask who ya are?" Aidan says with distrust in his voice.

I answer, "This is Maureen. Your da wanted me to meet with her. She's...she's a therapist." I don't know why, but saying it out loud suddenly feels funny.

Surprise fills Aidan's expression. He pins his gaze back on Maureen. "A therapist, huh?"

She beams. "Yes."

He hesitates, then asks me, "Is it helping?"

I nod. "It is."

He looks back at Maureen. "Okay, then. It's really awesome to meet ya. And ya know my dad?"

She states, "I do. Tully and I go back a long way."

"Funny, I've never met ya."

"Well, ya know your father. He likes to keep his people on the down low," she jokes.

"Aye, I guess so."

Her smile grows. "Alrighty, then. Well, I'll see ya in a few days unless something changes, okay, Scarlet?"

"Sure. That'd be great. Thanks, Maureen."

"Nice meeting ya," Aidan adds.

"Ya too," she chirps, sliding past us and out the door.

It shuts, and I toss my arms over his shoulders, lacing my fingers around his neck. "I'm so glad you're home. I was so worried."

"Shh. Ya don't need to worry about me ever. And I have something for ya. Well, if ya want to see it." His face darkens, and the crazed look in his eyes appears.

The hairs on my arms rise. "Why am I scared to ask what it is?"

He stares at me for a moment.

"Aidan, what do ya have for me to look at?" I question.

He lowers his voice. "Ya don't have to see it if ya don't want, but I brought ya back the proof."

"Proof?"

"That he's dead."

My heart beats harder, and my chest tightens. "Ya brought his body back?"

He shakes his head. "Not all of it. I burned most of it."

A chill runs down my spine. I admit, "Then I don't understand."

He confesses, "I brought his head back. Again, ya don't have to see it, but do ya want to?"

"Ya think that's a good idea?" Brody's voice booms.

I spin.

Alaina appears. "Is what a good idea?"

"Showing Scarlet Tommy's cut-off head," Brody answers.

Alaina's eyes widen. She opens her mouth.

"Don't," I warn before she can say anything.

She pauses, then snaps it shut.

Aidan taunts, "Well, go ahead and say whatever it is ya want, Alaina. Get it over with. But at the end of the day, Scarlet's going to do what she wants to do. I'll make sure of it."

My sister looks at me, lifts her chin, and states, "It's your decision, not mine."

"Sorry, did I hear ya right?" Aidan questions.

She smirks at him. "I'm not sure. Maybe you're losing your hearing in your old age."

"Watch it," Brody reprimands.

She laughs and grabs his hand. "Let these two figure this issue out on their own." She winks at me and pulls him down the hallway.

Aidan watches them disappear, then asks me, "Am I in the twilight zone?"

"Nope. I trained her while ya were gone."

"Well done," he praises.

I laugh again, and he gives me another kiss. When he pulls back, he puts his hand on my cheek and states, "Ya don't have to do anything ya don't want to, but I've got to send the head where it needs to go. So I need ya to make a decision."

"Where are ya sending it?" I ask.

His lips twitch. "To the registrar."

I gape at him.

He chuckles. "There won't be any question that he's dead and you're free to marry me."

"Won't they be suspicious?"

He grunts. "I'm adding O'Leary fingerprints to the box."

I stare at him.

He leans closer. "And now I just told ya all my secrets, so ya have to marry me."

"Are ya worried I won't?"

He kisses me. "Maybe a tad."

"Don't be!"

He kisses me again, then says, "Would ya rather see the head or not?"

"I've never followed through on any Would Ya Rather questions."

"This one, ya have to."

I lock eyes with him, my insides slightly quivering in debate.

He cautions, "Ya don't have to. I won't lie, it won't be pleasant to look at, and I rather ya didn't, but I didn't want to get rid of it in case ya needed to see it. I don't know what the right thing to do here is, but it's your decision to make."

I blurt out, "I want to see it."

He studies me. "Are ya sure?"

I swallow hard and nod. "Yea, I am."

He kisses me again, then puts his arm around my waist. "It's in the garage."

He leads me through the house, and we pass Devin and Tynan.

"There's the lass we can't ever stop hearing about," Tynan teases.

"Hey, glad ya guys are back," I say.

Devin just nods as they pass us.

"Something wrong with Devin?" I question.

"Nah, he's an ornery bastard."

"I heard ya," Devin calls out.

Aidan ignores him and continues moving me toward the garage. We step inside, go over to a car, and he opens the trunk. A steel box is the only thing inside it.

I hold my breath, my hands shaking. I point at it. "Is...is it in there?"

"Yea, petal. Are ya sure ya want to see this? Once ya do, ya won't be able to unsee it."

I stand straighter, but I'm glad he has his arm around my waist, supporting me. My knees wobble and my mouth turns dry, but I affirm in my strongest tone, "Yes, I want to see it. I *need* to see it."

He scans my face, looking for any uncertainty.

"Aidan, ya brought it back to me for a reason. Why are ya hesitating?"

"I just want to ensure I'm doing the right thing, Scarlet."

"Ya are," I insist, then order, "Now open it."

Another moment passes, and I wait. He finally puts on black gloves, takes a key, and unlocks the box. A putrid smell wafts into the air as he lifts the lid.

I put my hand over my nose and mouth.

"It's bad, I know," Aidan states.

"Ugh," I groan.

"Are ya sure ya want to see it?" he asks again.

"Don't ask me again," I warn.

"Okay, petal." He lifts the lid higher, and my stomach flips.

Tommy is barely recognizable. His bald head is a purplish-white color. Dried blood and dirt cover his hair and are caked into his wrinkles. His bloodshot eyes are half open, staring at me.

Aidan starts to shut the lid, and I demand, "Don't."

He freezes.

I continue studying Tommy's lifeless face. My insides quiver harder, and then tears stream down my cheeks. I apologize, "I'm sorry. I'm not crying because I'm upset. I'm...I'm just so relieved."

Aidan shuts the lid and pulls me into him.

I start to sob, crying for I don't know how long, until I don't have any tears left.

"Shh," he says the entire time, rubbing my head and kissing my hair, telling me occasionally, "Everything is okay now."

When I finally calm, I look up, questioning, "It's really over now?"

His lips twitch. "Aye, and ya know what that means?"

So much happiness radiates inside me. I don't remember ever feeling it before. I chirp, "I do. Ya get to marry me!"

30

Aidan
One Month Later

"The lasses in Belfast are getting old. I need a change in scenery," Devin complains.

"Let's go to Dublin for a night out," Tynan suggests.

"Are ya crazy?" I scold them.

They turn toward me. "Why are we crazy?"

"Ya know going to Dublin's a bad idea," I snarl.

Devin snorts. "There's nothing to worry about. We've taken out a ton of those bastards."

"Aye. The O'Learys are dwindling in numbers. It's about time we started claiming parts of Dublin anyway," Tynan chimes in.

I smack him across the head.

He scowls, barking, "What the fuck, Aidan!"

I reprimand, "Ya don't go into Dublin without Brody's or my permission. And ya definitely don't start deciding which O'Leary territory we're claiming as ours."

"Someone needs to," Devin mutters.

More anger fills me, which only pisses me off further. I shouldn't be anything but elated today, yet my brothers have to show their stupidity. I point at both of them. "Don't ya dare step foot in Dublin without orders. We don't need trouble there right now."

"So hypocritical," Tynan claims and drinks the rest of his stout.

I cross my arms. "What's that mean?"

Devin tosses his whiskey back and states, "It was fine when ya went all over Ireland, wherever ya wanted to go. But we're supposed to just stay in Belfast."

My rage intensifies. "Doing what I wanted to do? Ya mean keeping my woman safe? Protecting her from that thug?"

They stay quiet.

I growl, "It's not the same thing. And both of ya better watch your tongues."

Brody's voice interjects as he shouts from across the room, "Cheers to Scarlet, the only woman on the planet who'd ever say forever to this plonker." He holds his shot glass in the air.

The room erupts in cheers.

I call back, "Watch who you're calling a plonker."

"Aye, mate." Brody grins, then downs his shot of whiskey. I grab one off the table, do the same, then glance at my watch.

Two hours to go.

Time to remind my petal what I bring to the table.

My cock starts to ache again. It's been killing me all morning. I push past all the men and leave the bar Brody created in his house.

I move through several wings to the other side of the mansion, gripping my matches. If I don't see her, I'm going to have to go outside and burn something.

It's been a month since Tommy's death. We haven't tied the knot sooner because Scarlet's dress had to be flown in and then tailored.

Alaina pulled me aside one day and told me that Scarlet was upset because the dress she wanted would take a month to be ready, even with the rush fee paid. So she chose another one she wasn't as keen on since it could be ready in a week.

After everything my petal experienced when her da forced her to marry Tommy, I wasn't going to stand by and not give her everything she wanted for her day. So I ordered the dress she wanted and canceled the other one.

Scarlet was upset when she found out. She argued, "I don't want to wait another month to become your wife. I want to become Mrs. Aidan O'Connor now."

We debated for a while, but I wasn't backing down and finally won.

The month ironically passed quickly but also seemed to crawl at the same time. Both of us felt it, but when Alaina announced at breakfast that she got notice Scarlet's dress had arrived, the way my petal's face lit up was worth it.

And I need to see it again.

Now.

Not waking up next to my bride-to-be this morning was torturous. My sister Bridget got to town, and she implemented all the traditional rules a bride and groom are supposed to follow.

I wasn't happy. Scarlet kissed me good night, and I grumbled, "This is a stupid tradition that doesn't apply to us."

Scarlet laughed and teased, "Good things come to those who wait, Aidan."

But I'm done waiting. I want to see my bride without anyone else around. And there's something I need to give her, or I'm going to go outside and burn everything in my path.

I turn the corner and don't bother knocking. I enter the suite. Alaina, Bridget, and my niece Fiona gape at me.

Bridget scolds, "What is wrong with ya? Did Dad not teach any of you wedding etiquette? You're not supposed to see your bride before the ceremony."

"Tough shit. Get out," I order.

"You get out," she demands.

Alaina laughs and grabs her bicep. "It'll be all right, Bridge. Let them be."

"First, Brody can't obey the rules, and now you," Bridget reprimands.

I glance around the room. "Where's Scarlet?"

"In the loo," Fiona states.

I glance over at her, dressed in her pale pink cocktail dress. "Ya look really nice," I declare and kiss her on the cheek.

She straightens out my bow tie. "You look nice too, Uncle Aidan, although you really shouldn't be in here."

I groan. "Thanks for the advice, but time to leave. Everybody out."

"This is really not right, Aidan," Bridget tries again.

"Ya mind helping me out?" I ask Alaina.

She laughs and takes Bridget and Fiona's hands. "Come on, ladies, let's go. It'll be okay."

"Thanks," I state, as she pulls them away.

It's weird. Alaina and I have come to an understanding. It's more about making sure that whatever's right for Scarlet, we're on the same page, but she knows I get the final say. But she also appears to finally trust that I have her sister's best interests at heart. We still taunt each other from time to time, but it's mostly for fun. And it's easy to see that Scarlet's relieved we're not fighting anymore, as is Brody.

The door shuts, and I lock it. I remove my tux jacket, bow tie, and shirt. Then I sit down on the armchair, waiting for my petal.

She calls out, "I forgot about the garter! Does anyone know where it went?" She steps out of the bathroom and freezes. Her eyes dart between my naked torso and face.

I slowly whistle. My blood races through my veins, and I don't think I've ever been so hard in my life. "Jesus, petal. Ya look like a fucking angel." I gaze over her vintage lace, chapel train, long-sleeve, off-the-shoulder gown.

It fits her perfectly. By the time my eyes travel back up, her cheeks are on fire.

She states, "That's the dirtiest look you've ever given me, Aidan."

I pat the armrest. "Why don't ya come here for a minute?"

She glances around the room and nervously asks, "What are ya doing here? I thought this was bad luck."

I grunt. "That's an outdated myth. Besides, I came to give ya good luck."

She tilts her head, her lips curving into a smile. "Oh? How are ya going to do that?"

I curl my finger. "Come over here and find out."

She hesitates, then slowly saunters across the room.

My erection strains against my zipper. I mutter, "Oh, you're a fucking little vixen."

She softly laughs, batting her eyelashes. "Am I?"

"Ya know ya are."

She stops in front of me and coyly questions, "Now what, dear husband-to-be?"

"One step closer," I order, then scoot to the end of the chair.

"What for?" she asks.

"This is the time ya obey, petal."

She smirks. "But I haven't said my vows yet where I promise to obey ya for all eternity."

My lips twitch. I tease, "Would ya rather have good luck or bad luck?"

"Good, of course."

I announce, "Well, ya don't get my good luck present if ya don't step forward. And it would be a shame to have bad luck, wouldn't it?"

"It sure would," she coos, then slinks another step forward. Her body stops an inch from my face.

I reach for her ankles and slowly slide my hands up the outside of her legs.

She inhales sharply. Her voice shakes as she asks, "What are ya doing, Aidan?"

I slide my palms to the back of her thighs and cup her ass cheeks. "What do ya think I'm doing?"

"Getting me all worked up before I walk down the aisle," she breathes.

I softly chuckle. "My tongue missed ya last night and this morning."

Her cheeks heat further. She swallows hard. "Oh?"

I grunt. "It seems to me that I need to take care of this before ya walk down the aisle."

Need and worry swirl in her emeralds. "But ya don't want a messed-up bride, now, do ya?"

I move my hands off her ass and slide them between her thighs. Her breath hitches as I vow, "I promise I won't touch your hair."

She subconsciously reaches up and pats her locks. "Umm...that would be bad. But I'm unsure how ya can keep your word on that."

I slide my thumb inside her.

"Oh shit, Aidan," she blurts out.

"Such dirty language for a bride," I scold, then curl my digit inside her.

"Jesus Christ."

"Don't let Father Michael hear ya say that. He might change his mind about marrying us. We wouldn't want that, now would we?" I move three fingers over her clit.

Her mouth falls open.

I circle her clit and order, "Answer me."

Her face turns the color of her hair. She whimpers, "Ah, no, that'd be very...oh...oh...."

"That'd be very what, petal?"

"That'd be so bad. So...oh God... So very bad," she declares.

I take my other hand and move her dress up until it's bunched at her waist. I state, "There's something I need ya to do."

Her voice cracks as she asks, "What?"

I circle faster with my thumb and fingers.

She moans, "Jesus, Aidan."

I put my face closer to her center and glance up, locking eyes with her. "Tell me how badly ya want my tongue on your pussy."

She looks at me with wide eyes, but I see the lust in them. It's an expression I love, and I crave it almost every hour of the day.

I slowly flick my tongue across her clit, then pull back.

She whimpers, and her knees wobble. She places her hands on my shoulders.

"Tell me. And say please," I demand.

She swallows hard. Her voice is barely audible as she begs, "Please lick my pussy, Aidan."

I put my hands on her hips, my face to her pussy, and start flicking my tongue on her clit.

"Oh my God," she cries out. Her breasts hit the top of my head and her dress falls over me as she bends forward.

I take my time, inhaling her, rotating between licking and sucking until she's digging her claws into my shoulders and I can't understand a word that flies out of her mouth.

Sweat drips down my chest. I hold her hips steady, cursing myself for keeping my pants on. It's hotter than a fire pit under her dress.

"Don't stop! Oh God!" she yells, then a chain of tremors erupts in her.

After a few moments, she tries to pull back, but I don't allow her to. I hold her tighter and suck.

"Aidan! Oh...my...Jesus!" she moans, unable to hold herself up and convulsing harder.

I don't show her any mercy. I eat her out until she's spent. I wait for her to stop shaking, then slowly lift my head from under her dress. I take my arm and wipe the sweat off my face.

Her face is fire-engine red, and her eyes glow like a wild animal at night. She tries to catch her breath, and I tug her onto my lap.

She puts her arms around me.

"Fuck, ya taste good, petal," I praise, then slide my tongue in her mouth, kissing her with everything I've got.

She retreats, fretting, "I'm going to need a shower now."

"Don't ya dare!"

"But I smell."

"Ya smell exactly how I want ya to smell before I marry ya."

Her lips twitch. "You're so dirty."

"Ya love that I'm dirty."

She doesn't say anything, but she can't stop her smile. I kiss her again.

Her tongue slides against mine with a new intensity, driving me crazier.

She reaches for my zipper, but I grab her hand, questioning, "What are ya doing, petal?"

"What do ya mean? I need it. Ya need it," she declares.

Jesus, I love this woman.

It takes everything within me not to let her sit on my cock.

I shake my head. "You're not getting this until you're Mrs. Aidan O'Connor."

She pouts. "That's not very nice."

"Ya want it, ya got to marry me," I assert.

She laughs. "Is that so? Are ya worried I might say no?"

"No, not at all," I confidently declare, but it's a lie. A huge part of me thinks that she won't show up or that she'll change her mind during the vows.

I know I'm not normal. She's always accepted my faults, the way no one else ever has, but she also does everything in her power to try and understand me. And somehow, beyond all rationale, she seems to. So the fact she chooses me still blows my mind.

She leans close and caresses the side of my head. "Let me tell ya something, Aidan O'Connor."

"What's that?" I question, my heart racing faster.

"There's nothing in this entire world that would make me not want to be yours forever. So ya should let me have ya right now. Let me show ya what you're missing so I can ensure ya show up."

I chuckle. "Oh, I know what I would be missing, and I guarantee ya I'm showing up. Now, give me that tongue of yours again." I press my lips to hers.

She kisses me back and tries to unzip my pants again.

I stop her. "You're not getting it until you're Mrs. Aidan O'Connor, petal. Now, give me one last kiss and then I'm leaving. I need a shower."

"No, don't go," she whines.

"If I don't go, my sister will behead me."

She groans. "Bridget has good intentions, but really, she should mind her own business."

"Well, ya trained Alaina. Maybe ya can train her?" I suggest.

"Hmm, would ya rather have my sister or your sister?" she asks.

I think about it. "I can't answer that."

"Ya have to answer it," she claims.

"No, petal, I'm not answering that."

"Um, if ya don't answer it, how can I marry ya?"

"What?" I blurt out, worried she's serious.

She laughs. "I'm just teasing. But ya really should answer Would Ya Rather questions. It's kind of a cop-out."

"Well, I guess I'm going to have to take the cop-out on this one," I state.

I move her off me so she's on her feet. When I make sure she's steady, I rise. I lean down and peck her on the lips. "Make sure ya show up, okay?" I state, my nerves filling my chest.

"Make sure ya show up," she tosses back.

"Ya never have to worry about that, Scarlet." I kiss her again and start to leave.

She calls out, "Hey, Aidan."

I spin. "Yea?"

"One more thing ya forgot."

I arch my eyebrow. "What's that?"

She pulls her dress up and puts her foot on the chair, exposing her thigh. She wiggles her eyebrows, beaming. "There's a garter that's going to be on here. Have ya thought about what you're going to do when ya take it off?"

EPILOGUE

Scarlet
One Month Later

The car pulls up to the front door. Aidan reaches for the door, but I grab his arm. He turns his head. "What's wrong?"

My belly erupts in butterflies. I admit, "There's something I've wanted to tell ya all night."

His eyebrows pin together. "What is it?"

"Nothing bad," I insist.

"Then tell me."

I swallow. My mouth turns dry.

He orders, "Petal, tell me what it is. You're worrying me."

I take a deep breath and put my hand on his cheek. I ask, "How do ya feel about being a daddy?"

He freezes. "Are ya—?"

"Yea, I am," I blurt out. Excitement fills me with nerves.

He grabs me and pulls me onto his lap. "Seriously? You're pregnant?"

"Yea. Well, I peed on the stick. I haven't told anyone. I know I should go to the doctor to confirm it, but I took two tests. They were both positive. Then I bought another box and took two more. I got the same results. And I thought maybe I should go to the doctor and confirm before telling ya, but then I worried about finding things out that maybe I shouldn't without ya," I say in a rush.

Amusement fills his face. He kisses me. Then studies me.

My butterflies grow. I order, "Say something."

"You're pregnant."

I laugh. "Don't be so shocked."

"I... Holy fuck. You're pregnant. We're going to have a baby," he says, grinning. Then he kisses me quickly and pulls back. "I can't believe ya kept this from me all night."

"I'm sorry. I've been trying to find the perfect time to tell ya, but I don't know. I mean, the food was good, then we were playing Would Ya Rather, and I was really, really hungry."

"Is that why ya didn't drink your wine at dinner?" he questions.

"Ya noticed?"

"Ya didn't touch it all night. But sometimes ya don't drink, so I thought ya just didn't feel like drinking."

"I was trying to figure out how to tell ya. I wanted it to be special. Plus, I didn't know how you'd take it."

He jerks his head backward. "Did ya think I wouldn't be happy?"

I toss my hands in the air. "I wasn't sure. No, wait! I knew ya would. I just... I don't know. It's just... We're going to have a baby!" I exclaim.

He chuckles. "Let's get out of this car and go celebrate."

My insides light up. "I'm not going to complain if ya want to do that thing to me ya did the other night."

He grins. "You're referring to Thursday?"

My face heats and I nod.

A light in his eyes sparks. "Noted." He chuckles and gets out of the car. He reaches in, helps me out, and leads me into the house.

I've never been so happy. I might as well be floating in fluffy clouds. Aidan's the best husband ever. And now, we're going to have a baby. Plus, our baby can play with Alaina and Brody's baby, which seems too perfect.

We walk through the door, pass several rooms, and Brody shouts, "Aidan, we need to talk to ya."

My gut drops. I glance up.

Aidan closes his eyes and shakes his head. He mutters, "Always something. We have to get our own place." He leads me into the den.

Alaina paces with her arms crossed.

Brody's scowling.

"What's wrong?" I ask.

His face darkens. He announces, "Those dumb brothers of ours went to Dublin for a night out."

Aidan snarls, "I ordered them to stay in Belfast."

"Brody, where are they? Can ya pull it up?" Alaina questions.

He glances at his phone and scrunches his face. "Somewhere called The Confessional."

"They went to church?" Aidan blurts out.

The blood in my face drains. I look at my sister, and she has no color either. We lock eyes, and I reach for Aidan's arm.

He asks, "Petal, what is it?"

I swallow hard, answering, "That's an O'Leary pub."

Brody claims, "It's not on our list."

"That's because it's an Ahern pub. Tommy's sister, who got married and has a different last name, owns it," I inform them.

A tense silence fills the room.

Brody seethes, "They just turned their phones off and are ignoring my orders to return to Belfast."

I turn my head, feeling sick, and squeeze my eyes shut. I say to my sister, "This isn't good."

She agrees, "No. It isn't."

"If it's not on the list, then hopefully they can fly under the radar," Aidan states.

"No. They...oh jeez," I fret.

"Petal, what aren't ya telling us?"

I stare at my sister.

Alaina answers with disgust in her voice. "It'll be swarming with Ahern and O'Leary men. One thing I can guarantee ya is they won't be too kind to O'Connors paying any attention to their lasses."

Thank you for reading Illicit Captor!
I hope you loved Aiden and Scarlet's story!

Are you ready for Illicit Heir?
Download it here!

ILLICIT HEIR

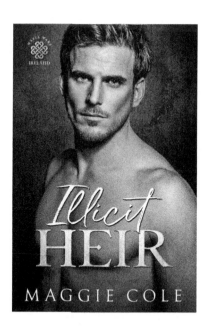

*H*e won an hour with me from a stupid bet.

We were several shots of whiskey and two pints of Guinness in when Devin suggested we play his game.

That hour turned into the next morning.

Then all hell broke loose.

I ransacked his wallet to find his identification card.

Our bliss disappeared into anger, hate, and accusations.

When he rejected me in that room, he didn't just leave me with a pounding headache and remorse.

He left me with a forever reminder of that night—the mix of two enemy bloods.

And now no one can ever know...including him.

READ ILLICIT HEIR-BOOK THREE OF MAFIA WARS
IRELAND

DEVIN O'CONNOR

ILLICIT HEIR PROLOGUE

Devin O'Connor

*T*he ball flies past the goalie, and the pub erupts in ear-shattering noise as everyone jumps into the air.

It's the All-Ireland Senior Football Championship, one of the biggest sporting events of the year, and I've never seen the pub so packed. Normally, the energy would pump up my adrenaline, even though I'm not a huge fan of the sport.

My brothers and I grew up mostly in New York but spent summers and long periods in Belfast. Our father tried to instill the love of what he calls football, and we still want to call soccer, into our heads. Yet none of my brothers are overly enthusiastic about the sport.

Boxing's the thing we love more than anything. We've spent countless hours in the ring, so all of us would rather see a boxing match. Or, we'd get more excited about American football or even rugby. At least there's more aggression in those competitions, but when we're in Ireland, there's no choice but to embrace what they call football.

Usually, a few pints of Guinness will get me into the sport, and I'll cheer with the other lads, especially for this big of a game. Yet all I keep thinking is one thought.

I'm bored and over Belfast.

I scan the crowd for the hundredth time, and my frustration only grows. There are at least a dozen women I've conquered in this room. Most of them several times, a few only once. Yet not one of them currently does anything for me.

And I'm antsy.

I down my Guinness and glance at my brother, Tynan. He scans the room and then meets my gaze.

One thing is clear.

He's just as fed up with Belfast and the current selection of birds as I am.

Cathal steps next to me, his eyes buzzing with alcohol and the excitement only victory can bring, and he wraps his arm around my shoulder, shouting, "Greatest day of the year, mate!"

I scoff, muttering, "Sure it is."

He pins his eyebrows together and leans closer. "Did ya not see that winning shot?"

"Aye. Course I did."

"Then why aren't ya ordering another round?"

Brogan steps on the other side of me and hands me another pint. He grins, "The lasses are going to be wild tonight. I'm calling dibs on..." He glances around and then sets his eyes on a brunette he often takes home. He eyes her over and declares, "Her."

Tynan groans. "Mate, you're so fucking predictable."

Brogan's grin widens. "Predictable is good when ya got a lass that can do the things she can with her pretty little mouth."

"Here we go again," I mumble, and down half my pint.

"Which one ya taking home tonight?" Cathal questions.

I study the pub for another moment, then finish my pint. I set the empty glass on the table and shake my head. "No one."

Brogran taunts, "Is your cock not working? Got issues ya need to discuss?"

"Fuck off!" I scowl.

Brogan, Cathal, and Tynan all chuckle.

I point at my brother. "What are ya laughing at? There are no birds in here you're interested in leaving with tonight either."

Brogan looks at Cathal and states, "Have our O'Connor boys switched sides?"

Tynan slaps him on the side of the head. "Watch your mouth."

"Ouch!" Brogan grunts.

Cathal asks, "What's wrong with you two? The pub's crawling with lasses ready to spread their pretty legs. It'll never be easier than tonight to get what or who ya want."

I cross my arms, sniff hard, and scan the room once more. Then I announce, "I've reached my limit of boredom. I'm heading to Dublin tonight."

Tynan's eyes light up, and his lips twitch in approval. He declares, "Thank fuck. Let's get on the road."

"Dublin? Have ya gone mad?" Cathal accuses.

"Why would ya go to Dublin when ya can get everything ya need right here?" Brogan questions.

I shake my head. "You two need to expand your horizons."

"My lass over there will expand my horizons just fine tonight," Brogan insists, then winks at her.

Tynan groans and scrubs his face. "She'll be here tomorrow too. And the next day. And then the day after that, dumb ass."

"Your point?"

"Exactly what Devin said. Ya need to expand your horizons, and it isn't going to happen here."

Cathal cautions, "Dublin's asking for trouble."

I lock eyes with him and can't stop my grin from growing. "Exactly."

His eyes darken, turning to slits. "Brody and Alaina won't give us approval to go down to Dublin."

"That's why we aren't telling them," Tynan interjects.

Cathal's head jerks backward.

Brogan blurts out, "Have ya both gone mad?"

My brother and I exchange glances as my adrenaline finally kicks into high gear. I nod at everyone's pints, ordering, "Drink up."

"Ya have to be joking," Brogan mutters.

I grab his pint.

"Hey!" he protests.

I down it, set it next to my empty glass, and state, "Grab a couple 8-packs from Sarah, and let's go."

Cathal whines, "If Brody and Alaina find out—"

"They won't. Now are ya going to be a pussy, or are ya coming along?" I insist.

"He'll be a pussy," Tynan declares.

"You're asking for it," Cathal warns.

"Ya have two minutes to get your asses in the car," I assert and push through the crowd, ignoring everyone. I get to the front door and step out into the brisk air, taking several deep breaths.

My vehicle isn't far since all my brothers have designated parking spots. I reach for the door and pause, almost forgetting I'm not in America.

I spin, and before I can ask anything, the parking lot bouncer Declan informs me, "No one's been near it."

I nod, then open the door. After a few seconds of quiet, I relax, even though he gave me the all-clear. If my guys I trust aren't watching my vehicle, I usually take out my special pen that can detect bombs. Even though we haven't had an incident in a while, you can never be sure in Ireland. The O'Leary's will do anything to kill us off, just like we'll do the same toward them.

Which is why Brody and Alaina will have a fit if they find out we went into Dublin. Our other brother Aidan's also warned Tynan and me several times to stay in Belfast in our territory.

But a man has to do what a man has to do, and I have to get out of here. Plus, we took a lot of O'Leary's out when we hunted down Tommy Aherne. Over the last month, we've claimed some of the territories on the outskirts of Dublin, but my brother and Alaina need to be more aggressive. The window to seize the O'Leary territory could close at any time. So it's time we start taking over whatever we can, and I don't understand why they're not capitalizing faster on our opportunity.

Tynan opens the passenger door and slides in with an 8-pack. Cathal and Brogan get into the back seat, each holding another box of Guinness.

Brogan mutters, "Can't believe ya made me leave my lass."

"She'll still be here tomorrow," I reiterate, turning on the engine. Then I order, "And stop your bitching." I reverse out of the spot and pull onto the road.

"How deep into Dublin are we going?" Cathal questions.

I glance at Tynan's mischief-filled grin. I assume it matches mine. My endorphins ignite, and I answer, "Pick a pub in Coolock."

"Coolock? Have ya lost the plot? We only took over the territory north of there!" Brogan points out.

Tynan turns his head, smirking, "Such a pussy."

I add, "It's prime to take over. The O'Leary's have no one there based on all the intel Alaina received."

"But they haven't ordered the clan to move on it," Brogan argues.

"Pussy," Tynan taunts again.

"Shut up," Brogan scolds.

The pop of a Guinness can fill the car. Cathal mumbles, "I need more alcohol for this."

Zings fly down my spine. I veer onto the motorway and head south, finally feeling alive for the first time in months. I demand, "Find a pub, Tynan."

He pulls his phone out of his pocket, and several minutes pass. Then he declares, "Got it."

"Where to, little brother?" I ask.

He programs an address into the GPS and states, "The Confessional."

Brogran grumbles, "Reconciliation would be a better decision right now."

I snort, claiming, "Oh, we're going to need reconciliation. But not until after tonight."

Tynan chuckles and opens a can of Guinness.

"There's going to be O'Leary women in that pub. This really isn't a good idea," Cathal points out.

Tynan and I exchange another glance. The heat in my blood grows hotter. He says, "Guess it's time."

"Time for what?" Brogan questions.

I grin at my brother, answering, "Time to learn what it's like to be inside an O'Leary lass."

READ ILLICIT HEIR-BOOK THREE OF MAFIA WARS IRELAND

CAN I ASK YOU A HUGE FAVOR?

*W*ould you be willing to leave me a review?

I would be forever grateful as one positive review on Amazon is like buying the book a hundred times! Reader support is the lifeblood for Indie authors and provides us the feedback we need to give readers what they want in future stories!

Your positive review means the world to me! So thank you from the bottom of my heart!

CLICK TO REVIEW

READY TO BINGE THE ORIGINAL MAFIA WARS SERIES? GET TO KNOW THE IVANOVS AND O'MALLEYS!

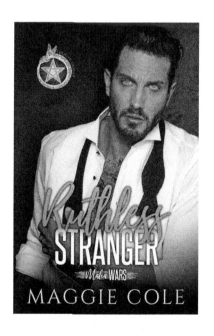

He's a Ruthless Stranger. One I can't see, only feel, thanks to my friends who make a deal with him on my behalf.

No names. No personal details. No face to etch into my mind.

Just him, me, and an expensive silk tie.

What happens in Vegas is supposed to stay in Vegas.

He warns me he's full of danger.

I never see that side of him. All I experience is his Russian accent, delicious scent, and touch that lights me on fire.

One incredible night turns into two. Then we go our separate ways.

But fate doesn't keep us apart. When I run into my stranger back in Chicago, I know it's him, even if I've never seen his icy blue eyes before.

Our craving is hotter than Vegas. But he never lied.

He's a ruthless man...

"Ruthless Stranger" is the jaw-dropping first installment of the "Mafia Wars" series. It's an interconnecting, stand-alone Dark Mafia Romance, guaranteed to have an HEA.

Ready for Maksim's story? Click here for Ruthless Stranger, book one of the jaw dropping spinoff series, Mafia Wars!

MORE BY MAGGIE COLE

Mafia Wars Ireland

Illicit King (Brody)- May 1, 2023

Illicit Captor (Aidan) - June 15, 2023

Illicit Heir (Devin) - August 15, 2023

Illicit Monster (Tynan) - TBD

Club Indulgence Duet (A Dark Billionaire Romance)

The Auction (Book One)

The Vow (Book Two)

Standalone Holiday Novel

Holiday Hoax - A Fake Marriage Billionaire Romance (Standalone)

Mafia Wars New York - A Dark Mafia Series (Series Six)

Toxic (Dante's Story) - Book One

Immoral (Gianni's Story) - Book Two

Crazed (Massimo's Story) - Book Three

Carnal (Tristano's Story) - Book Four

Flawed (Luca's Story) - Book Five

Mafia Wars - A Dark Mafia Series (Series Five)

Ruthless Stranger (Maksim's Story) - Book One

Broken Fighter (Boris's Story) - Book Two

Cruel Enforcer (Sergey's Story) - Book Three

Vicious Protector (Adrian's Story) - Book Four

Savage Tracker (Obrecht's Story) - Book Five

Unchosen Ruler (Liam's Story) - Book Six

Perfect Sinner (Nolan's Story) - Book Seven

Brutal Defender (Killian's Story) - Book Eight

Deviant Hacker (Declan's Story) - Book Nine

Relentless Hunter (Finn's Story) - Book Ten

Behind Closed Doors (Series Four - Former Military Now International Rescue Alpha Studs)

Depths of Destruction - Book One

Marks of Rebellion - Book Two

Haze of Obedience - Book Three

Cavern of Silence - Book Four

Stains of Desire - Book Five

Risks of Temptation - Book Six

Together We Stand Series (Series Three - Family Saga)

Kiss of Redemption- Book One

Sins of Justice - Book Two

Acts of Manipulation - Book Three

Web of Betrayal - Book Four

Masks of Devotion - Book Five

Roots of Vengeance - Book Six

It's Complicated Series (Series Two - Chicago Billionaires)

My Boss the Billionaire- Book One

Forgotten by the Billionaire - Book Two

My Friend the Billionaire - Book Three

Forbidden Billionaire - Book Four

The Groomsman Billionaire - Book Five

Secret Mafia Billionaire - Book Six

All In Series (Series One - New York Billionaires)
The Rule - Book One
The Secret - Book Two
The Crime - Book Three
The Lie - Book Four
The Trap - Book Five
The Gamble - Book Six
STAND ALONE NOVELLA
JUDGE ME NOT - A Billionaire Single Mom Christmas Novella

ABOUT THE AUTHOR

Amazon Bestselling Author

Maggie Cole is committed to bringing her readers alphalicious book boyfriends. She's an international bestselling author and has been called the "literary master of steamy romance." Her books are full of raw emotion, suspense, and will always keep you wanting more. She is a masterful storyteller of contemporary romance and loves writing about broken people who rise above the ashes.

Maggie lives in Florida with her son. She loves sunshine, anything to do with water, and everything naughty.

Her current series were written in the order below:

- All In (Stand alones with entwined characters)

- It's Complicated (Stand alones with entwined characters)
- Together We Stand (Brooks Family Saga - read in order)
- Behind Closed Doors (Read in order)
- Mafia Wars (Stand alones with entwined characters)
- Mafia Wars New York (Stand alones with entwined characters)
- Club Indulgence Duet
- Mafia Wars Ireland

Maggie Cole's Newsletter
Sign up here!

Hang Out with Maggie in Her Reader Group
Maggie Cole's Romance Addicts

Follow for Giveaways
Facebook Maggie Cole

Instagram
@maggiecoleauthor

TikTok
https://www.tiktok.com/@maggiecole.author

Complete Works on Amazon
Follow Maggie's Amazon Author Page

Book Trailers
Follow Maggie on YouTube

Feedback or suggestions?
Email: authormaggiecole@gmail.com

twitter.com/MaggieColeAuth

instagram.com/maggiecoleauthor

bookbub.com/profile/maggie-cole

amazon.com/Maggie-Cole/e/B07Z2CB4HG

tiktok.com/@maggiecole.author

facebook.com/authormaggiecole

Printed in Great Britain
by Amazon

25245476R00243